Against the Boards

by

Melinda Di Lorenzo

Copyright Notice
This is a work of fiction. Names, characters, places, and incidents are either the product of the author's imagination or are used fictitiously, and any resemblance to actual persons living or dead, business establishments, events, or locales, is entirely coincidental.

Against the Boards

COPYRIGHT © 2024 by Melinda Di Lorenzo

All rights reserved. No part of this book may be used or reproduced in any manner whatsoever without written permission of the author or The Wild Rose Press, Inc. except in the case of brief quotations embodied in critical articles or reviews.
Contact Information: info@thewildrosepress.com

Cover Art by *Lisa Dawn MacDonald*

The Wild Rose Press, Inc.
PO Box 708
Adams Basin, NY 14410-0708
Visit us at www.thewildrosepress.com

Publishing History
First Edition, 2024
Trade Paperback ISBN 978-1-5092-5618-1
Digital ISBN 978-1-5092-5619-8

Published in the United States of America

Chapter One

My fists hit the punching bag with numbing fury, the steady smack filling my ears and blocking out the other sounds of the gym.

Bam-slap.

Bam-bam-slap.

I rotated through a series of jabs and swipes and uppercuts in perfect sequence, pummeling the leather with most of my strength and all of my grace. My movements were rhythmic. Hypnotic. Beautiful. But aggressive. More importantly, it reeked of careful control. I was utterly in charge of my body. Utterly in charge of the bag. And by extension, utterly in charge of the space around me.

Bam-bam.

Slap-bam.

Bam-bam-slap.

I'd gone over my allotted thirty minutes at the station, but no one was going to ask me to stop. The gym was male dominated, and I knew I scared the shit out of most of the men. Primarily because once upon a time, one had made the mistake of deliberately sneaking up on me. He thought he was being funny. Impressing his buddies. Instead, he'd gotten himself a broken nose, a black eye, and a bruised rib. The story was legendary. And it hadn't earned me any friends.

Bam-bam-slap.

Bam-bam-bam.

I didn't care. I wasn't there to pick up any of the assholes—or even *non*-assholes—who sweat out their aggressions on a speedbag or in the ring. I was just there to stay strong. To get stron*ger*. To maintain tight lines of muscles in my body, and to know I could sleep at night without fear. If being intimidating helped me along, then so be it.

Bam.

Breathing quickly—but not too heavily—I dropped my fists to my sides and executed a roundhouse kick instead. The punching bag practically wheezed. I let myself smile the smallest smile, then threw my left foot forward in a series of hard slams at varying heights. Knee. Groin. Stomach. Chest. When that was done, I bounced on the spot and prepared to do the same with my right foot.

Before I could lift it, though, a wry voice almost made me stumble.

"Easy there, Pint-Size," it said in a familiar timbre. "Those things are expensive to replace."

The tension in my chest eased. I snorted, steadied myself, and performed my kicks without further acknowledgement. For good measure, I added another five-punch sequence before turning around.

As always, facing my oldest brother was kind of like looking into a funhouse mirror. His features were undeniably similar to my own. He had the same wide brown eyes and the same too-long lashes. His nose was like mine as well—it was narrow and just a tad too sharp to be called elegant. I could see myself in Charles's smattering of freckles, in his smirking mouth, and even in his strong jawbone—though mine had a hint of delicateness, while his had a hint of stubble instead. But it wasn't any of that which made the resemblance cartoonish. It was my older brother's size.

Charles was a big dude. Six-foot-one, two-hundred and fifty-eight pounds. And no, he never let anyone forget that final eight. It was some mark of honor for him. One that just made me roll my eyes. His height and broadness were a sharp contrast to my five-foot-two, hundred-and-twenty-pound frame. But my compactness was deceiving. I was wired with muscle. And I sure as hell wasn't going to let my brother forget it.

Grinning, I drew back a fist and aimed it right at his shoulder. "Better to be pint-sized than to look like I'm getting ready to fight a grizzly bear."

"Hilarious." Charles rubbed the spot I'd punched. "Is there somewhere we can talk?"

"That sounds ominous. Did you have a billing emergency? Forget to expense your monthly steak allowance?"

Half of me really *did* think his emergency might be food related. The other half was pretty sure he needed help filing something. Par for the course in my life. I had five brothers. All older. All bigger. All convinced they needed to keep me wrapped in marshmallow. Which was at least one reason that—despite my P.I. license and extensive self-defence training—I'd been relegated to the role of glorified office assistant at our family business, Ames Security.

Sometimes, I chalked it up to plain old misogyny. Other times, I knew it was far more than that. My brothers loved me. They wanted to protect me. And once upon a time—not too long after we lost our dad—

I'd given them a good reason to think they needed to. Never mind that more than three years had passed since then. Closer to four years, really. But until I unequivocally proved otherwise, all five of my siblings would see me as nothing more than their little sister. So if I wanted to make slightly snide jokes about it, then that was my prerogative.

Except judging by Charles's expression, he wasn't in the mood to be bugged.

Sighing, I snagged my towel off the rack, slung it over my shoulders, and gestured to one of the unoccupied benches lining the gym walls. "Will that do, Chuck, or should we find a creepy alcove somewhere?"

He grunted but didn't comment on his most-hated nickname, and instead strode to the bench and folded his over-sized frame down onto it. He tried to get settled, couldn't, adjusted his position again, then finally just stuck his long legs straight out in front of him. I held in another teasing comment and positioned myself beside him. My body fit much better in the space, and I bit back a remark about that, too.

"What's up, oh mighty brother of mine?" I asked.

He muttered something unintelligible, then cleared his throat. "I need you to work a case."

My heart did a hopeful little leap, but I quelled it. "Some more utterly enthralling internet research?"

Charles let out another grumble.

"Seriously?" I said. "If you're just going to sit there and make like an ogre…"

"Fieldwork!" He snapped the word abruptly, his reply so loud that three other boxers turned and looked our way.

I blinked, and a single word popped out before I

could stop it. "*Why?*"

"Seriously?" He echoed my earlier disbelief perfectly.

I made a face. "Okay, but can you blame me for wondering? Like…did hell freeze over? No, wait. Is it Toby? Is he okay?"

Toby was our middle brother. The one who filled in most often when Charles—who let out a sigh now—was tied up.

"Toby's fine," he said. "And hell is still nice and toasty. Could you at least hear me out before you start waxing sarcastic?"

"Waxing sarcastic. Ha. Good one."

"Look. If you don't want the chance to do a job, Ivy, then just say so."

I eyed him suspiciously. Part of me really *was* tempted to refuse. After all, if it was a prime case—or one that held even the vaguest bit of real interest—and Toby wasn't around, then Charles would likely have outsourced. It wouldn't be the first time he'd overlooked me and hired a goon to do something on behalf of our company. So, the fact that he'd approached *me* with this—whatever it was—made me nervous. As did the fact that he hadn't yet disclosed a single detail. But the moment he started to push to his feet, I saw the already-tiny window of opportunity begin to close. And my mouth immediately overruled my brain.

"Fine," I said. "I'll come. I'll hear you out. But I swear to God if you're about to ask me to go dumpster diving…"

"I'm not," he replied, dry and relieved at the same time. "But remember Dad always said to be careful what you wish for, Pint-Size."

I rolled my eyes. "Great. That's super reassuring. Give me a sec to get changed, okay?"

Charles nodded, and he made no move to get up. But I still hurried. There was a 90 percent chance my brother was going to change his mind, so I didn't even let myself wonder what the assignment was. I just quickly peeled off my sweaty gym shorts and sports bra—my preferred minimalist workout gear—then slid into a sleeveless, jersey knit dress in bright yellow. I switched out my running shoes for a pair of classic high-tops, tossed my cellphone into the dress's zip-up pocket, and cast a single, scrutinous look at myself in the mirror.

"Not exactly dressed for success," I said, smoothing the fabric a little. "But better than boxing stuff, right?"

As satisfied as I could be, I hurried back to Charles, who was still waiting on the bench, bobbing one of his feet impatiently. He gave my dress a raised eyebrow but said nothing. In fact, he was unusually quiet. Even after we'd climbed into his very practical sedan, he offered no hints about our intended destination or the job. He said almost nothing as he navigated away from the gym and started through the Surrey streets. Not even an update on his weekend or a comment about something one of our brothers was up to. Five minutes went by before I finally had enough of the silent treatment.

"Okay," I said. "Spill it. You can't expect me to just walk in somewhere clueless."

He gave me a look that told me he was actually kind of hoping to do just that, but he also shook his head and relented. "I'm assuming you've heard of TJ Jones?"

"No. Should I have?"

"Really?" The word was infused with genuine surprise.

"Yes, really," I said. "Why? Is he an actor?"

"No, Pint-Size. He's not an *actor*."

"Is the disparaging tone really necessary?"

"I'm not being disparaging. I just forget sometimes that you're…" He trailed off, and I knew exactly what he'd been about to say.

"Go ahead, Chuck," I said as we came to a stop at a red light. "Finish it. You forget that I'm a *girl.*"

"You always make that seem like an insult."

"Because it *is* when you say it like that. Just like when I reply by calling you a sexist jerk, it's also an insult."

My brother threw up his hands in a rare moment of defeat and faced me. "Okay, fine. You know what? You're right. I'm totally a sexist jerk. Happy?"

The concession—even if he was kidding—startled me. "You are?"

"Yes." He gripped the steering wheel again as the light changed to green. "But only where my baby sister—who is totally irreplaceable and who I love so dearly despite her generally prickly nature—is concerned."

"Apology accepted," I said with a frown. "Sort of. But it doesn't change that I don't know who TJ Jones is."

"He's a hockey player. Pro. One level below the NHL." He flicked on the righthand turn signal and steered in the same direction, taking us into a section of mid-rise commercial buildings. "To be more specific, he's the newly appointed captain of the Surrey Slammers. The expansion team that started up this season."

I felt my frown deepen. "Ohhh-kay. And he's the client?"

"Yes, he's the client," Charles agreed, sounding oddly sour.

"All right." My head was starting to ache from how hard my eyebrows were knit together. "What does TJ Jones, captain of the Surrey Slammers, need?"

"A bodyguard."

"A...what?"

"A bodyguard," Charles repeated.

"I *heard* you," I said. "I'm just confused. You're asking *me* to guard someone?"

"Yeah." The word was heavily grudging and weirdly...a little reluctant. "He's got a stalker, and TJ's concerned things might escalate. I've gone over the details, and I agree. He needs twenty-four-seven protection while we work on figuring out who's behind this."

He signaled again, then pulled the vehicle into an underground parking lot at swanky-looking hotel. My fingers strummed my thigh. It wasn't unusual to meet a client on neutral ground. But this didn't seem usual at all.

"Just so we're clear," I said. "You want *me* to be the brawn while *you* take on the brain side of things?"

"Christ, Pint-Size. You're making this really hard."

"Yeah, I am. What are you leaving out, Chuck?"

Without answering me, my brother brought the car to a halt, cut the engine, and opened the door. He even went so far as to climb out before finally speaking.

"I'm not leaving out anything," he said. "Except the part where TJ Jones is about to become your new boyfriend."

Then he slammed the door and took off so quickly that all I could do was draw in a sharp, startled breath as his back receded into the dimly lit parking lot.

Chapter Two

For several seconds, I was stuck. Stunned into immobility and glued to the seat with my hands curled into fists at my sides.

"He's got to be kidding," I said under my breath. "Like...*really* has to be."

A small chill, prodded more by memory rather than by the current moment, crept its way along my shoulder blades. It made my palms sweaty. And the control I relished while beating on the punching bag at the gym was quite suddenly a slippery thing.

My brother knew better than to put me in a situation like the one he'd just described. He knew why, too. But Charles showed no sign of turning back to tell me it'd been a prank. I had no choice but to unstick myself, climb out, and scramble to catch up to him. And unfortunately for me, my shorter legs had me at a disadvantage. By the time I got to my brother's side, he was not only at the elevators, but he'd already pushed the button, too. The light above the doors indicated the car was on its way down from the fourth floor.

"This is a joke, right?" I asked.

He turned a grim eye my way. "Did I sound like I was joking? *Would* I joke about something like this?"

The chill came back, and I fought to keep it at bay. "I don't think you would. But I also don't understand why you'd even suggest it."

"You wanted fieldwork."

"That's a low blow, Chuck. And did you think for one second I'd go for it? And besides, that—"

A ding announced the arrival of the elevator, and the doors whooshed open, giving my brother a momentary reprieve from the rest of my intended verbal attack. But the second we stepped inside I started up again. Or I tried. I only got as far as opening my mouth before snapping it shut again. We weren't alone in the small space. A tall brunette who had a baby on her hip, a frazzled look on her face, and a preschooler at her knee, stood in one corner.

"Hi!" greeted the little girl right away. "I'm Josie."

"Josie!" admonished her mom.

"What?" said preschooler.

"I've told you a hundred times not to talk to strangers."

"Oh. Well. How was *I* supposed to know they were strangers? They got into *our* elevator."

Her mom made an exasperated noise, then directed her attention to me and Charles. "Sorry. My husband gave her blueberry pie with ice cream for breakfast. And be forewarned, my beautiful little monster pressed all the buttons before I could stop her. Then we missed our floor twice and—well, here we are. So. Sorry. Again."

"No trouble at all," my brother replied, all congeniality. "We'll get where we're going eventually."

"I like your dress," Josie told me.

I managed to smile at her. "Thank you. I like yours, too."

She twirled, sending her flowered ensemble spinning. "Thanks! It was a present!"

I exhaled a slow breath and mentally maimed my brother with a rusty spoon. Outwardly, I carried on a conversation with Josie. I learned she was four years old, and her baby sister's name was Rai. And by the time we reached our stop on the eleventh floor, I also knew they'd joined her father on a business trip, and were staying in room 1212, which was just two from the top. And as it turned out—after a painful stop at every floor—it was also a level above our own destination.

Josie waved a cheerful goodbye, her mother apologized again, and Charles and I exited onto floor eleven. I expected my brother to at least say something, but he didn't even pause. His feet hit the ground—his steps muffled by the wine-red carpet under his shoes.

"Hang on," I said, chasing him once again. "We have to talk about this."

Now he *did* stop, and for a second, I was relieved. But then he glanced at his watch and shook his head.

"Sorry," he said. "We're already ten minutes overdue, and I wouldn't want Mr. Jones to think we're unprofessional."

"You wouldn't want him to..." I trailed off practically in a sputter as my brother lifted his hand and knocked on the nearest door.

Rap-a-tap. Rap-rap. Rap-rap. Pause. *Rap-a-tap. Rap-rap. Rap-rap.*

It was clearly a predetermined pattern. A code to the person on the other side to let him know who to expect. Immediately, it reminded me of my rhythmic punches at the gym. A fact which distracted me just long enough that the door had time to swing open before I could make another protest. The dimly lit entryway appeared to be empty. But only a heartbeat went by before a voice—which was strained and relieved at the same time, and presumably belonged to the pro-hockey player client—carried out to issue a greeting to Charles.

"Afternoon, Mr. Ames," he said. "Please. Come on in."

Charles offered a responding nod and stepped forward. Gritting my teeth, I followed him in. Mostly because it was a choice between that and making a scene in the hallway.

"Sorry about the wait, Mr. Jones," said my brother. "Took a little longer than I hoped to secure your secret weapon."

"My secret weapon?" replied the still unseen man.

Charles took another step and angled himself so that he no longer blocked the space between me and TJ Jones. And of course, the new position gave me a full view of the hockey player. My assessment was automatic. A protective reflex that occurred more often than not when I came in contact with a new face. Particularly if that new face was male. And there was certainly no denying that TJ Jones fit the mold for the traditional masculine form.

He was tall. Wide-shouldered. Lean across the middle in a way that would've made me sure of his fitness level even if I hadn't known about his chosen career. His clothes were simple. A heather gray, zipper-front sweatshirt overtop of a T-shirt in the same shade, a pair of faded jeans with slightly frayed cuffs, and leather-strapped flipflops. He had the sweatshirt pushed up to his elbows, and his arms were tanned enough to be called olive. I caught a flash of ink on his left wrist.

Dark hair—visibly damp—capped his head in a floppy, carefree style. A bit of stubble covered a strong, square jaw. And pair of very blue eyes stared back at me. He was clearly making a reciprocal assessment, but I wouldn't exactly have called his examination unabashed. If anything, he looked as though he might be fighting his interest in my appearance. Nonetheless, his eyes roaming over me hyped up my self-awareness. I was suddenly very conscious of the fact my dress was extra short, I was braless underneath it, and I hadn't properly brushed my hair before coming. All of which set off the familiar alarm bells in my head.

I gave myself a mental kick in the ass and ordered my brain to get to work.

"No," I said.

I meant it to sound firm, but it came out more as a petulant snap. And my sharp tone made the hockey player blink.

"No?" he echoed.

"I will *not* be your fake girlfriend," I stated.

He blinked again, dark lashes moving across his blue gaze. "Uh. What?"

Shit.

I rounded on my brother and spoke through my teeth, trying to keep my tone as civil as possible. "You didn't even *tell* him, did you?"

Charles shot an exasperated look my way, then addressed TJ instead of me. "Apologies, Mr. Jones. Creative differences on the team."

I plastered my best approximation of a sweet smile onto my face and spoke to the hockey player, too. "Do you mind if we take a quick minute to ourselves?"

TJ's face was one-part puzzled and one-part

concerned, but he still swept his arm wide, gesturing for us to use the other side of the good-sized room. "Whatever you need."

"We'll only be a second," I promised. "Really."

I grabbed my brother's arm and led him away from TJ with as much aplomb as could be had under the circumstances. But when we were about ten steps away, Charles spoke before I could, his voice low, his tone blunt.

"You're not exactly making us look good here," he said.

"Me?" I replied incredulously. "You *ambushed* me with this."

"You wouldn't have come if I'd explained the details."

"No shit."

"TJ Jones is a minor celebrity. This is perfectly safe."

The way he said it—as if *I* were the unreasonable one—made my teeth clench. I cast a quick glance toward the hockey player to see if he was listening, but he'd ambled over to a set of sliding glass doors, and he was studying the panoramic view of the mountains in the distance. His hands were in his pockets, his eyes faraway.

I dropped my voice to a whisper anyway. "We both know why I don't *do* relationships. I'm honestly stunned you'd even suggest it."

"It isn't real, Ivy," my brother replied. "But it *is* really unprofessional to sneak away to argue in a corner."

I ignored his second comment in favor of the first. "Real or not, this isn't what I had in mind when I said I wanted field work."

"Field work is uncomfortable sometimes."

"Oh, great. Now you sound like Dad."

Charles let out a muted sigh. "Listen, Pint-Size. You have to know I wouldn't have asked you if the situation wasn't desperate."

"Ouch."

He winced. "That's not what I—"

I waved my hand, cutting him off. "Yeah, I get it. But to be fair, you *didn't* ask me. And you haven't explained a damn thing."

He inclined his head toward TJ. "Our client here isn't able to go to the police, and he hasn't disclosed why. That concerns me. He's made it clear he can't have a bodyguard in any official capacity, and he hasn't given me a full reason for that, either."

"Those are all big, giant red flags."

"I know," said my brother. "Any other time, I'd already have cut him loose. But I just have this gut feeling that if we don't help him, he won't *get* help."

His words were heavy with worry, and I couldn't help but steal another look at the man in question, searching for an explanation for my brother's unusually personal desire to help. TJ's position hadn't changed, but I could see that his body was practically rigid with tension. His strong jaw was set, too. And his handsome face—yes, there was no denying his good looks—had taken on a brooding quality. It did tug on my heart a little. But could I really put aside my past and do this? My pulse pumped a nervous beat at the mere thought of it. I flexed my hands, trying to dry them of the sudden, light sweat that covered them, then redirected my attention to Charles again.

"No," I said again. "I'm sorry, Charles, but your plan sucks. If you want me to be his bodyguard, then let me do it in a way that doesn't involve short skirts and making out."

The statement must've come out louder than I'd intended, because TJ spun toward us, shaking his head as he interrupted with a vehemence that might've even surpassed mine. "No. No goddamn way."

His tone got my back up, and my response just barely rode the edge of politeness. "I appreciate your input, but I can fight my own battle here."

"Pretty sure it just became *my* damn battle, too." His eyebrows bunched together in a frown that was nearly a scowl as he spoke to Charles. "Find another way."

My professionalism was teetering. But before I could demand to know what *his* problem was with the plan, a light rap on the door stopped me.

"Expecting company?" I asked tightly.

"Your brother instructed me to do whatever I'd normally do when I rented a room, so I did. I ordered some room service for lunch."

Exasperation made my words snappish. "By all means. Don't let us stop you from getting your food."

But I knew—even before Charles shot a look my way—I couldn't let TJ answer the door. In fact, I was already on the move, slinking toward the entrance as I finished speaking. But I didn't immediately go for the door. Instead, I pressed my back to the wall beside it, pushed my finger to my lips for silence, then shifted so I could press my ear to the wood. There was no sound on the other side. Not even the lightest footstep. I waited anyway, silently counting down from fifteen.

When I reached zero, I twisted my body again, this time to stand on my tiptoes and look through the peephole. Except for the room service cart and its silver-lidded tray, the hallway appeared to be completely empty.

I bit my lip and held my position for another ten seconds before finally sinking back down and spinning to face the two men again.

I pointed to the door. "All right. Go ahead and get your lunch."

He moved so quickly I didn't have time to get out of his way, and the result was that he brushed against me, filling my nose with a decidedly pleasant scent. It was clean and fresh, and definitely not created by any cheap hotel product. It made me want to draw in another breath. Which was weird on its own. But even stranger than that was the little voice in my head that piped up and asked if being his pretend girlfriend would be so bad after all.

Don't even, I said to my subconscious, taking a step back to give myself some space.

But as TJ swung open the door and closed his fingers on the rolling cart's handle, my instincts reared up a warning. Maybe it was the faintest buzz in the air. Or maybe there was another smell emanating up under TJ's nice one—a tinge of something foreboding. Either way, I knew I had to act. Without further thought, I threw myself toward the broad-shouldered man. Despite his size, I had both experience and surprise on my side. I hit him at just the right angle. Together, we toppled back into the room, my smaller body pressing to his in what would've been an intimate position under any other circumstances. It also would've set off my finely tuned self-defence mechanisms and earned him a knee in the groin. But there was no time to even think about that before a sizzle and pop sounded, and the air abruptly filled with a smoky, searing heat which pressed in, all around.

Chapter Three

Once upon a time, when I was about eight years old, my brothers were playing a game of touch football in the backyard. As usual, the five of them stuck me in a chair. Out of harm's way. They told me I was their water girl. Except, of course, they never actually let me *get* any water. But at some point, the game got out of control. Touches became tackles, and tackles became shoves, and one particularly aggressive maneuver sent Toby and Charles at me. The impact had launched me like a rocket. Up and out of my chair and straight toward our metal swing set, headfirst. And *boom!* My ears rang. The edges of my vision took on a weird blurriness that reminded me of a funhouse mirror. The pain was excruciating. But all of that had nothing on the current moment.

My ears weren't just ringing—they were consumed by a high-pitched whine that blocked out every other sound while simultaneously clogging up my ability to think. I wanted to put my hands up to stop the cacophony. But I didn't dare touch my head, because my brain felt like it was two sizes too big for my skull. On top of that, an onslaught of nettling stabs rained down over my back, poking through the fabric of my dress and hitting every inch of exposed skin along my neck and arms with a new jolt. Like I was being struck by shrapnel.

It feels like shrapnel because it is shrapnel, you dummy! That was a bomb. My brain paused, took a second to acknowledge it was true, then did its best to kick common sense to life as reality came rushing back. *Shit. Shit, shit,* shit! *This isn't good. Are we still under attack? We need to move!*

But as I rolled off the behemoth of a man underneath me then pushed to my feet, another problem struck. The hotel room *warped* around me. The walls looked like they were bending in and out, and no matter how many times I blinked, I couldn't clear it. A single step nearly made me fall. In fact, I likely would've hit the ground all over again—this time unintentionally—if not for the large hand landing on my elbow, steadying me.

I knew it was TJ who held me up. And a very illogical part of me wanted to pull away. I'd just saved *him,* dammit, not the other way around. But I was stubborn, not stupid. If I forced him to let go, I'd likely wind up on my ass. Anyway, what I did was adjust my arm so I was gripping him, too. A shared stability.

Using that, I took stock of the spinning room. I was sure the hotel staff would've started an evacuation the moment the resounding noise was heard. And it would only be a matter of time before the sirens began, and the authorities showed up. The fire engines would come first. But the police wouldn't be far behind. And cops meant red tape. Something I was familiar with. There'd been a number of instances over the years that Ames Security had faced having its investigations stonewalled. If I didn't want that to happen now, I needed to get some clues together. Prior to that, though, I had another obligation—to make sure the threat wasn't ongoing.

Five to ten minutes, tops, I told myself. *That's all I've got.*

I took a small breath and turned my throbbing head as fast as I dared. It was hard to keep my vision focused, but I did my best not to be perfunctory in my assessment. The first thing I noted was the door had closed behind us, containing the explosion. It wasn't necessarily a bad thing. Being cut off from the hallway meant if there was an immediate hazard out there, it would have to get through a wall. And there was no way that was happening without me noticing.

Unless the threat is already in *here.*

With the frightening thought in mind, my eyes slid over every probable hiding place in the immediate vicinity. Once. Then twice. There was no hint the bomber was present, nor that he had an accomplice waiting to strike again. It was a small relief, considering. But I didn't let myself relax even a smidge. Someone might bomb and run for the sake of saving their own ass, but that didn't mean there wasn't some other danger lurking. Possibly a secondary incendiary device, even.

I shifted my evaluation to the explosion's leftovers.

The source of the blast—the rolling room service cart—had been forced into the room, and it had miraculously survived. It sat on its side a few feet away. A charred mess spilled out around it. Food. A blackened tablecloth. Chunks of drywall. And some wires and metal likely belonged to whatever it was that had created the explosion. I noted it all, storing it away for later consideration. But when my study of the room widened, my heart dropped. My five-to-ten-minute window became the very last thing on my mind.

Fifteen feet away, my brother's prone body lay splayed out in front of the coffee table. He was partially obscured by the couch, and his navy pants blended in with the curtain that had fallen beside him. That, coupled with my still-fuzzy head, explained why I hadn't spied him right away. But now that I *had*...I couldn't understand how I'd missed him. From where I stood, I could just see the hem of his pale blue shirt, pulled free and hanging over his belt.

No. Please, no. Why didn't I look for him first?

For a moment, my feet remained rooted to the spot, frozen by fear of what I'd find if I got closer. But then protective instincts kicked in, and I moved toward him. Or I tried to. Something held me back. *TJ Jones.* I'd already forgotten he was holding me up. Without looking his way, I tried to shake him off. Instead of releasing me, his grip tightened, making me Yoyo on the spot. Damn him.

I tossed him what I intended to be a scathing look, but when I spoke, my accompanying words had an unmistakably plaintive ring. "Let me go."

Neither my expression nor my order had any effect. Either he didn't hear me—maybe he had the same thing going on in his ears as I did—or he simply chose to ignore my demand.

I flung my attention back to Charles then gave my arm another vicious yank. TJ still didn't budge in his hold. Instead, he shook his head and said something I couldn't make out.

Frustrated, worried, and getting angrier by the second, I used my free hand to point to my ear. "I can't hear you, dumbass, and that's my brother. So just let me go."

TJ shook his head again, and then—suddenly—his mouth was right beside the same ear I'd just pointed to, so close I could feel the heat of his breath as he spoke. And though his voice had a faraway, underwater quality to it, his words were discernible.

"You took the majority of the blast," he said. "Stay here for just a second. Hold the back of this chair to keep from falling over, and I'll go check him out."

An immediate protest started to form. "He's—"

"Your brother. I know." He dropped my arm, pushed my hand to the chair in question, then turned away.

I wanted to chase him. No. More than that. I wanted to push past him and drop to my brother's side. But fear of what I'd find held me rooted to the spot. I settled for following TJ with my eyes as he crossed the room. His movements held an undeniable grace. He easily picked his way through the debris, not tripping or stumbling or even pausing to avoid any of the rubble as he made his way over to Charles.

Because he's a hockey player, I recalled belatedly.

For a moment, my blurry brain imagined him on the ice. It was easy to picture him gliding through his opponents with the puck in front of him. Stick down. Head up. Untouchable. Not that I was a huge fan of the sport. Or any professional sport, for that matter. But I definitely understood the basics. Maybe a little more than that, even. Growing up in a houseful of boys had supplied me with an abundance of testosterone-fueled competitiveness and plenty of exposure to the zealous fandom of sports stars. I couldn't relate to the painted faces and the playoff beards, but I did have an appreciation of athleticism in general. Which in turn meant I had an appreciation for TJ's movements. Especially when those movements included bending over to gently touch my brother's back.

I held my breath as TJ leaned down even more. His big body blocked my view of Charles, but I didn't dare turn away in case something happened while my eyes were elsewhere.

Why had I been so stubborn about telling my brother to take his idea and shove it somewhere unpleasant? He was right. Field work was field work. It was short-sighted of me to let my emotions—to let my specific fear—rule my present. Hadn't I spent three and three-quarter years trying to get myself to a point where it didn't matter?

I'm sorry, Charles, I thought.

A sob was doing its best to work its way out of my throat. But the sound faded away before it could fully form. Because TJ was reaching down even more now, and this time, it was to help Charles get up from the floor. My brother's eyes were open and aware, if a little dazed. He pushed a hand to his side, then looked over in my direction. His expression was annoyed, in typical Charles fashion.

Oh, thank God.

As another bonus, in the few seconds it took for the two of them to get back to me—with my brother limping a little but not seeming to need any actual support—I started to feel slightly better. My head definitely wasn't unclogged. My back still stung where it'd been struck by the fallout of the bomb. But the room had stopped moving on its own, and when I took a step, I didn't feel woozy, which was a welcome improvement. Unfortunately, one thing that hadn't been restored yet was my hearing. So, when Charles said something to me in greeting, all I was sure of was his words included my hated nickname.

"*Hey, Pint-Size…*" And the rest was gobbledygook.

I frowned. "Sorry. What?"

But my brother had already looked away, his eyes roaming the room in an obvious attempt to inventory the situation. And it was TJ who leaned in to give me the direct-to-ear translation.

"He said he's fine, and it's not as bad as it looks," he told me. "He also said this shit is *exactly* why they don't want you in the field."

Despite my relief that my brother was okay, irritation pricked at me. So did embarrassment. My eyes narrowed, watching Charles as he did the same visual inventory I'd already done. A slightly childish tirade built up in my head.

Hadn't he *just* given me a lecture on professionalism before all this went down? How professional was it to make a comment like that about me in front of a client? And how *dare* he jump to the conclusion I hadn't made an assessment? If it had been one of my other brothers, he would've assumed a proper check had been done already.

I bit my lip to keep from letting any of it out. It would only make me sound like I really *didn't* belong there. I turned to TJ, ready to take charge. After all, he was my client, too. And even if I didn't like the modus operandi for making it that way, I was going to go ahead and claim ownership. But before I could speak up, a sound at last managed to break through the ringing in my ears. It was the wail of sirens.

TJ's attention swung toward the glass doors on the other side of the room, and his concern was obvious in the sudden tightening of his jaw.

"Charles said you called us because you're trying to avoid the cops, and I assume that's still true?" I asked.

He answered with a short nod.

"Then we should go before they get here and start asking questions," I told him.

My brother had rejoined us again, and the thin set of his mouth told me he was readying an argument. I put up hand.

"You might as well save it, Chuck," I said. "I won't be able to hear you anyway."

He spoke despite my warning, gesturing toward the sound of the sirens.

I shook my head and turned to TJ, weirdly sure he'd give me a straight answer. "Is he complaining about leaving a crime scene?"

TJ nodded, then leaned in. "He used the word 'fleeing' rather than 'leaving,' but yeah."

Charles said something else, his hands moving rapidly along with whatever irritated statement he was making. A command, undoubtedly. And the only part of it I thought I caught was his accusation of me being a numbskull. And that was simply because I knew what the insult looked like—it'd been my brother's favorite since we'd been kids. But I wasn't going to let him steamroll me.

"You made this my case," I reminded him. "If you don't like my decisions, you can leave by yourself. But it's my job to protect Mr. Jones. And I sure as hell wouldn't feel good about throwing the Ames name down the toilet in order to follow some moral code you've got. We'll work on our story and other logistics as soon as our client is in the clear."

Charles added something else.

I met his gaze. "If you're trying to argue it's against the law to leave the scene, I'll tell you that I know it's not. An enormous chunk of my job is becoming familiar with how the system works. I know all the rules and how to bend them to our advantage. Trust me…you can't beat me on this, Chuck. You might as well join me."

He threw his hands up.

"I'll assume that's an admission of defeat," I replied.

He jammed a finger in the direction of the exit.

"Glad we see eye to eye." I infused the words with extra sweetness, then turned to TJ. "Stay behind me as we move out, all right? I'm not armed, but I'm more than competent in a hand-to-hand fight. My brother will pull up the rear."

To avoid any further protest, I spun on my heel and strode to the door. But when I stood on my tiptoes and peered out the peephole, I saw that walking out wasn't going to be as easy as I'd assumed. The hallway outside the door was enveloped in black smoke.

Chapter Four

I gave the door handle a light touch, and when the metal came back cool, I almost wanted to cry with relief. Heat would've indicated a blast of fire—one that would've made a successful escape questionable at best.

Just smoke, I said to myself, looking through the peephole for a final second. *Which is bad enough on its own. But at least we have options. I hope.*

I dropped my hand and turned around, doing my best to school my face into a professional, in-control mask as I addressed TJ in a calm voice. "Is there another way to get out?"

He started to answer, saying something I still couldn't hear over the ringing in my ears, then he remembered my hearing issue without being reminded and stepped closer.

"Is there a problem?" he asked into my ear.

His clean scent invaded my senses once again, and I moved back a few inches. Out of smelling distance.

"Would I be asking for another way out if there *weren't* a problem?" I countered.

His attention flicked from me to the door then back again. For a second, I could've sworn he was about to move to check the situation for himself. My eyes narrowed, and I automatically took a more defensive pose, widening my stance and putting my hands on my hips.

Try it, I dared mentally.

His foot started to lift. But after an almost undetectable hesitation, he just lowered it down again and stayed exactly where he was.

Smart choice.

Unfortunately, my brother didn't do the same. Either he didn't notice the change in my body language, or he didn't care. Likely the latter. He brushed past me, took his own look out the peephole, dropped what could only be a muttered curse, then spun back to TJ and said something. I couldn't hear him, but if I had to hazard a guess, I'd say he was repeating my question about a way out. Probably almost word for word.

TJ cast a glance toward me, and I knew I was right. And I also knew he'd caught my brother's unconscious undermining as well as I had. But I kept my lips pressed together and refused to acknowledge it. It was a means to an end.

Charles spoke again, and this time I was sure it was just a prod. *Mr. Jones? A way out?*

A small frown creased TJ's forehead, and before he answered, he sidled up beside me and tipped down his chin so I could catch his words, too.

"There aren't any other doors out to the hall, but there's a balcony," he said. "I doubt it's much of an escape route, though. We're on the eleventh floor."

My brother replied, no doubt something to the effect of not ruling anything out, then he strode toward the sliding glass doors on the other side of the room.

TJ turned his attention my way.

"As far as I know," he said, "There's no way to get down from there unless we're planning on jumping."

He paused. "I *really* hope that's not the plan."

I shook my head. "Ames Security is good, but we haven't yet mastered the art of unassisted human flight."

My gaze sought my brother. He appeared to have finished his visual check of the patio doors, and he was now sliding them open in a very slow, very cautious way.

In a dry voice I added, "Not that I'm aware of, anyway."

TJ's mouth twitched with momentary amusement before he seemed to remember there was nothing funny about the current situation.

"What did you see out there in the hall?" he asked.

"Smoke," I admitted. "A lot of it."

"Well, shit."

"That's one way to put it."

TJ eyed Charles, who was only just stepping through onto the patio. "You want to go tell him to hurry up? Or you want *me* to?"

I sighed and shook my head again. "No, give him a minute. Trust me. He saw what was out there, too, and he seriously needs to do the balcony check himself. Even if that means wasting time that we could be using to get the hell out of here alive. And speaking of which…just because my brother is preoccupied doesn't mean we should be standing around. You want to give me a hand and grab three pillowcases off the bed then meet me at the bathroom sink?"

"Three pillowcases? Why do you…" He trailed off as I raised my eyebrow, then cleared his throat and adjusted his response to acquiescence rather than a question. "Yeah, sure. Three pillowcases, coming up."

I watched him only long enough to be sure he was going to do as I'd instructed and strip the pillows of their Egyptian cotton cases, and then I hurried to the bathroom. There, at the sink, I turned on the tap full blast. Moments later, TJ appeared at my side. The requested items were in his hands, and his face was scrunched up with puzzlement as he held them out to me.

"Okay," he said, standing close enough that he could be sure I'd hear him. "What now?"

"This," I replied, immediately holding the first bit of fabric under the tap and pretending I wasn't extraordinarily aware of how his large frame was practically spooning me.

He frowned. "Mind if I ask for any hints as to *why*?"

"You like breathing, right?" I finished with the first pillowcase then dropped it in a sopping mess on the counter.

"Don't we all?" he replied.

I held the second pillowcase under the tap. "And I'm guessing you don't have a bunch of oxygen masks kicking around?"

"Not something I generally carry with me, no."

I dropped the second, soaked pillowcase beside the first and repeated the routine with the third one.

"So barring the sudden, magical appearance of any mechanical breathing apparatuses…" I said. "We're going to need these to hold over our mouths and noses when we get out there."

"Will that work?"

"I sure as hell hope so."

I finished with the final pillowcase, and without

thinking about it turned around with the intention of handing it over. But TJ was still ultra close to me, and the wet fabric slapped into his T-shirt and stuck there. I winced as the water immediately soaked his stomach and began to drip on the floor.

"Whoops!" I said, my cheeks warming. "I hope you weren't too concerned about your damage deposit."

"Last thing on my radar," he told me, meeting my eyes as he lifted his hand to take the pillowcase from me.

For a second—with our nearness to one another and the way our fingers met—I could've sworn there was a double entendre in his statement. It was a ridiculous thing to even cross my mind. Despite the absurdity of the notion, my face heated even more. And the remarkable blue of TJ's gaze seemed to be pinning me to the spot. It was an odd moment. One that made my pulse thrum with nerves, and one that made me sure I should pull away. When was the last time I was this close to a man—one who wasn't one of my brothers or someone whose ass I was about to kick?

You know when, said my subconscious.

And the reminder should've been enough of a warning. But I just stood still, heart hammering, nerves alight. I don't know how long we would've stayed that way if not for Charles's appearance at the bathroom door then, his expression sober.

I just barely managed not to spring away from TJ.

My brother's mouth worked, forming more words I couldn't hear. And I didn't dare step closer to TJ again.

I blew out a breath. "I have no idea what you just said, but I'm assuming whatever it was, it was something that would lead to needing one of these?"

I grabbed another of the pillowcases and tossed it at my brother, who caught it in the air, then immediately dropped it. I smiled as he gestured angrily toward the sopping mess and said something that didn't make it past my blocked eardrums.

"Still can't hear you, Chuck," I reminded him. "But if you don't want to die of smoke inhalation, then I'd advise picking that up and using it to cover your face while we get the hell out of here."

I didn't wait for my brother to answer. I didn't want to waste any more time arguing. Instead, I did something else. Something small, but that I didn't really understand. I slung my own pillowcase over my shoulder, and then I closed my fingers around TJ's hand and pulled.

Chapter Five

I don't know what possessed me to take the hockey player's palm in mine. Excuses flitted through my head. Irritation at my brother, maybe? Something to prove? Or just a true need to get out of the hotel room as fast as possible? The last thing seemed the most plausible. Or at least I *wanted* it to be the most plausible.

Safety—mine, Charles's, and TJ's—was a genuine concern. I definitely didn't feel like dying in a fiery mess or sucking in a lungful of smoke. Not ever, of course. But especially not today. Not on a day I'd been invited to do field work. Was that a good enough reason to be clinging to a client as I pulled him from the bathroom and out through the room? I doubted it.

There was also a second factor to consider. I just plain *didn't* hold hands. In fact, under usual circumstances, the idea of being close to a man like that made my heart skip a nervous beat in a bad way. For a good reason. But just the same, I held on the whole time. My fingers stayed tight when I used my free hand to grab the closest thing I could use as a weapon—a long, narrow candy dish—and I continued the grasp all the way to the door. There, I finally let go. But only because I had to. And even then, what I felt wasn't quite relief. I actually had to order myself to forget it altogether, so I could push up to steal another look out through the peephole. As before, the hallway was clouded with smoke. The thick, acrid-looking kind. But as far as I could see, it was devoid of people.

Yeah, because anyone who was out there would've collapsed already. And if they didn't *keel over...it's because they* planned *to be engulfed in smoke, and they came prepared with more than a few wet pillowcases.*

I shook off the dark thoughts and put my hand on the knob, testing its heat once more. It was still cool, thank God. I squinted a little harder, straining to make sure I hadn't missed anything outside the room. I still saw nothing.

"Have the two of you got your DIY masks on?" I asked.

I sank down off my tiptoes and started to turn and confirm the answer to my query, but TJ moved quicker. He'd already leaned in—probably to get close enough that I'd be able to hear his response—and I fell into his chest. His hands came up, too, steadying me for the second time in the last short while. It was a momentarily intimate pose. Almost an embrace. In all honesty, it *would* have been an embrace if not for the candy-dish-weapon between us.

What's worse? This...or the hand holding?

Pretending my face wasn't as warm as the anticipated fire, I pulled away. "Mask?"

"Putting mine on now," TJ told me. "And Charles is good to go, too."

I turned a quick glance in my brother's direction. Though his eyes were pinched at the corners, he did have his pillowcase in place. Satisfied, but also worried he might try to take over, I spun to face the door again right away.

"All right, guys," I said over my shoulder. "Backs

to the wall, please."

I suspected Charles was either muttering a complaint or at least wanting to, but after less than a second, I felt them shuffle into place. Relieved at the lack of argument, I lifted my own pillowcase up and tied it into place so I could have two free hands. Then I adjusted my position, took a breath, slowly opened the door, and held it open just an inch. Immediately, smoke poured in. My eyes wanted to squeeze shut, and I had to fight off the automatic urge to protect my vision. I focused on counting to ten in my head. It was enough time for someone to pounce from out in the hall.

When there was no movement, I gave the door another little push and held it open about two feet more. I braced myself for some kind of attack. None came. But more smoke billowed in, enough to elicit a cough, even through the wet fabric.

I counted to ten again. Then cautiously moved forward. My first step into the hall made me blink. And not just because of the thick, smoggy air. I was also struck by a startling spray of water, cascading down from overhead and prickling my back, reminding me that I was injured too, albeit to less of an extent than Charles.

The sprinkler system.

The fire had obviously triggered the activation through its heat. Which was a good thing. A life-saving thing. Even through the smoke, I could see that the fire had burned quick and hot. The synthetic carpet below my feet was almost black. Charred. Melted in some spots. I didn't even want to think about what would've happened had the hotel not been properly equipped. The only downside was that as the water continued to hit the ground, the smoldering carpet hissed and sent up even more smoke.

Being careful to keep my head low and draw as few breaths as possible, I took a step fully out of the room. The carpet squished and crunched at the same time. It was disconcerting, and I was grateful when I felt TJ's brief but reassuring touch on my shoulder.

"Stairs are to our right," he said into my ear.

"Do they go all the way to the underground parking lot?" I replied.

"As far as I know. Is that our goal?"

"I think it'll be easier to get out unseen than if we try to go through the lobby."

I moved forward a bit more, still cautious. I paused and listened. I did my ten-count. Then I stepped again. I peered through the thick haze. I made sure Charles and TJ were still following me as closely as they should be. Three more steps. Then four. And at last, we seemed to be out of the worst part of it. Through my blurred vision, I could see the fire damage stretched from TJ's room all the way down the corridor.

Behind me, the hockey player dropped a curse that was actually loud enough for me to hear. And I couldn't blame him. Clearly, the bomb had done even more damage out here than it had on the inside. Looking at the destruction made me sure it was just sheer luck the majority of the fire power had been expelled outward. And even more randomly fortuitous the door had kept it from wreaking havoc in the room itself.

Or worse, I thought with a dark shiver.

I made myself keep going, quicker now. My throat was already raw, and a few small coughs escaped. The cuts on my back burned with my movements. But in just a couple more seconds, we reached the end of the hall where the wide, metal door beckoned with its bright red exit sign. I glanced back at Charles and TJ once more, then brought my arm up to the bar that would let us into the stairwell. I was still wary of moving without prudence, but I was also more confident now, that whoever had created the explosion was long gone. Sticking around past the initial ignition—or at least staying in close proximity—would be very risky. Assuming the bomber didn't want to get caught, of course.

Not even going to consider it, I said to myself. *If this was a suicide mission, they wouldn't have left things to chance.*

With that in mind, I pushed the door open. The action brought in a much-needed rush of fresher air, but I didn't pause to appreciate it. Any second, the fire fighters could be on their way up. And if they suspected anyone was trapped up on the higher floors, they'd probably try to get up even faster. I pulled off my mask and picked up the pace.

My brain churned to match the new speed. Because it had just occurred to me that TJ wasn't some average hotel guest. He was a celebrity or at least a somewhat prominent sports figure. And while that didn't render his life more important than anyone else's, it did make him more noticeable. Someone was bound to realize the hockey player was missing, sooner rather than later. I might not know much about how hotels ran, and I had no clue what the protocol was for evacuation, but I had a feeling accounting for people was high on the to-do list. As I made a mental note to let the staff know TJ was alive and well, the man in question gave my shoulder a tap, somehow magically avoiding my injuries.

I turned. "What is it? We're only at the fifth—"

Before I could finish, TJ stepped aside and pointed. And my breath stuck in my throat worse than it had in the smoky hallway. Charles was hunched over, one hand on the railing, the other squeezing his side. When he looked up at me, his face was pale and pinched. And very defensive.

He was faking being okay, I realized belatedly.

Angry and scared at the same time, I stepped toward him. "Let me see it."

My brother started to shake his head, then seemed to think better of it. Wincing visibly, he eased away from the railing, and with shaking fingers, he lifted the hem of his shirt up to chest level.

I sucked in another breath, and this time it was sharp. Charles's ribcage was covered in fresh, wickedly blue bruises, and when he turned to the side, the new position showed off a gash that wrapped around to his back.

Chapter Six

For a good ten seconds, my concern for my brother's well-being won the battle for supremacy over my emotions. His injuries were obviously far worse than he'd let on. He needed help. Badly. He probably shouldn't have been walking around, let alone traipsing down multiple sets of stairs. I didn't even know how he'd managed to get this far. I opened my mouth to tell him we were going to get some medical help before we did anything else, but TJ touched my elbow, drawing my attention away.

I turned to see what he wanted, and frustration—no doubt both a deflection and misplaced, but overwhelming and impossible to ignore—surged up.

"You could've warned me," I said, my tone just shy of snappish.

Surprise flashed over his features. "Me?"

For the first time, I could hear without having to have him right beside me. It was a relief. But it was also secondary at that moment.

"You said he was fine," I reminded him. "Clearly, he's not."

"To be fair, I said that *he* said he was fine."

"Really? You're going to get nit picky about it now? You—no. Never mind. I don't even have time to argue with you about it." I turned to my brother. "And you need a doctor. Stat."

Charles's expression soured further. "I just—"

"A doctor," I repeated firmly. "Which means we're going to have to get you into an area where there are people. Which also means my plan has to be adjusted."

"Yeah, and the second the paramedics finish with me, the cops will want to talk to me, too," my brother said.

It was obvious his concern about the police was for TJ's benefit, and I wanted to tell him I couldn't care less about any contractual obligations right then. I would have, but I knew Ames Security meant everything to him. It mattered to me, too. And I had a feeling that if I wanted Charles to comply with me in any way at all, I needed to keep TJ's case at the front of our discussion.

"If that happens—if you *do* have to answer any questions—just stall them," I replied with as much patience as I could muster. "Tell them you bumped your head and don't remember. We both know they'll believe you. Or if you really can't lie, exercise your right to say nothing. I don't care." I paused and shook my head. "It's going to have to be the lobby. At least for you." I held out my hand. "Come on."

Charles gave me a doubtful look, and I expelled an exasperated noise.

"It's not a contest right now, Chuck."

"I'm not trying to beat you, Pint-Size. I'm just pretty sure you can't carry me."

It gave me a pang to hear him admit—even in a roundabout way—that he needed so much assistance.

"Here," TJ interjected. "I'll help him the rest of the way."

"Fine." I exhaled again, gratefully this time.

"Just…be careful. He's a pain in the ass sometimes, but I'm kind of attached to him anyway."

TJ nodded and slung his arm very gently across Charles's waist, and after a few seconds of adjustment, we resumed our downward trek. I kept the pace slower now, worried any amount of speed might further exacerbate my brother's injuries. It made descending the last of eleven flights of stairs take far longer than it ought to. But finally, we reached a landing with a door labeled *Lobby*, and right away, TJ shifted to let Charles stand on his own, who then reached for the door handle.

"Wait," I said.

"Wait?" TJ echoed.

"I need to think about how we're going to do this."

My brother spoke up, his voice laced with poorly disguised pain. "You already said we had to go through the lobby."

"I said it had to be the lobby for *you*," I corrected, waving my hand as he tried to add something else. "Just give me a second, okay?"

I pursed my lips and narrowed my eyes at the door. There'd probably be chaos on the other side. Or if not—if everyone in the hotel had already managed to be filtered to the exterior—then the first responders would be on site. Either scenario was fine for getting Charles the help he needed. But conversely, either scenario was bad for TJ if he didn't want to get spotted.

Which leaves us with only one option.

"We have to split up," I stated bluntly.

"Split up how?" My brother's reply was laden with suspicion.

"I think you already know the answer to that," I told him.

"Christ," he muttered. "You can't seriously expect me to—"

I cut him off. "To do what? Let me do my job? It's not like you're in any shape to take over."

"We can find an alternative."

"Ames Security *is* the alternative. The only other possibilities are either giving up the case to the police, or letting TJ try to find someone else to take this on."

Charles sighed. "You know why I'm worried, Pint-Size."

"I do know," I said. "We've been over this. But you can't make my decisions for me."

My brother's eyes sank shut. I just had to wait it out, and I stole the briefest glance at TJ. His expression was decidedly neutral, and I suspected he was trying to pretend he wasn't curious about what we were alluding to. I couldn't blame him. I'd have been curious, too. And for the briefest second, I had half a mind—*half a crazy mind*—to just blurt it out.

It might save all three of us a hell of a lot of awkward trouble.

Of course, I kept my mouth shut. There was no reason to drag a client into our personal business, and there was every reason to keep him out of it.

At last, my brother opened his eyes, and he addressed me in a grudging tone. "You'll need to find somewhere safe to hang out."

"Yes, I know," I replied.

"And once you've gotten all the details from TJ, you need to come up with a plan."

"I know."

"As much as you might not like it…mine was a solid one. So, if you're not going to use it, you'll need something equally workable."

"I know, Chuck. I know all of it." I felt affectionate and impatient at the same time. "I've been in this business for just as long as you have."

Charles didn't argue. Instead, he reached out and, with a pain-tinged grunt, pulled me into a hug. Tears tried to spring up, but I fought them off.

"You'll be safe, right?" I said, close to his ear.

"I promise," he said, giving me an extra squeeze.

He pulled away and looked over at TJ. And I fully expected him to extract a promise from the hockey player that his little sister would be well-taken care of. But when Charles spoke, it was to say something almost the opposite, really. And it surprised me in a good way.

"Ivy will take care of you," he stated firmly.

TJ nodded. "What about you? Do you want a hand getting out there?"

Charles shook his head, moved haltingly toward the door, then pulled it open, speaking as he did it. "I'll be able to make it as far as the lobby on my own. And once I'm out there, I'll have more help than I'll know what to do with."

"Before we head down to the underground lot, I'm going to wait thirty seconds," I told him. "Just in case you need to come back."

"Better make it a full minute." He winked in his typical, big brotherly fashion, but his face was drawn as he made his joke. "Hurrying probably isn't in my best interest."

I forced a light tone, too. "And that reminds me…call me as soon as you've seen a doctor, okay? I want to gloat about how right I am about how badly you're hurt."

"I will," he assured me, pausing once more before he stepped out of the stairwell. "But not so you can gloat. I need to make sure you're doing everything right."

"Shut up," I replied without any venom. "I'll do everything better than you would."

Charles smiled, then limped away, leaving the door to whoosh shut behind him with an ominous bang. For a second after the sound echoed off the concrete, my gaze hung on the space he'd vacated.

"I swear to God..." I muttered. "If he dies, I'm going to find someone to resurrect him so I can kill him again myself."

"I take it you two don't always see eye to eye on things?" TJ replied.

"It would be really unprofessional of me to answer that honestly."

"Would it be more or less professional than calling me a dumbass?" he asked teasingly.

My face warmed. "I didn't mean that."

He raised an eyebrow. "You didn't mean it, or you didn't mean for me to hear it?"

I was sure my blush was deepening. "Both. But in my defense, I was a little worked up because I thought my brother might be...well. You know."

"In need of a resurrection?"

"Yes. Exactly." My attention swung to the door for another moment, then came back to TJ. "Sorry for snapping at you before. I know it wasn't your fault he was covering up his injuries."

He shrugged. "I'm a hockey player. I get paid to take hits."

"I'm serious," I told him. "Thank you for checking him out when I couldn't."

There was no disguising the slight break in my voice as I spoke, and for a second after the words left my mouth, the look on TJ's face made me think he was about to pull me into an embrace just like my brother had. I almost wanted him to. But then he gave his head a shake.

"Anyone would've done the same thing in that situation," he stated.

Maybe he was right. Maybe anyone *would* have done it. But I found myself brushing off an unexpected flicker of disappointment that it wasn't about *me,* specifically. I ordered myself to get it together. I needed to be thinking of a good way to get my client out of there, not wishing he would hug me.

Okay, Ivy. You've got this. Prove to Charles you really are *as good as him.*

I straightened my shoulders and nodded a firm, quick nod—both to my absent brother and to TJ—then let out a breath. "Nonetheless, thank you. And I promise you, our success rate is phenomenal, and I don't mean that in a braggy way. It's just a statement of fact. I'll get you out of here safely. You have my word. And speaking of which, we should go. Our minute of waiting is up, and if we don't manage to get clear of the building, then I'll have sent Charles off on his own for no reason."

"You're the boss," said TJ.

His words were a little too quick. And I knew exactly what it meant.

"You don't have to do that," I said as I started down the stairs.

"Do what?" he replied, hurrying to catch up to my quick steps.

"Go out of your way to make me feel like you think I'm in charge."

"You *are* in charge," he hedged.

"Oh, I am," I agreed as we rounded a landing with no door and continued down the next set of steps. "But that doesn't mean *you* believe it. I have five older brothers. And when we were kids, they took turns letting me win at cards or boardgames or arm wrestles. I figured out their trick by the time I was about five. Now I'm pretty much an expert at recognizing fake deference when I see it."

"Look. I'm—"

"Don't apologize. It's fine. And I'm used to it. I'm a tiny woman with a pretty face. People underestimate me all the time."

We reached the final landing, and I started to reach for the door labeled P1, but TJ shot out a hand and stopped me. Startled, I spun back. My hand tried to close into a ready-to-punch fist, and I willed my fingers to stay open.

"What's wrong?" I asked.

"Nothing. I just wanted to say I guess we have that in common," TJ told her. "People underestimate me, too."

I looked his big frame up and down with dubious scrutiny, then met his eyes. "Yeah, no. Sorry. You're definitely *not* a tiny woman with a pretty face."

Despite everything going on, he chuckled. "I wasn't saying we have *that* part in common. I just meant because of my career choice and the way I play the game, some people assume I'm not the brightest crayon in the box."

I could feel the two spots of color rise in my cheeks. "I already said I didn't *mean* to call you a dumbass."

"That wasn't what I was thinking of, I swear. Now that you've brought it up, though..." His smile widened to a cheeky grin.

I shook my head. "Any chance you can forget that I reminded you?"

"Probably not."

"Dammit."

"But I meant what I said. I know what it's like to have people make assumptions. And you probably saved my life up there in that room, Ms. Ames. If not, then at the very least, you protected me from some kind of physical damage that could've ended my career. I'm sure as hell not going to insinuate that you're incapable of continuing to do so."

I met his eyes again. Only this time, it was different. I was genuinely studying him. Weighing what he'd said. He didn't waver in his returning stare. For some reason, it seemed important to him that I believe him. Imperative, almost.

And do *you believe him?* I wondered.

I tried to tell myself I was completely overthinking it. There was no reason for a client *not* to have confidence his bodyguard would protect him. But this felt like more than that. As though TJ was asking *me* to put my faith in *him.*

The seconds were ticking by, and with each one, the silence between us seemed to take on even more meaning. Complete trust was a leap I wasn't entirely sure I could take. But I thought I should at least try.

"Okay," I finally said. "How about we make a deal? I won't underestimate you, and you won't underestimate me?"

"Sounds good to me," TJ replied immediately.

"All right. Let's get the hell out of here," I said, pulling open the door.

Chapter Seven

As we stepped into the parking garage, darkness pressed in. I had to blink a few times before my vision cleared enough to see that the concrete space appeared to be suffering from an electrical short-out of some kind and was only brightened a bit by emergency lights.

"Not exactly welcoming, is it?" TJ's voice was low. "Even by parking lot standards."

"It'll be okay," I replied. "We're going to be in here for only two or three minutes."

Despite the firmness of my words, I had an unsettled feeling in my stomach. And try as I might, I couldn't shake it. Even with the distraction of my primary focus—the urgent need to find a safe, undetected route out—the unease insisted on sticking around.

Yeah, I think I have a pretty good excuse for that, I reminded myself as I took an initial look around. *I was just bombed. My brother was badly injured, and I had to send him off alone. Oh. And on the subject of being alone…I'm alone in the almost dark with a man who's a virtual stranger. And he's built like a tank, so. There's that.*

The churning thoughts were all valid. Any of those things was a good enough reason for the jump of nerves. Even the last one. Maybe especially the last one, actually. Regardless as to whether TJ was client.

But it wasn't something I wanted to dwell on. Particularly not since it made my brother's worry seem all the more accurate.

"That's not the problem anyway." I made the statement under my breath, but TJ still heard me.

"Sorry," he said. "I didn't quite catch that."

I felt the heat rise in my cheeks—something that seemed to be happening more and more frequently in the last short while. I brushed off his question and took a couple of steps forward in the dark.

"It was nothing," I said. "Just talking to myself."

"Regular habit of yours?" he asked, following closely behind me.

"Only when my head is ringing so badly I can't hear myself think."

I meant it as a joke, but his response was infused with concern. "Do you think maybe *you* should've seen a doctor, too?"

"I'm fine," I replied, pausing behind a cement column and peering through the dimly lit area in search of a way out that wasn't the main exit. "And before you ask, I don't mean that in the same way Charles did."

"I wasn't going to ask," TJ replied. "We literally just agreed not to underestimate each other. Unless you want to retract that deal already?"

My stomach did another strangely nervous flip, and I shook my head. "No, of course not."

"Good. But just in case…as a person who's been hit in the head with a puck on more than one occasion, I'm fully versed in concussion care."

"I'm fine. I swear."

It wasn't a lie. I felt physically okay. Not perfect, of course. My ears still had their buzz, and I was starting to ache a little, the same way I did after I'd gone too hard at the gym. Not to mention the sting from where the bomb's pieces had cut through my dress and singed my skin. But the butterflies in my stomach were the only real problem. They were pounding their wings so hard that they felt more like birds.

What is wrong *with me?*

I very nearly lifted a hand to still the inexplicable sensation. In fact, the only thing that stopped me from pressing my palm to my abdomen was spying a possible exit right then, and thankfully my finger pointed toward it instead of to my stomach.

"Does that look like a service ramp to you?" I asked.

TJ stepped closer, his shoulder brushing mine as he attempted to follow my sightline. "Where those yellow poles are?"

I nodded, but my mind was suddenly elsewhere. It was asking me when I'd stopped being good at avoiding touchable distance. Because since the moment the bomb had gone off, TJ seemed to have stayed within arms' reach. And right now, I could feel the heat of his body. I could smell his lightly fragranced soap again. And I didn't even have an urge to inch subtly away.

"Ms. Ames?" TJ prodded.

I was deeply thankful that the darkness was enough to cover my expression, and I feigned a small cough before answering. "Yes, by the yellow poles. See how they angle up a bit? I think they go into the cargo bay."

"You mean the kind a semi pulls up to?"

"Exactly. And there should be a door there so they can do direct unloads. Rollup, I'm guessing. Let's go check it out."

As we started off, I had a reprieve from the fluttering nerves. It was good to have a specific aim. But as quick as the tension abated, it came back again, spurred by the way TJ's hand bumped mine. Twice. I immediately remembered I'd grabbed hold of his fingers earlier and held them for far too long. It almost seemed like a good idea to do it again.

No, I told myself. *It's most definitely not a good idea to do it again. Not now. Not ever.*

Except as soon as I thought it, I realized that if I was going to proceed with my brother's plan, I was probably going to *have* to hold his hand again. After all, how convincing would I be as his supposed girlfriend if I refused even the smallest physical contact?

Hang on, interrupted my subconscious. *Since when did Charles's plan become a real option?*

It wasn't. It couldn't be. I just hadn't come up with an alternative yet.

But what if it's the only option?

The butterflies came to life again. Thankfully, we'd reached the yellow-painted poles, which gave me an excuse to forcefully stuff aside the unsettling sensation. Without looking at TJ, I quickly stepped up the stairs and onto the metal platform, then made my way to the door. It was a rollup, just as I'd expected. It was also sealed with a padlock at the bottom.

"I don't suppose you have a key hidden in that dress of yours, do you?" TJ's dry question announced that he'd joined me on the platform, once again making the space between us quite small.

I pretended not to notice his proximity as I answered. "No. No key. But that's fine. I don't need one."

I reached up and pulled two bobby pins from the back of my ponytailed hair. Without pausing, I used my nails to pinch off the protective plastic tips. Next, I bent them in just the right way. Then I knelt and took hold of the lock. It was a simple one. The most basic, really, and not at all designed to properly secure the door. Probably there only to discourage vandalism more than anything else. With a practiced motion, I inserted the first bobby pin, then the other. In under twenty seconds, I found the locking pins, released them, and pulled the padlock off. I stood up and held it out, and TJ took it with raised eyebrows.

"I don't know if I should be impressed or concerned," he said.

"Maybe stick with impressed," I replied. "At least until you're trying to keep me out of something yourself."

"Noted."

I smiled, then sidled past him to get to the panel attached to the platform's railing. I flipped up the plastic cover, pressed the button there, and turned to watch the corrugated steel curl up. When it had reached a height of about two feet, I pressed the button again to stop it. I surveyed the opening I'd created. It was wide enough for us to slip through, but hopefully not so wide as to immediately draw attention from any casual passersby on the other side.

With that done and with a possible unwanted audience in mind, I dropped down and took a careful look without fully pushing my body outside.

My view was limited, but I still managed a basic inventory of our surroundings. We appeared to be at the end of an alley. Two short rows of commercial buildings—rear sides facing in—gave it away. The structures led up to the loading dock, creating a dead end. I could see a large garbage bin on one side and no fewer than three *No Parking* signs along the other. I imagined when a semi-truck backed up to deliver its load, there was little more than walking room between it and the backdoors of the other business. It was good, though, because it meant that so long as TJ and I could get out undetected, we'd be well-sheltered from street view. And hopefully, if anyone happened to spy us from inside any of the buildings, whoever it was would be more concerned with the commotion going on out front than with what was happening in the back.

That hope's all well-and-good...Unless the someone who sees us is the same someone who planted the bomb, and they want to use the layout to box us in.

I shook off the thought. If someone *did* try to trap us, we had the option of diving back into the loading bay. Or if really necessary, we could pound on one of the doors in the alley. Yes, it would draw the attention we were trying to avoid. But it was better than the alternative. Not ideal, but still a workable option.

I made a mental note to arm myself in some way as soon as I could, then drew my body back into the dark so I could explain everything to TJ.

"Okay, pretty straightforward plan," I told him. "We'll slip into the alley out there, then make our way up to the end. We'll decide which way to go once we're there. Path of least resistance, I'm thinking. It won't matter too much anyway because we can always wind back around if need be. Once we're far enough away, we'll come up with a more concrete destination."

TJ nodded. "Sounds good. Except for one thing."

"What's that?"

"It feels a little wrong not to offer to go first in case you need a human shield."

Despite the fact that his comment both made me worry about an immediate attack *and* bordered on undermining the deal we'd made, I felt a smile do its best to make its way onto my face. Mostly because he sounded genuinely conflicted. But also because it was such an absurd thing to say.

"A human shield?" I repeated.

His brown creased. "Isn't that what it's called when someone uses their body to protect someone else?"

"Well, I guess so. But who actually *says* that?"

"Me, apparently."

I fought a laugh. "Okay, then. I guess you *could* still offer."

"Yeah?"

"Sure."

"All right. You want me to go first?" he said, gesturing to the opening.

"To be my human shield?" I replied.

"Didn't we establish this already? Yes."

"Okay, then," I said again. "No, you may *not* be my human shield."

"Wait. What?"

"I told you that you could offer. Not that I'd accept."

The smile and the laugh won out, curving my lips up and making me chuckle as I ducked down and slid through the opening at the bottom of the door. But my amusement was forgotten as I slipped all the way out and nearly fell off the narrow platform on the other side. I probably *would* have fallen—and dropped down the full five feet or so to the ground, too—if TJ's arm hadn't shot out and pulled me back.

"Guess I misjudged how much space we had," I stated, my heart thundering as I tried to catch my breath. "And how far away the ground was."

"Guess you did," TJ replied. "Guess you're sorry about me and my offer to be your human shield, too, hmm?"

His voice was in my ear again, but this time, without the excuse of my temporary deafness, hearing it so close had a different feel. An intimacy.

An unexpected flash of warmth slid up my body. And then I clued in. The unease. The butterflies. They weren't coming from the fear of some unseen danger. They were coming from something far more basic. I was attracted to him.

Dammit. No. Hang on. More *than dammit. Shit on a fresh slice of toast.*

How had I not seen it before? I'd fully acknowledged his good looks, hadn't I?

But that's not the same thing, is it?

"Ms. Ames?" said TJ, and I knew I'd been silent for a few seconds too long.

"Just thinking," I replied quickly.

"Without taking this as me doubting your ability to climb down a height that's almost as tall as you are...do you want me to go first, then give you a hand?"

"Yes, sure. That sounds like a good idea."

It was a relief to have him break our physical contact. I needed the space to breathe without drawing in his scent. And for a few seconds, the reprieve hung on. TJ's feet hit the ground with a light thump. I sat up and I swung around for assistance, taking his outstretched hands. But as he helped me to the ground, the respite was yanked away, because I stumbled forward hard enough that he had to steady me. His warm hands gripped my arms as my face slammed into his solid chest. Immediately, my stomach fluttered.

Trying to calm the thump of my pulse, I eased myself away from TJ. But instead of giving myself the separation I was aiming for, I found myself staring up into his blue eyes. And I could swear I felt a physical pull.

It was almost embarrassing that I hadn't recognized the attraction for what it was before. The only excuse I could come up with was that it had been so long since I'd given a man more than a passing glance that it was the furthest thing from my mind. Add that to the fact that I was riding the kneejerk reaction of total protest to a fake girlfriend plan, then throw in a bomb, and apparently, I'd become completely out of touch with my own feelings.

Or maybe you just blocked it out.

That would make sense, too. But either way, it was bad.

"You okay?" TJ asked, his voice low and gruff.

I tried to nod, but the slight downward tip of my head brought my eyes to his lips. Which were full. And an appealingly ruddy shade of pink.

Shit.

Forcefully, I jerked my attention up again. Only now I found those blue eyes again. They were staring down at me, and I could've sworn I found open interest in them. Unmuted heat that matched what was running

through me. But it was mixed with something else.
Pain.

Identifying the emotion provided for a momentary buffer for my nerves. And I was compelled to know where it came from. Why would it hurt TJ—this strong, capable man—to find me attractive? Except I no sooner wondered about the source of the obvious feeling than his face changed again. There was no less kindness or concern in his gaze. But the desire I'd spied was now stowed so well that it made me think I'd imagined it.

The moment broke. And I probably should've been grateful. But quite suddenly, I found a new reason to worry. Standing at the end of the alley was a hooded figure. Watching us in eerie silence.

Chapter Eight

Every instinct I had told me the person watching us was the bomber. And I knew I had to give chase. It was the perfect chance to end this case, here and now. Before I had to deal with my attraction to TJ Jones. And before I had to enact my brother's plan, too. But I was frozen to the spot. A remembered fear surged up then dominated my body. It paralyzed me. Mere seconds were passing, but they felt like an hour.

Blood rushed noisily through my head, drowning out the pervasive ringing. Invisible hands gripped my neck. The memory of dark, dangerous eyes hovered around the edges of my mind. I was so lost in the shadowy fright of my past that I almost didn't notice the change in my current reality. The hooded figure's stance had become more alert. More focused on us. And then—without further warning—he bolted.

Shit! He's going to get away! my brain hollered. *Do something!*

It was enough to bring time back to a normal speed. But it wasn't enough to unstick my feet. Not quite.

See, Pint-Size? said Charles's voice. *You aren't ready.*

I could picture his headshake, too. Not gloating. But pitying. And at last, that was just the motivation I needed.

"I want you to get out of sight," I said to TJ.

His eyes flicked toward the other end of the alley. "What? Why?"

"No time to explain," I said, pushing him toward the loading dock.

"Ms. Ames..."

His concern was evident, but my legs were already moving.

"Out of sight," I repeated over my shoulder. "And wait here until I come back."

With that, I took off at a run. I didn't look back to make sure he was listening to the order. I had to trust he'd meant it when he'd said I was in charge, because my focus needed to be entirely homed-in on catching up with the stalker.

My high-tops slapped against the cracked cement, and in seconds, I reached the end of the alley. I turned right just in time to see the hoodie-wearer reach the end of the very short block. He swung his gaze back, spotted me, then sprinted away to the right once more. He was moving fast.

But not fast enough.

I ran as often as I boxed, and even in my dress, even with my injuries, it was easy for me to follow him. I stretched my stride. And as I rounded the next corner, I noted with satisfaction that I'd halved the distance between myself and the wannabe assailant. If there were other people on the street, I didn't notice. I pushed myself even harder. I was almost there. Almost on him.

C'mon, c'mon, I urged myself silently.

He clearly felt the pressure, too, because he quite abruptly jerked to the side. My automatic assumption was that he was heading into one of the shops along the sidewalk. Could it work in my favor? But my assumption was off. I was suddenly facing down a flying bicycle he'd grabbed from God knew where, and I had no choice but to dive out of the way. My knees hit the ground, my skin scraped over the sidewalk, and a cry escaped my lips. But I didn't give in to the pain. Or give up on catching him.

Fighting the sting of road rash, I staggered to my feet, took a deep breath, and kept going. My fresh injuries slowed me only marginally, but the extra few seconds had given my target enough time to get out of sight. As I reached the end of yet another block, I thought maybe I'd lost him altogether. But when I paused to try and make an educated guess on which direction he'd gone, a quick glance to my left revealed we'd come around in a square. The hotel and its chaos were right there. Staff and guests and first responders milled around. Emergency vehicles blocked the road. And the news guys were there already, too.

So not that way, then, I decided. *Too many eyes.*

I turned sharply to the right and lifted my foot, intent on resuming my chase. But my intuition was suddenly screaming at me.

If he's really trying to get away from you, the crowd is the perfect place to disappear.

I stopped. I shifted my gaze to the right. And I was immediately rewarded with a clear view of the gray sweatshirt and jeans. He was definitely making his way toward the dozens and dozens of people who surrounded the front of the hotel. Could I catch him before he got there? Before someone saw us? Would someone in the throng become collateral damage? But the questions fell aside as I realized he was right near the alley where I'd left TJ.

"Shit," I muttered.

For some stupid reason, it hadn't occurred to me that he'd make his way back there. I tensed, ready to launch myself forward. If he made a single move towards the alley, I'd have no choice but to make a move. And probably to punctuate my maneuver with a scream. TJ's life trumped exposure.

But as I watched, the guy in the hood circled as wide as he could around the opening to alley, then ducked back toward the mayhem once more. On the very edge of the crowd, he paused and turned. Like he could feel my eyes on him. I caught the quickest flash of a pair of dark sunglasses. Then he spun back again and disappeared into the flood of people.

"Shit," I said again.

I bit my lip, and I eyed the mix of people. *Do I go after him now?*

He could easily ditch the sweatshirt. The glasses, too. He could find and put on a hat. Or just about any other disguise, for that matter. I really had no idea what he looked like. And now that I didn't have eyes on him, I needed to get back to TJ.

I could hear my brother's voice again. *Leaving him alone was a terrible idea to start out with, Pint-Size. What if the bomber had an accomplice? Or what if the guy in the hoodie* was *the accomplice?*

"Shit," I repeated for the third time, this time more forcefully.

I gave the crowd another frustrated look before starting toward them myself. But unlike the hooded man, I kept myself close to the building. I still moved swiftly, but I made sure not to be seen. I reached the corner of the alley, then cautiously turned and stepped into it. The space was empty. My heart tripped a little before I remembered I'd specifically told the hockey player to stay out of sight.

"TJ?" I called softly as I approached the rolling cargo door. "Are you there?"

There was a little light clatter from inside, and then his flipflop-covered feet appeared first, followed by the rest of him. He hopped down, eyed my torn knees and sweaty face, then lifted his eyes to mine. His expression was neutral.

"You're hurt," he stated, his tone matching his look.

I waved off the observation. "Nothing worse than before."

His attention flicked to my scrapes, then came back to my face once more. "Have you got time now to tell me why you ran off?"

"There was a guy in a hooded sweatshirt at the end of the alley. A suspect," I said. "I went after him."

"And?" The word was strangely tight.

I frowned. "And I'd bet my entire life savings he was the one who set off the explosion. I chased him around the block, and then he disappeared into the crowd outside the hotel. But there's an upside. Now that I've seen him once, he'll probably be more reluctant to show himself again anytime soon."

For a second, TJ went silent. Too silent. A hint of unease crept along my spine. I opened my mouth, but before I could say a thing, a sentence burst from his lips.

"I don't care," he said, his words a vehement growl that surprised me so badly I almost jumped.

"What?"

"About any of that. Your life savings. The upside. The whatever else. What the actual *hell* just happened?"

"I just told you."

He ran a hard hand over his jaw. "Yeah. A guy in a fucking hoodie. I heard that part."

"Probably the bomber," I reminded him, speaking calmly in an attempt to assuage some of his hostility.

"I caught that, too."

"I don't—"

"You scared the hell out of me."

I blinked, caught totally off-guard. "I'm sorry?"

"Is that an apology or a question?" TJ replied. "You just told me to *hide,* and then you took off. Not armed. No explanation. No contingency plan that I'm aware of. And in a goddamn dress, to boot."

Irritation prickled at me. "I'm perfectly capable of doing things in a dress the same way I'd do them in pants."

"That was the least important part of what I said. If you're going to be my bodyguard, we need to have some ground rules."

"That's not how this works," I told him.

"Really?" His skepticism bordered on sarcasm. "Are you sure? Because some of the stuff I heard you and Charles say to each other makes me think this side of the business isn't your usual thing."

I felt my face heat yet again. Only this time, it wasn't so much of a blush as it was anger. TJ met my eyes, challenging me to disagree. I drew in a deep breath and ordered my temper to stay back.

"You're right," I admitted. "I presently do most of my work from behind a desk. But I also manage all the nitpicky details of my brothers' cases. I know *exactly* how they do things. In fact, I direct them a lot of the time. If you can't accept that, we can go our separate ways. Once I've gotten you out of here safely, I mean. Then I can either refer you to one of my other brothers, who I'm sure will be glad to take over. Or you can wash your hands of Ames Security altogether with no hard feelings."

"None of that is what I'm after." He blew out a breath, his frustration almost visibly deflating with the exhale. "I don't have any interest in not using Ames Security, and I'm not trying to undermine your authority, either. It wasn't an ultimatum."

I crossed my arms over my chest. "Then what was it?"

"I just don't want to be worried you're going to run off at any given moment and get yourself killed."

"Then you can relax, because I happen to like being alive, and I have no intention of doing anything that will jeopardize that fact."

"You're seriously stubborn, aren't you?"

"So I've been told a time or two," I replied.

TJ surprised me then, by stepping forward and putting his hands on my folded elbows as he spoke in a soft voice. "Ms. Ames, you can't protect me if *you* get hurt. And I know what you said a second ago about that not being your intention. But I also know what I just witnessed. I have to trust that you're not going to take unnecessary risks with your life, because my safety is contingent on yours. I need a bodyguard for more than five minutes."

I stared at him. There was something more than general concern behind what he was saying. Despite his words, I was certain he was worried about my safety for reasons that had nothing to do with his own life. I knew it as surely as I'd known that the hooded figure was the bomber. My mind slipped back to the pain I'd spied in TJ's eyes right before spotting the probable assailant. What was the source?

Whatever it is, Ivy...it's personal. And unless it's related to the case, you don't need to know.

"Fair enough," I made myself say grudgingly. "But let me ask you something then."

"Go ahead. Ask away."

"Would you be making the same request for ground rules if I weren't a woman?"

He hesitated, and I tensed for a denial that would undoubtedly be a lie. One I was overly reluctant to hear for some reason. But right then, a noise rattled from up near the end of the alley, making me whip my head over my shoulder while I took on a defensive stance. There was no one there, but it was enough to remind me of what I was supposed to be doing. We'd wasted enough time already.

I shook my head. "Look. Just forget it, okay? We have to get out of here before someone spots us. We need to pick a destination and figure out a way to get there without drawing any attention."

"Are you still considering using your brother's plan?" TJ asked, seeming happy enough to let the other conversation go.

"I haven't come up with anything better yet. But when we were up in your room, I got the feeling it wasn't your favorite idea."

"It's not," he admitted.

I waited for some further explanation, but he just

shook his head.

"I can't think of anything better either," he said. "So maybe you'd better tell me how you feel about country retreats."

"Um. What?"

"I know a good place to go, and I've got a reasonable way to get there, too," he told me, pulling out his phone out of his pocket and dialing before I could argue.

Chapter Nine

I had a brief urge to yank the phone from TJ's hand. Particularly when he turned away and started speaking in low, quick sentences. But as quickly as the impulse came, I stowed it. Yes, I was technically the one who ought to be making the arrangements for a getaway car—which appeared to be the intent of TJ's call—but I also knew the last short while hadn't been my finest example of professionalism. Fighting with my brother. Insisting I was in charge. And while I wasn't going to lump in chasing the bad guy with those other things, I did feel like I owed my newest client at least a bit of leeway for the way I'd run off. Because it had clearly upset him.

More than upset him, I thought.

I bit my lip a little guiltily and studied his broad shoulders. His reaction really *had* been strong. And it had gotten my back up. Another kneejerk reaction, created by too many years of being babied by my brothers. But I expected it from them. A virtual stranger, however, was a whole different thing. Where had TJ's reaction come from? Maybe it really *was* about him not wanting to lose his bodyguard. The claim made at least some sense. But something else tickled at my instincts, and I couldn't stop myself from thinking there was some underlying reason for his concern about my well-being.

You can ask him all the important questions once you're somewhere safe, I told myself. *Including finding out exactly where that will be. And speaking of which...*

TJ's conversation had already wound down, and he was tapping off his phone.

"That was my agent," he told me as he stuffed his cell into his jeans pocket. "He's got a car coming for us in ten to fifteen minutes. We just need to start walking in the opposite direction of the crowd you mentioned, and he'll find us."

My worry about where we were going was replaced with a new one—the fact that TJ was far more traceable than he ought to be under the circumstances.

"He'll find us?" I echoed.

TJ nodded like it was no big deal. "I've got the location services activated on my phone. My agent will forward the coordinates to the driver."

"Seriously?"

"What's the problem?"

"I'm just wondering it you *want* it to be easy for a stalker to track you," I said, gesturing for him to start walking.

"I don't have the location services on for everyone," he replied as we headed up the alley, side by side. "Just my agent. And trust me, it's not by choice."

The last statement made me curious. *More* than curious, really.

"What does that mean?" I asked. "He forces you to share your location with him?"

TJ's expression turned pinched. But he didn't look angry. He actually looked a little embarrassed.

"It's a long story," he said.

The rueful-sounding statement sparked even more

curiosity.

Professional detachment, I reminded myself. *Unless...*

"A long story that's relevant to the case?" I asked.

"I doubt it," he replied.

A flash of mild disappointment hit, but I brushed it off. We'd reached the end of the alley anyway, and I needed to concentrate on getting us out undetected. I put my arm out to indicate we should pause. And when TJ complied, I carefully eased forward to steal a look. I was well-aware that my caution was contradictory to my minutes-earlier run after the suspect, but there wasn't anything to be done about that now.

First, I turned to the left and did another study of the crowd on the corner down the road. It was still more than mild chaos. In fact, the number of people seemed to have grown. Hotel guests jostled shoulders with reporters. A man with a baby on his hip fought to soothe a toddler who clutched at his knees. The flash of emergency lights provided an intense backdrop for the whole scene. I even spotted Josie, the little girl from the elevator, and her mom. But thankfully, not a single person was interested in what was going on behind them.

I swung my attention to the right. The street on that side was blissfully empty. There were a few businesses, all of which I'd run past before without noticing. If there were patrons or staff around, they'd either joined the group of bystanders, or they were keeping themselves safely inside. There was no sign of the hooded figure in either direction. But I wasn't going to rule out the idea we were being watched. Our best bet was to move quickly.

"You ready?" I asked in a low voice.

"Guess that's a relative question," was TJ's reply.

"As ready as you can be," I amended.

"Then yes. But hang on for a sec."

"What are we waiting for?"

He shuffled, then slipped off his sweatshirt and draped it over my back. "There. Now no one will wonder why you're walking around in a dress full of burn holes."

I tried unsuccessfully to look over my shoulder. "Shit. Is it bad?"

"Not bad anymore."

Unexpectedly, his hand found mine. And while it definitely wasn't unpleasant to have his warm palm pressed to my own again, it *did* go against the professionalism I'd just promised myself I'd maintain. I started to pull away, but TJ spoke again, stopping me.

"If we're going to be a fake a couple," he said, "then we might as well start now."

He sounded almost resentful, and I couldn't stop myself from searching his face for an explanation. "Are you sure that's what you want to do?"

His mouth opened then closed, and his expression tightened. "No, I'm not certain. But at least this way, if anyone sees us out there together, we've got a valid excuse."

His tone only added more questions to my ever-growing list. But we were short on time, and truthfully, it made sense to do things like this. It was entirely logical, so I just nodded, then stepped forward, pulling him with me. Once we were around the corner, I was careful to start off at a steady pace, not too leisurely but not too hurried. We were just a pair of lovers on a stroll through the city, totally oblivious to everything but each other.

"Tell me about hockey," I said as soon as we were a reasonable hundred feet away from the excitement behind us.

"About hockey?" TJ replied, sounding surprised.

"Well, yeah. Because normal people don't just walk along in complete silence. And we probably shouldn't discuss your case until we've got some real privacy. So we might as well talk about something you like."

"All right, then…let's see…" he said musingly. "Where should I start? At the beginning, maybe? Hockey is a sport played on ice, with six—"

"I know what the sport *is,* TJ. I just—" I cut myself off as I caught his grin. "Okay. Very funny."

"Well, *I* thought so."

I rolled my eyes. "What I *meant* was…tell me about *you* and hockey. What made you want to start playing?"

"Honestly?" he replied with a chuckle. "It was because my dad hated it, and it piqued my curiosity."

"You don't get along with your father?"

"Oh, no. We got along fine," he said. "He passed away twelve years ago now."

My heart panged. I knew the loss well.

"I'm sorry," I said, meaning it.

"Yeah, me too. He was a good man. A good dad." TJ's hand gave mine a squeeze. "But we had this neighbor who was an absolute nut of a hockey fan. The guy would lose his shit every time his team got beaten on the ice. He threw a puck out his window one time, and it smashed my dad's windshield."

"That's crazy."

"Yep."

"And your dad blamed *hockey*?"

"Oh, yeah. He was far too good of a neighbor to blame the angry, puck-throwing dude."

I laughed. I couldn't help it. And I listened with genuine interest as TJ described how he'd sneakily purchased his first pair of skates, and how his father had eventually found his stick hidden in the basement. His dad had called him a traitor. Then promptly went out and bought TJ all new gear. But even with the levity in our conversation, I remained alert. My ears were open for any unusual sounds, and my eyes took in everything in my field of vision. I was poised to run or to dive in front of TJ—whatever was necessary.

Quite quickly, we made it one block west, then another block north. From there, we slipped up a narrow, one-way street and cut through a tiny, single-swing, five-tree park. Finally—once we'd made it two more blocks without incident—I was almost ready to let myself breathe.

And you still haven't asked where, exactly, you're going, I reminded myself. *And you should probably do that now.*

But as we crossed the road at the lighted intersection and took a few more steps, I forgot again. Because my nerves came to life. I could feel invisible eyes tracking our movements, and I was 100 percent certain it was more than paranoia.

I paused and turned to TJ, whose gaze widened with surprise as I put my arms over his shoulders and pushed to my tiptoes to murmur into his ear.

"I'm pretty sure someone's watching us," I said.

To his credit, TJ didn't look around in search of confirmation. He just set his palms on my hips and leaned down.

"Watching us from where?" he asked.

"I don't know. Not precisely," I replied. "But the second we stepped out of the crosswalk, I felt someone's eyes on us."

He still didn't question my certainty, and I was grateful. The last thing I wanted was to be forced to come up with an excuse for how well I knew what it felt like to be followed.

"What do we do?" said TJ. "Try to find him? Or just get out of sight?"

"Well, I'd like to do both," I told him. "It's a hell of a lot easier to mount a defense against an enemy I can see. But I think it's in our best interests to minimize exposure, so I'll settle for ducking into one of those shops up there."

"Sounds like a plan."

I started to move away, but TJ held on for a second longer, and then reached down to brush away a strand of hair from my forehead. His touch was gentle, his fingers warm. But not quite as warm as what followed. His head dipped down, and his lips found the spot his hand had just left. It was the lightest brush. Almost not a kiss at all. But it also left the most searing heat.

"Now that the illusion is complete..." he murmured, finally letting me go. "I see a *very* colorful sign up the road. *Bea's Emporium* is calling our names."

For a single, wild moment, I wanted to point out that he was wrong. The illusion wasn't *quite* complete. In order to actually make it look real, a kiss on the lips would've gone a lot further. But thankfully, common sense overrode the crazy urge.

"*Bea's Emporium* it is," I said with a hint of breathlessness.

We locked fingers and started off again. We made it only five steps more, though, before the source of my instinctive unease became visible. It was a man in a hooded sweatshirt, standing just outside an open-air café. He was making no effort to hide his presence, nor any attempt to disguise his attention, which was zeroed in on the hockey player with unsettling intensity. Was it the same figure I'd chased before? It was impossible to know for sure. But one thing was certain. Unlike what had happened in the alley, when he realized he'd been spotted, his reaction wasn't to turn and run. Instead, he started toward us.

With my heart in my throat, I gave TJ's hand a sharp tug. But the entryway for *Bea's Emporium* was still too far away. And the man in the hoodie was already almost on us.

Chapter Ten

For a second, fear dominated. My feet threatened to do their freezing act once again. The man striding toward us presented an undeniably forbidding figure. He had a scar running from his eye to his lip and fists the size of Toronto. The invisible hands clawed at my throat in a repeat attempt to subdue me. But I felt TJ shift a little beside me, and I realized I needed to gear up for a fight.

I took a deep breath.

I steadied myself.

I squared my shoulders.

"If I tell you to run," I said quietly, "then you run."

TJ made a noise that could've been a protest or and agreement. I chose to believe it was the latter.

But then something unexpected happened. The imposing man stopped a couple of feet away, a grin splitting his face.

"Hey, man!" he called, his tone ripe with enthusiasm. "Don't take off! I'm not going to ask for an autograph or a selfie or anything weird like that. I just want to shake your hand."

Puzzlement made me speak up. "What?"

Mr. Meat Fists appeared not to hear me, and his full attention stayed on TJ. "You *are* the Troublemaker, aren't you?"

I wasn't yet convinced the stranger and the hooded

figure weren't one and the same, but TJ's body language changed, and he smiled back at the man. "Last time I checked, yeah. Although I mostly I try to avoid trouble when I'm not on the ice."

Mr. Meat Fists let out a guffaw. "Oh, man. I *knew* it was you. I was *at* that game where you and those four other guys started the brawl."

"Oh, yeah? Not my finest moment."

"Are you shitting me? It was insanely awesome. When that dude from the crowd jumped in? That was the best fucking thing I've ever seen happen at a hockey game. Hands down."

TJ chuckled. "Guess I'll take props wherever I can get them." He reached out his hand, and the other man clasped it and gave it a solid pump. "You sure you don't want a picture, bud?"

"Wish I could take you up on that," the guy replied. "I really do. But I dropped my fucking phone in a glass of beer last night and fried it. My lady just about killed me. Swear to God, though, it's just an honor to meet you."

"The honor's all mine."

"Hope you do all the same shit this season, bro." The other man clapped TJ on the shoulder, then turned and strode away without even looking at me as he kept muttering in awe. "The Troublemaker. *The* fucking man. Awesome."

I let out a breath and tipped my gaze up to TJ, who was rubbing the back of his neck in a sheepish way.

"Sorry about that," he said.

"It's fine," I replied. "Better than what was going through my head."

"Mine, too."

"Is that a common problem for you? Being accosted on the street by rabid fans?"

"Well, I prefer to think of it as being recognized like a rock star rather than being accosted, but..." He trailed off and gave me a slightly cheeky smile.

I rolled my eyes, but my reply was serious. "Because if it *does* happen all the time, then it changes how I have to do my job. And it also makes me wonder if your stalker is someone like that."

He let out a sigh. "You can rest assured, Ms. Ames...I'm very seldom recognized, and if I am, it's not like that. I also somehow doubt I have a fan who cares enough about my career that he's set out to destroy me."

"You don't know that for sure."

"No, I don't. But I'm a thirty-seven-year-old hockey player who didn't make it in the big leagues. I had to restart my career in a place that favors guys who're damned close to being young enough to be my sons. I don't exactly attract big-time obsession."

The way he said it rendered me momentarily silent. It wasn't that he sounded bitter; he really didn't. His speech wasn't even quite matter of fact. It was more genuine than that.

That's really how he sees himself, I realized.

I stared at him, trying to reconcile the idea that a man who looked like TJ—visibly fit, totally attractive—would think he was somehow past his prime. I knew it was partly a career thing. A lot of pro athletes retired before forty. But I still felt like he was wrong. And I also felt like I should say something to contest his statements. Except I couldn't think of a way to do it without coming across as either completely flirtatious or disingenuous.

I was almost grateful to be saved by the arrival of a sleek black car, which came to a rolling stop beside us. The window eased down, and the driver—a sixty-something man with a full, gray beard and equally silver, closely clipped hair—greeted TJ with friendly professionalism.

"Good afternoon, Mr. Jones. It's nice to see you, as always," he said. "Mr. Armstaad sent me to pick you up." He flicked an almost imperceptible glance in my direction. "But he didn't mention that you wouldn't be alone."

TJ didn't look at me as he answered. "Sorry, Eldon. I didn't get a chance to explain it to him. And actually…I'd appreciate it if you could keep this little detail between us. At least for now."

The uniformed man's professional demeanor didn't falter, but his response held a hint of hesitancy. "You know I'm not here to spy for Mr. Armstaad, but he *is* my boss."

"I know. All I'm hoping is that unless he questions you about it directly…"

"I'll do my best, Mr. Jones."

"That's all I can ask." TJ quickly reached for the handle on the rear door before the driver could hop out and do it for him, then turned to me. "I'm assuming 'ladies first' is okay in this case?"

The exchange between the two men made me frown. But right then, I just nodded and climbed in. TJ was quick to follow.

"Where are we headed today?" the driver asked over his shoulder.

"Home," TJ told him. "But not to the apartment.

You remember the way to the other place?"

"South Langley near the vineyard?"

"That's the one."

"I'm on it."

With that assurance, Eldon pressed the button that slid the privacy glass into place, and a second later, the smooth roll of the tires heralded our departure from the street. I kept quiet for a minute before nodding toward the opaque window.

"Is that soundproof?" I asked.

"Pretty sure it is," TJ replied.

I kept my voice low anyway. "I'm going to hazard a guess and say you don't want your agent to know about your current, problematic situation."

"Your guess is correct."

"So, if we do this…he's not going to be looped in."

"*If* we do it?"

My face heated. "Sorry. My opposition to the plans must be sneaking in subconsciously."

"I'll do my best not to be horribly offended by just how repugnant you find my company," he replied dryly.

"It's not you. It's—Okay, look. I know exactly how this will sound, but just suffice it to say that in this case, it really *is* me."

He studied me, his curiosity obvious. And I felt my chest tighten in response. The last thing I wanted to do was to rehash my past or to explain why I would make a terrible girlfriend. Even of the phony variety. It wasn't as though it was relevant to the case. Thankfully, TJ didn't push it.

"All right," he conceded, his lips curving up. "I'll make a mental note. You're defective."

"Very funny."

"If it makes you feel any better, my record isn't exactly spotless, either."

"You're a professional athlete," I said sweetly. "You're *supposed* to have a checkered past."

"Now who's funny?" he replied.

"Humor is the basis for any happy, fake relationship."

"Good to know."

My eyes caught our reflection in the privacy glass, and for a second, it looked real. We were both smiling, our shoulders almost touching. I looked cozy in his sweatshirt, and there was no reason to suspect that my back was stinging again from sitting with it pressed to the seat behind me. I tried to tell myself that was a good thing—we needed to be convincing if we wanted people to buy our story—but my pulse was jumping too erratically for any kind of rational thought to stick. And the irrationality was probably the reason it took so long for me to notice he was looking at me, too. There was a slight softness in his gaze. The kind that made me think despite his protests over the situation, he liked the realness of the illusion, too.

Dammit. Are you really doing this, Ivy?

I didn't know how I could even consider it. And having my leg pressed to his wasn't helping my lack of clarity, either. I wanted to lean in even closer. It was a dangerous feeling. One that made me order myself to ease away a little and direct my attention to the window, my fingers strumming my thigh in tap that was far slower than my heartrate.

For a few moments, I watched the scenery whip by. We were well into the countryside now, with fields and livestock dominating the view. It always amazed me how quickly the landscape changed. From the thick cityscape of downtown Surrey to the suburbs of Cloverdale and Langley, and then straight into farmland.

"It's like two different worlds, isn't it?" said TJ.

I nodded my agreement, but decided it was a good idea to steer the conversation back where it needed to be—on the case.

"Is he a suspect?" I asked. "Your agent, I mean."

He shot a startled look my way. "Bram?"

"Assuming that's your agent's name, then yes...Bram."

TJ shook his head. "No. Not a chance. If he wanted to ruin my life, he could do it in a far easier, far more torturous way than just trying to blow me to bits."

"Well. That sounds pleasant."

"It's complicated."

"But not so complicated that he'd have you killed?"

"If I'm dead, I don't make him any money," TJ pointed out.

"Valid argument," I conceded. "And it begs the question...*Is* there anyone who would profit from your death?"

His expression turned strained for a moment before he cleared his throat and said, "No. I can't think of anyone who'd like to see me dead."

"If you aren't honest me," I replied, "it's going to be a lot harder for me to help you."

He sighed. "I'm being honest. And I did go over this a bit with your brother. I don't have much in the way of family, and I did a pretty good job of driving away the majority of my friends over the years. There're definitely a few guys on the team who don't exactly love me, but I doubt they'd go to the trouble of trying to scare me with notes. They'd just coldcock me in the dressing room."

"Hang on. What notes?"

"Your brother didn't explain how this all started?"

"Not specifically." I made a face. "I think his focus was on tricking me into coming to your hotel room so he could blindside me with his plan. Some of the finer details were probably meant to come later."

"Right." TJ gave his chin a quick scratch, then launched into an explanation.

There were three notes altogether, with the first one turning up eleven days ago. It was on plain white paper. And the words were made of letters clipped from magazines and newspapers.

"Like a kid had watched an old ransom movie or something and decided to use the same technique to slap it together," he said. "My first thought was that it was some kind of joke."

TJ had almost thrown it away. He admitted he probably *would* have tossed it, if not for where he'd found it—directly at the bottom of his personal locker at the gym. Inside his *combination sealed* locker, to be more accurate. It'd been easy enough for him to dismiss the idea that someone had simply slipped it through the cracks. The scotch tape holding it in place gave it away.

TJ described the tickle of unease that had slid between his shoulder blades, and how he'd been unable to stop himself from jerking his attention around to see if anyone was there, watching. He'd even gotten up and *looked* around. When he'd found the locker room empty, he'd come back to the paper, rereading the single sentence there.

WATCH YOUR STEP.

He'd told himself it was no big deal. It's not as though the words were a death threat. Or any kind of threat, really. Just a weird but vague warning. So he'd tucked the paper away, not thinking of it again until he'd tripped down the stairs two days later, when he'd wondered ruefully if the glued-on letters had been a prediction. After that, the note had gone out of his head. Lost in the slap of pucks and a TV interview, and the big win his team had earned that night.

"I thought it was a one-off, which probably sounds naïve," he said. "But I guess it was just wishful thinking. Then I got the second note, two days after the win. It was in an envelope with my name on it, and it was taped to the bathroom mirror at a restaurant where I was having dinner with a potential sponsor."

"What did that one say?" I asked.

"Don't get stuck," he replied with a little shrug. "Again, not all that threatening."

"No. But still…"

"I know."

"And the third note?"

"It said not to play with fire," he told me. "And I found it in my wallet the day before yesterday."

My instincts lit up. "And where was your wallet?"

"In my goddamn pocket."

As soon as he'd said it, a chill washed over me. "Where were *you*?"

He met my eyes. "In my goddamn apartment."

The chill deepened. And I knew TJ was experiencing a similar feeling because his expression reflected as much. Automatically, I reached out to cover his hand with mind.

"We'll find out who's behind this, and we'll make sure they're dealt with accordingly," I promised.

He twisted his hand to clasp mine properly, and he stared down at our hands. I followed his gaze. The contrast was striking. His fingers looked almost comically large when meshed with mine. But there was something nice about it, too.

"I'm not afraid to admit the last note scared the shit out of me." TJ's voice was gruff. "And that's coming from a guy who's taken a skate to the kidneys."

"I get it," I replied.

The statement drew Travis's eyes up to my face, and I realized belatedly my words were probably full of far too much conviction. My pulse did its increasingly familiar jump as I stared back at him. I knew he was probably wondering exactly why my words sounded like more than a platitude. I opened my mouth, an excuse on my lips. But my attention was quickly diverted. The car had slowed down, and we were pulling up along a winding driveway. And I could already see the house at the end of it. It was a huge, sprawling rancher with a wraparound porch, quaintly shuttered windows, and a rooster-shaped weathervane sitting atop the roof.

"Well, Ms. Ames…" said TJ. "Welcome home."

Chapter Eleven

I hadn't had time to stop and think about where TJ might live. Nor had it really occurred to me to do so. But if I *had* taken a moment to consider it, maybe a stereotypical bachelor pad would've popped to mind. Framed movie posters. Hockey paraphernalia. A foosball table where there should be a dining room set. And most definitely a big screen TV. But a hobby farm wouldn't even have been on my radar. Which is probably why a surprised question escaped from my lips before I could stop it.

"This is your place?" I asked.

"Sure is," he replied. "But don't worry. The property is tied to my dad's cousin's business. Second cousin? I can never keep it straight. Anyway, he's got a different last name. It would take more than your average stalker to figure out the connection."

I didn't tell him my question hadn't been prompted by that concern, and I didn't mention that most stalkers didn't exactly fall into the "average" category. Instead, I used his explanation as a segue.

"I should still make sure the house is secure before we go in," I said. "But preferably not while the driver is watching. He might think it's a little strange for your new girlfriend to be doing a perimeter check."

TJ's expression momentarily darkened. "So, we're really going that route?"

I tried not to be curious about the look on his face. He still hadn't told me why it bothered him so much. And even thought it was literally my job to explore the majority of the facets of his life to determine which ones were a threat, it felt a bit invasive to pursue that line of questioning.

"Aren't we?" I said instead.

"It's still probably the worst idea I've heard." His words were a mutter.

"Have you come up with another one?"

"Wish I had. But no."

There was a moment of awkward silence before I cleared my throat.

"So," I said. "Perimeter check?"

TJ rolled his shoulders as if clearing his sourness, then nodded. "Yeah, sure. And you're right—it might not be normal relationship behavior. How about I take you on a tour of the property? At least then you have an excuse for looking around."

I considered the suggestion. It wasn't ideal. But then again, nothing about the situation was. Proper procedure would be to make sure TJ was guarded while I perused the entry points.

"Okay," I said. "That's probably our best option."

We were almost at the house now, and I eyed the empty driveway.

"Do you happen to have a secondary vehicle?" I asked. "We might need a quick way out."

"I've got a dirty old truck out by the barn," he replied.

"A dirty old truck?" I repeated.

"Yep."

"Does it run?"

"Like a dirty old truck dream."

"I have no idea if that's a good thing or a bad thing," I said.

"Hopefully you won't have a reason to find out," he told me.

The car eased to a halt, and TJ slid over to open the door right away. He swung his legs out, stood up, then turned to bend down and offer me his hand.

"Ms. Ames," he said.

I closed my fingers on his, and he helped me step from the backseat to the driveway. As soon as I was standing on the ground beside him, he closed the door behind us. Eldon had climbed out of the front seat, too. The driver was shaking his head.

"You do know that my contract includes a clause about opening car doors for people, don't you, Mr. Jones?" he said.

TJ grinned, stepped forward, and clapped the other man on the shoulder. "And you *do* know my nickname is the Troublemaker, don't you, Eldon?"

Eldon sighed. "I'd say it was well-earned, but that would be overstepping."

TJ laughed. Then—in a smooth, practiced move—slipped a twenty out from somewhere and clapped it into the driver's palm.

"I hope this isn't a bribe to keep me from mentioning your lovely new lady friend," said the other man, his voice full of good humor.

"Would it work if it was?"

"Not a chance, Mr. Jones."

"Damn it," said TJ, slinging an unexpected arm over my shoulder. "But you can keep it anyway, Eldon. Just for putting up with all my shit. And now I'm going to take the lovely lady friend on a walk around the property in hopes of impressing her with my material wealth. Maybe it'll help her stick around in spite of my bad attitude."

Eldon smiled. "Best of luck."

"I'm probably going to need it," TJ told him as he slid his hand down to mine. "Have a great day, Eldon!"

The older man winked, got back into his car, then closed the window. As the vehicle rolled away smoothly, barely making a sound, I noted a small smile on TJ's face. It was genuine. Open. One I fully appreciated. Which is likely why I didn't stop myself from commenting on it.

"You like him, don't you?" I said.

TJ turned his attention my way, and I was sad to see his lips go flat again. "I didn't grow up in a house where we could afford to have people driving us around. I forgot that once. Guys like Eldon help me remember not to do that again."

I wanted to know more. But he didn't elaborate, and it felt wrong to ask.

"Should we start the tour?" I asked instead.

TJ glanced down at our hands, and I was sure he was going to let me go. But he didn't. He just gave my palm a squeeze and started pulling me up the driveway. He guided me wide to the left of the house and across a small field of overgrown grass. From there, we made our way through a patch of mature apple trees, slipped past an unused chicken coop, and started toward a well-weathered building. I knew it had to be the barn, because the dirty old truck TJ mentioned, which looked more like a jacked-up four-by-four, sat to one side of the structure. But the barn wasn't like any I'd ever seen before. From a distance, it appeared as though someone had stuck two contrasting buildings together. One half was short and outfitted with a peaked roof. The other half was far taller than the first, and it looked to be completely flat on top.

As we continued our trek, I did my best to keep an eye on our surroundings, searching for anything out of the ordinary. But truthfully, it was hard. TJ moved quickly, with the assurance of someone who had travelled this same path many times. And he kept hold of my hand, steadying me when—no fewer than four times—the uneven ground tried to get the better of me. By the time we reached the barn, I hadn't seen much more than a blur of greens and browns, and I was a little nervous I'd missed something. TJ, on the other hand, seemed to be enjoying himself.

He finally released my fingers and gestured to the side of the building, where a rusty metal ladder hung from the eaves. "You want to go first, or should I?"

"Hang on," I said. "You want to climb up *there*?"

"Says the woman who was happy to run through a burning building and chase after a potentially armed bomber."

"Yeah, because both of those were safer than *that*." I pointed at the ladder, and then pointed up to the roof, too. "*And* that."

His mouth twitched with amusement. "Trust me. It's safe. I used to come up here when I was a kid so I could spy on my dad and his cousin."

"You mean it was safe two decades ago. When your breakfast didn't consist of a six-egg omelette, and you probably weighed half of what you do now."

"Cut me some slack. I never have more than four

eggs at a time, and I was almost as big at fourteen as I am at thirty-seven."

I eyed him skeptically. "Still."

"C'mon. You'll have a perfect view of the whole house. If there's anyone casing the place or has a car hidden somewhere, you'll be able to see them or it. If they decided to book it on foot when we got here, you'll be able to see that, too."

I bit my lip. Heights really weren't my favorite. He was right, though, it would be good to get a view of the house and the immediate surrounding area. I'd still need to check the doors and windows to see if any had been compromised, but at least I'd have a warning if someone was lurking around.

"All right," I said. "But you can definitely go first. And I'll make sure to steer clear of the bottom of the ladder so I don't become a pancake when you come crashing down."

He laughed. "Your confidence is encouraging. Thank you."

"You're very welcome," I said, stepping back, as promised.

I couldn't help but cringe as TJ turned and grabbed the rickety-looking rung just above his head. And I fully held my breath as he lifted his foot and placed it on another, even rougher-looking one at shin level. I waited for a collapse. But instead, the ladder just let out the smallest creak. And TJ zipped up the side of the barn like it was no big deal. At the top, he pushed his hands to a lip on the roof, then pulled himself up and over. When he slipped out of sight, my pulse jumped with worry. But a moment later, his face appeared again.

"Care to join me, Ms. Ames?" he called.

I stepped forward and gripped the nearest rung. It was cool under my palms. And it didn't feel sturdy in any way, shape, or form. I took a breath, closed my eyes, and started my ascent. Slowly.

"You should probably start referring to me as Ivy," I told him, trying to distract myself from the increasing distance between my feet and the ground. "People might think it's weird for you to call your girlfriend Ms."

"Hmm," he replied. "Maybe I should skip over Ivy and go straight for a cutesy nickname."

I moved up a bit more. "Do I seem like the kind of woman who goes for cutesy nicknames?"

"I don't know you well enough to make that judgement. But I did hear your brother tossing one around."

"Don't even think about it."

His chuckle carried down. "Don't worry. The last thing I want is to call my girlfriend by the same name her brother uses."

"Fake girlfriend, real-life bodyguard," I reminded him. "If we go that route."

"If we do," he agreed.

I was almost at the top when I made the mistake of glancing down. Vertigo hit immediately, and my breath sucked sharply into my lungs.

It's not that far, I told myself. *Not even two storeys. That's just broken wrist height. Maybe a leg if I land wrong.*

But my vision did its best to wobble anyway. As I struggled to regain my equilibrium, one of TJ's warm hands landed on my wrist.

"Look up here," he said.

I lifted my face and found his eyes just eighteen inches from my own. Their azure hue held me as steadily as his grip did.

"Just one more rung," he added, his voice both encouraging and firm at the same time. "I swear you'll be over the top. Then you can decide what you like better—baby or sweetheart."

With what felt like a Herculean effort, I brought my foot up once more. At the same time, TJ gave my arm a hard pull. And just like he'd promised, I found myself on the roof. Well. Half on it. And half on him.

"TJ?"

"Yes?"

"Maybe we should just stick with having you call me Ms. Ames," I said, closing my eyes and leaning into him, not caring at all about the momentary lack of professionalism.

Chapter Twelve

I let myself breathe in and out for several seconds before taking control again. And TJ was right. It was a little weird to be afraid of heights—and not even *high* heights—but to feel totally secure in chasing after someone who'd just set off a bomb in a hotel room.

But since when is fear about logic? I thought as I opened my eyes.

TJ was staring down at me, a mix of amusement and concern playing over his features. "You good, babe?"

I gave him a dirty look, then extricated myself from the awkwardly close position. "Yeah, that is *not* happening."

"I'll keep trying," he said.

"You go ahead and do that," I replied, shifting again so I could survey our surroundings.

I was surprised and more than a little relieved to see we weren't simply sitting on top of the flat roof. Instead, we were about one foot down, inside some kind of cordoned off area. For several moments the space puzzled me. It wasn't big. If another person had been sitting beside us, we wouldn't have been able to move without touching each other. The surface underneath us was hard, but gravelly. A large plastic container that looked almost like an oversized bucket took up one corner. And when I studied it for a second,

I noticed a spout sticking out of the side. From that, a pipe led out through a hole in the roof. Then it clicked.

"That's a rain barrel," I said.

TJ nodded. "Out of commission, though. It was put in by the people who owned the place before my dad's cousin bought it, but he never used it."

I swiveled my head and turned my attention to the yard. Having the one-foot lip all around me eased a bit of the fear of falling, and I was able to look around without any dizziness. TJ's description of what we could see was accurate. The fields were open and empty, the forested area appeared sparser from up high than it had as we'd walked through it. The house was set at an angle, and our vantage point allowed an unobstructed view of the front, side, and back of it. The side that I *couldn't* fully see appeared to be covered in some kind of shrub so thick it looked like anyone trying to get through it would need a machete.

"What do you think?" asked TJ. "Not a bad substitute for a regular old perimeter check, right?"

"Not bad at all," I agreed.

"Here. Let me show you something else. Lie on your stomach."

"What?"

"Indulge me. It's not like we're going anywhere fast."

I fought my usual need to be prickly and conceded. "Fine."

Being careful not to get close to the edge, I shuffled around so my stomach and thighs were pressed awkwardly to the cool rooftop. Seconds later, TJ joined me, his position matching my own. He held something out to me, and it took me only a moment to realize it was a pair of binoculars.

"You keep these up here all the time?" I asked as I took them. "Or only when someone's been trying to kill you?"

"Well. If you *really* need to know…I stored them up here in an airtight container for a large chunk of my childhood years."

"Wow. You took your spying seriously when you were a kid, didn't you?" I said.

"It was in the days before I discovered hockey. Imagine how weird I might've become if I hadn't found sports." He dropped a wink then gestured to the expansive yard. "Have a look."

I did as he suggested, and I was rewarded with an even better view. The details of the house became vividly clear. I could see a long split in one place on the wooden siding, as well as a splatter of white paint below one of the windows. As I adjusted both my focal point and the lenses, I was able to scan the doors and the windows. I found no visible sign of forced entry. I moved on. Without rushing, I scanned the surrounding area. Though the property was too large to see everything, I could see enough. It was devoid of movement and evidence of life. If someone was currently on the property, they were an absolute master of hiding.

"This is good, TJ," I said, letting out a breath as I made another, quicker, visual sweep. "Really good."

"Shit," he replied.

Concerned, I lowered the binoculars. "What's wrong?"

"I was only aiming for mediocre," he told me. "But if I've been elevated to *really* good…"

I groaned, but a smile fought its way onto my face. For the first time since my brother had said the word "girlfriend" to me, I felt a modicum of tension leave my shoulders. Of course, as soon as I thought of Charles, my worries redirected. Why hadn't he called yet? Was he done with the doctors? Had something gone wrong? I could feel my phone in my dress pocket, digging emphatically into my hip.

Maybe I should see if it's working, I thought. *It could've been damaged in the blast.*

"Hey." TJ nudged my shoulder. "You thinking about your brother?"

"Yes. Why? Did a neon sign start flashing on my forehead just now?"

"No. But you were making the same face you made when you realized how badly he was hurt, so I took a guess."

I pretended not to be flattered he'd so astutely picked up on my facial expressions.

"Have you got brothers and sisters?" I asked.

He shook his head. "My mom passed when I was too young to remember, and my dad never remarried, so it was just me."

I was struck, for a moment, by the commonalities in our pasts. Aside from the largeness of our families, of course. My own mother was nothing but the vague memory of a smile and a laugh, and I'd lost my dad, too. I had to work to push away the desire to comment on it.

"Well, what can I tell you, then?" I made myself say in a light voice. "Siblings are basically simultaneously the most annoying people in the world, and the ones who also have your back under every circumstance. At least that's what it's always been like for me."

"Hence the face?" he replied.

"Hence the face," I confirmed.

I felt a strong urge to tell him more. Like how the youngest of my older brothers had—in the same week—stolen my allowance *and* given a black eye to a boy who spread a rumor about me around my middle school. Or how Charles had tried to play the father-figure role since our dad's death. I normally kept the details of my family life close to my chest, but I actually had to press my lips together to keep from letting the words roll out. Maybe it was our oddly parallel pasts. Or maybe it was just because of the way TJ's blue eyes seemed to hold true interest in what I had to say. They hung on me, patiently waiting.

But interest doesn't always mean good intentions, I reminded myself.

I cleared my throat. "Speaking of phone calls that need to happen...I meant to tell you to let the hotel know you're okay. Even if you just leave a voicemail, it's better than nothing. The last thing we need is the police trying to hunt you down to make sure you're not hurt."

TJ frowned, and for a second, I thought he was going to persist with the other line of conversation. But he just adjusted his body again, this time to sit up and pull his cell from his pocket. He dialed quickly, and he left a calm message explaining he'd met a friend for lunch at the last minute, and he'd been out when he heard the news. He said in a very genuine tone that he hoped everyone was okay, and he added that he had no concerns at all about the belongings he'd left behind in his room. He closed by saying he'd continue to recommend the hotel to his friends. But he no sooner hung up than his phone buzzed to life with an incoming call.

"Shit," he said as he glanced down. "It's Bram. My agent. I have to take this."

The way TJ announced it, a little regretful and a little resentful at the same time, made me think there was something more than the usual, professional courtesy behind his words. But even if I'd been about to voice my curiosity about it, I wouldn't have had a chance to do it. TJ answered his phone too quickly.

"Hey, boss," he greeted, his voice betraying none of what his expression had held a moment earlier. "What can I do for you?" He paused and listened. "Yeah, I told you I needed to get out of there quickly, didn't I?" He paused again, for a little longer this time. "How was I supposed to know that? I just saw all the hordes of—" His jaw ticked with irritation. "Yes, I'm aware." He closed his eyes. "She is." Another brief, painful-feeling silence. "That's unreasonable. I—" He stopped, opened his eyes again, and fixed me with a gaze I couldn't quite interpret. "Christ, Bram. Yes, I heard you." The next pause lasted close to a full minute before TJ finally snapped, "Yes. Goodbye." He gave the phone's screen a wince-worthy tap to end the call, then growled a low, "Fuck!"

"I'm guessing the driver told him about us after all?" I asked.

"No. It was my number one fan back there. Dude might not have wanted a selfie, but he was happy to post on social media about meeting TJ the Troublemaker Jones and his new girlfriend."

"Shit. I wasn't even sure if he even noticed I was there."

"Apparently, he did."

"Well, I guess that takes away *not* playing the fake girlfriend angle," I said, wondering why I didn't feel *entirely* disappointed. "Does your agent have any idea it's a ruse?"

"No," said TJ. "Not at all."

As if to match the dreariness on his face, a drop of rain plopped down to the gravel in front of me. Then another. A quick look up told me the sky was darkening with the promise of an incoming storm. I dropped my gaze back to TJ. He still looked upset. Was it just having the choice taken away from him, or was it something more?

"What else did your agent say?" I asked, careful to keep my tone dispassionate.

He shook his head. "I told you things with him were complicated."

"Yes, you did. But I still don't really understand."

"'Complicated' might've been an understatement."

"An understatement how?"

The rain was cascading down now, running unimpeded over TJ's face, and reminding me that I still wore his sweatshirt,

"How do I explain it?" he said, shaking his head when I tried to shrug off the hoodie. "Keep it. You might *want* me to suffer once I've told you that if we really want to keep up this ruse of ours, I'm going to need to ask you to do something for me."

"What kind of something?"

"Move in with me."

The statement was as confusing as it was

unexpected. Startling enough that I couldn't even pause to panic. And if I hadn't already been blinking away the ever-thickening rain, I would've blinked about that, too.

"I'm sorry, but…what?" I managed to say.

He scrubbed his hand over his chin. "I probably should have said something before."

"Back it up a sec," I replied. "You should have said something before about asking me to move *in* with you?"

"About why I initially rejected the fake girlfriend idea," he replied, shaking his head again. "I'll explain it better. But how about I do it once we're inside and out of the rain?"

Overhead, an ominous roll of thunder sounded, and despite my concern about the whole thing, I nodded my agreement.

Chapter Thirteen

The only good thing about the rain was it was blinding enough that I couldn't see the ground as I made my way back down the ladder. It also helped that my mind was on TJ's so-called complications. I couldn't think of a single reason any kind of complication would turn moving in with me, a supposedly real girlfriend, into an obligation to his agent. It was hard not to demand an immediate answer.

But for a couple of minutes, I was able to distract myself with my closer examination of all the windows and doors. TJ stuck close to my side, showing me each possible entry point, and it didn't take long to decide everything was secure. There were no broken latches. No tampered-with locks. If anything, there was evidence that the home wasn't regularly opened up. A bit of extra dirt on the sills. A tucked away spiderweb collecting droplets of rain that sprayed its way. It was a relief. And I was glad it went quickly as well as in our favor. But in the short time it took to make sure it was safe to go into the house, TJ and I both got soaked. And that meant getting warm and dry took precedence over asking questions.

It wasn't until I'd bandaged up my scraped knees, examined the cuts on my back—which turned out not to be as bad as I'd thought—and we'd both changed—him into a fresh shirt and new jeans, and me into a small pair of sweatpants and fitted V-neck that he dug up from somewhere—that I finally opened my mouth to try and gain some further insight. But I no sooner started to speak than TJ ushered me into the living room, then disappeared with the promise of returning with something hot to drink. I wasn't sure if he was stalling or not. But I didn't argue. I did, however, stare after him, a frown making its way onto my face. I was truly baffled.

No point in worrying about it until he finishes doing whatever he's doing, I told myself, taking a look around the room instead of dwelling impatiently.

Two of the four walls were painted a soft shade of creamy white, while a third was wood paneled with inset shelves, which were laden down with dog-eared books and random knickknacks. The fourth wall had floor to ceiling windows that were presently covered up by a set of taupe drapes. One corner of the room held a freestanding, gas fireplace. Another was home to an antique radio, on top of which sat a vintage record player. It was a large area, and even with three, full-length couches—dark brown leather—and two coffee tables, it felt spacious. Despite that, it didn't have any kind of opulence. Instead, it was homey. Inviting.

I sank down onto the nearest couch and squinted at the books on the shelf, trying to make out the titles. They didn't seem to be ordered in any particular way. I spied some classics, some contemporaries, and a few non-fiction titles. A cookbook was jammed in between a volume of poetry and a title that appeared to be a how-to guide for bathroom renovations.

Idly, I wondered how many, if any actually belong to TJ. He definitely didn't fall into the dumb jock stereotype. He was far too well-spoken for that. Not that I put much stock in stereotypes, but still. I tried to picture him opening up a copy of *Jane Eyre* while he sat by the fire. It was an entertaining image. The big man with big hands wrapped around the feminist classic. Then again, it was impossible to judge from someone's outside what their reading habits included. When my ninety-year-old, great nana died, we found a collection of erotica so wild that my brothers and I didn't dare try and donate it anywhere. Even now, thinking about it made me want to giggle. Which made *Jane Eyre* plus hockey star a little less far-fetched. I eyed the shelves again. I was about to stand up to take a closer look when TJ's voice just about made me jump.

"Hey," he said.

I turned and found him standing in the doorframe with two mugs in his hands.

"Hey," I echoed.

He stepped into the room and held out the cup. "Hot chocolate?"

"Thanks."

I took the mug, wrapping my hands around the warm porcelain. I waited expectantly for him to take a seat, too. But he didn't. Instead, he stepped over to the gas fireplace, flicked on a switch, then fiddled with the settings for an excessive number of seconds. Even once the flames were flickering brightly, he didn't say anything else to me. Most definitely stalling. Finally, I decided if I just left it, he might never offer up anything else.

"So…" I said, taking a small, careful sip from the mug full of steaming liquid. "Are you avoiding talking to me, or are you just a big fan of creating ambience?"

The question earned me the barest smile, and the curve of his lips made was definitely strained.

"Maybe both," he told me. "Can't hurt to be comfortable when I reveal my deepest secrets, right?"

My chest constricted as I nodded. Not because I had enormous concerns about TJ's secrets—although there was a tickle of worry there—but because it made me think of my own. I pushed off the anxiety and made myself answer in a light, calm voice.

"If this is the part where you confess you're an axe murderer…" I said, "then I'm out. And fair warning…I can disarm most men faster than they can draw their weapons."

His mouth tipped up a little bit more. "Is that where you draw the line? Just this side of axe murderer?"

"Even private security people have their limits," I replied.

"And just like that, I'm suddenly feeling pretty good about my secret." Despite his words, his expression drooped again, and he sighed, then sat on one of the other couches. "I'm not a bad guy, Ivy," he said, looking down at his hands. "Which I'm sure is exactly what every douchebag tells people. But I have to put it out there anyway."

His plaintive tone made my heart ache, and I had to steel myself against a need to move closer to him. "I'm not here to judge you, TJ."

He lifted his eyes and smiled again, this time without a shred of good humor. "You say that now."

"I don't say things I don't mean." The statement felt a little too personal, and I took a breath and added, "It's my job to keep you safe. And to find out who's behind this. So if there's something I need to know…"

His nod was tight, his words all but robotic. "A few years ago, I wasn't the same person I am now, and I'm not proud of who I was then. I partied more than I want to admit. Far more than was acceptable for my career choice. And it bit me in the ass. I went to a bar. I met a woman. She was beautiful. Fun. Flirtatious. Danced with ten other guys before coming my way. That was fine with me because I wasn't after something serious. Neither was she. Mostly because she was already married to another player on my team. I swear I didn't know. But what was done was done. And here I am."

I waited, sure he was going to add something more. Something worse. Something awful and deviant. I was physically tense with the anticipation of a larger reveal. But he stayed silent, his gaze now fixed on the fireplace.

"So you had an accidental affair?" I said, trying not to sound like I was minimizing his feelings on the matter. "And that somehow translates to me—a girlfriend, I mean—moving in with you?"

"Yeah. I guess that's one way of putting it."

"I'm still not quite following."

"Let's just say it was the culminating moment of some bad decisions and reckless behavior," he replied. "It destroyed my relationship with that teammate. The tension between us tore apart the team."

TJ went on, his voice quiet, resigned, and clipped at the same time. He explained how his team lost game after game after game. The frustrations boiled over onto the ice. Massive blowouts. Hollering matches.

As he spoke, a possibility bubbled up.

"Can I stop for you one second there?" I asked.

"Sure. But I know what you're going to say—that

it sounds like my former teammate might think he's got a pretty good reason to come after me," TJ said. "If he were alive, I might agree. Unfortunately, he passed away. Natural causes. His wife remarried. Younger man. I think they live in Bermuda."

"Ah. Okay."

He resumed his story, starting with a description of his final bit of ice time that season. He got into a fight with an opponent, and it earned him a concussion, a broken wrist, a fractured collarbone. And no hope of contract renewal. He needed an entire year off, just to recover. Rumors spread. A blackmark formed. TJ spiraled. No one wanted to touch him. Cue Bram Armstaad.

"He's a shark," TJ said. "He got me back in the game, but with stipulations."

He reeled off the list. No alcohol. No public appearances in bars or clubs or unsanctioned events. Media attention was to be strictly regulated. And there was a clause about relationships. No one-night stands. No casual hookups. No room for a repeat of the previous error. Any infractions would lead to the termination of his deal. And there was also the possibility of having to pay back any earnings he'd made up to that point.

He exhaled and met my eyes. "So. Now you know why I don't want my agent involved in what's going on with the threatening notes, why I can't let myself get involved with the police, and also why my initial reaction to your brother's suggestion was strong opposition."

I nodded. "Yes, I do understand. But TJ…why would you agree to all of that? It's excessive. It doesn't even sound legal."

His expression was practically a mask, and what he offered me was nothing more than a clichéd reply. "There was no other choice."

"There's always a choice."

"Sure. I could've sharpened skates for a living."

"Or gone back to school," I argued. "Or looked for something else."

"I hardly know you at all, Ivy," he said, "but one thing I'm sure of is that you're pretty damned determined to do your job at Ames Security. *So* determined that you're willing to fight with your brothers, put up with their shit, and do work that's probably beneath you just for the chance to get out there."

I fought a small wince. He was right about all of it. But he didn't know where *I* was coming from.

"I'm not sure what *I* do is on the same level of unreasonableness," I said, my tone carefully schooled to reveal none of my self-doubt.

"Maybe. But it's the only comparison I've got. I put everything—*everything*—I had into going the route of professional player. Stupid as it may sound, I didn't have a backup plan. I didn't even have a backup education. I only finished high school because my dad made me."

The admission surprised me. "You didn't do any kind of post-secondary at all?"

"Nope. All my brilliance is self-taught. Books and the wonderful world of the internet." The barest smile graced his face before slipping away again. "My dad wanted me to go to trade school, like he did. I just assumed I'd play until retirement, then pursue some secondary job in the business. Coach, manager, whatever. My life got messy and complicated, and my career fizzled right when it should've been rising to its peak. No way in hell was someone going to take me on in one of those roles, or anything even close." He stood up, moved from his couch to mine, and took my hands. "So here I am, sitting across from you, begging for you to help in keeping me in line with my contract."

I couldn't stop myself from feeling the heat of his palms travel up my arms. "And you really want me to do that by moving in with you?"

"Bram said it's the only way to make a hundred percent sure that my contract isn't viewed as violated. People won't be able to accuse me of being in a casual relationship if my girlfriend is living with me." His eyes closed for a second, and when he opened them again, his expression was raw. "I'm sorry, Ivy. If this is going to hurt you…"

My throat constricted, and if I hadn't known myself better, I would've sworn I'd been about to cry on TJ's behalf.

"It sounds more like it's going to hurt *you*," I stated softly.

There was no denial in his gaze. But his responding words weren't exactly an affirmation, either.

"All of that stuff I just told you about my contract?" he said. "No one knows about any of that except Bram, me, and the owner of the team. The guys on the team have no clue. My coaches don't know. Neither does my manager. I sure as hell didn't tell your brother when I was hiring Ames Security. I'm trusting *you* with it, and I don't even know why. But I *do* know it's not just because I don't have much other choice.

Trusting you with that information takes a hell of a lot more than trusting you with my life. So, if you can't do this, just tell me."

I swallowed.

It's just another level to the same plan, I told myself. *And it's a temporary arrangement. A fake one.*

It sounded very reasonable when I thought about it like that.

But I had other motivations to reject the suggestion. Ones that kept me up at night and made my brothers think I ought to stay away from field work. The same past that made me a less than ideal choice for the fake girlfriend fiasco. Despite all that, though, what popped out of my mouth was something else entirely.

"Where will I sleep?"

The expression on TJ's face might've been comical under other circumstances. His eyes went wide with surprise, and his mouth dropped open silently. Probably because it was the last question he'd been expecting to hear. Which really made two of us. I could feel every inch of my face burning. But thankfully, I was saved from having to backpedal or make an excuse. In my pocket, my phone vibrated softly, and when I freed my hands to pull out the slim, electronic device, my embarrassment faded into relief. Charles's name scrolled across the screen.

Chapter Fourteen

I didn't let myself feel true relief until I heard my brother's voice.

"Hey, Pint-Size," he said, sounding tired. "Turns out I'm good at *not* puncturing any major organs while breaking a few ribs."

I closed my eyes and leaned back against the couch. "It's good to have a talent."

"Agreed," he replied. "Oh. It also turns out I developed an allergy to penicillin sometime between my tenth birthday and today. Hives are fun."

"You're never boring, are you, Chuck?"

"Nope. Always trying to keep things lively. What about you?"

"No penicillin allergy here," I joked.

My brother laughed. "I meant are you keeping things lively in other ways. As in…with our client?"

"TJ the Troublemaker Jones is alive and well. We're in a secure spot, and we're discussing our next move."

"I take it your relationship is progressing well, then."

"So well, we're moving in together."

There was a pause on the other end, and I could easily picture my brother's face pinching up in puzzlement. I smiled at the thought. And I opened my eyes again to cast a glance toward TJ. His lips were

113

curved up, too.

"Okay," said Charles with a sigh. "I'm not even going to ask. I just wanted to make sure you got out okay, and to let you know they want to keep me here in the hospital overnight, and that the meds make the accommodations more bearable."

"And as a bonus, you won't be able to break any *more* ribs," I replied, and then, in a more serious tone, I added, "I'm glad you're okay."

"Me, too. And ditto."

"Is there any news on what happened at the hotel? Is anyone saying anything about TJ?"

"Just that the police investigation is ongoing," he told me.

"Good," I said. "Maybe we can dodge the attention for a little while longer."

In the background, I heard the overlap of voices, and when my brother spoke again, it was to tell me he had to go because the nurses were there for a check. He promised to call me again if he heard anything. I assured him I would update him with any news on my end, too, and then we hung up.

"Your brother's doing all right?" TJ asked as I tucked my phone back into my pocket.

I nodded. "Thank God."

"Good." He paused. "Not to make things all about me, but did I hear you right? You're going to go along with the moving in plan?"

"This *is* all about you," I reminded him. "And I'll do what I have to in order to keep you safe."

Relief dominated his features. "Thank you. You have no idea how much this means to me. And to answer your question from before, I have a spare room.

And probably a spare toothbrush, too."

My cheeks warmed, but I ignored the sensation. "Great. I'll probably need a little more of my own stuff. Pants, for example. But it can wait a bit. At least until the storm is over. And in the meantime, I'd like to take a look at the notes you received. I'm assuming you still have them?"

"I do," said TJ. "I'd have preferred to toss them into a bonfire, but I've got them stowed in a very ugly shoebox instead."

"Burning evidence is generally frowned upon," I replied. "Is the ugly shoebox here, or at your apartment?"

"Here." He hesitated. "I haven't been back there. Not since I found that third note. It just felt like it was too risky. I stayed here the night before last, and in the hotel yesterday."

"I don't blame you."

"I also had this weird thought that whoever left the notes might try to come back and take them," he admitted. "Which is why I brought them with me when I came here two days ago. You want me to grab them for you now?"

"Please."

He stood up, and I watched him go, trying to make my mind churn out a few ideas about who might be behind the whole thing. It was pretty much a futile effort. Usually, we came at our cases in a tidy, formulaic way. We interviewed the client. Assessed the angles. Came up with theories. Ruled things out and focused on the probabilities. It was what I needed to be doing now. But my brain wandered onto something else entirely. The woman on the other side of TJ's

accidental affair. What was she like? Blonde? Brunette?
Why does it matter?

For a moment, I stalled on an answer. Then I realized I had logical one staring me right in the face.

"It matters because Bermuda or not...she could be the one who wrote the notes and set off the bomb, that's why," I said under my breath.

Except as soon as the claim left my mouth, I could tell that it had a ring of falsehood. Why would a woman who'd inherited a hockey player's fortune turn around and threaten another man's life?

So ask yourself again, Ivy...why does it matter?

I wasn't sure if I wanted to know the answer. Because the only one I could come up with was green-tinged, made no sense, and was utterly misplaced. So I was thankful that TJ was quick to return. He held the promised shoebox, with its garish clash of colors and asymmetrical designs making it fully blink worthy.

I eyed it skeptically. "That really *is* ugly."

He stepped over, set the box on the table, and sat down beside me. "I told you so."

"What kind of shoes were in there?"

"I honestly have no idea. Nothing good, I'm sure."

The words were a joke, but they had a portentous undertone, and neither of us touched the box for a moment after that. Apprehension hung in the air. Except looking at the notes wasn't a choice; it was a matter of necessity. I gave in and pulled the box closer to wiggle off the tightly fitted lid. Inside, curved against the cardboard, were three medium-size, clear plastic bags with zip-up tops.

"Sorry," said TJ right. "I think I've probably seen too many crime shows for my own good."

"No," I replied. "It was smart. Preserving the evidence. Far better than burning it in a bonfire."

Carefully, I lifted out the first note. It was slightly crumpled, and I could easily imagine TJ balling it up in his hand after reading it, then smoothing it out again later. My eyes ran over the message. The warning was displayed just as he'd said. *WATCH YOUR STEP,* spelled out in magazine and newspaper lettering. There was nothing distinct about it. Which, of course, was the intention. I had no forensics expertise, and I suspected that's what would be needed to identify the sender. I bit my lip to keep from suggesting to TJ that the police might be able to figure it out by simply trying to lift some fingerprints.

"I know it would be easier to just let the cops do their thing," he said, reading the turn my thoughts had just taken. "But if there's a chance I can figure this out without risking everything…"

"That's why I'm here," I told him.

I set down the first note and pulled out the second one. *DON'T GET STUCK,* it read in its pasted-on letters. The message was so innocuous that the only thing that made it a threat was the manner in which it was delivered.

Frowning, I moved on to the third and final note. *IF YOU PLAY WITH FIRE,* is all it said.

"There's not much to go on, is there?" TJ sounded understandably frustrated. "The last one isn't even a full sentence. They could've at least finished it with 'then you're going to get burned.'"

His facetious statement made me pause. Something tickled at my brain.

"But you *could* have gotten burned today." I lifted

my gaze to his face. "If the bomb had blown into the hotel room instead of out of it. Or if the sprinkler system had malfunctioned."

There was a flicker of unease in his eyes. "That's true."

"You said that this last note came two days ago, right?"

"Yes."

I did a quick calculation in my head. "Did you get stuck anywhere, a week ago?"

His brow wrinkled. "Did I get—" He stopped short, his attention flicking to the second note before coming back to me. "What are you saying?"

I held up my fingers, tapping them as I counted off. "Day one, you got a note telling you to watch your step. Day three, you tripped down the stairs. Day five, you got a note telling you not to get stuck. Skip ahead to day nine, and you got a note saying not to play with fire. Day eleven—today—you were on the receiving end of an explosion. So…what were you up to on day seven?"

TJ's eyes widened. "Shit. My truck wouldn't start. I had to call a cab to get to my training session. But the cab couldn't get to my building because a couple of moving vans had the place boxed in. I was an hour late. You don't seriously think someone orchestrated all of that?"

"It wouldn't be all that hard, really. Easier than a bomb. Just pull a few wires from your engine. Hire a moving company to come, give them special instructions on where to park. Even if they never actually have to move anything, they've served their purpose."

"Shit," he said again, more emphatically this time.

"After your truck wouldn't start, did it need to be repaired?"

"No, actually. It started up fine later on that night."

"So, you assumed it was nothing."

"Yes."

My mind was moving quickly now, putting the pieces together. "And when you tripped nine days ago, how did it happen?"

"It was a skipping rope, tied to the handrail at the bottom of the steps. Figured it was some of the kids in the building, goofing around." His worry was evident in the tightening of his jaw. "Why the hell didn't I make the connections?"

"Why would you?" I replied. "The first two incidents were beyond subtle. My head wouldn't have gone there either if the notes weren't laid out like this."

"Still. I should've clued in."

"It's my job to find connections like this, TJ. Even if it'd been more obvious, I wouldn't think you should've come up with the link. Just like if you threw me onto the ice with a puck, you wouldn't expect me get a hat trick. In fact, I'd probably just fall over because I can't skate."

"Wait. You can't skate?" he asked.

I couldn't stop a laugh from bubbling up. "That's the part of what I just said that you're focused on?"

"It's important."

"While we're trying to figure out who's stalking you?"

He gave a dismissive wave. "It'd be important at any time. Have you *tried* skating?"

"Not since I had to use one of those bar things to

hold myself up," I said. "Can we go back on the case?"

"As soon as you agree to give it another try."

"Skating?"

"Did we switch to talking about something else?" TJ countered.

"We were already talking about something else," I reminded him.

"And now we're talking about skating," he stated. "It's important."

"Are you serious?"

"Deadly."

"We don't have time for me to learn to skate. We have a bomber to track down."

"Are you, or are you not my fake, live-in girlfriend?"

"I am. Apparently."

"People will think it's weird if my girlfriend doesn't skate," he said. "I'm a professional hockey player."

I tossed him a look but also realized it wasn't a battle I was going to win. "Fine."

"You're just saying that because you think you won't have to follow through."

"Okay. Look. If we *happen* to get near the ice—and I don't mean in the middle of one of your games—then I will commit to ten minutes of sliding around and falling on my ass."

"Fifteen minutes," he replied.

I rolled my eyes. "Fifteen minutes then. Now can we get back to work?"

"Sure."

His grin was infectious, and I looked down so that he wouldn't notice that I was smiling, too. There was no way in hell I was going to lace up. But it was impossible not to enjoy his misplaced enthusiasm at the idea.

I tapped the notes. "If we follow the pattern, it goes like this. A note is delivered. Then two days later, the setup to match the note comes. Two *more* days go by, then the next note is delivered. Right now, we're on day eleven. A setup day. Which means that the day after tomorrow, we can expect another note."

"Oh, good. Something to look forward to."

"It *is* good. At least insofar as it gives us some predictability."

TJ's hand slid over his chin. "What should we expect? More banana-peel slips, or more bombs?"

I hesitated. The escalation was not only obvious, it was also very quick. A fall. An inconvenience. An explosion. The stalker was gaining momentum. Probably wanting more attention.

What comes after trying to blow someone up? I thought. *Nothing good, that's for sure.*

Aloud, I treaded more carefully. "I'm not going to jump to any conclusions. And my hope is that we figure this out before we even *get* the next note. But if we don't...I think we should analyze it very carefully. Look for clues in the wording—like 'fire' or 'fall' in the last ones—and come up with some plausible scenarios based on what we infer. Agreed?"

"All right," he said. "But that means we have a day and a bit to kill. What do we do in the meantime?"

I started to say that we needed to stay focused. To come up with a list of every person he'd possibly affronted in the last decade. To call around to see if we could find out who hired the moving company that had blocked his road, and to check if there was any kind of CCTV to be accessed in the spots where the notes had been left. But as I eyed TJ's face, I changed my mind. The corners of his eyes were pinched, and exhaustion rolled off him. I could relate. The last couple of hours felt more like an extremely trying month. Neither of us would be very effective if we kept going until we dropped.

"First…" I said, "we get some food. Then we see about moving me in. After that, we'll get back to work."

His nod was eager, his relief palpable. And I was glad I'd decided to err on the side of taking some time. But as TJ asked what I liked better, pizza or Chinese food, there was also a little part of me that silently asked if I was motivated by something more personal.

Chapter Fifteen

The next few hours passed at ten times the rate of the previous ones.

After a quick discussion, both of us decided we weren't in the mood for Chinese food *or* pizza, and we settled on cooking for ourselves instead. The house was only in semi-regular use—a little getaway when TJ needed it—and as such was only stocked with the basic necessities. TJ joked that unless I wanted to eat pasta with plain tomato sauce every day for as long as we were "shacking up together" then we definitely had to make other arrangements. But I didn't think it was in our best interests to make a trip out in public. Not yet anyway. After a brief discussion, we opted for getting a few groceries delivered. And then we settled down to make a list together.

I pretended not to notice that it felt abnormally normal. I didn't tell TJ that I'd never lived with anyone other than my family before, and I didn't ask if he had, either. I just added my preferred brand of soup to the notepad and acted like it was no big deal. Because it *wasn't* a big deal. It was just a part of my everyday job. That is, if a regular job included making a bed with a virtual stranger.

The whole time, I kept hearing Charles's voice in my head. He alternated between telling me to be careful and reminding me that this was work.

There was one, very nervous moment when the delivery guy arrived. The second that the bell rang, TJ and I looked at each other. And neither of us had to say anything. We were both thinking about the last time food had supposedly been waiting on the other side of the door. But thankfully, a quick check through the window revealed a van wrapped in the grocery store logo and a teenager laden down with plastic bags.

By the time the food—burgers and a salad, washed down with sparkling water—had been cooked and eaten, and the post dinner dishes had been washed and put away, the bungalow was swathed in darkness. And both TJ and I were yawning.

I decided picking up my things could wait until the morning, and I suggested we spend a few minutes trying to compile a list of people who might not hate TJ, but who might not exactly love him. It was a short-lived endeavor. TJ couldn't come up with more than a few names—prior teammates and a couple of opponents. None of whom he could see having a true vendetta. I was really starting to lean toward the idea he'd royally pissed someone off without even knowing it. Which wasn't exactly the best-case scenario, assuming there *was* a best-case scenario where stalking and bombing were concerned. With no viable suspects, I was going to have work with evidence rather than by following a flashing arrow that would lead me to the culprit. It was a frustrating roadblock. And when TJ had snapped his fingers and produced another name to add to the list—a restaurant server who'd given him a bad sandwich the week before—I knew it was time to call it a night.

I did a second perimeter check, both outside and

inside. When I was satisfied that everything was secure, I took the new toothbrush that TJ offered, said a goodnight that managed to be only slightly awkward, and then slipped into the guest bedroom.

Once I'd closed the door behind myself, I leaned against it and wondered if I'd gone off the deep end. Maybe I'd bumped my head harder than I'd thought. Because the me I knew would never agree to sleep at a stranger's house. And if that same me was forced to for some reason, then she'd be barricading the door and tensing for the possibility of a fight. But what I felt as I stood there was…what?

Relaxed, said a little voice in my head.

I was warm and dry. My stomach was full. And despite everything, TJ's company was enjoyable. When his mind wasn't on the imminent threat, his sense of humor slipped through. I'd enjoyed making dinner with him. Several times, I'd almost forgotten my purpose in being there. And weirder than that was the fact my past had been far from my mind. Not that I normally spent time dwelling on it, but it was always just…*there*…under the surface, waiting for an excuse to rear up. But not so much tonight.

"Yeah, I've *definitely* lost it," I said, pushing up from the door to flick on the light and move more fully into the room to get ready for bed.

Though really, "room" wasn't the most accurate room to describe it. Suite would've been a better word. It was spacious. Tastefully decorated in neutral colors. The bed was a king size, the pillows and bedding more luxurious than the ones I had at home. And it also had its own sitting area, as well as full bathroom with a tempting spa tub that seemed to be calling my name as I brushed my teeth. I resisted. As much as I ached all over, the whole situation was weird enough. I settled for changing into yet another of TJ's shirts—the new one smelled like the fabric softener—then grabbed my phone and sent a quick text to Charles. I wasn't expecting a reply. The nurses probably had the patients all tucked in at a reasonable hour, and with any luck, my brother was full of enough painkillers to help him sleep well through the night. But I knew he'd appreciate being looped in when he got up in the morning.

Not that it's much of an update, I admitted ruefully as I slipped into the bed and stared up at the textured ceiling.

I wondered guiltily if I should be staying up all night in search of more answers. For more than three years, my part of Ames Security's cases stopped at the office doors. Sure, sometimes my brothers had some kind of emergency that required some late-night assistance, but not often. What did *they* do if there was a need during non-standard hours? Did they stay up? Prop themselves in a chair in a doorway and wait vigilantly for something to go wrong? Maybe they did, in the case of overnight jobs. But there was a difference between a shift that started at dusk and ran until dawn and what I was doing.

Besides which, I honestly couldn't remember a time when one of them had been hired for a 24/7 thing like this. Our paid security details usually involved specific events for short periods of time. A few hours at a conference. An escort from the airport to a hotel, or a day spent guarding an apartment building for some specific reason. Other than that, most of our business focused on the P.I. side of things.

Self-doubt nagged at me.

What if I'm doing this wrong?

A need to seek Charles's advice—something that would undoubtedly make him gloat—seeped in.

I rolled over and eyed my phone. It was silent. And I was sure that if I picked it up and looked, I'd see that my outgoing message to my brother remained unread.

I rolled over again, and this time my gaze found the door. It was closed. And in the dark, it wasn't much more than a silhouette. But I could easily picture what was on the other side.

One step out. Three steps over. TJ's door.

I'd gone into his room out of necessity, just like I'd gone into every other room in the house. And even though I knew that it wasn't his primary residence, I hadn't been able to stop a bit of personal curiosity from rearing up as I made my professional sweep.

Without meaning to, I closed my eyes and went over it in my mind.

The walls were painted the palest gray, the baseboards and crown molding were black, and the furniture was a very dark red, deeper than crimson. The contrast was striking but not jarring. The accoutrements were minimal. A broken hockey stick hung like a trophy on one wall, and a piece of abstract art dominated another. A framed photo sat on the long dresser, and that had held my gaze the longest. I'd known right away that the young boy in the picture was TJ, and I was sure the man beside him was his father. The family resemblance was uncanny. And of course, TJ's wide smile and blue eyes were the same now as they'd been back then.

Through the fuzziness of encroaching sleep, I

thought about that smile, and about the man attached to it. Who would want to harm him? And why? Not the bad sandwich girl that he'd tried to add to the list, of that I was pretty sure.

Is he keeping something from me?

Normally, I would just assume the answer was yes. It was common for clients to try to protect themselves by covering up parts of their lives, and it was often hard to convince them that secrets were detrimental to their cases.

But for me...secrets were also bad on a personal level. They set off the deepest of alarm bells. Particularly where men were concerned. In every case we'd take on since my life had unraveled almost four years ago, it had been a struggle to keep that panic at bay. It was pure instinct. Except right then, I was too close slumber for my usual, self-preservation to dominate.

If he is *hiding something, what is it?*

My wakefulness dwindled even more. Possibilities flitted in and out, but none of them stuck. I tried to make a mental note to ask him directly. But that slipped away, too. Instead, my mind drifted to the way TJ had looked when I'd finished doing my check. He'd been leaning against the doorframe, his eyes on the photo that had captured my attention for those extra moments. His expression had been sad. Almost pained. And I'd had to shut down a desire to step over and pull him into a hug.

Does his secret have something to do with that look?

I wasn't sure where that particular thought came from, but unlike the others, it seemed less elusive. For a moment, I clung to it. But it didn't last long. Sleep overtook me, washing away any semblance of coherence.

Chapter Sixteen

I was trapped in a familiar dream. One I knew well. One—despite that knowledge—I could never escape, no matter how many times I experienced it.

In it, I wore a floral dress, and I was approaching a man outside an expensive restaurant. I knew the man. He was expecting me. He smiled, and I smiled back. Though his face wasn't quite handsome enough to be the sort that would draw attention in a crowd, the overall pleasantness of his features was undeniable. It was clear that he cared about his appearance. His hair looked freshly trimmed, his face was cleanshaven. And there was something comfortable about his slightly crooked nose and his nondescript hazel eyes. Maybe because the lack of perfection made him seem accessible. It helped that he held a bouquet of pink roses in his hands. My favorite.

A little flutter of anticipation danced in my chest. I started to hurry.

But as I got closer to the man, things changed. First, I noticed that the roses were far from fresh. They were wilted and edged with brown. My steps faltered. I stopped. And as I watched, a petal dropped to the ground. The flutter became a wild kick.

Run! said a voice in my head.

But my reaction came too late. Because the restaurant had already faded away, and now I was in an alley. The air was rank. I spun in a circle, searching for the man and his roses. He was gone. I called out, but I was unsure if I actually wanted him to answer. Fear took hold. And when I spun around again, that same fear came to life in the form of a pair of hands around my throat. I wanted to scream. I couldn't. The fingers were tightening, blocking my airway. Silencing any sound that might otherwise escape. Dark was going to win.

But suddenly—unexpectedly—another hand landed on my shoulder. I heard my name. And was ripped back to reality. I sat bolt upright, my heart slamming against my ribcage. There really *was* a hand on my shoulder. And a pair of blue eyes were staring down at me, too, concern evident in their vivid hue. It took a good moment to orient myself.

TJ the Troublemaker Jones. The hockey player. The case.

"You okay?" he asked, his tone matching his worried expression.

The last vestiges of the bad dream faded away, leaving me with just a bit of hovering unease. I knew from experience that would dissipate before long, too.

I exhaled, nodded, then leaned back. And belatedly realized that I was on the floor. My shoulders were pressed to the side of the bed, and my bare legs were sticking out along the floor. The borrowed T-shirt was pushed up so high that it all but exposed the rest of me. My bandaged knees. My thighs. One little move, and TJ was going to get a very special show.

Dammit.

As quickly as I could, I yanked the fabric down. And I did manage to cover my*self*. But there was no way to cover the fact that I'd fallen out of bed. Not that TJ was looking anywhere but my face. Why *wasn't* he looking anywhere but my face? His attention hadn't even dropped to the expanse of skin on display.

Seriously, Ivy? I chastised silently. *You're worried that he's* not *a pervert?* But my sub-conscious answered that with a slightly snide, *Well, there's* not-a-pervert, *and then there's disinterested, isn't there?*

I shoved aside the ridiculous internal argument and said, "I guess I'm not used to sleeping somewhere other my own place. And apparently, I'm not very good at it, either."

"No shit," TJ replied. "The thump was so loud that I thought maybe you were fighting off my stalker."

"That'd be far less embarrassing."

"Then I probably shouldn't tell you that you were hollering. Something pretty fierce, too."

My face heated. "Did I say anything particularly interesting?"

"If you did, it was in a language I didn't understand."

"Small mercies."

He eased up from his crouched position, then held out his hand. I took it and let him pull me to my feet. As I did, I noticed that—unlike me—TJ was fully clothed. He wore a pair of sports shorts and a fitted, athletic shirt.

"Is it morning?" I asked.

"Very early," he replied. "Like 5:30."

"That's not just very early. That's very, *very* early."

"Yeah. Coach sent me an angry text last night. Said he didn't buy that I was all that sick, and if I didn't show up for the team skate this morning, I could kiss some of my ice time goodbye."

"Damn. What time is the skate?"

"Starts at 7:30. I like to eat a full breakfast a couple of hours before that. Hence the ridiculous hour," TJ explained.

"Okay. I should probably see about getting some clothes, then," I said.

"Clothes?" he echoed.

I lifted an eyebrow. "Unless you think I'll be warm enough in the arena in nothing but my yellow dress with all its holes?"

Surprise played over his features. "You're coming?"

"It would be a little hard for me to protect you if we were in two different places," I pointed out. "Is that a problem? Are the sessions closed?"

"To the public," TJ said. "But the guys occasionally bring guests."

"I guess you're the guy today. Do we have time to stop by my place? It's not too far from the arena, and it won't take me more than ten minutes."

"Sure. We can do that."

"Perfect." I paused as my stomach let out a small grumble. "Did you say something about breakfast?"

"Yep. Eggs, sausage, toast, and fruit. Some bacon, too. Sound good?"

"Sounds better than good."

"Then follow me."

He gestured to the door, and I took a couple of steps before remembering that I was pants-less. I stopped, mid-stride.

"I should probably make myself a little more

decent," I said.

For the first time, TJ's eyes traveled to my bare skin. He quickly jerked his attention back to my face, but not before I saw his Adam's apple bob in his throat.

"I'll see you out at the kitchen, then," he said.

When he spun and headed out of the room, I felt both a tingle and a small bit of misplaced relief. He *had* noticed me.

"You've got a problem, Ames," I muttered at myself as I grabbed the sweatpants that I'd discarded last night and slid them on.

And truly…no one knew as well as I did just how much more than a "problem" things could become. If I wanted proof, all I had to do was to acknowledge the dream that had landed me on the floor of my current client's guest room. As I thought about it right then, the residual fear crept up again. Unconsciously, I brought one of my hands up to my throat. When I clued in to what I was doing, I quickly forced my arms to drop.

This isn't the same thing as what happened back then. In fact, it's not even close.

"TJ isn't some freak with an ulterior motive. He's a legitimate, vetted client," I asserted quietly.

And he was. He had to be. Charles had done he due diligence. Of that, I was sure. Because if he hadn't, there was no way he would've involved me. Which was just another reason to not be thinking about whether TJ was checking out my legs.

I stepped over to the mirror, combed my fingers through my hair, then twisted it into a bun. As I finished securing it with the ponytail holder I'd had on my wrist, TJ's voice carried in from the hall.

"Ivy?" he said. "You coming out here anytime

soon? You might wanna hurry. I finished my bacon, and yours is starting to look pretty appealing."

I smiled because I couldn't help it and called back, "Don't even think about it!"

Then I forced my face into a stern glare—directed at my own reflection—and took a slow breath before exiting the room to make my way to the kitchen, where TJ waited with a plate. The food was heaped on—two slice of toast, two eggs, two sausages, and a bowl of chopped fruit.

"Wow," I said. "You weren't kidding about the full spread."

"Some of my teammates like a protein shake. Me, not so much."

As I approached, he sat at the breakfast bar and motioned to one of the tall stools. I immediately grabbed one of the pieces of bacon and gave it a quick bite while raising a challenging eyebrow at TJ, who chuckled.

"What?" I said when I finished chewing. "I wake up hungry."

His smile became a grin. "Well, I don't want to be one of those guys who says he loves to see a woman eat, but apparently…I'm one of those guys."

"Trust me," I said. "I had to fight five older brothers for food when I was growing up. I like to eat."

He laughed. "Coffee to wash that down?"

"Please."

As he poured a mug for me, I finished off the bacon and moved on to a slice of toast. With the dream now stuffed back in the proper compartment in my brain, I was more alert, and I was eager to get back to work.

"Do you know the name of the moving company?" I asked. "The one whose trucks were blocking the road to your apartment, I mean."

TJ frowned. "I can't remember. But I bet you ten bucks the doorman at my building does. He called it in."

I reached across the counter to grab the pen and notepad that we'd used to make our grocery list, and I made a note.

"Do you have the doorman's number?" I said. "Or do you think we'll have time to swing by and talk to him today?"

"Either or."

"Okay, good." I made another note. "Does your building have cameras?"

He nodded. "Yeah, it does."

"What about the locker room where you found the first note?"

"Does it have cameras? Jesus, I hope not."

I lifted my head up sharply. "Why? Is there something going on in there?"

TJ's lips curled up. "Uh, no. Just a shitload of naked and half-naked hockey players."

My face heated. "Right."

He chuckled. And in a belated—and failed—attempt to cover my embarrassment, I stabbed a strawberry with my fork. But I only got the fruit halfway to my mouth before TJ cut me off with an unexpected question.

"Was it a nightmare?" he asked.

Automatically, I started to deny it. But for some reason, I couldn't quite manage the lie, and I nodded instead.

"I get them sometimes," I admitted. "Occupational hazard, I suppose."

"Do you see a lot of bad things in your line of work?"

I bit down on the strawberry and hoped my slow chewing didn't come across as exaggerated. I still didn't want to lie. But however-relaxed I'd felt the night before, the thought of explaining the truth behind the dream still sent my heart racing.

"Not a ton," I said with casual vagueness. "But now and then something sticks with you."

Understanding passed over TJ's face, and it made me curious. Did he really get it? Had something stuck with him in the same way? If so, what was it?

You could ask, I pointed out to myself. *In fact, you probably* should *ask, in case it's related to the case.*

But I didn't get a chance to do it. His face changed to utter neutrality, and he stood up abruptly, cleared his dishes to the sink, then excused himself to get ready for his early morning skate.

Chapter Seventeen

By the time I finished breakfast, TJ was all but ready to go. I was glad when he told me he'd called a cab to pick us up and take us back into Surrey to retrieve my stuff from my apartment. Had he not done it already, I would've suggested it myself. There would've been absolutely no way to travel subtly in the beast of a truck I'd spied out near the barn. And it was my intention to keep as low a profile as possible for as long as possible.

The only negative about taking the taxi was that it meant we weren't alone. Unlike Eldon's car, there was no privacy glass between us and the driver, and that meant keeping our conversation at the surface level. We talked about the weather. About a movie we both happened to have watched the previous month. About the merits of cold pizza. Each topic was less consequential than the previous. And the entire time, the last moments of our breakfast interaction—mostly TJ's final expression, really—hovered in my brain, demanding attention. The more I forced myself to ignore it, the surer I was that I should be exploring it further instead. When we pulled up to my building, I was so frustrated that I wanted to throw the door open and let out a scream.

"Are you doing all right?" TJ asked as the taxi came to a halt. "You look like you swallowed a fly."

"I'm fine." I said it with as much lightness as I could muster. "I just want to get in, get my stuff, and keep going."

His forehead wrinkled, but he didn't argue. "Okay. You want me to come in with you, or should I wait out here?"

I briefly debated the question. On the one hand, I couldn't remember what kind of state I'd left my apartment in. And I wasn't in the habit of having people inside it to begin with. Most definitely not clients. But on the other hand, I'd spent the night at TJ's house. I was currently wearing TJ's clothes. So worrying about whether or not I'd left a towel on the bathroom floor seemed like an overly superficial point. I could also picture the look on my brother's face at even the *idea* of leaving a client on his own in a taxi.

"Come with me," I said. "The elevator in my building is broken, and I might need someone big and strong to carry my bag down the stairs."

TJ's mouth quirked up, silently calling out my bullshit. I covered my own smile with my hand, and I swung open the door.

"We'll be back in less than ten," I told the driver.

The cabby shrugged. "Take as much time as you want. I'll leave the meter running."

We climbed out and stepped toward the front doors, where I plugged in my code on the keypad.

"You aren't worried about someone following us here?" TJ asked as the lock buzzed its open signal, and I pulled on the handle.

"What was that thing you said yesterday about needing more than the average stalker to figure out who owns that house of yours?" I replied, motioning for him to move into the lobby.

"Oh. You mean your dad's cousin's uncle's brothers' dog owns this place?"

"Ha-ha. I happen to rent it under a pseudonym. My pseudonym has an entire, well-crafted life."

I led him past the built-in mailboxes and the elevator with its out-of-service sign, then turned to the right in the first-floor hall.

"Hang on," TJ said as we bypassed the door marked with the word *STAIRS* and kept going. "I thought you said we were going up?"

"Did I?" I replied innocently. "My bad."

We reached my door then—apartment 109—and I punched in another code on my personal keypad.

"Welcome to the home of self-employed typist, Godiva Ravensberger," I said as we stepped inside, and I flicked on the light.

"*Godiva Ravensberger?*" TJ repeated.

"Well, when you say it like that…it sounds fake."

"Yeah, the way I said it…*that's* what added the element of fake-ness."

We moved from the small entryway into the living room. It felt good to be home. But it also felt strange. Like I'd been gone for a year instead of a day.

I shook off the internal disquiet and said, "Godiva makes it make sense when I answer to Ivy. And if it'd been up to my dad, they fully would've named me that. My mom vetoed it."

"And Ravensberger?" TJ asked.

"When I was in third grade, we made family trees. There was a girl in my class—Emily—whose paternal grandmother had Ravensberger as her last name. I was insanely envious," I explained.

"So you stole it."

"Yes."

"Like…twenty years later."

"Yes. I'm very patient." I pointed to the couch. "Have a seat. I'll pack my stuff and come right back."

As I made my way to my bedroom, I realized something. I'd just disclosed more personal details to TJ the Troublemaker Jones than I'd told anyone in the last four years.

They were small things, I said to myself.

And it was true. There was no enormous reveal in that brief conversation about my fake name. But still. It *felt* enormous.

It's not, I insisted. *Stay focused.*

Nervously biting my lip, I threw open my closet doors. What did someone pack when she was starting the moving-in process with her fake boyfriend? I had no idea. Then again, I also didn't know what someone would pack when she was moving in with her *real* boyfriend.

A sudden flash of lacy lingerie popped to mind, and despite the fact that I was alone, my face warmed. I didn't own a single piece of lingerie. Boy-cut underwear and practical bras. And if I *had* been the proud owner of satin and lace, I sure as hell wouldn't have been packing it to take to TJ's place.

I grimaced at myself, then reached into my closet and yanked out my suitcase. Haphazardly, I tossed in yoga pants and T-shirts, flannel pjs and a few other things that I barely looked at. I grabbed my toiletries from my tiny ensuite bathroom—my own toothbrush included—then moved on to getting changed. I slid into some dark wash jeans, tossed on a bra and tank top, then added my favorite, button-up flannel, hoping it would be warm enough to stave off the cold in the arena.

It felt good to be dressed in fresh clothes.

"Almost ready," I murmured.

I just needed to think about the business side of things. What items I would need that were more about doing my job and less about playing the role of girlfriend? I didn't own a gun. Even Charles—who was the one most often responsible for bodyguard work if it arose—had never pursued the "Authorization to Carry" permit. My preferred weapon was my body. Fast hands and feet. I didn't spend all those hours working on self-defence for nothing. Right now, I wasn't sure that it was enough.

With a sigh, I decided that my usual means of protection would have to suffice. The last thing I needed to do was to jeopardize the status of my P.I. license by breaking weapons laws. I'd bring my laptop in case I needed the resources I kept on there, and other than that, I'd stick to using my wits and my experience.

I zipped up my suitcase, set it on the ground, then wheeled it down the hall and back to the living room. TJ was no longer sitting on the couch. Instead, I found him standing in front of the small shelf beside my TV. He had his fingers wrapped around the only photo I had that showcased my entire, immediate family. It was also the only picture I had on display. And it made me think of how I'd zeroed in on the shot of him and his father that he had in his bedroom. I felt another thread of commonality wrap itself around me. It was a strangely warm sensation. But I no sooner acknowledged that I kind of liked having things in common with TJ than he turned and threw me for a loop.

"Do you want kids?" he asked abruptly.

The question startled me. "What?"

And apparently, he'd startled himself, too. "Shit. Sorry. That wasn't a very appropriate question, was it?"

"Not really. But now I need to know where it came from."

"I was thinking about what kinds of things people who were moving in together needed to know about each other before that happened."

"And that was the first one you came up with? Not, like…favorite color?"

He set the framed picture down and swept a hand over my small living room. "I didn't have to ask about that. Blue is clearly your favorite."

I wrinkled my nose. But he was right. Everything from the couch—in the darkest navy—to the tiny sconces on the wall—in the palest powder—was some shade of blue.

"And yellow is your second favorite," TJ added, jerking his thumb toward the sunshine-colored bits and pieces dotting the room.

My toes did a weird tingling thing, and I ordered them to stop. "Okay. My tastes give away my fondness for blue and yellow. But having children is the next thing on your list?"

He shrugged. "I'm guessing that your favorite hobby is some kind of martial art. And I already—"

"Wait."

"What?"

"I like to box," I said. "And I've studied mixed martial arts for over three years. But how did you know that?"

"Your thing about disarming a man," he told me with another shrug. "I pay attention."

My toes tingled again. "Now I feel like a pretty shoddy P.I."

He grinned. "Why? You don't know my favorite color or my hobby?"

I started to shake my head, then stopped. The crimson accents in the bedroom at the rancher sprung to mind. So did the shelves of books.

"You have a preference for red," I said quickly. "And since hockey's your job, it doesn't qualify as a hobby. But you like to read."

"Correct on all accounts. And I'm impressed that you caught the last one. Sometimes my blue-collar mouth hides the fact that I've managed to make my way through a big chunk of Dickens. But the real question is…do I want kids?"

The tingle traveled up my legs, and I knew the only way to stop it from heading even farther was to get moving.

"We should go," I said, avoiding the question. "We don't want to spend your entire investigation budget on a taxi that we're not using."

TJ pointed to my bag. "Would offering to take that be a violation of our underestimation agreement?"

"Probably. But the driver will also probably think you're a shitty boyfriend."

"Don't sell the cabby short. He might just think you're a controlling girlfriend."

I fought a laugh. "I can live with that. And it might even be a little bit true."

He made a face, then stepped over and closed his fingers on the suitcase's handle and tipped it onto its wheels. "Yeah, well...maybe *you* can, but I don't want him to think that *I'm* an asshole."

"Your prerogative."

With him towing the bag, we exited my apartment and started back to the lobby. But TJ wasn't quite done with the discussion.

"On the subject of getting to know each other..." he said. "You should probably give me syncopated version of your life story. In case I have to answer any questions."

"Are we expecting an interrogation?" I replied.

"Possibly."

"It's a short-term, fake relationship. Not a marriage for the sake of gaining citizenship."

"Yeah. I know. But you haven't met Bram yet."

We reached the front doors, and TJ moved ahead so that he could open the door for me.

"Is he really that bad?" I wanted to know.

"Just you wait," he said.

"Great. No pressure or anything."

We paused a few feet from the taxi.

"Okay," I said. "You want my life in thirty seconds or less?"

"I'd even accept forty-five seconds," he told me with a smile.

I took a breath. "Born and raised in the Vancouver area. Youngest in a family of six. Only girl. My brothers are—in order of oldest to youngest—Charles, Callum, Jensen and Riley—they're twins—and Toby, who everyone calls 'the baby' even though that's technically me."

I went on quickly, explaining how my mom contracted meningitis when I was two, and she didn't make it. I told TJ that up until then, my dad was a cop. But it didn't take long for him to figure out that it was too hard to juggle that kind of schedule with having six kids, so he quit and started Ames Security. He used to take us into the office with him when we were too young to be left alone. Aside from the large family and not having a mother-figure in my life, everything else had been pretty normal. I'd graduated high school on time. Studied criminology for a short while, then dived right into P.I. work myself.

"And here I am now," I said. "Good enough?"

"Not really," said TJ.

"What do mean? That's my whole life, right there."

"That was a regurgitation of facts. There was nothing in there about *you,* personally."

My instinct was to argue. Except a nagging voice pointed out that he might be right. But what had he expected to hear in under a minute? My hopes and dreams? My biggest fears and greatest regrets? All my heartache? The secret I kept? I opened my mouth to tell him that what I'd said would have to do, but another sentence escaped instead.

"I do want to have kids," I declared.

"That's good."

"It is?"

"Yeah. It'd be weird if my girlfriend moved in with me, and we didn't want the same things." One side of TJ's mouth turned up. "But not quite as weird as her not knowing how to skate."

Then he opened the cab door and asked the driver about using the trunk, forestalling further personal conversation.

Chapter Eighteen

We stayed mostly silent for the rest of the trip to the arena. And I should've been glad of the reprieve because it gave me time to think about the case, and it saved me from anything other than superficial chatting. Instead, my brain refused to stay where it ought to. It drifted to unreasonable things. Like how *many* kids TJ wanted.

It didn't help when he reached over and took my hand, threading our fingers together so that the soft dips between them were meshed together. I couldn't pull away. Not under the possible scrutiny of the cab driver. And in all honesty, I didn't truly want to, anyway. In the quiet car, I couldn't even manage to deny it.

You're going to have to curb this, Pint-Size, said my brother's voice in my head.

I knew it was true. But it would have to wait until later.

At least the drive was over quickly. In just under fifteen minutes, we were unloading ourselves in the private, rear parking lot of the newly minted home-ice for the Surrey Slammers. And as TJ grabbed my suitcase from the trunk, I eyed up the location. When the zoning and permits had gone through, more than a few local residents had worried that the arena would be an eyesore. But looking at it now, it looked like something just shy of majestic. Its exterior was brushed steel with black accents. A decorative spire topped the oval structure. And black and red banners, emblazoned with the Slammers' exploding puck logo, hung from tall posts along every side of the building.

"It's almost the same colors as your bedroom." I made the observation without thinking, and I felt my face go pink.

But if TJ noticed my discomfort, he didn't comment.

"I thought it was a good omen when I signed with the team," he told me. "Maybe not quite so much right now, though." He set down my bag and took charge of pulling it again. "Come on. Let's get you checked in as an authorized visitor and ask guest services to stow your suitcase."

I followed him up a nearby ramp that led to a door marked with the words *Passholders Only* and watched as he pulled out an ID card and swiped it over a small, black panel. The red light turned green, and the door swung open on its own, revealing a lounge-style lobby, complete with couches and a big screen TV. Just inside, behind a desk, sat a petite blonde woman in a uniform. Her gaze was cool but sharp, and when she spied TJ, a smile broke out over her face. She stood and walked over to greet him with easy familiarity.

"Travis James Jones," she said in a friendly tone that irked me for no good reason. "I wasn't expecting to see you today. I heard from Lee that you were sick."

"Wasn't feeling the hottest yesterday," TJ replied easily. "Much better now. How's your mom?"

"Cranky as always." The woman laughed. "Last night, she told me that she birthed me. Nothing else. Just that. She made it sound like a favor. How do I even argue against that? Assuming it *is* something to argue against."

"True story," said TJ, then shifted slightly on the spot to give my elbow a light squeeze. "And speaking of favors…do you think you could do a fast track on a guest pass for me? I'm already running a few minutes behind."

As though noticing me for the first time—when clearly that wasn't true—the woman turned my way. I studied her as she studied me. It was hard to say whether she was security or some kind of concierge, though I mentally leaned toward the latter as she continued to eye me up and down for a moment more. Finally, she nodded once, then stepped back to her desk, retrieved a clipboard and pen, and handed them over to me.

"Fill this in, and I'll be right back with the guest pass," she told me, her voice flatter now.

"Do you mind if we stick Ivy's bag in the storage room as well?" TJ added as she spun away.

"You know you don't even need to ask, Travis." The concierge-slash-security-guard smiled at him over her shoulder, then clicked away on her high heels.

I hope to God she's not *a security guard,* I thought. *Because Lord help her if she has to fight someone off while wearing those shoes.*

While TJ rolled my suitcase over to a narrow door on the other side of the room, I stared after the other woman, wondering where the weirdly unkind feelings were coming from. I had no reason not to like her. And yet…I didn't. In fact, I was so wrapped up in my mild animosity that it took a nudge from TJ to pull my gaze away from the spot where she'd disappeared.

He nodded toward the clipboard in my hands. "You gonna fill that out, or…"

I jerked my attention down, then started scrawling in the answers to the very basic personal questions.

"Not a very hefty screening process," I grumbled.

"To be fair, most of the people who come in are *already* pretty well-known to the players."

"Still."

Grumpily, I finished the paperwork and set it down on the desk, then took a more thorough look around. It wasn't at all what I'd pictured. In my head, I'd imagined walking straight into something similar to what I'd experienced at the ice rink as a kid. Hard wooden benches to sit on while changing skates. Scratched plastic that tried to pass itself off as glass. Maybe the stench of too many bodies and too little air. This place looked more like a high-end airport lounge. In one corner, there was even what looked like a full bar.

"Pretty state of the art, huh?" said TJ.

I nodded. "Not as totally gross as your average men's locker room."

He chuckled. "Don't worry. There's plenty of sweaty grossness to be had. This is just what they use to lull us into complacency. We have our team meetings here. They give us appetizers and the occasional highball. Or in my case, some virgin cocktail. Then they immediately demote us to stinky gym sock territory."

I started to laugh, but my amusement faded as the blonde woman reappeared. Her presence immediately dampened my mood. I even had to force myself to reach out and take the lanyard and visitor's pass she held out, and my "thanks" wasn't more than a mutter as I slid the item in question over my head.

"Enjoy your practice," the other woman said to TJ, her smile bright. "Oh. I also radioed in to let Lee know you'd be bringing a friend today, so he's going to meet her outside the changeroom and show her where to go."

"Thanks, sweetheart," TJ replied.

And when the casual endearment made me cringe, I clued in as to what was bothering me.

He didn't call me his girlfriend when he was talking to her. He didn't correct her when she referred to me as his friend. And I'm jealous.

It was a stupid thing to feel. And as misplaced as every other odd emotion I'd felt regarding TJ over the last day. Jealousy over a client. Over a man I barely knew. Nonetheless, it was true.

Shit.

I watched the blonde woman flip open a laptop and clack something onto the keyboard. The sensation didn't dissipate in the slightest. In fact, a compulsion to do something about it surged up alongside it. Like I had something to prove. Without stopping to think about it, I reached out and took TJ's hand. And thankfully, he didn't react in any way except to lead me out of through the lobby to a swinging door, then out into a corridor. I knew I should probably let him go. And maybe I would've. But right then, another man—short, round, bald, and visibly furious—burst through a set of doors at the other end of the hall, startling me. My fingers tightened on TJ's instead of releasing them.

"Don't say I didn't warn you," he murmured into my ear as the angry man strode toward us.

As soon as he said the words, I knew exactly who

was approaching.

Bram Armstaad. TJ's agent.

He held his shoulders straight. His suit looked bespoke, and the watch on his wrist had the flash of money while his whole demeanor exuded an abundance of confidence. His eyes slid from me to TJ, then back again, and I was sure that he was assessing me as some kind of commodity.

"What the hell are you thinking, Jones?" he demanded as he came to a stop in front of. "How long has this been going on?"

"We just made it official yesterday," TJ replied smoothly.

"Yesterday. And you already got caught," his agent muttered, shaking his shiny head. "Discretion has never been your strong suit."

"It wasn't a secret, Bram."

"Then why the hell wasn't I informed?"

"It seemed like a good idea to convince the lady in question first." As TJ made the statement, he freed his fingers and slid his arm around me, resting his hand on my hip.

My heart immediately jumped up to my throat, and my pulse tapped so noisily that I missed whatever it was that Bram said next. But I didn't dare pull away. Not even a bit. I took a careful breath and focused on the continuing exchange.

"You didn't give me a chance to explain when we were on the phone," TJ was saying. "I'm not even sure if you let me finish a sentence."

"I was hoping it would go away."

"Not happening."

"Does she understand what this means for you?"

Bram asked.

Irritated by the way he spoke about me, as though I weren't even there, I cut in. "*She* is capable of answering for herself. And *she* is well-aware of what this—what *I* mean for TJ."

The agent spun his attention my way. "You say that, but do you? Do you *actually*?"

Wondering how the hell this man effectively negotiated deals for his clients, I ordered myself to channel some on my inner, P.I. calm as I answered him. "TJ went over the terms of his contract in detail. And while I think some of them are asinine and bordering on illegal, I most definitely understand them."

"What're you? A lawyer?"

"A typist."

His responding glare might've made someone else relent. I didn't even flinch.

"I'm going to need to verify that," Bram told me.

"Go ahead. How deep do you want to go? Because I should warn you, my browser history will show off both my fondness for kittens *and* my predilection for men performing domestic duties."

I heard TJ muffle a laugh. The bald man, on the other hand, didn't appear impressed. His invisible eyebrows shot up, and he addressed TJ once again.

"She doesn't fuck around, does she?" he said.

"No," TJ agreed. "I'd have to say that she most definitely does not. And…now that we've had this lovely meeting, I *really* need to take Ivy to Lee so I can go lace up."

Bram looked at me again. "Fine. But just one more thing."

"What's that?" replied TJ.

"You'd better have a good plan in place for how to spin it when you break up." He paused dramatically, then spun on his heel and strode away.

Chapter Nineteen

As TJ's agent stormed off, a newly unsettled feeling took root in my gut. What *were* we going to do at the end of all this? Would our "break up" negatively impact TJ's contract? His whole career? Would it do the exact opposite of what he was trying to avoid?

Why the hell did I agree to this charade in the first place?

But if TJ himself had any concerns over the matter, he didn't show it as he led me the rest of the way up the hall. I didn't get a chance to ask him what his thoughts were, either. Because when we reached the two-way split at the end of the corridor and turned right, another man was there, waiting.

The contrast to Bram Armstaad was immediate and obvious. This man was smiling. He had a full head of salt-and-pepper hair, and while his slim frame was clad in the same uniform as the blonde woman in the lobby, it somehow managed to look relaxed on him. In fact, *all* of him seemed to lack tension—even his greeting.

"Mr. Jones," he said, soft and enthusiastic at the same time. "So glad to see you *and* your lovely company."

"Always a pleasure, Lee," TJ replied.

He offered a quick introduction, describing Lee as the Surrey Slammers' Super Host. And this time, I noted, he did remember to refer to me as his girlfriend.

I was more pleased than I ought to have been. But I had to pretend it didn't make me wonder why he hadn't done the same with the woman.

I let go of TJ's palm so that I could shake hands with the uniformed man. "Nice to meet you."

"Ditto, Ms. Ames," Lee said.

"Lee will be *much* more pleasant to deal with than Bram," TJ added. "Won't you, Lee?"

"Well, Mr. Jones..." the Super Host replied. "I would never presume to pass judgement on Mr. Armstaad, but I do like to think of myself as a rather congenial chap."

"See?" TJ added. "Who else would refer to themselves as a congenial chap?"

From the other end of the hall, a raucous laugh carried out of some unseen room. It was followed by a string of enthusiastic curses. Then a door slammed. And for the first time, I caught a whiff of hockey smell.

"Guess that's my cue to get going," said TJ. "You're going to show my girl how to get to the proper zone, Lee?"

"Happy to," the other man agreed. "Say your sappy goodbyes, and I'll whisk her away."

Blushing a little, I turned to wish TJ luck in his practice. But he surprised me by stepping forward first. His fingers came up to gently clasp my chin while his face dropped down to mine. With the contact, a rush of anticipation rolled in. I remembered the way he'd pressed a kiss to my forehead the day before. I recalled the warmth of his mouth on my skin. I thought about how it would feel if our lips met. And I automatically stilled, waiting for it. Wanting it, even. But TJ's mouth aimed for my ear instead.

"Don't let the players' wives get to you," he said. "Babe."

Then he ran a thumb over my cheek, let me go, and headed for what I assumed was the locker room. The disappointment was physical. It was stupidly—embarrassingly—hard not call him back. I even had to force myself not to stare at him until he disappeared. And a lightheaded feeling reigned as I followed Lee to yet another hall, then through a door that led into a concrete staircase.

I almost wanted something to go wrong so that I had some motivation to think about TJ-the-case instead of TJ-the-man.

There is *something wrong,* I thought as we stepped from the stairwell into the chilly air of the rink. *Only it's something wrong with* me.

"Right this way, Ms. Ames," said Lee, pointing ahead.

My heart danced nervously against my ribcage. The spot he was indicating was located at center ice, and it wasn't empty. Two women about my age—one short, plump, and cute and the other statuesque and regal—sat in one row. A third woman—not much more than a teenager, I thought—was in the row in front of them, typing away on her phone. To top it off, there were three toddlers there too, bouncing in their seats and squealing as the Zamboni slid by.

And when Lee's two-way radio squawked to life, and he excused himself to answer it, every single pair of adult eyes turned to look at me.

Showtime! said my brother's voice in my head.

I straightened my shoulders and stepped into their little sphere. "Good morning. Mind if I sit with you?"

The plump woman was the first to reply, smiling as she greeted me. "Morning! Sit anywhere you like. You must be Rio's new girlfriend?"

I smiled back and shook my head. "TJ's."

Now the statuesque woman spoke up. "TJ *Jones*?"

"Is there another TJ?" I asked.

"No," said the plump woman quickly, shooting her companion a look. "Ignore Heather. There's no other TJ. It's good to meet you. I'm Charlene. Igor Stravinski's wife." She swept her hand toward the bouncing kids. "The girls are mine—they're twins—and the boy belongs to Lisa."

"And Lisa is me," added the woman on her phone. "And I'll save you the trouble of asking all the questions everyone thinks but it too afraid to voice. No, I didn't have the kid when I was still in high school. Not that there'd be anything horrible about it if it were true. But I'm twenty-one. Blaine is my stepson. Ryder Black—the goaltender—is his dad."

Wishing for one of the notebooks I used during my in-office inquiries, I did my best to mentally inventory all the information being hurled at me. But my brain wanted to stick on the evident surprise at my association with TJ. How could I ask for more info without sounding like an interrogator? It was new territory. And not at all how I was used to doing business. But I was saved the trouble of it anyway, because the taller woman, Heather, was clearly hung up on it herself.

"So…" she said, sounding falsely innocent. "How did you and the Troublemaker meet?"

Charlene gave her another dirty look. "You could try to cover up your nosiness a little, and at least start by asking her name."

I cleared my throat. "It's okay. I'm Ivy. And TJ and I met at a hotel. My brother introduced us."

"Did your brother know who he was?" Heather asked.

"Heather!" Charlene admonished.

I forced out a laugh. "It's fine, honestly. Ask whatever you like. And yes, my brother knew who TJ was. Charles was doing some contract work for him."

Heather opened her mouth again, but the younger woman, Lisa, beat her to it.

"They have a bet," she told me. "Heather thinks TJ is gay, and Charlene thinks he swore a vow of celibacy."

Both women in question grumbled a protest, but Lisa waved it off.

"You know it's true," she said. "And I guess either of you could still be right." She focused an openly curious look at me. "Are you TJ's beard?"

It took my brain a second to catch up to the question. "Am I…no. I'm not his beard."

"And is he celibate?" she asked.

I could feel the heat trying to creep up my throat. Was there a proper way to answer that? A no was an admission to intimacy. And feigned or not, my sex life was definitely a private thing. But a yes seemed like an equally inappropriate answer. Could I simply say that I didn't know?

Or how about telling them that I don't know, yet?

For some reason, that made me feel even more uncomfortable. And they were all looking at me expectantly.

Maybe I should've just grabbed a coffee and set up

camp outside on a bench. That would've been good enough, wouldn't it?

Thankfully, an abrupt blare of music saved me. It boomed out of the arena's sound system, drawing everyone's attention to the ice. I followed suit as the Zamboni finished its last round then disappeared through the gates. The first skater came out onto the ice. And even though he was covered in gear and his face was obscured by the mask attached to his helmet, I knew with 100 percent certainty it was TJ.

My heart did a funny little jump, and as I watched him, the idea of *not* being there became foreign.

He blasted by at full speed, not stopping until he was dangerously close to the boards on the other end of the arena. A spray of ice sailed up, then cascaded down.

"Someone's showing off," said one of the women beside me.

I didn't turn to see which one it was, because I was too busy watching TJ's graceful, powerful display. He did the same move a second time in the opposite direction. Only this time, instead of just stopping, he spun to the left. And faster than I could blink, he rocketed across the width of the ice toward us. Toward me. Maybe he *was* showing off. But as he paused in front of me for the barest moment before zigzagging away, he met my eyes. And in that heartbeat, I saw true joy. And freedom.

Something in my brain clicked. Hockey was more than a job to TJ. It was a passion. One he was at risk of losing because of the stalker, and because of the method we'd chosen to pursue the criminal in question.

Bram Armstaad's question jumped to the front of my mind.

Does she understand what this means to you?

I realized that despite what I'd claimed, I *hadn't* understood. Not until right that second. There was much more on the line for TJ than I'd assumed. And the realization came with a pressing need to make sure he got to hold onto all of it.

Chapter Twenty

Taking things to an even more personal level wasn't exactly what I'd had in mind when trying to motivate myself. It certainly wasn't in line with TJ-the-case versus TJ-the-man. Nonetheless, it worked. As the men skated around on the ice, casually tossing pucks back and forth, I made small talk with the women around me.

From them, I learned that Surrey Slammers practiced six days a week, most weeks. There were casual sessions, like this one, where the focus was on team building and movement. There was dry land training. Weights and varied cardio. And of course, more intense practices, where their coach worked them until they dropped. On game days, the players got out to skate twice.

The rigorous schedule made me wince, even from an outside perspective. When I confessed as much to the other women, they just laughed and told me I'd either get used to it, or I'd move on. Which provided the perfect segue into a discussion about TJ. Except there was surprisingly little gossip to be had.

Heather, Charlene, and Lisa were all aware of his past on a surface level. But as we sipped on the hot chocolate brought in by Lee, the three women agreed that so far, they'd seen nothing that would come even close to earning him his nickname of Troublemaker.

Charlene described him as a loner. Heather jumped on that and told me that it wasn't in a *bad* way. But TJ never joined in on any of the guys' nights out. Despite his status as a single man—until now, Lisa was quick to interject—he never went on dates or took advantage of the fact that there were a lot of more-than-willing girls hanging around after games.

No one disliked him. But he was private, so no one really knew him.

I couldn't exactly say I was disappointed to hear all of that. Yes, I'd been hoping for some clue as to who might be behind the letters and the increasing violence. A little nudge in the right direction would've been good. But it made me happy to know that there was no rampant hatred for TJ on the team. I had a feeling he'd like to know it, too, and I made a mental note to bring it up.

After two hours, the skate finally wound down. I didn't have anything huge to add to the investigation, but I did have more suspects on the way to being eliminated. And maybe once I'd actually spoken to the players themselves, I'd fully be able to cross the team off my list, which would mean concentrating my efforts elsewhere.

And that's still a step forward, I told myself as I followed the other women and the three kids out of the stands and back to the lounge.

"The guys take a little bit to come out," Charlene stated, sinking down into one of the couches and flicking the TV to a children's program. "It's a pain in the you-know-what, waiting. But it's better than the alternative of having them show up un-showered." She shuddered theatrically. "Hockey stink. Yuck."

"Have you had the pleasure of smelling that particular stench yet?" Heather asked.

I thought of TJ's pleasant, understated scent. I couldn't even imagine him smelling bad.

"No," I said. "I can't say that I have."

"Give it a year," Lisa interjected. "That's around the time when they give up. Then they're perfectly happy to throw a dirty hockey sock on the bathroom floor."

"Better a sock than a jockstrap," Charlene said.

The other ladies all laughed.

"But anyway…" said Heather. "Back to the good stuff before we scare you away. Are we going to see you tomorrow night?"

"What's tomorrow night?" I asked.

"The Surrey Slammers Gala," Charlene explained. "It's a charity event, schmoozing type of thing. Pretty much everyone who cares about the sport and the teams will be there. They'll have silent auctions. You get to wear a fancy dress and eat ridiculous food. And most of the time, at least a few celebrities show up."

"TJ didn't mention it," I told the two of them.

"Yeah, he wouldn't have," Heather replied. "It's not his usual thing. Or at least that's what I assume, since he didn't show up to the event we did in Toronto last month. But the coach always calls these things voluntarily mandatory."

"And so far, TJ has leaned toward the 'voluntary' part," Lisa added. "But now that he has *you* in his life, maybe that'll change."

"I'll ask him," I promised.

"Ask me what, babe?" TJ's voice startled me, but not as much as the fact that his arm encircled my waist and pulled my back against his chest.

I drew in a sharp breath, and as soon as I did, I recalled what Charlene and Lisa had just said about the stink. But all I smelled was TJ.

"Don't tell him now," suggested Lisa. "You don't want him to say yes just because *we're* listening. Trust me. I learned that the hard way."

"It's true," agreed Charlene. "Wait until after you leave. Then you can butter him up a bit first. If you know what I mean."

My cheeks warmed, but TJ chuckled.

"Now that we're on the subject of leaving and being buttered up," he said, "I've got a cab coming any second."

"You do?" I replied, wiggling a little so that I could look up at him.

He inclined his head. "Yeah. No offence to the guys, but I want you all to myself."

If I hadn't been fighting a frown, my toes would've been tingling. But I made myself answer lightly.

"Well, then. I guess that settles it." I directed my attention back to the hockey wives. "Thanks for the conversation."

They offered a chorus of reciprocal thanks, and then TJ grabbed my hand and whisked me—and my bag, which he'd already retrieved—from the lounge to the hall, then straight out into the open air.

"Sorry about that," he said when we hit the parking lot.

"About what?" I replied.

He gestured back toward the arena. "Sticking you with them."

I shook my head. "Don't be sorry. I actually kind

of liked them."

"Yeah?"

"Yes. They're nice. And funny. And I don't think any of them are behind your little issue."

"That's good, isn't it?" he asked.

I nodded. "It's always good to know who your enemies *aren't*. But it might've been a good idea for me to me meet your teammates, too."

Unexpectedly, TJ's face darkened. "Another time."

"Did something happen?"

"No. Nothing important."

"It doesn't help if you're not honest with me."

He looked away, then sighed and met my eyes again. "Look. It's stupid, okay? One of the guys on the team—Keegan Michaels—asked who the hot brunette in the bleachers was, and I just…"

"You just what?"

"Defended the honor of my completely fake girlfriend with a little too much enthusiasm."

A seconds-long conflict waged in my head. As dumb as it was, I liked that he'd defended me. But dumber than that was something else—the fact that I *dis*liked that he'd just make a point of reaffirming the phoniness of our relationship.

Let it go, Ivy.

I exhaled and kept my tone neutral as I asked, "So does that mean you started a fight?"

"No. But I got a bit carried away. To the point that I was *actually* pissed off." He ran a sheepish hand over his damp hair. "On top of that, Michaels is the kinda guy who likes to dig, so if I'd brought him out to meet you, he would've flirted with you, and I would've had to do something about it."

"I'm pretty capable of taking care of myself," I reminded him.

He gave me a small smile. "Even more reason why *I* would've needed to be the one doing the defending. Michaels might be a bit of an asshat, but he puts the puck in the net. We need him in one piece."

"All right," I conceded. "Point taken. But I'm probably still going to have to meet the team."

"I see those guys more than I see my own reflection. You'll get another chance."

"So how about tomorrow night at the Surrey Slammers Gala, then?"

His expression darkened marginally. "Is that what they were wanting you to ask me about?"

"Yes. Don't you want to go?"

"I hadn't planned on it. Black tie. Champagne I can't drink. Corporate sponsors whose asses I don't want to kiss. Why the hell would I *want* to be there?"

"I don't know. Maybe because it sounds like a mandatory team event?"

"Voluntarily mandatory," he corrected. "And I can get out of it."

I frowned. "Maybe you *can.* But I don't think you should."

He sighed and gave his chin a scratch. "For the sake of the case, you think I should put on a monkey suit, smile at strangers, and spin you around the dance floor?"

"Yes. Except for the last part. I dance about as well as I skate."

"You're not exactly selling me on the idea here, Ivy."

"You're trying *not* to draw attention to yourself," I

reminded him. "And won't your agent be mad if you don't go?"

TJ's attention flicked to the road. I followed his stare. The familiar yellow car was making its way toward the parking lot. His gaze came back to me again.

"He won't be delighted," he admitted grudgingly. "But then again, he never is."

"Well, *I'll* be unimpressed, too. Because the hockey wives said every person who matters in the hockey world—in *your* world—will be there. It's perfect opportunity for me to do a wide assessment."

"Or the perfect opportunity for someone to try to blow me up again."

"I honestly don't think that's going to happen. It would be outside of your stalker's schedule. People like this stick to a routine."

"You mean a ritual," he said.

"You could say that I guess."

"Like a serial killer."

The further upturn of his lips made me sure he was kidding. But the dark words made my throat go dry anyway. It was a fair, if somewhat exaggerated analogy.

"Let's not go that far, okay?" I said, "I wouldn't put you at risk. Trust me, TJ, it's a good idea for you to be at the event."

"I do trust you," he replied just as the cab rolled to a halt in front of us. "But I'm also wondering if you've thought this all the way through."

"What do you mean?"

"Did you pack a ballgown into this suitcase?" he asked, rattling the bag in question before reaching for the cab's door handle.

I opened my mouth. Then closed it as my nerves lit up for some other reason. I spun, seeking out the source. And I saw it. Or to be more accurate, I saw *him.* An unwelcome, familiar figure in a gray hoodie, standing behind a minivan on the other side of the street in the overflow parking lot. Something metallic glinted in his hands. Aimed in our direction. And for the second time in two days, I launched myself at TJ the Troublemaker Jones, sending him to the ground.

Chapter Twenty-One

I braced myself for the thunderous crack of a gun. For the bullet whizzing by. Or maybe even for the searing metal to strike some vulnerable part of my body. But the air was silent. The objects around me and my skin, too, remained unmolested.

What the hell.

I didn't move. Not yet. Three heartbeats went by. I was afraid that the attack was yet to come. At the same time, though, I was sure that if I didn't react quickly, I'd lose the assailant again. Another heartbeat.

You're wasting time.

My subconscious was right. I freed myself from my position on top of TJ and pushed to my feet. Feeling a bit guilty about it—but not having much of an alternative—I used the taxi as cover and sought out the hooded man. He was utterly still, his stance wide, his ballcap pulled low. I had no clue why he hadn't bolted yet. Or why he hadn't fired. Maybe it was simply too far to make a good shot. But I *did* know that I couldn't just stand around pondering it.

I put one foot out before remembering my promise not to go running off and putting myself in danger. I spun back and held out my hand. Ignoring the confused complaint made by the cab driver, TJ took my fingers and stood up. Together, we moved to face the hooded figure. As we started to run, the man took a step backward. Except instead of sprinting away, he spun to the van beside him. Then he swung open the driver's side door, tossed in his weapon, and climbed in behind the wheel.

TJ and I were getting closer.

In the reasonably silent air, the van's engine sputtered.

With TJ on my heels, I pushed for another burst of speed. I hit the street between the two sections of the parking lot, and narrowly missed getting swiped by a passing hatchback. I ignored the driver's fierce honk, and I kept going.

The van made a whirring noise.

I was near enough now that I could see the outline of the driver's profile. Definitely male. Nothing else currently distinguishable under the shadow of the ballcap.

Dammit.

The engine growled, turned over, then went dead.

Yes!

My high-top-clad feet slammed to the blacktop, and my heartrate surged. I'd only been going for seconds. Logically, I knew it. But it was taking far too long to get to my target.

Another sputter.

Come on!

The engine roared noisily, and this time, it stayed on.

I knew that it was too late before I even heard the curse that TJ dropped. But I didn't let it stop me from making a final attempt to reach the vehicle. I lengthened my stride and ignored the burn in my chest.

Almost. There.

The van's tires screeched. Its body shuddered. And a burnt rubber smell filled the air as it flew from the lot.

I slowed down, then came to a complete halt. I made a last-ditch effort to make out the license plate number. Unfortunately—unsurprisingly—it was obscured by caked-on mud.

"Shit," I said breathlessly.

I put my hands on my knees and bent over to suck in some oxygen. A second later, I heard TJ stop beside me, his inhales and exhales heavy with exertion. For several long seconds, we didn't move or speak.

Then TJ let out a mutter.

"Golden opportunity...wasted," he said.

"I'm fast," I replied, straightening up. "But I'm not faster than a speeding van, apparently."

"I didn't mean it was your fault."

"No, I know. I'm just frustrated, too." I stared at the now-empty parking stall. "Maybe we can take something away from this, though."

"Did you get his license plate number?" TJ asked. "Because I didn't."

I shook my head. "No. But now we know what he's driving. And what he can *afford* to drive."

"How do we know it's not a second vehicle?"

"Because if he could afford another vehicle, he'd buy one that stood out less. And one that was more reliable. Even an older sedan would blend in better," I explained. "I also have a few sources that might be able to give us a hand figuring out who the van belongs to. Assuming it's legally owned, that is."

TJ nodded, but a horn blared in the distance, and he jumped a little, then sighed. "I know he's my own personal stalker, Ivy, so this is a totally ridiculous thing to announce, but Jesus…whoever the asshole is, he's really *following* me."

Though he was right that the statement was redundant, I understood—fully and all too well, in fact—the need to say it anyway. And I recognized the emotions in his voice, too. Fear. Disgust. A feeling of violation. There wasn't much I could say to drive it away. And my brain seemed to have stalled anyway, stuck on an empathy that I didn't dare share.

TJ's eyes hung on the tire skids. "I don't get it. If the notes and the tricks and the bombs aren't enough for this guy, then what the hell is he after?"

The desperately edged question helped me find my voice again. "He wants you to be scared shitless. He wants you to feel powerless.

My claim was full of conviction, and TJ's gaze swung my way once more. He was curious. I could feel it rolling off him. But he didn't voice any of it.

"Come on, then," he said instead. "Let's take that away from him. Let's show him we're *not* scared. We'll get my other truck from the hotel he bombed. We'll go to the most stupidly expensive dress shop in town, where we'll buy you the most beautiful fucking dress you've ever owned. I'll drag out my best suit, and I'll make sure every single person at the Surrey Slammers Gala knows exactly how happy and in love we are."

With each word, his tone grew more fervent. He paused for breath, and I blinked at him. I tried to reply. But I only managed to get in one word.

"You'll—"

Then he was off again.

"Hell. Maybe I'll propose. I'll pull you up to the damn podium and kiss you in full view of the entire room." He opened his mouth like he was going to keep going, then stopped as though he'd just realized what he'd said. "Shit. That was taking it a bit too far, wasn't it?"

"Getting engaged wasn't exactly on my to-do list this week."

I deliberately left out the part about the public kiss. Probably because in all honesty, I wasn't sure if the thought of it made me uncomfortable, or if the imagery brought all kinds of pleasantness to mind. Maybe both. But I didn't get much time to think about which had more weight. Because once again, TJ caught me off guard with a question.

"Was it on your to-do list at some point more recently?" he asked.

"Sorry, but…what?"

"Being engaged."

"I mean, it's not on my *never-to-do* list, but…"

He pointed to my left hand, and I looked down, then flushed. There was the slightest, barely noticeable bit of a tan line there on my ring finger. For a good few seconds, I couldn't believe it hadn't crossed my mind since Charles's arrival at the gym. There were a hundred reasons why it *should* have come up. At least to myself. And yet, it had gone out of my head completely. Self-consciously, I tucked the hand against my side.

"That's not what it looks like," I said, fully aware that the claim made me sound guilty of something.

TJ's eyebrows lifted. "It's not a tan line left by a ring?"

"No," I said. "I mean, yes, it *is* that. But not from a real engagement ring."

Understanding marked his eyes right away. "A deterrent?"

I lifted my chin a little defiantly. "Yes."

"Because of something specific, or because of something general?"

My mouth somehow managed to feel dry and sticky at the same time. But I made myself answer honestly.

"Something specific," I admitted.

TJ studied me for a moment, his expression unreadable. Had it been what he'd expected to hear? Did it matter to him? Did I *want* it to?

More importantly…Am I going to answer him if he asks the right question?

I didn't know. My thumb found its way between my ring and middle fingers, rubbing the spot where the gold usually sat while my pulse thrummed nervously through my veins. But TJ didn't push it.

"All right," he said after another heartbeat. "I promise that I'll do my best not to ask you to marry me tomorrow night."

I exhaled and forced a smile. "Thanks for that."

But as he turned and started to walk back toward the cab, a tiny wave of disappointment hit me, and I had to remind myself that I had no interest in expounding upon the details of my past. I kept them inside for a reason. And despite my attraction to TJ—and even though the more time I spent with him, the more I found to like about him—there was no excuse to change that. In fact, it was probably a pretty good reason *not* to discuss my personal life. The last thing I needed was to form some kind of attachment to my fake boyfriend. The goal was to get the case solved as fast as possible. To get paid and cut ties. I just wasn't sure why that truth gave my heart a pang.

Chapter Twenty-Two

I wasn't a girl who liked to shop. Racks of clothes made me want to turn and run in the other direction. Maybe it was because I grew up around brothers who were loath to set foot in any store that didn't sell track pants. Or maybe it was because I preferred the sweatpants, too. Either way, I was only three dresses into TJ's big plan of buying me an overpriced ballgown when my frustration with the whole thing got the better of me.

"You can just stop looking at me like that," I muttered to my own, miserable-faced reflection. "I already know how much this sucks."

And I *did* know.

I'd been forced to cast aside my usual preference for shorter dresses after putting on the first one and realizing that my scraped knees were a problem. The next dress had a hem that cascaded past my feet and made me look three feet tall. Now I was in a skin-tight, calf-length number that prevented any normal movement whatsoever, and the dress waiting on the hanger looked like a teal puff of cotton candy.

Getting TJ's truck out of the hotel parking garage and thoroughly checking for any kind of bug or tracking device then making sure we weren't followed had *all* been easier and less stressful than this.

I glared a little harder at the mirror. I was most

definitely not giving the salesclerk free reign to pick the next set of items to try on. In fact, I would've preferred rifling through the options on my own. But as the cheerful woman had informed me, I was "lucky" to have come at such a slow moment. Normally, they asked patrons to make an appointment. Especially when needing one-on-one service. And the slightly askance look she'd tossed at my plaid shirt told me that she truly believed I was in need of the assistance, even if I was just buying off the rack instead of custom ordering.

But even worse than her so-called expertise was her initial assumption for why we were there. She'd taken one look at my finger and my ring—which I'd retrieved along with my gym bag from my brother's car—and started gushing about our big day. It was impossible to say which one of us was the most embarrassed—the woman, me, or TJ. Personally, I wanted to vote for myself. Especially when the clerk's eyes strayed to my ring a second and third time before she stumbled through her apology for misunderstanding.

The only small blessing I could find in the whole situation was that the swankiness of the dress shop—which was primarily a higher-end bridal gallery—meant that TJ and I had been given a private, two-room changing area. It was at the back. There were no prying eyes. No blushing brides pitying me for *just* needing a gown. And since there was no other way of exiting or entering, I wasn't too worried about leaving my client out of sight. If I wanted to be sure he was still alive and well, all I had to do was glance at the space under the door. I could see his feet, sticking out from the designated "man-chair" outside my little space.

As though he could feel me thinking about him, TJ called out just then, his voice sounding *extra* manly in the cream-colored, tulle-heavy room.

"Hey, babe?" he said. "You wanna ditch this place and go see if we can chase a few gun-wielding maniacs through the streets?"

"Don't make promises you can't keep," I replied. "And stop *calling* me that."

His laugh was a pleasant echo in the reasonably small space.

"It's not funny," I told him. "We should see how *you* like being stuffed into a sausage suit like the one I have on right this second."

He chuckled again. "It can't be that bad."

"It is. Trust me. If could see it, you'd agree."

"Then let me look."

"No!"

But it was too late. Before I could even think to react, I heard his feet move over the carpet. And as much as I wanted to dive over to hold the door shut, the dress had me in its death grip, and I didn't have time. The hinges rattled. And a heartbeat later, TJ was looking over my shoulder to meet my eyes in the mirror.

"Go ahead," I said, my face heating as I swiped a hand toward my reflection. "Mock it all you want. You can't make it any worse than it already is."

And he *didn't* make it worse. Not exactly. His gaze swept over the dress, and by extension, it swept over me.

For a few seconds, it was just awkward. I was ridiculously conscious of the unflattering nature of the dress. The color was best described as silver, the fit best described as a second skin. While the salesclerk had called the sheath a sex-bomb option—her exact words—it didn't work. On me, it just looked like an attempt to be something I wasn't. My curves were there. But there was no way I could get away with trying to be viewed as voluptuous. And the dress was pretty much crying out for an hourglass figure. Not to mention a bit of height.

Unconsciously, I straightened a little. Then—realizing what I'd just done—I met TJ's eyes again in the mirror and fixed him with a challenging look. Silently, I dared him to make fun of me like I'd suggested moments earlier. As he stared back at me, something shifted. The awkwardness dissipated, and it was replaced by another sensation. *Heat.* And slowly, his stare moved over me once more.

Now I could feel every inch of the dress. The places where it pulled tightly over my skin. The areas it *did* accentuate. And I could also feel how TJ saw the same spots. How he appreciated them.

Shouldn't you be scared?

Mentally, I shook my head. Yesterday morning, the fear might've reared up in a situation like this. The conditions were exactly right for a panic attack. Small space. No real way out. A man's eyes roaming over me with interest. In fact, it would've been strange if I hadn't been scared. I would've been tensing, my body and my brain automatically moving into fight-or-flight mode. But I wasn't afraid. Not today. Not like that. Not with TJ. If anything, I was relieved to know for sure that the attraction wasn't one-sided.

I held very still, enjoying the way the warmth spread with his perusal. Almost revelling in it. Finally, his attention came to my face again. His expression was a touch. A caress. And before I could pause to gain some self-control, my lips parted in a small gasp.

"The dress isn't my favorite..." TJ said, his voice husky and teasing at the same time. "You, wearing it, on the other hand..."

I inhaled. He was going to move closer. I could sense it. His hands were going to find my skin for real.

And I want them to.

I waited. Breathless now. Urging him to hurry. Wondering why the world was moving in slow motion.

TJ's eyes stayed locked on mine.

He took a step.

The changeroom was a sauna.

His hand came up.

I tingled, outside and inside.

And then the salesclerk's cheerful voice cut through the moment.

"Mr. Jones," she said, "I took your suggestions and found two dresses that—oh!" She paused and sent a startled look between the two of us, then added, "Sorry. I didn't mean to interrupt. I'll just put these down and—"

"It's fine," TJ replied, his voice as neutral as his face had abruptly become. "My girlfriend was just showing me one of the dresses you picked out."

Doubt flashed over the clerk's face, but she covered it with a look in my direction. Right away, she shook her head and made *tsk-tsk* noise.

"Oh, that's all wrong, isn't it?" she said. "I mean, it's the right size, but I didn't realize how petite you were under that plaid. I should've insisted on taking your measurements. Don't worry. I can find something else that's more suitable." With that, she stepped past TJ, stuffed two zippered dress bags on the hook in the changeroom. "Go ahead with these. I'll see what else I can do out there."

Then she backed out quickly and slipped away. Immediately, I focused on the mirror again. But TJ was already heading back to his spot on the chair.

I bit my lip. There was a big part of me that wanted to call him back. But I made myself step over and close the door instead, then took a breath and turned back to the mirror. Once again, the silvery dress looked ridiculous. My narrow hips didn't fill out the stretchy fabric. My chest was far too subtle. And I wasn't being overly critical of my appearance; it was just the reality. Except, of course, when TJ had been looking at me. Then reality had changed. The blatant attraction rolling from the blue-eyed hockey player made the dress's fit unimportant.

But he's fighting it. As quickly as the thought came, another, counter-thought followed. *And so am I. Because it's the right thing to do.*

I eyed the closed door anyway. I very nearly caved in and opened it. What would happen, if I did? Something good, or something bad? Or would it be a something good that then *became* something bad?

"You need to let it go, Ivy," I whispered in a voice so low I knew only I would hear it.

Struggling to hold onto my resolve, I nodded firmly at myself, then stripped out of the sheath and faced the two dress bags. Carefully, I unzipped the first one. Fabric in the softest shade of yellow spilled into my hands so quickly that trying to contain it was impossible. I gave up and let it fall. When it was done, and I had a full view of the dress, my heart skipped a little beat.

It was stunning. The bodice was strapless and stiffened and marked with tiny jewels. The skirt fell prettily from the waist in multiple layers, and a little tag—which had been secured to the subtle belt with a piece of ribbon—announced that the garment had pockets.

I smiled and tried not to feel greedy as I released it from the hanger.

For some reason, I knew even before I slid it on that it was going to be a perfect fit. And my instincts were right. The dress hugged me just where it ought to and showed off my cleavage in a way that managed to be alluring rather than gaudy. The gentle flow of soft yellow over my hips didn't add any bulk, and the hem sat just between my ankle and mid-calf.

I couldn't help but stare at it in the mirror for a few prolonged seconds. Much like my aversion to shopping, I'd never been particularly partial to putting on fancy things. Besides the one I'd tossed on after my boxing round, I owned a single other dress. Little. Black. Full utility. I'd worn it to weddings, funerals, and out for dinner.

This dress, on the other hand...

I liked it so much I almost forgot I was only buying it for show. Wearing it made me want to spin in a circle. Something I might have done if not for a light knock on the door just then.

"Ms. Ames?" said the saleswoman. "How are you doing in there?"

"This is the one," I told her, trying to stop myself from sounding too pleased. "I don't need to try on anything else."

"Is that the yellow, then?"

"Yes."

"Did you try the other one, too?"

"Not necessary," I stated.

"Wonderful!" She sounded truly pleased. "Whenever you're ready, I'll meet you at the front while one of the girls packs it up for you."

"Thanks."

As she tapped away in her sensible flats, I waited for a comment from TJ. Or maybe a request to see the dress. But there was no sound.

"TJ?" I called.

I got no response.

"Shit," I muttered, then added more loudly, "TJ?"

When he still didn't answer, I stole a look under the door. His feet were decidedly missing. Nerves made my pulse jump, and hastily, but still carefully, I peeled out of the dress and slipped into my own clothes. I flung open the door, stepped out, then strode into the main part of the shop. It wasn't particularly big, but it was crowded with satin and lace and tulle. All of which felt overwhelming at that moment.

I froze for a second, eyes narrowed. I cursed myself for momentarily forgetting that TJ was my job, and the dress was a part of that. Then, ignoring the startled look on one of the other two saleswomen's faces, I swung to my right and began moving urgently between the racks, calling TJ's name in a whisper. Finally, I spotted him. Partially blocked by a shelf of sparkly stilettos, he stood near the very front of the store beside the cash register.

I was relieved. But annoyed, too.

"What just happened?" I demanded as I got closer.

He shot a puzzled look at me. "Rosette said you picked your dress."

"What?"

He inclined his head toward my cheerful clerk, whom I belatedly realized stood on the other side of the till.

I turned back to TJ. "Okay, yes. But why did you leave the changeroom?"

"To pay," he said.

"To..." I trailed off, eyed Rosette, and modified my tone to something sweeter. "You didn't have to do that."

"I wanted to."

"But seriously. You *didn't* have to."

"What kind of boyfriend would I be if I didn't pay for my girlfriend's dress for our very first formal event together?" His hand found the small of my back as he said it, and the touch was just distracting enough to make me forget about arguing.

It wasn't until we were climbing back into the truck that I remembered something important the salesclerk had said. It was TJ who'd given the suggestions that led to the yellow dress. And I couldn't help but wonder how he'd known just what to pick.

Chapter Twenty-Three

Against my better judgement—but maybe still under the influence of the dress—I let TJ talk me into making a stop at his apartment before we headed back to the country house. He promised me a box of newspaper clippings about his career, a chat with his building manager, and a sandwich. And I couldn't pretend the last thing wasn't a factor.

On the quick trip from the dress shop to TJ's city home, I placed another call to Charles, who told me the hospital was insisting he stay another day or two, just to be safe. I made him swear up and down that his injuries weren't any worse than he'd already confessed. When I was satisfied he was telling the truth, I promised to call again soon, then said goodbye. Before I could click the phone off, though, my brother's voice called out again.

"Hey, Pint-Size?" he said.

I put my ear back to the phone. "Yes?"

There was a prolonged pause on the other end, and I tensed, certain I knew what was coming. And sure enough, Charles's next statement confirmed my suspicion.

"I just want to make sure you're still being safer than you were four years ago."

My teeth clenched, and I had to forcibly loosen my jaw in order to reply. "I'm fine, Chuck. It's not even comparable."

"Would you tell me if it were?"

It was my turn to pause. Would I?

Would you even know?

Self-doubt nagged at my brain, and I just barely managed to keep from looking over at TJ.

I would know, I told myself. *And this most definitely isn't the same at all.*

I cleared my throat and lowered my voice. "I'll never be in that place again, and I have a job to do."

"I'll probably keep asking," Charles admitted.

"I know."

"Call me again if you have any updates?"

"Bye, Chuck."

"Talk to you soon, Pint-Size."

I tapped my phone off and sighed.

"You okay?" TJ wanted to know.

I was again struck by an urge to blurt out the reason behind my brother's concerns. And weirdly, it wasn't just professionalism holding me back this time. I was actually a bit worried what TJ would think if he knew the truth. What kind of judgement would he pass, if he knew about the biggest mistake of my life?

Don't risk it, Ivy.

I made myself nod. "Just the usual brother-sister stuff."

"You sure?" TJ replied.

"Would I lie to my fake boyfriend?"

It took him a second to answer, and when he did, it was in a thoughtful tone. "You might. If it meant doing your job."

I couldn't argue with that particular statement. But thankfully, I didn't have to. Because right then, TJ flicked on his turn signal and guided the truck into what looked to be the parking lot for a small cluster of low-rise, brick front condos.

"My second home-sweet-home," he announced as he cut the engine and opened his door.

Frowning a little, I climbed out, too. But when my feet hit the ground, I stopped short. I hadn't been paying a lot of attention to where we'd been headed, and until right then, I hadn't taken a close look at what was around me. It wasn't what I'd been expecting. We were on a dead-end street that backed onto a thicket of trees. There were no single-family houses in sight, nor what would normally come to mind when thinking of apartments. Instead, there were just three of the matching buildings, their positions spread out along the block to form the points of a triangle. An enclosed playground and grassy area took up the space between the farthest building and its counterpart on our left, while a basketball court dominated the other space beside the condos on our right.

"What's wrong?" TJ said when he came around to my side of the truck and found me standing there staring.

"Nothing." I nodded toward the red brick structures. "You just keep surprising me."

He looked from me to the buildings and back again. "You're surprised by where I live?"

"Twice," I agreed. "First with the hobby farm and now with the family-friendly choice."

"I *did* say I wanted kids," he reminded me.

"I know, but this is so…"

"What?"

I'd been about to say "immediate," but something about the carefully neutral expression on his face stopped me. I just shook my head, smiled, and amended my words.

"So un-bachelor-like," I said.

"Ah. But you're forgetting something."

"What's that?"

"I'm *not* a bachelor at the moment." He offered me a wink, then held out his hand.

I took his fingers, only realizing once our palms were together that I hadn't even stopped to think about it. But it would've been weird to pull away, so I held on and let him lead me to the nearest building and distracted myself from thinking about it by flicking a look around as we approached the stairs. The most suspicious thing I saw was a crow with a shoelace in its beak. That is, until we reached the door, and a big man—bigger than Charles, even—stepped in front to block our path. He was dressed in a black suit, and he obviously wasn't the man in the hoodie who'd been pursuing us, but that didn't mean he wasn't dangerous. Automatically, I moved to reposition myself between TJ and the potential threat.

"Are you human shielding me?" TJ asked in a low, teasing voice.

I refused to sound defensive as I answered. "I might be."

"Well, you can probably save it for another time. That's our onsite security guy."

On cue, the big man stepped forward again, this time to open the door.

"Afternoon, Mr. Jones," he greeted with a nod.

"Is it afternoon already, Jerry?" TJ replied.

"It was 12:03pm when you pulled up."

"Explains why I'm starving." TJ put his hand my

elbow. "Jerry, this is my girlfriend, Ivy. Ivy, this is Jerry."

The big, intimidating man remained expressionless, but he nodded again, this time in my direction. "Miss."

"Sir," I replied awkwardly.

I heard TJ muffle a laugh, but when he spoke, his voice was even. "Ivy's probably glad to see you. We're moving in together, and she's a bit scared about a report of suspicious behavior in the neighborhood."

I picked up on where he was going with the statement, and I shot a dirty look his way. "You're the one who *gave* me the report. You said you saw a weird guy hanging around a few days ago."

For the first time, Jerry's face changed. It was marginal, but there was definitely a slight flicker of concern.

"Which day?" he said.

TJ paused as if he had to think about. "Uh. Pretty sure it was a week and half ago. I could probably pinpoint it so you could check the security footage to ease Ivy's mind."

"No need," Jerry replied right away. "I know exactly what day you mean. There were some punk-ass teenagers messing around down here. One of them threw a rock and hit the camera above the door. I chased them off, and when I got back, there was a dude in a hoodie skulking around. Booked it when he saw me."

I exhaled a tiny breath. "Did you call the police?"

"You have nothing to worry about, Miss," the security guard told me. "We have a protocol, which I followed to the letter. The appropriate reports were made, but if it would make you feel better about living here, I can pull up the footage and email it over to Mr. Jones."

I feigned a weak smile. "Could you? I know I'm being paranoid, but…"

"No apologies necessary," said Jerry. "In my business, there's no such thing as too much caution."

Don't I know it, I thought.

TJ shifted to sling an arm across my waist. "Really appreciate it."

The other man issued another of his nods. "I'll get it done ASAP, Mr. Jones. You two have nice afternoon."

I waited until we'd reached TJ's spacious, fourth-floor apartment—if it could even really be called that—before speaking up again.

"That's not a coincidence," I said as soon as he'd locked the door behind us.

"No shit," he replied. "Are you thinking my friendly stalker paid the teenagers to wreck the camera?"

I nodded. "It has to be true. Just like the moving trucks."

"This guy is smart." The statement held a hint of bitterness.

"He might not be a complete idiot," I said. "But there's a difference between intelligence and cunning."

"Probably a fine line that doesn't even matter."

"It *does* matter. Whatever's driving this guy, it's not intellect. He'll make a mistake. He's probably *already* made one. They always do."

TJ sighed heavily, but he didn't argue. "You want that sandwich before I get the box of stuff?"

"I'm always up for eating. Which I know is your

favorite quality in a fake girlfriend."

My joke didn't even elicit a smile, and my heart dropped a little in sympathy. I knew how TJ must be feeling. As though the criminal was a step ahead. I also knew that all the assurances in the world wouldn't do much good. So, I kept my mouth shut, seated myself at table in the kitchen, and watched as he went through the motions of putting together our lunch.

We both stayed silent when he was done, too. It gave my mind a moment to wander, and as I bit into my turkey sandwich, I randomly considered what might be on the menu for my brother at the moment. Charles was a big fan of food. Enormous family barbecues and appetizers that went on for days. I couldn't imagine whatever they were feeding him was satisfying. Guiltily, I swallowed my mouthful of sandwich, thinking maybe I should wrap up the other half and bring it to him.

"You want to swing by the hospital to visit you brother?" TJ asked just then.

I was immediately grateful for the offer. But it also made me blush a little.

"Why? Am I making the face again?" I replied.

His mouth quirked. "Maybe, maybe not."

"Yeah, well…I was never all that good at poker."

"That's okay. At poker tournaments, hockey players' girlfriends are more about being eye candy than they are about playing the game itself."

"Shut up."

He grinned. "It was a compliment."

"Calling a woman 'eye candy' is *not* a compliment," I told him.

His eyes widened innocently. "Implying that a

woman is beautiful is an insult?"

I ignored the pleased flutter in my chest at his use of the word beautiful. "Implying that a woman isn't good for anything *but* her beauty is an insult."

"You're also very smart," he said.

I rolled my eyes. "And you're very funny."

"I've always thought so." He paused. "But seriously, Ivy. If you want to check on Charles, then we should do it."

I shook my head. "I love his annoying self, and I want to be sure he's okay, but there's nothing I can do that the doctors can't do better."

"Emotional support?"

"You met my brother, right? He'd probably just be pissed off because I was taking time away from the case."

TJ laughed, but his thumbs drummed the countertop lightly at the same time, and it made me sure his levity was a front for tension.

"Is there something else you want to talk about?" I asked.

His *tap-tap-tap* stopped immediately. "Just thinking about tomorrow."

I knew he didn't mean the gala. "And wondering whether or not the suspect will bring another note?"

His responding nod was curt, and he didn't say anything. Automatically, I reached over and put my hand on his wrist.

"Either way, TJ, we'll take care of this. We'll look at whatever video footage Jerry sends over, and we'll go through the box of stuff you want to show me.

His arm turned over, and his hand found mine. "Ivy…"

The way he said my name—intense and slightly raw—made my breath catch. "Yes?"

His Adam's apple bobbed up and down in his throat.

This is it, I thought, even though I wasn't sure what "it" was.

The seconds ticked by as I waited for a revelation of some kind. Something about the case. Or maybe something personal. I honestly wasn't sure what I wanted more. But I didn't get the satisfaction of hearing either.

"I'll go get that box," he finally said.

Then he let go of my hand and stood up and walked away, leaving me feeling oddly bereft.

Chapter Twenty-Four

By the time we were on our way back to TJ's truck, the weather had turned temperamental once again. Dark clouds blotted out the sun, and the formerly blue sky was now an icy shade—one that reminded me of the rink where TJ and his teammates had done their morning skate. Except it was definitely colder than it'd been in the arena. Wind drove straight through my plaid shirt. Thankfully, the first drops of rain didn't splatter down until we were already seated in the cab once more. But things only got worse from there.

The downpour thickened, then turned sideways. Tree branches battled to stay attached to their trunks, while the leaves had no choice but to concede the loss. Horns honked. Tires splashed. And as we moved through the traffic, two types of drivers—those who took the storm as a challenge, and those who were scared of it—fought for dominance. It quickly grew so dark that it might as well have been midnight when we hit the Surrey-Langley border, then began to head south toward farmland.

The journey wasn't quite harrowing. But only because TJ didn't seem to be bothered much by the way Mother Nature battered down on us. He made all the turns smoothly and kept the truck from hydroplaning when we hit a particularly deep pool of water covering the road. That didn't mean the drive was fun. We had to pull to the side twice to let emergency vehicles go by, and we spotted the aftermath of no fewer than three accidents—two minor, and one that made me wince as we took a wide berth around it.

The stormy drive *did* curb conversation. I didn't want to distract TJ from his focus on the road, and the torrential rain seemed to be demanding my attention anyway. What little we said was kept to small details. The location of the following evening's event. The home game he would play on the night after that. The fact that this was a rare week with only four practices rather than six. Not much more.

Several times, my eyes strayed to the box—a large, round one designed for holding photos—that now rested on the console between us. I was curious about the contents. And possibly more interested than I ought to have been in seeing how TJ's career had built up.

"Don't worry," TJ said when he caught my gaze lingering on the glossy cardboard lid. "I'm not actually a narcissist."

My attention flicked back to him. "What?"

"The newspaper clippings. They're courtesy of my dad," he explained. "He cut out everything he could find. I mean *everything*. I swear you're going to find a picture of me, buying a car in that box. Said he might take up scrapbooking someday, and I was never sure if he was kidding or not."

I could easily imagine his dad, an older version of TJ, sitting at a table, meticulously pasting articles into a bound book. And I liked it.

"You should do it," I told him spontaneously.

"Me? Scrapbook?"

"Yes."

"I did just say I wasn't a narcissist, didn't I?"

"It's not narcissistic," I argued without force. "It's honoring your dad's legacy. Even if he *was* kidding about doing it, your career obviously mattered enough to him that he spent time documenting it. Plus, when you eventually have those kids you want so badly, they'll love to look through it."

TJ's hands tightened on the wheel, and even though he smiled, I could see something was still nagging at him. What was it? Had what I'd said offended him? If so, I wasn't sure how. He was the one who'd started the whole having-kids discussion. And when he'd talked before about his dad, he hadn't looked upset.

The feeling I was missing something—or that he was keeping it from me—resurfaced. Frustration bubbled up. I understood the need for privacy. I held things in, too and with good reason. But we were talking about a dangerous situation. Possibly life or death.

And more specifically, TJ's life or death.

The thought quite suddenly and unexpectedly made my heart do its best to claw its way up to my throat. It bordered on unreasonable. And it definitely felt like more than just a general concern for another human being. I let out a tiny breath and balled my hands into fists to keep from pressing a palm to my chest to ease the ache.

I had to continue to assume that whatever TJ was keeping buried, he wouldn't hold it in if it meant the difference between living and dying. But it bothered me anyway. What was he waiting for? Some sign I could be trusted with his secret?

Would you trust him with yours?

Of course, the answer was obvious. I wouldn't. I hadn't. And that made sense. It was logical. Because TJ Jones was a man I'd known for a day. A client. A person who was paying for my professional services. Someone to whom I owed nothing personal, and vice versa. That didn't stop it from nagging at me for the duration of the drive. And my mind wandered to the way he'd said my name back in the kitchen at his apartment, too. It was so obvious that something was holding him painfully captive.

From the corner of my eye, I stole another quick glance his way. TJ caught me looking and offered me a small, strained smile, then flicked on the turn signal and slowed the truck as we approached his ranch. The house was dark, and the storm had done a number on the surrounding trees. The ripped-away leaves danced viciously over the driveway.

"Gotta love the Lower Mainland and its never-ending monsoon attempts," TJ said, inclining his head toward the wild display.

The words echoed with banality in the cab of the vehicle. I didn't reply. Right then, I didn't feel like talking about the weather. My thoughts and the accompanying emotion were too complex for that. So instead, I waited until we'd come to a complete stop, then opened the door and hopped out into the rain.

"What are you doing?" TJ called over the howl of wind.

"Perimeter check!" I called back.

"Now?"

"Yes, now. And every time we go in, here or anywhere, really—until your case is solved."

"Okay. Give me a second, then. I'm coming with you."

I thought about arguing but quickly decided against it. Leaving him unguarded in the truck came with about the same amount of risk as having him alongside me. I nodded then closed the door.

Hopping from foot to foot to try to retain a bit of warmth as I waited for him to climb out, I squinted at the house. It looked much dimmer than it had that morning. Which shouldn't have been surprising. After all, blackness reigned overhead. Still. It seemed darker than it ought to have been. Another moment of staring provided a possible explanation.

"I think the power's out," I stated when TJ reached my side.

He surveyed the house. "I think you might be right. Happens a lot here, to be honest. Should we go back to the apartment?"

I shook my head. "No. I think we're still safer here than we'd be in the city. Let's just hope hydro gets it fixed before too long."

Lifting a hand to shield my eyes as best I could, I stepped forward into the watery onslaught. I was already drenched, but I made myself ignore it as I performed my perusal of the exterior of the house. It went more quickly this time. I knew already where all the entry points were, and I'd mentally cataloged the most vulnerable spots when I'd done my initial search. Thankfully, nothing had changed. The windows and doors still showed signs of disuse. There was no evidence of tampering and no indication that anyone had been on the property since we'd left it hours earlier.

I told TJ I was satisfied we could safely go inside,

and we dashed back to the truck to grab my bag and the photo box, then hurried up to the front porch. There were a few moments of chaos when he opened the door. A particularly forceful gust flew up, simultaneously sending a barrage of leaves in our direction and loosening his grip. The door clattered backwards against the siding, then wildly swung back and forth before launching away from the house and whipping toward us again. Just in time, TJ gave me a nudge forward. As we stumbled over the threshold together, the door slammed to a shuddering close behind us. Immediate darkness enveloped us, and after the rigors of the storm, the stillness was deafening. I let out a breath just for the sake of making a noise.

"You okay?" The question came from a place just above my ear, and the vibration of TJ's voice brought a tingling heat that overrode the permeating chill.

"Fine," I replied softly. "I mean, as fine as I can be considering I'm cold, wet, and pretty much blind."

His chuckle drowned out the staccato beat of my heart, and I felt him shuffle beside me. A second later, there was a click, and a yellowish light illuminated a small circle of space around us. TJ held up a battery-operated lamp.

"Better?" he asked.

I started to nod, but my teeth chattered instead.

"I guess that's a no," TJ said dryly. "C'mon. I'll bring your bag to your room, then leave the lamp with you so you can get changed."

I was too cold to insist on dragging my own suitcase, so I just followed along behind him, took the handheld light, then stepped into the guestroom and closed the door. My whole body was shaking now, and

I cast a regretful look toward the bathroom and its soaker tub. A hot bath had even more appeal than it had last night, and my chilly brain insisted there had to be *some* way, some excuse to climb in before the job was through.

"H-how are y-y-you g-going to d-do that?" I muttered to myself as I dug through my suitcase. "Ask TJ t-t-to p-pay his b-balance in b-bubbles?"

I tried to snort and wound-up sneezing instead. Rolling my eyes, I tossed aside everything in the bag until I had what I wanted—the flannel pajamas. With quivering hands, I stripped down and then slid into the soft fabric, desperate to be warm again. It wasn't enough. If I'd been at home in my own apartment, I would've dragged all the blankets off my bed so I could make myself a cozy cocoon where I could wait out the storm. But I somehow doubted I could even *pretend* to be professional if I did that at TJ's house. A woman in a down comforter didn't exactly command respect.

With a sigh, I settled for squeezing my hair with a towel, pulling my pjs a little tighter, and silently insisting that if I believed I wasn't cold, then I really wouldn't *be* cold.

Mind over matter.

It didn't work, of course. But when I made my way back to the living room, it became moot anyway.

I immediately stopped short; the chill forgotten. Though TJ wasn't there, the gas fireplace was on, the flames licking as high as they go behind the glass. He'd pushed the coffee table to the side, and he'd tossed some of the couch cushions on the floor, too. Between those sat the photo box. I could tell what he'd been trying to do. He'd obviously wanted to create a warm, comfortable space for us to go over the newspaper clipping. But the arrangement had a side effect. It was...*romantic.*

Chapter Twenty-Five

There was zero possibility of denying the potential ambience. And for a moment, I considered just solving the problem by hastily undoing the whole setup. Putting the cushions back. Dragging the table to its appropriate place and setting the box on top of that.

Because rearranging things wouldn't make TJ ask any questions? my subconscious said, heavy on the sarcasm.

"It might be better than the alternative," I replied under my breath.

Awkward questions were one thing. But it would be something else entirely to be snuggled up beside a man who pushed all my attraction buttons while simultaneously being unattainable.

My eyes roved over the cozy space. And as much as I willed it not to happen, the vision filled my head anyway. TJ, leaning back against the pile of pillows. Me, curled against his solid frame. Newspaper clippings discarded. Case forgotten.

Stop it! I ordered.

But another look toward the setup made me flush, and I knew I had no choice. I absolutely *had* to undo it all. Just shy of stomping, I moved to the closest cushion, snagged it by the corner, and started to lift it. That was as far as I got before TJ interrupted my plan.

"Ivy?"

At the sound of my name, I dropped the cushion and spun guiltily to face him.

"Here!" I said, groaning inwardly at the fact that I sounded like I was answering a rollcall.

TJ, now clad in black, knee-length sports shorts and a deep blue T-shirt—gave me one of his half-smiles. "Yes, you are. What're you up to?"

I made myself shrug. "Just rearranging."

"Rearranging?"

"Trying to optimize the light."

His forehead creased as he glanced to the well-arranged pillows, then back to me, but if he doubted my claim, then he didn't pursue it. "Hot chocolate?"

Belatedly, I noticed he once again had two mugs of steaming liquid in his hands.

"You made hot chocolate without electricity?" I asked, hoping the question covered my embarrassment.

"I did," he said. "Do I want to know how?"

"That sounds like a trick question."

"I'm just looking for an excuse to brag, actually."

My discomfort eased a little, and I laughed. "Then by all means. Tell me how you made the hot chocolate."

TJ nodded toward the fire. "Have a seat, and I will."

I obliged, but I was also careful to put myself at the very edge of the pile of cushions.

"Well?" I said as I closed both hands around the blissfully warm mug.

TJ sank down, his long legs and wide shoulders effectively reversing the illusion of space I'd just created.

"Camping stove," he told me.

I heard him. But his very thorough nearness made me answer as though I hadn't.

"What?" I replied blankly.

He took a small sip of his hot chocolate. "Camping stove. I was staring into the pantry, wondering how the hell we were going to get something warm to drink when I remembered that last time I stayed out here, I found a stash of gear in the storage closet by the front door. So I thought I'd check, and *voilà*. Hot chocolate."

His triumphant look made me smile. "Not normally a camping kinda guy, I'm guessing?"

"God, no. When I was a little kid, my dad used to force me to go on these weekend trips with him. To build character, he'd say. I was always either too cold or too hot. I hated sleeping in a tent. I swear the s'mores were the only thing that kept me from trying to run away in search of suburban comfort."

"And you didn't get *any* character building out of all that?"

"Are you mocking me, Ms. Ames?" he asked teasingly.

"Quite possibly, Mr. Jones," I responded.

"So then. I take you *are* a camping kinda girl?"

"Family of six kids on a single income. Pretty much the only vacation we could afford was a tent in the woods."

He feigned a wince. "Ouch. Sorry to hear that."

I swatted his knee. "It was *fun.*"

"Yeah, no. Theme parks and five-star hotels and beaches are fun. Camping? Not so much."

"How will we *ever* decide where to take *our* children for vacation?" The joke slipped out before I could stop it, and I felt my face go pink.

TJ didn't seem to notice. "Don't worry. I have every intention of putting my son through the same 'character building' experience my dad provided for me. It's the only way he'll know just how great an all-inclusive resort is."

His tone was so serious, almost vehement, that I blinked. But as quickly as his intensity came, it also left.

"And while we're on the subject of fatherly duties," he said, "I guess it's probably time to start looking through my dad's clippings?"

I nodded, set down my mug, then pulled the box closer and opened the lid. Immediately, an overflow of newsprint spilled out.

"Shit," I muttered as a few pieces fluttered to the ground.

TJ shook his head as he picked them up. "Don't say I didn't warn you."

I made a face at him. "Less talk, more sorting."

I was kidding when I said it, but it quickly became reality. TJ's dad had literally clipped and kept every mention of his son. Anywhere. And anything he hadn't found in physical form—internet-based items, for example—he'd gone ahead and printed off as well. It created a startling volume of stuff.

The earliest item was a birth announcement from the thirty-seven years ago. The most recent one was a draft notification, dated just a few months before his father had passed away.

"When he was dying, he talked to me about these two pieces," he told me softly. "He called these ones the bookends of his life. The moment that made him a father, and the one that made him the proudest father in the world."

Automatically, I slid my hand to his, and he let out a small sigh before tightening his fingers around mine.

"He'd hate this," he said. "He'd hate that I let myself get to a point where I'm having to cling to the threads of my hockey career, and he'd hate that I've put myself into a position where I can't even call the police to help me."

"I'm sure he'd still be proud, TJ. No one is perfect. And I don't think anyone knows that better than a parent."

He shifted. Just marginally. But it was enough to change our pose into something more intimate. He was looking down at me, his stare earnest, his blue gaze locking me in place.

"Do you believe that, Ivy?" he asked. "Or are you just telling me that because it's what I want to hear?"

It wasn't a personal query. Not really. And it certainly had nothing to do with the reasons for my erratic pulse. But something in his tone made it seem like a request for a glimpse into the most private recesses of my mind. Or maybe my heart.

"I'm not the kind of person who says something to someone else just because they want to hear it." My reply came out with a breathlessness that didn't match my words.

"No..." TJ's eyes dropped to my lips for a fraction of a second. "I really don't think you are."

"I'm not," I stated unnecessarily.

His head dipped down a little, bringing his face a fraction of an inch closer. I could smell a hint of cocoa and also the muted scent of bodywash that emanated pleasantly from TJ's skin. If I could've swallowed, I would've. But my throat was too dry, my lungs too tight with nerves.

I hadn't kissed a man in more than three years. I hadn't even *wanted* to kiss a man in that long. There was too much fear attached to it. Too much to lose. But in the last day and a half, I'd been tempted to press my lips to TJ's more than once. And right then, I didn't just *want* to kiss him. It was a physical need. Which is probably why, when he pulled away, it was like have a bucket of ice water thrown at me. I might even have shivered. And goosebumps definitely slid over the entirety of my body when TJ's hand came up to my cheek and stroked my skin in a gentle caress.

"Ivy…"

Once again, my name was filled with emotion. Only this time, I could understand it. Or at least read it.

Regret. Sadness. Hurt.

I knew it wasn't specifically about kissing me. Or *not* kissing me, as the current case was. But that didn't quite take the sting out.

I leaned away and mentally shook off the renewed chill. "C'mon. Let's have another look through all of this."

"Ivy," he repeated plaintively.

I met his eyes, issuing him the smallest challenge. Asking him if he really wanted to discuss a thing that never happened. He backed down, his attention dropping to the newspaper clippings.

He cleared his throat as he picked up one of the articles. "Hey. Here's something."

Hope surged up. "Really? What is it?

"The time I won a debate against a very angry boy from a rivaling high school."

"What?"

"He was pretty pissed off."

I groaned. "Not funny."

His smile was a little weak. "A *little* funny."

"Not in the slightest," I said.

I sighed, dropped the clipping down to the table again, and studied the remaining stacks, wondering if anything would come from them. So far, I hadn't seen a single clue. And another forty-five minutes of sorting and combing over the various articles brought nothing else I could relate back to TJ's stalker, either. I did get a deeper glimpse into his life through his father's eyes, and as much as I inappropriately enjoyed that aspect of our search, I was nearing the end of my effort rope. My years in the business had taught me when to admit that something was a dead end. And I was getting surer by the second that this was one of them. So I didn't protest when TJ excused himself to take a call from the Surrey Slammers' manager. I didn't want to give him the bad news.

I exhaled and stared at the spread in front of me. I willed a clue to jump out at me. Nothing did. I flipped through the pile again, hoping a word or phrase would pop up. Still nothing.

"Sorry, TJ," I murmured to the empty living room. "We'll have to try something else."

But as I pushed to my knees and started to stack up the newspapers with the intention of putting them away, I spied a missed item in the bottom of the box. It was another piece of paper. It wasn't a newspaper clipping. It was white, faded, and printed with both handwriting and typed lettering.

For a second, its presence puzzled me. How had we

missed it when emptying the box? A tickle of unease slid between my shoulder blades.

Frowning a little, I peered down at the paper, trying to decipher what it might be without touching it. But the glow of the fire didn't offer enough visibility, and after another moment, I realized it was ridiculous to do anything but reach in and take it out. So I did. And as I scanned it in the flickering light, I almost immediately identified it for what it was—a police report on a woman's death.

Chapter Twenty-Six

For some reason I couldn't pinpoint, my recognition of the sheet of paper made me draw in a sharp breath. I almost dropped it, and I actually had to force my hand to squeeze tightly, crumpling the edge a bit as I continued to stare at it. An apprehensive pit had already formed in my stomach. Maybe it was because of the contrast between the death and the vibrant details of TJ's life. Or it could've just been because I hadn't been expecting to find something quite so sad or grim. All I knew for sure was that something felt off.

My eyes skimmed the information.

Skye Marie Swinter.

That was the name of the deceased, and she'd died almost a decade earlier. She wasn't someone I'd known. Not that I'd expected her to be. But the details of her death struck me. They were the kind a newscaster would undoubtedly call a senseless waste.

Twenty-five years old. Two days shy of her twenty-sixth birthday, in fact. Had Skye Marie Swinter been alive, she would've been only a couple years older than me. Which made that thick feeling of wrongness that much stronger. The cause of death was listed a car accident. And according to a note that had been scrawled along the bottom, Skye had been the driver, she was the sole victim, and her blood alcohol level was twice the legal limit. A preventable tragedy.

Who was the dead woman to TJ?

I lifted my gaze to the spot where he'd disappeared a couple of minutes earlier. For a moment, I wondered if she was the one who he'd had the accidental affair with. But I quickly dismissed the idea. The timeframe didn't add up. But whoever she was, she had to be important in some way. Otherwise, why would her information be in the box?

Two primary explanations came to mind—a family member or an ex. Either one was potentially heartbreaking. And either might also fit with whatever it was TJ was doing his best to keep hidden.

I churned over the idea in my head. There was one fact that bubbled to the top and stayed there.

Ten years ago.

Closing my eyes, I recapped the last thirty-six hours of conversation. There had to be something in there that connected to this. I wished—again—that I had access to the organizational board in my office. But nothing came to me. After another second of trying to find a clue, I gave up and opened my eyes. And I found myself looking at TJ. He was standing at the edge of the living room, watching me in silence. When he saw that I'd spotted him, he nodded toward the paper in my hand.

"What is that?" The question was tinged with poorly hidden suspicion.

I didn't see a point in lying. "It's a death report for someone named Skye Swinter."

TJ's face went very, very still for a moment, and when he spoke again, it was in a cool, almost wooden tone. "That shouldn't be in there."

I had a feeling he was about to stomp over to me

and snatch the paper from my hands. I pulled it a little closer to my body. But he stayed where he was, and his continued muteness made me nervous.

"Who was she?" I blurted.

"She was someone important to me," TJ said, his voice all but expressionless. "But she died a long time ago, which makes it impossible for her to have anything to do with what's going on now."

He was right. Indisputably. And I was 99.9 percent sure his secretive moments were related to this woman. Which should've eased the feeling that something was eluding me. Instead, the niggling questions remained. Maybe they even became more insistent. But TJ cut me off before I could ask for a little more clarification.

"I'm going for a run," he said abruptly.

"A run?" I echoed, puzzled. "But…"

"What?"

"Now? In the storm?"

"Indoors, Ivy."

I fought an urge to tell him there was no need to be curt. "I didn't see a treadmill anywhere when you gave me the tour."

"Guess I forgot." He shrugged the world's smallest shrug. "If you want to come, meet me at the mudroom door off the kitchen. I should be ready in five minutes."

I opened my mouth to try and talk some sense into him. I wasn't even sure how he *was* going to run on a treadmill with no power, but he was already striding away once more. I stared after him. My head reeled with questions. None of which he'd even given me a moment to ask.

My eyes dropped to the death report again. It was clear that Skye Marie Swinter was an unhealed wound for TJ. And his reaction to my single-query curiosity about it…about her…made me lean toward the idea that she was an ex rather than family.

Ten years, I thought again, my heart aching.

It was such a long time to hang on to that kind of pain. Far too long to suffer. It made me want to chase TJ down and pull him close and tell him everything was going to be all right.

That's not a part of your job. And it's not reasonable, either.

But I was already pushing to my feet. My hand was already closing on the battery-operated lamp. And I was already moving toward the kitchen and the adjoining mudroom, too.

Somehow, TJ had managed to beat me there. And if I'd thought my concern for him was high before, it had nothing on the way my stomach dropped when I spied him right then.

He sat on a storage bench. His elbows were on his knees, his face in his hands. One white ankle sock had been pulled onto his left foot, while his right foot remained bare. His hunched shoulders made him seem smaller than he was, which only increased my need to wrap my arms around him.

I took a step closer, and he spoke to me without looking up.

"Have you ever loved someone so much it made you do unreasonable things?" he asked softly.

The question stilled me. Not because it had dark undertones, but because it echoed my moments-earlier thoughts about *him.* How my feet had moved on their own while my brain protested. It was a ridiculous comparison. My rather fervent desire to help TJ didn't come close to that overpowering kind of love, but it left me tongue-tied anyway. And it gave time him time to speak again.

"I can't explain how things were with Skye," he told me. "I don't even want to."

I found my voice, albeit softer than usual. "You don't have to, TJ."

He brought his gaze up, and I could physically feel the relieved expression on his face. Like a touch. But despite both the look and his claim of not wanting to explain, when he reached down to grab his other sock, he started talking.

"I met her on her eighteenth birthday. I was twenty-one, almost twenty-two. I was still fresh into my first contract, and my dad had just died," he said, the words strained. "I didn't…I don't know. My head wasn't right. Neither was my heart. I had this gaping hole, and…Skye was troubled, but she filled that hole, I guess."

I moved closer. This time near enough to reach out and put my hand on his shoulder. I gave him a reassuring squeeze, then dropped my hand to my side and balled it into a fist to keep from turning the touch into something more.

"I just want you to understand," he added. "When she died, it messed me up. And it would kill me to drag her name through the mud for no reason. She had enough bad shit already hanging over her when she was alive. She doesn't need to have anything else added to that. Especially unnecessarily."

"I get it."

"Yeah?"

"Of course, I do."

He let out a breath and silently looked down at his hands again. My heart panged. It was obvious TJ wasn't over Skye Marie Swinter, no matter how much time had passed.

No wonder he didn't jump on the chance to kiss you. It was a self-centered thought, and it was followed by a worse one. *He had no problem jumping into bed with his teammate's wife though, did he?*

My face got hot, and I was desperately glad his attention wasn't on me. I was being ridiculous. Maybe even childish.

Let the whole thing go, I ordered silently. *Shift gears. Like. Now.*

"Are you still going for that run?" I asked, my tone neutral.

"Pretty sure my treadmill doesn't work without power," he replied. "But I'm guessing you already thought of that."

"Possibly," I said.

He groaned. "Shit. You must think I'm some crazy asshole."

"I think you're a guy under a lot of pressure, who's had some seriously scary things happen to him over the last little bit."

"So, then...yeah. Definitely a crazy asshole." TJ finally looked up, and he smiled for a second, but his expression almost immediately turned serious again. "Do you think we could just..." He trailed off, ran a hand over his hair and shook his head. "Never mind."

"Can we just what?" I prodded gently.

"Forget I started to say anything. It was a ridiculous thought."

"Tell me anyway."

He sighed. "I just wondered if we could pretend—just for tonight—that none of this is happening?"

"None of what?" I replied with a frown.

"Any of it." He swept a hand across the space in front of him. "The stalking. The violence. You, finding out about Skye. Can we put it aside for a few hours?"

I could tell he was serious. And maybe a little desperate for me to agree. And of course, I *couldn't* agree. There was no way I could just pretend his life wasn't in danger. He was paying me to do the opposite.

I didn't realize I'd said the last bit aloud until TJ answered me.

"But it's my money, right?" he said.

"Yes, it's your money," I agreed. "But it's *my* job."

"Then you're fired from this and hired to do nothing." He sounded utterly serious.

"I...what? You can't pay me to do nothing," I argued.

"Fine." He crossed his arms over his chest in a quintessential show of stubbornness. "Then I'll pay you to do something else."

"Like what?" I replied, frustration seeping in.

"To eat dinner with me. To talk about normal things. Maybe watch a movie."

"That's basically a date, TJ."

"Yeah, okay. I'm paying you for a date."

"I'm a private investigator and a bodyguard, not a call girl."

He didn't back down. "Take it or leave it, that's my final offer."

I exhaled a huff. He was being unreasonable. And I was sure he wouldn't *actually* fire me if I didn't agree. Or almost sure. But when I opened my mouth to say as much, I saw TJ's nearly indiscernible flinch, and I stopped myself.

He's paying you to protect him, I thought. *And if this is what he needs, right now…then who are you to fight that?*

"What movie?" I said.

TJ's jaw relaxed. "You can pick."

I lifted an eyebrow. "What if I choose a chick flick?"

"Then I'll suffer through it. But I suspect you're more of the apocalyptic zombie type."

"Guess you're about to find out."

A charming grin split TJ's face, and I was immediately glad I'd relented. And truth be told, the rest of the evening gave me nothing to complain about.

We played several intense rounds of rummy.

We ordered a pizza from a place where I knew and trusted the owner, and who had a driver willing to brave the storm.

The power came back on, and we settled on a movie that included both the brain-eating undead *and* a love story.

And we talked. About everything that had nothing to do with the case and nothing to do with my secrets or his.

Chapter Twenty-Seven

Our conversation flowed through the rest of the storm. I told TJ every ridiculous, growing-up-with-five-brothers story I could think of. He recounted a few tales from his not-so-fine high school years. We compared notes about living in single father households, and he laughingly admitted he'd often felt infinitely confused about the so-called fairer sex. I confessed I'd often longed for a woman to talk to when I was a kid. Things never felt unnatural. And the talking never lagged. The sun set. We were both yawning with every second word. But it wasn't until I complained of a small ache in my shoulder, and TJ jumped up to grab an ibuprofen from the medicine cabinet in his ensuite that there was even a moment of proper silence.

With him gone from the room, the space seemed emptier. And not just in a literal way. I was eager for him to come back. A story I hadn't yet told him, one that involved an oversized, stuffed spider and a lot of screaming sprung to mind. I smiled at the thought of how he'd react. I glanced at the time. He'd been gone for a minute already, and it was too long.

Am I seriously missing *him right now?*

Mentally, I tried to deny it. After all, it was a bit ridiculous to miss someone when they'd been gone for sixty seconds. And it was even more ridiculous to miss someone who was literally paying me to keep him company, and who I barely knew. Nonetheless, when I probed my mind a little, I had no choice but to admit it was true. TJ the Troublemaker Jones had been thrown into my life less than forty-eight hours earlier, and somehow I liked him enough that when he left the room…I missed him. It made me feel strangely good. Oddly open.

So maybe you really should tell him.

I knew right away what the silent, half-idle suggestion referred to. My past. Four years ago, to be specific. The incident that had changed every aspect of my life. And while the thought was unnerving, I realized that the number of times I'd had it over the last day and half, it had to mean something. And it felt right.

"So maybe I should do it," I said aloud to the empty living room.

For some reason, voicing it made it seem like an even better idea. I decided I didn't want to wait. I pushed to my feet and stepped from the living room into the hall. My feet moved quickly. Eagerly.

It wasn't until I was almost at TJ's door that it occurred to me that I was about to pour out my deepest secret to a man who I was very attracted to while *inside his bedroom.* And when it belatedly struck me that it might not be such a good idea after all, I paused. And the pause gave me long enough to realize the air around me was silent. Worry zinged through me. I had to quickly remind myself that I'd been thorough in my perimeter check. But I made myself hold my still position for another moment anyway, listening for any true sign of danger. There was nothing. No noise, no movement. I took a step forward, placed my hand on the door, and gave it a gentle push.

"TJ?" I called, just above a whisper.

I heard something that sounded like a mutter, and I took another step. This time, my movement brought me just inside the bedroom. There, I paused again. I'd spotted TJ. And not at all in a way I expected to find him. His long, well-muscled body sprawled across his bed, face up. His eyes were closed, his mouth a little slack, and his chest slowly rising and falling.

Sound asleep.

In one hand, he clutched the bottle of ibuprofen he's promised to me. His other arm was thrown up over his head.

I stepped closer yet again and spoke softly. "TJ?"

He didn't react, and I gave my head a small shake, smiling a little. The last day and half had been harrowing for him—not to mention the week and a bit leading up to yesterday's explosion. Add an early morning, an intense hockey practice, and a trying evening, and I couldn't blame him for accidentally crashing out.

Which means I probably shouldn't wake you, should I? I asked silently.

But I *did* feel like I ought to make him a bit more comfortable. Taking care not to disturb him, I extracted the ibuprofen from his hand. After setting the bottle on the nightstand, I reached for the duvet that sat in a scrunched-up pile at the foot of the bed, then tugged it up over his reposed body. I released the covers, then thought better of just letting them go, and instead tucked them in around his shoulders. TJ shifted. Just a smidge. But enough that I winced guiltily and counted slowly to ten in my head before I started to ease away.

And I only managed to put an inch between us before I was stopped again. This time because he freed one of his hands from the confines of the blanket and closed it around my wrist. My breath caught in a surprised gasp, and my gaze jerked up to his face. He was staring back at me, albeit with heavy-looking lids.

"Sorry," I murmured automatically.

TJ blinked slowly, his blue eyes visibly blurred with sleep. "Hey, you."

"Hey yourself. I didn't mean to wake you up."

"S'okay."

He eyes sank shut, and for a moment, I thought he'd nodded off again. But when I moved to separate my wrist from his warm palm, his grip tightened.

"TJ?"

"Stay here," he replied groggily.

"Stay...*here*?"

"Mm. Safer with you close."

My face warmed. Did he really expect me to stay in his room by his bed all night? Not that I wouldn't do it for the sake of the case. But to keep him feeling safe?

All the more reason to do it, actually, argued a voice in my head. *He's a client. You do what needs to be done to protect him, even if that's just providing him with a sense of security. Besides which. If it weren't TJ, would this even be a question?*

My subconscious was right. So I opened my mouth to tell him I'd stay if that's what he really wanted. But he spoke before I could.

"Animal crackers," he muttered.

I frowned, sure I had to have heard wrong. "What was that?"

"An anteater."

"Um."

His lashes fluttered, and then he directed his gaze at me. And as I studied his expression, I belatedly clued in. My internal argument over keeping him safe versus making him *feel* safe didn't matter in the slightest. Because TJ wasn't actually lucid. That sleepy stare of his was just that—the stare of someone caught in the throws of sleep. However relevant his statement about me being there might've seemed, it was nothing more than a coincidence. Just part of a dream that I wasn't inside.

Unless I know more about animal crackers and anteaters than I think I do, I thought, smiling again as I watched his lids sink shut.

I tried once more to subtly loose myself from his hold. And this time, a few seconds of effort did earn me physical freedom. But then TJ spoke up once more, his words stilling me.

"You're beautiful," he said, his voice throaty. "I wanted to tell you that."

He was asleep. I *knew* he was. The compliment wasn't intended for me. In fact, if I were to stop and think about, I'd have to acknowledge its target was, in all likelihood, TJ's long-passed girlfriend. She had to be on his mind. But much as I knew all of that, it was impossible to stop myself from *wishing* he was speaking to me. And it didn't stop a little wave of tingles from starting at my toes again, too.

Lay off, Ivy, I ordered sternly. *Turn around and leave.*

And I tried. I needed sleep myself. Especially considering that the next day would likely bring a new, vaguely threatening note along with the gala. I'd need my wits sharp, and my body needed to be prepared for a fight, too. But as I turned toward the door, TJ's voice stopped me again.

"Ms. Ames," he murmured.

Startled—and feeling a little whiplash-y—I spun back. I fully expected to find him sitting up and looking at me this time. But he was still tucked in, his eyes still closed.

A reply slipped out anyway. "I'm right here."

"Ivy." My name was a thick, relief-filled exhale, and the barely subsided tingle came back with a vengeance.

"Yes?"

"I'm sorry."

You're having a conversation with a man while he's sleeping. That's a new one. And maybe even a little unethical?

But apparently common sense was out of reach.

"What are you sorry for?" I asked softly.

His response was utterly unexpected. "I would've kissed you, if it weren't for him."

I sucked in a breath. "TJ? Are you still dreaming? Because I'm not sure if I'm all that flattered about being lumped in with the anteaters and the animal crackers."

"So complicated."

I stared at him, wondering if any of what he'd just said held any truth. Knowing I wanted it to. Half wishing I had the guts to wake him up and ask. And chastising myself for continuing to stand there. Finally, the last thing won out.

"Goodnight, TJ," I whispered.

"Night, babe," he said back.

And the words almost made me fall over as I hurried from the room.

Chapter Twenty-Eight

Feeling discombobulated—a word I'd never thought to apply to real life before—I closed the door and sagged against the wall in the hallway. My face was flaming hot. I was unsure whether I ought to laugh or cry. A bit of both, probably. I had to take several deep breaths before the unusually lightheaded sensation faded. And even then, the warmth in my cheeks refused to abate.

"What the hell is wrong with me?" I muttered, but then immediately shook my head. "No, actually. Don't answer that."

I eyed TJ's door one more time, then ordered myself—extra firmly—to get it together. I decided to make a quick detour to the living room so I could tidy things up before grabbing a shower and jumping into bed myself. And I did get as far as packing up the playing cards and straightening the couch cushions. But before I could do anything else, the box full of newspaper clippings caught my attention. Automatically, thankfully my brain shifted gears, settling back on the case.

Is there something in there that I missed?

I felt so strongly like there had to be, because my tiredness faded. I grabbed the box and sat down to go through it again. It was easier this time; everything was already in order. Despite my determination, my resifting brought a frustrating amount of nothing. I had to acknowledge the possibility that my intuition was off. Or maybe it was clouded by hope. Heaving a sigh, I started to put the clippings away once more.

I couldn't help but pause on the police report about Skye Marie Swinter. Sorrow on TJ's behalf nagged at me. There was such a small gap between his dad's death and Skye's accident. It must've hurt to lose his father and his girlfriend so close together. By his own admission, TJ hadn't coped well. The double whammy was likely the catalyst for the dark years and bad decisions he'd talked about.

I paused with my hand hovering over the box. My gut told me there was something there to grasp, if only I could break it down.

TJ's dad died, I mused. *And that was what messed him up enough to get involved with the wrong woman.* I flushed guiltily at the slightly unkind thought, then firmly reminded myself it was TJ who'd referred to her as troubled, and I pushed on with my mental cataloging. *Skye Swinter was killed, messing TJ up even more. Then came the affair. The collapse of his hockey career.*

"What *un*-messed him?" I wondered aloud.

Was it the repercussions of his actions? Had the accidental affair been rock bottom for him?

I tried to picture TJ as he'd described himself back then. Young and reckless. Drinking too much. Acting without thinking. But it was hard to reconcile the TJ who I'd been getting to know with a man whose nickname was the Troublemaker. Everything I'd seen of him made me think he maintained careful control of his behavior. He'd had a few moments of frustration—my chase of the hooded figure came to mind—but he was predominantly reasonable. He was kind to his agent's driver. Polite to the staff at the arena.

"He made me hot chocolate with a camping stove, for crying out loud," I muttered.

Yet if I had to guess, I'd say his quick summarization barely scratched the surface of his bad years. Questionable backgrounds were a common theme in my line of work. Sometimes, they were literally the *source* of my work. And one thing I knew about people with reformed lives was that they didn't typically want to dwell on their *past* lives. They left things out. Glossed things over. Which meant I needed more details about what, exactly, TJ had gotten up to following Skye's fatal accident. And there was nothing about it in the pile of stuff sitting in front of me on the coffee table. I needed a different source—the good old-fashioned internet.

Once again being cautious about making any noise, I finished putting the newspaper clippings back into the box where they belonged, set it all aside, and made my way to the guest suite. There, I retrieved my laptop from my bag, plugged it into the outlet beside my bed, and sought out the Wi-Fi. For a second, I puzzled over the password. But on a hunch, I typed in the word "hockey." And I was immediately rewarded with access.

I had to shove aside a guilty twinge as I plugged TJ's name into the search engine. Normally, I didn't feel bad about probing a client's online life. But with the strange intimacy of our setup, it felt a little wrong to do it. The bout of conscience quickly abated, though, when the very first article popped onto the screen, and I read the headline.

TJ the Troublemaker Jones: Can the former bad boy of hockey redeem himself with the Surrey Slammers?

The date was a bit old—probably from around the contract signing time—but it still seemed ultra-relevant. So, I clicked. And I wasn't disappointed. Not at first, anyway.

The journalist recounted the story in a succinct, easy-to-read way. First, there was an overview of TJ's career. Highlights. Big wins. An award. And following that, there was an outline of his negative trajectory. His dad's death. The briefest mention of a relationship, then his devolution into a brawler. His troubles off the ice. Partying his time away, and a question about how anyone could keep up that lifestyle while also maintaining the job of a professional athlete. From there, the article jumped to the information about TJ joining the Slammers and speculated on whether the past would come into play.

"Okay," I said. "But what happened in *between* the time he got booted from his old team and the time signed with his new one? That's what I really want to know."

He was a badass troublemaker. And then he suddenly decided to stop.

I frowned at the computer and sucked my lower lip between my teeth. For some reason, I didn't believe it was as straightforward as the affair and the consequences. Maybe it wasn't enough. Yes, losing his career, his status, and his reputation added up to something enormous. But in my head, it didn't fit right. I felt like there had to be something more. A specific trigger. And I also thought that whatever it was, it might lead me closer to the person who was stalking him. If I'd been at my office with my giant organizational board, I would've tacked up a giant, red question mark right in the center of it.

My eyes drifted toward the hall that led back to TJ's bedroom. As tempted as I was, I wasn't going to wake him up to ask. I did make an underlined mental note to find a way to bring it up—preferably one that didn't set him off the way the conversation about Skye had.

I released my lip, which was burning a little from the pressure of my teeth, then clicked out of the current article and slid my gaze down the list of other TJ-focused links. There was plenty of information there. Except, a few quick checks told me none of it was what I was seeking. It was as though a certain time period had become a blank in his life.

My fingers tapped the bottom edge of my laptop. It seemed unrealistic, if not impossible. Briefly, I considered whether it was *literally* orchestrated, that TJ had somehow paid to keep his name out of the press. But common sense overruled the idea. There were far too many news avenues—traditional, indie, alternative—for someone to pay off every single one.

He must genuinely have stayed out of the limelight, I concluded with a frown.

My fingers tapped the plastic for a second more, and I typed in a new search, this time including the estimated date range. Unsurprisingly, the information didn't change much. In fact, the search engine went so far as to offer to eliminate the added dates. But when I scrolled down a little farther, there *was* one headline that immediately made my throat thicken.

Car Crash Victim Identified.

Even though no names were mentioned, I knew right away it couldn't be a coincidence. The article was about Skye. My hands wanted to shake, and it took some effort to hold them still when I clicked. I blew out a breath as I started to read the short, post-death biopic.

The identity of the female victim who perished in last week's widely publicized crash on the Highway of Heroes has finally been released. Twenty-five-year-old Skye Marie Swinter was a local columnist at The Artist's Rendering, an online magazine that bills itself as the premier source for edgy, upcoming talent. Though Ms. Swinter was on her way to becoming known in her own right, at the time of her death, her largest claim to fame was through her status as a troubled, teenage heiress. The only child of acclaimed modern artist Harlow Lawless (deceased), Ms. Swinter was no stranger to the wrong side of the law, particularly in her formative years. Eighteen months prior to her death, Ms. Swinter was also briefly associated with professional hockey player, Travis James Jones. Mr. Jones was not available for comment on this tragic loss.

My eyebrows knit together. If the article was correct, then Skye and TJ had split a year and a half before her death. Which made little sense. Or at least *less* sense. I could still understand why TJ would be upset over an ex's death. But to that spiralling extreme?

"C'mon, Ames," I said. "You've got to—"

The words caught off in a yawn, and I immediately forgot what I'd been about to tell myself I had to do. I pinched the bridge of my nose, trying to remember. But my brain was fuzzy, and I knew I was long overdue to call it a night. It was time to concede temporary defeat. Closing the laptop, I resigned to pick up my search the next day.

It wasn't until I'd brushed my teeth and tucked the duvet up around my chin and very nearly drifted off that my mind dredged up one more wondering. *TJ said he would've kissed you if it weren't for 'him.'* What did that mean?

Chapter Twenty-Nine

Thankfully, the rest of my very short night was dream-free and uninterrupted. But with the dawn of the next morning—which came far sooner than I would've liked—my late-made, sleep-tinged plans quickly got pushed to the wayside with a flurry of back-to-back activities.

First, TJ woke me with a smoothie and the suggestion of an outdoor run. I drank half of the former and groaned at the thought of the latter. But I laced up my runners anyway, and I powered through. And by the end of the jog, I was grateful for the dose of fresh air, the vitamin D brought in by the crisply sunny morning, and the burst of energy provided by the endorphins.

After that, TJ insisted we pick apples from the overgrown orchard. It seemed like a bizarre task, but he promised the mysterious surprise at the end wouldn't disappoint, so I acquiesced. There was a lot of leaves-in-hair laughter attached to the chore, but the cinnamon-laced apple crumble that resulted from the labor was nothing short of heavenly. Especially when TJ added some fresh coffee to the mix.

With the second breakfast complete, I decided it was time for a much-needed shower. I hesitated before I left the kitchen, contemplating whether I ought to say something about my online delve into his life the night before. But TJ made a blush-inducing joke about joining me while I bathed, and I scurried away instead.

It wasn't until I'd finished with the hot water and was already toweling dry that I realized something. The busyness was intentional. A distraction. A means of keeping us from talking about the past.

"Shit," I muttered into the steamy air. "You're a sneaky bastard, aren't you, Mr. Jones?"

And if I had any uncertainty about my conclusion, it was firmly washed away when I completed my get-clean routine and headed back to the main part of the house. TJ, who also appeared to be shower-fresh, was waiting for me in the living room. The box of newspaper clippings was gone, and in its place was a small stack of envelopes, which were undoubtedly yet another distraction of some kind.

I met TJ's eyes. "Catching up on a little correspondence?"

"I was thinking about what you said the day before yesterday," he replied. "About a crazed fan? And I thought we could explore that avenue, however unlikely. This is a sampling of stuff I've received."

I bit my lip. His suggestion was spoken carefully, if not robotically. Like he'd been rehearsing.

I exhaled and decided to be straightforward. "Look, TJ...if you'd rather leave certain subjects off the table while I do my damnedest to solve this for you, that's fine. But don't treat me like I don't know you're avoiding something. Because it definitely violates the whole underestimation deal we made."

For a second, his expression remained painfully impassive, and I thought he was going to deny it. Then his face drooped, and he scrubbed a hand over his chin.

"I want to take Skye off the table," he admitted.

"All right," I said.

He studied me for a second. "Now *you're* violating the deal by pretending that's okay with you when it's not."

I sighed and sat down beside him. "Are you really going to fight with me about agreeing to do what you want?"

"No." TJ paused, a smile ghosting his lips. "Well, yes. But only because I want it to *actually* be okay with you."

"I'm not dissecting every part of your life because I want to," I reminded him. "It's my job."

"So you keep reminding me."

"TJ…"

His hand slid over to clasp mine. "I know. It really *is* your job. I'm sorry if I'm being a stubborn ass. I'm letting everything get to me. Seeing that death report yesterday…I think it messed my head up. I had a shitty sleep and weird dreams, and I'm dreading this gala tonight."

At the mention of his dreams, a blush threatened to creep up, and I ordered my skin to refrain from getting any pinker, and I dredged up some genuine sympathy. "We'll get through it. And you'll be back to sleeping like a baby in no time."

"Awake and hungry every few hours?" he teased.

"Very funny," I said with an eye roll. "Didn't you say something about fan mail?"

"Actually, this is the opposite," he replied. "Anti-fan mail."

"You mean hate mail?"

"I like my term better. It's less aggressive."

I made a face and freed my hand to reach for the

first envelope. "Do you always keep your anti-fan mail at your dad's uncle's cousin's dog's son's house?"

TJ chuckled. "No, actually. I usually don't keep any of it anywhere. The team manager has a guy who sorts through anything that comes in—not that there's much of it—and he passes along the relevant stuff, or things he thinks one of the players should answer directly. He keeps the bad stuff, just in case. When I clued into what was happening, I asked to have a look at it. This is what he gave me."

"You weren't worried about making him suspicious?" I asked.

He shrugged. "He didn't seem to care one way or the other. I told him I was trying to track down an angry reference to one of our first games."

Nodding, I slid my finger under the envelope's flap and pulled out the first letter. It was easy enough to dismiss. The sender was angry that TJ had "stolen" the jersey number of another player. I moved on to the next one. It was full of barely coherent sentences, and it took me three reads before concluding that the writer blamed TJ for a game loss. The next few letters were more of the same. TJ should've shot left when he went right instead. He checked an opponent too hard, and the guy in question was going to be out for multiple games, pissing off his number one fan.

When I got through the contents of the eleventh—and final—envelope, I had to agree with TJ's conclusion. His stalker hadn't decided to take up letter writing. Well, not this kind, anyway. But just to be thorough, I did what I could to track down the supposedly anonymous sources of acrimony. Using my Ames Security contacts and a few trade secrets, I was able to put a name to every writer except one. And the ten I could trace were all exactly as they appeared to be, disgruntled hockey fans. I was sure that had I been able to pinpoint the eleventh one, I would've gotten the same result. It was frustrating. And the hours it took to do it all brought us to the point where, when TJ pointed out the time, I couldn't say no to getting ready for the charity event that evening. Any argument would mean missing the opening.

I was annoyed at the situation. Frustrated with myself for not being able to ask the questions I wanted ask. And doubting my ability to continue to do the job effectively. Not because of my capabilities, but because of my feelings. Something I'd promised myself would never, ever come into play while I worked.

*Once burned...*I thought with far more lightness than I felt as I made my way up the hall toward guestroom.

I wondered if I should call Charles and admit defeat. It would be humiliating. And he certainly had enough on his personal plate at the moment. He didn't need some business-related stress added to that.

Short-term loss, long-term gain, I told myself, pushing open the door and stepping through the frame. *He'd be far happier to have to scramble now than he will be if Ames Security's reputation takes a hit.*

I moved to grab my cellphone from the spot where it sat charging on the nightstand. But I didn't quite make it. Because the dress box from the day before sat in the middle of my temporary bed, drawing my attention. Somehow, I'd all but forgotten about it.

My eyes strayed to the door. TJ must've sneaked it in somehow. And admittedly, the thought of pulling out the beautiful yellow fabric filled me with more than a bit of girlish giddiness.

With eager hands, I slid my nail under the stickers holding the lid in place and opened the box. Then blinked. Instead of a sea of sunshine greeting me, I was met with a sultry shade of the darkest crimson.

Puzzled, I reached in and folded back the tissue paper. And my actions revealed a surprise—it didn't just contain the yellow dress; it contained a red one as well.

The one I didn't try on at the shop, I realized, remembering that although I'd almost immediately made my selection, the clerk had brought in two for me to try on.

Belatedly, I saw a note taped to the inside of the boxes lid. It was written in tidy, all-caps printing.

I'M NO EXPERT, AND I WOULD NEVER CLAIM TO BE ONE, it read, *BUT FROM WHAT THE SALESPERSON TOLD ME...WOMEN LIKE TO HAVE A CHOICE. SO JUST IN CASE YOU CHANGE YOUR MIND...OR SPILL SOMETHING ON THE YELLOW ONE...OR ALMOST GET BLOWN UP AGAIN AND NEED TO COVER THE BLOOD...HERE'S AN ALTERNATIVE.*

"You really *are* a clever bastard," I grumbled at the absent hockey player, rereading the note as I spoke. "And macabrely obnoxious, too."

But truthfully, I was pleased by the gift. With a pleasant warmth in my cheeks, I lifted the crimson garment from its wrapping. It was as stunning as the yellow one. It was also very different. It had long sleeves and a high neckline that, at first glance, gave the appearance of modesty. Upon closer inspection, though, that illusion faded. The chest area plunged into a lace-covered V, so low that it nearly touched the waistline. The back matched that, only it was lace-free, and when worn, it would expose an expanse of skin. The gown was floor-length. And cut with a slit on one side that I knew would reach higher than mid-thigh on me. Where the first dress was fluttery and sweet, this one was undeniably sexy. The material was shimmery, and when it caught the light, I saw tiny flecks of near-black. It was unique. Undeniably beautiful.

My fingers ran over the fabric, being careful not to snag it with my touch. And as the smoothness met my skin, I recalled again that the two dresses were selected based on TJ's suggestions. The yellow had been perfect. Which made me want—no, *need* to know—if the red was the same.

Fueled by the compulsion, I quickly stripped out of my yoga pants and T-shirt, then slid into the dress and stepped into the bathroom to have a look. And it *was* perfect. Especially once I'd reached around to do up the small zipper at the back. It hugged where it ought to. The slit bypassed my skinned knee. And the style was flattering, even if it did make me feel a little like I was wearing a glamorous disguise.

Which begs the question...which one do I wear?

I turned to the yellow dress and pursed my lips. Just looking at it made me want to smile. But since TJ had gone out of his way to pick this other one—in *his* favorite color, no less—there was a big part of me that leaned toward choosing it instead.

Deciding to give myself a few more minutes to think about it, I focused on my hair and face. The former was an easy enough problem to solve. I simply dampened my locks then slicked them back into an easy version of a French twist. I secured the look with a half a dozen bobby pins—one of my few staple beauty-related products—I found at the bottom of my suitcase. The end look was just shy of chic, and certainly more than passable. The latter of the two style issues, on the other hand, wasn't quite so straightforward. I hadn't thought to bring makeup. And in fact, even if I *had* wanted some, I probably would've needed to purchase it. I couldn't remember the last time I'd so much as looked at my one and only mascara. But after some digging around in my bag again, I did find a small bottle of moisturizer and a tube of lip balm in the side pouch. It wasn't much. But I used both, and hoped that a fresh, natural look wouldn't be too bizarre at the fancy event.

"It'll have to suffice," I told my reflection.

I slid my gaze from my hairline down the length of the red dress, thinking I probably should've taken it off before securing my hair. Except the thought slipped away as I spied a new problem. Namely…my feet.

"Shit," I said, looking down at them.

It hadn't occurred to me until right that second that I was going to need something other than my trusty old high-top runners.

The dress isn't going to matter much if I'm running around barefoot, is it?

And high heels weren't exactly something I could expect to borrow from TJ. But I was definitely going to have to stop and grab a pair from somewhere before we got to the gala.

I groaned at the idea of last-minute shoe shopping, cast one final dirty look at the mirror, then hurried out to tell TJ the bad news. As I stepped into the hall, hearing a sharp intake of breath made me jump.

Heart thumping, fists ready, I turned and found TJ standing just outside *his* door, his eyes fixed on me. I expected him to tease me about being ready for a fight. But he surprised me with a sincere-sounding compliment.

"You look…amazing." His voice was more than a little rough.

Accompanying admiration coursed through his gaze, too. My palms quite abruptly grew sweaty, and as I relaxed them, I had to command myself not to wipe them on the delicate fabric of the red dress.

I mustered up some lightness. "Like an imposter, you mean?"

He didn't buy into my jest. "No. Like yourself. But amazing."

"And here I was, just aiming for mediocre."

"Trust me. You're beautiful."

I couldn't stop the blush now. And I also couldn't help but notice that his tone was similar to the one he'd used while sleep talking. Did that indicate he'd meant it? Did it mean he meant the other things, too?

Like that he would've kissed you if not for 'him,' Ivy? Get a grip.

I cleared my throat. "Thank you." I gestured to the tux he wore. "You clean up pretty well, too."

It was an understatement, of course. His shoulders filled out the suit while the crisp collar of his shirt contrasted perfectly with his tanned skin. His bowtie was both endearing and sexy, and his pants couldn't have fit better if he'd been born wearing them. And— unlike me—he'd already donned a pair of suitable shoes. A fact which hadn't slipped by him, either. He pointed to my polish-free toes.

"Did you bring something else to go with that dress?" he asked. "Because I don't think what I picked out is going to match."

The question and the statement both confused me. "What do you mean?"

"Wait here a sec," he replied. "I'll show you."

He turned around, stepped into his room, then reappeared a moment later with a pair of pale-yellow ballet flats dangling from his fingers. They were a perfect match for the other dress. But I still didn't understand.

"You bought those for me?" I asked.

TJ nodded. "I saw them sitting on a display shelf while I was paying, and I thought they'd suit you. I sneaked a look at your shoes for the size. Not indicative of a foot fetish."

"They're really perfect," I agreed. "And I appreciate it, and you probably shouldn't have gotten them. But since you *did*...you didn't also get something to go with the red dress?"

"I would have. If I'd know you were going to buy something other than the yellow, too."

"Me? You bought this one."

"It's beautiful. But I didn't buy it," he argued.

I laughed. "Riiiiight. So then I guess it just appeared randomly in my—"

His expression cut me off. His eyebrows were drawn together, his mouth set. He was serious.

If TJ didn't buy it...who did?

The answer was as obvious as it was chilling. And as TJ's eyes scanned me once more, I knew he'd come to the same conclusion.

Chapter Thirty

TJ was talking. Cursing. Looking up and down the hall like he might find his stalker lurking there. But I was underwater. Or maybe encased in ice.

Cold fear swept through me. The seconds hand on my personal clock seemed to have gone still.

TJ's stalker knew about us. And as a result, he was targeting me.

Me.

The frightened girl who'd been through it before tried to rear up and take charge.

Run! she urged. *Run now!*

But even if I'd been inclined to listen to her, that didn't mean I was capable of complying.

Flashes of my recurring nightmare surfaced. My floral dress. The smiling man. The dead flowers. The horror that came after, but which I always managed to keep buried, even in my sleep. Except right now, it didn't seem to matter that it was buried. Because it was on me anyway. In me. Surrounding me and drowning me. I needed to save myself. To do something. Anything.

Yes! the frightened girl in my head agreed. *I said run!*

She seemed to mean it quite literally. But I remained stuck. Bare feet glued to the ground, sweat slicking the folds of my elbows and the backs of my knees. My muscles cramped. My chest ached so badly that it felt like a heart attack.

Because you have to breathe, dammit.

It was true. My lungs burned from the lack of oxygen. And yet I still couldn't seem to draw in any air.

It's the dress, I thought suddenly.

And that made me want to pull it off right then and there. My hands finally came to life, reaching up to grip it, and if TJ hadn't stepped forward and put his fingers on my wrists, I might've torn the red fabric in an attempt to rid myself of it.

"Ivy?" he asked, his voice slicing solidly through my panic and yanking me back to the present. "You okay?"

At last, I inhaled. I deliberately savored the oxygen for a moment, proving I was in control.

Never again, I reminded myself. *I'm not a victim.*

I blew out the breath and shook my head. "I'm not okay. *You're* not okay."

Maybe it wasn't what he was expecting to hear because he blinked. "Sorry?"

I kept my voice steady as I answered him. "We haven't been taking this seriously enough. As much as I know you needed the break last night, we can't afford to become unfocused like that again."

TJ's expression changed. His blue eyes flashed. And for a second, I thought he was going to argue with my statement. Instead, his head dipped in a vicious nod.

"You're right," he told me, his tone as furious as his expression. "Abso-fucking-lutely right."

Now it was my turn to blink, startled by his vehemence. "I am?"

His eyes flicked up and down the hall again.

"Yeah. We need to get the hell out of here. We can get another hotel room. Or an Airbnb."

"We're fine where we are for the moment. He's not at the house, TJ."

"How the hell can you be sure? That fucking dress... *Jesus.*"

"I'm sure because the box was taped shut with the dress shop's logo sticker."

"He could've—Christ." He said something in an incomprehensible growl, then added, "Who knows what he's capable of?"

"We can call the shop to be sure," I said.

"We can call the shop to get all the staff fired," he corrected.

"I'm sure our friend gave them a good enough excuse for adding the dress to the box."

"Don't call him that, even sarcastically," TJ snapped.

I understood his anger. I understood his need to find someone to cast blame on. The dress was more than a pieced together note. It was more than a skipping rope prank and a blocked off driveway, and somehow, it was even more than a hotel bomb. It was a violation.

And no one knows better than I do what that invasion of privacy feels like, I thought, covering a shiver as the dead flowers from my dream tried to surface.

TJ exhaled, and when he spoke again, it was in a more restrained voice. "Look. I know I sound like I'm freaking out here, and shit, maybe I am. But there's just no way I'm letting that asshole get any closer to you, let alone close enough to *hurt* you."

It took me a second to process his words. He

wasn't mad about his own situation. At least not solely. He trying to keep me safe. And admittedly, there was a not-very-subtle part of my brain that *liked* that. But I didn't need to be a flattered-girl version of myself right now anymore than I needed the frightened-girl version of myself. I needed to be the kickass woman who made men step wide of her at the gym.

I squared my shoulders. "I'm not worried about getting hurt. I'm worried that if we keep making hot chocolate and sitting by the fire, then this guy is going to amp things up even more and get away with it."

TJ didn't let it go. "Call it what you want, Ivy, but that doesn't change the fact that whoever this douchebag is, he's threatening you now."

I pushed down a sliver of fear—a muscle memory brought on by my own past trauma—and answered him in a firm, even voice with what I knew logically to be true. "He's doing it to get to you."

"It's working," he muttered.

"This is *all* about you," I reminded him. "Chances are he has zero interest in harming me at all."

He met my eyes, and I saw a spark of something fierce and protective that made my heart skip a beat. But as quick as the look came, it was gone—covered in a glare.

"I'll call Bram," TJ said.

"Your agent?" I replied. "Why?"

"We're obviously not going to the gala now, and I need to let him know."

"We have to go. They're expecting you."

"Yeah. And so is the man who's trying to destroy my life."

I touched his forearm, trying to sooth him. But he

was so tightly wound that he flinched back at the contact.

"TJ..." I said gently. "There's a chance this guy *wants* you to cancel."

"How the hell do you figure?" he asked.

"Just think about it. He's *watching* you. Clocking every move you make. And this dress..." I swept a disgusted hand down my body. "It means he wants you to know it. He followed us to the shop. He might've been inside while we were there. All it would take is a quick internet search to figure out why we were buying it. But if he wanted to cause harm during the event, why draw attention to his foreknowledge that we're going to be there?"

His hand found his jaw. "Shit."

"Yes. Shit, indeed."

"So we really have to go."

"But we should be extra vigilant while we're there. I think we should also be careful to stay side by side, whenever we can."

His eyes slid over me and the red dress. "And you have to get out of *that,* too."

The reminder made the fabric feel tighter and more cloying, and I nodded. "Give me five minutes."

"Sure." He offered me a half-hearted smile. "I'll give you ten if it means we can burn the damn thing."

I made a face and turned to go. But I only got two steps before I realized he was right on my heels.

I spun back. "What are you doing?"

"Coming with you," he replied matter-of-factly.

My face pinked. "You can't come with me while I get changed, TJ."

"You literally just told me we need to stick side by

side until this is done."

"I literally said that," I agreed. "But I didn't *mean* it literally."

His jaw had a stubborn set. And I was suddenly too tired to fight with him about it.

"Fine," I said with a sigh. "But you're going to stow your TJ the Troublemaker self, and you're going to sit on the bed with your *eyes closed* while I get changed in the bathroom."

His face finally relaxed, and he even raised an eyebrow. "If you're in the bathroom, why do I need to close my eyes?"

"Take what you can get, TJ."

"Roger that."

I spun again, ignoring him this time as he followed closely behind me. I pushed down further embarrassment when we entered the guest room, and I pointed at the bed.

"Sit," I ordered.

He smiled and plunked himself down. "Sitting."

"Eyes closed."

He obeyed, but I waved my hand in front of his face, just to be sure, before I made my way into the bathroom. Why it mattered so much, I didn't know. He was right that it was overkill. But the vulnerability I'd be feeling over the past few minutes, the outright exposure and the reminder that I'd once been the victim, left me raw. I needed control.

Like that's *new, Pint-Size*.

I pretended not to hear the brotherly manifestation of my subconscious Because there was nothing *wrong* with wanting to be in control. It wasn't a failing. It was a necessity. Especially in this job.

I straightened my shoulders and reached for the dress's zipper. But as I did, I caught sight of my reflection in the mirror, and I paused. The dress was still perfect. It still looked as good as it had when I'd put it on and done it up. *Amazing.* That had been TJ's descriptor. His slightly breathless compliment filled my head, and a flash of anger zapped through my chest.

How *dare* this asshole stalker use me like this? How dare he force me to remember the terrible things I'd been through? How dare he ruin this perfect dress in TJ's favorite color that made me look *amazing*? And for a second, I was half-tempted to leave it on, no matter how it made my skin crawl to know who'd paid for it. But as much as I liked the idea of giving the stalker a metaphorical middle finger, I didn't think he really needed any further provocation. I could have *self-*control as well as control.

I let my eyes linger on the dress for a single moment more, then shook my head and reached for the zipper once again. But as I gave yank, I had to groan. It was stuck. Because of course it was. I floundered, trying to get a better grip on the pull. No luck.

"Come on," I muttered.

I kept working at it. And working at it. And working at it some more. I made so much of an effort and took so long that sweat beaded along my forehead, and TJ finally called out to me from the bedroom.

"Ivy?" He sounded genuinely worried, and I groaned again. "You okay in there?"

"I'm fine!" I called back.

"Are you sure? Because—"

"I'm *fine!*"

But actually, my arm was starting to ache from the

weird angle. And my hair had loosened from its updo, and it stuck to my face and my back.

I gave up on my efforts for a moment, trying to catch my breath. I cringed at what I saw in the mirror. My face was red enough that it nearly matched the crimson of the dress. And now—because I felt like I was being *forced* to stay in it—I wanted to get it off even more than I had before.

Drawing a breath, I reached back around to give it another go. Immediately, the zipper pull came off in my fingers.

A frustrated cry burst from my lips. "You've got to me shitting me!"

"Ivy?" TJ repeated, no less urgently.

To his credit, he still sounded like he hadn't moved from the bed. Dollars to donuts, his eyes had stayed closed, too. But I wished for a second he wasn't so gentlemanly and that he'd go against my orders and burst through the door to see what was wrong. It would've saved me from having to answer him with an admission I didn't want to make. I even counted to ten to see if he'd do it. He didn't, of course.

"TJ?" I said. "I think I need a little help."

"From me?" he replied.

"You're the only other person here."

There was a pause, and I wondered if he'd keep sitting right where he was until I specifically asked him to open his eyes and get up to come to the bathroom. But another few heartbeats passed, and the door opened an inch.

"What can I do?" TJ asked through the narrow crack.

"The zipper's stuck. It broke, actually. I can't get it

to undo."

"Oh."

"Can you...?" I trailed off and gestured toward my back.

He pushed the door open the rest of the way and met my eyes in the mirror. "Hey."

"Hey."

"You want me to—"

"Yes, please," I said quickly. "Let's not make this any more embarrassing than it is, okay?"

He stepped closer. One hand pressed to my back while the other sought the offending zipper. It was impossible not to feel the heat of TJ's palm. Impossible to pretend it didn't shoot heat *through* me, too.

Stop it, Ivy.

And I tried to listen to myself. I swallowed and stayed as still as I could. I even closed my eyes so I wouldn't have to look at him in the mirror, but all that did was make me even more aware of just how close TJ was, and his now-familiar scent seemed to fill all my senses.

"Sorry it's taking so long," he said, right beside my ear. "Thing's a bugger."

I made a small, noncommittal noise and hoped he took it as an agreement rather than an inability to speak properly.

Finally, the telltale *ri-i-i-ip* of the zipper coming down filled the small space. It should've been a relief. He was done. I was free of the stalker's dress. But there was zero relief. Zero reprieve. Although TJ's hands had stopped moving, they hadn't fallen away from my body.

"Shoddy workmanship," he said.

"Overzealous undressing," I managed to get out.

"In any case, we should be able to return the fucker."

"Yes."

"Ivy…" My name was hot on my neck, and in contrast to that, I shivered. "You really do look beautiful despite where the dress came from."

My eyes opened. TJ was staring at me through the mirror. His gaze was appreciative to the point of looking hungry. And three days ago, being looked at like that—looked at with a tenth of that want—would've sent my fight or flight response into overdrive. Right now, I just watched him watching me.

I wished he wasn't a client.

I wished I'd met him in the produce section of a grocery store where we fought over the last cantaloupe until we had no choice but to agree to share it.

I wished he was removing the dress for any reason other than this.

All of which was ill-placed and unreasonable and—

"Ivy," TJ repeated.

"Yes?"

"If I let go of the dress, it's going to fall off."

I think he meant it as a joke. Except when I met his eyes in our mutual reflections again, it seemed more like a question. *Do you* want *to let it fall off?* And wildly, I did. But I made myself shake my head, forced down the unexpected desire, and put my hand up, careful not to touch *his* hand, then smiled.

"Let's try to avoid any further fashion disasters," I said. "And thank you."

A flash of something, possibly disappointment,

crossed his features before he smiled back. "Happy to help. See you in a minute."

He slipped back out of the bathroom, and when he'd closed the door, I let out the longest sigh of my life.

TJ the Troublemaker Jones was under my skin. And somehow, that felt more dangerous than the person who was out to get him.

Chapter Thirty-One

After I'd put the yellow dress on and tucked the red one back into the box—somehow managing to stow thoughts of TJ's hands unzipping the latter of the two at the same time—I called the dress shop. It was after hours, and I knew I'd get their voicemail. It was still a bit of a letdown when the automated voice on the other end told me to leave a message.

I explained who I was, then—careful to put nothing more than an eyeroll into the rest of what I said—I delivered a story about an ex trying to win me back. I suggested that maybe he thought "gifting" me the red dress was a good way to show up my new boyfriend. I punctuated that part with a laugh.

What is he…crazy? Like a dress is better than TJ the Troublemaker Jones? Like anything is!

Finally, I told them I just wanted to make sure it wasn't a mistake on their part, and I asked them to call me as soon as they could.

"Good enough," I said when I tapped the phone off.

"Do you think they saw him?" TJ asked.

I shook my head. It was another reason I wasn't all that concerned about getting in touch with someone at the dress shop.

"This guy is too clever to simply walk in and pay," I said. "I mean, there's a chance the clerks may have talked to him if he had to pay by card, but remember how he used those kids to break the camera at your apartment? He could've done something similar."

TJ's shoulders drooped. "Dammit. I was hoping it'd be like a golden goose."

"It still might be," I replied. "Maybe he left behind some small tidbit of info." I stood up a little straighter as I realized something else. "I wasn't part of his plan."

"Sorry?"

"He's only after *you*, TJ."

"Gee, thanks."

I shook my head. "Seriously. When he started whatever this is, he had no idea I'd show up. Buying me a dress? That couldn't possibly have been included in his original plans. He's had to adjust."

TJ's blue eyes got a bit wider. "Shit. You're right."

"He's been meticulous and careful, but I'm a wild card. He couldn't have preplanned for my existence, so if he's going to make a mistake…"

"That means *you're* the golden goose, babe."

Despite the use of my so-called nickname, I smiled. Some of the tension even managed to leave my shoulders.

"Let's agree not to tell Charles his idea was a good one," I said.

Unexpectedly, TJ reached over and pulled me into a hug so hard it crushed my ribs and lifted me from the ground. When his cellphone buzzed in his pocket, I could feel it in my teeth.

"Shit," he groaned as he let me go to tug out the device and read his incoming message. "Bram is already on a rampage. He says half the team is there already, and to quote him, 'TJ Jones isn't fucking one of them.'"

"I guess that's our cue."

"Do we *have* to go?"

I laughed. "You sound like a five-year-old being dragged off to his least favorite great-aunt's house."

"I basically am," TJ replied, one corner of his mouth turning up. "Only it's my great uncle's widow, and her house is in the middle of nowhere, smells like mothballs, and has a bad draft. Also, it might be haunted, and she might be a demon."

"Very dramatic."

"Very accurate."

"Come on," I said. "Now that we're using me to throw the stalker for a loop, being out in public together is even more important."

The twinkle in his eyes faded. "I don't want you to be bait, Ivy."

"It's my job," I reminded him.

He put his hand on the back of his neck. "I know. Christ. I *do* know. I'm not underestimating you. I just really hate the idea of you getting hurt."

I swallowed against a sudden tightness in my throat. "Yeah, well. Ditto."

He reached up and touched my cheek for a heartbeat. And as his hand fell away as quickly as it'd come up, I heard his sleep-tinged voice in my head again.

I'd have kissed you if not for him.

I swallowed again. "We should go. Before your agent sends another mean text."

"Mean texts are the worst," he replied a little dryly. "Mind if I drive us there? I didn't arrange a car."

"No, that's probably a good idea."

I didn't add what I was thinking, which was that the reason it was good was because it might be best to have a quick way out, if we needed it. Maybe I didn't need to add my thoughts anyway. TJ tipped his head and narrowed his eyes, and he seemed to read my carefully neutral expression for what it was.

"You know we can be proactive about this, right?" he said. "Avoid the need for a getaway car altogether."

"Stop stalling."

"All I'm saying is we could just ditch the gala before we even get there and go for some fast food instead."

I made a show of rolling my eyes. "If you think for a second I'm wasting this dress on a burger and fries, you've got another thing coming."

He flashed his teeth. "From my perspective, you're wasting it on the gala."

"Ha. Very funny."

"For real. I mean, *all* of the women at the gala will be fancy. None of the ones at a burger place will come even close. Think of how much more the staff and other customers will appreciate you."

But the back-and-forth teasing felt forced. More unnatural than anything we'd said to each other since I first walked into his hotel room. And it continued as we left the house and climbed into TJ's truck. He made a joke about me arriving naked because the hem of my dress got caught up on the bottom of the door and had to be pulled free. I retaliated with a threat to make *him* wear the dress, while I took over his suit. Exaggerated, all of it. And I couldn't help but notice his hands were tight on the steering wheel before we even made it all the way out of the driveway. It was almost funny that the gala would be more stressful than being stalked. But not quite. And worse than the artificial banter was the silence that followed. TJ must've been feeling the same way because after five or so minutes of driving, he reached over and clicked on the stereo. Classic 90s rock blared out of the speakers, and he didn't bother to turn in down, and I didn't bother to complain.

For a good forty minutes or so, we drove just like that. His attention on the road, mine turned inward while Kurt Cobain's voice provided a soundtrack. I kept my thoughts on the case. Or I tried to. But with no conversation, it was embarrassingly hard not to remain utterly focused. I reasoned with myself that it was only a natural progression. How could I think about who might be out to get TJ without thinking about TJ himself? Except it was an excuse, and I damn well knew it.

You wanted fieldwork, Pint-Size, my brother's voice reminded me once again.

I silently grumbled at him to shut up. I *did* want fieldwork. I had to expect some curve balls.

You mean curve...pucks? The suggested adjustment came into my head in TJ's voice rather than my brother's, and I almost snorted at the lameness of the joke. Still, I did smile a little. Until we rounded the next street corner, and the full impact of what I was getting myself into hit me. Which, apparently, was a *lot*.

Limos and town cars and Ubers and taxis lined the block. Cameras flashed and caught the light of sparkling dresses as fancily clad women exited the vehicles. There was also a line for valet parking, and TJ guided us there. While we waited for our turn to hand over the keys to the next available agent, he was visibly rigid with tension. A spark of guilt wormed its way under my skin. He *really* didn't want to be here.

Forgetting my own discomfort, I reached over and put my hand on his forearm to reassure him. "It's going to be okay."

"Is it?" TJ asked without turning my way.

"Yes," I replied firmly. "We're going to go to this party. See the people here and let them see us. We'll solidify our relationship and show your stalker we aren't scared."

"And if that doesn't fucking work out?"

"Then we'll leave."

Now he did look toward me. "I *am* scared, Ivy."

His voice was gruff, his tone raw, and as he shifted in place, I realized I was still holding onto his arm. My fingers tightened.

"I'll keep you safe." I sounded so fervent that it might've been comical to an outside observer—me, the "pint-size" protector making the promise to TJ, the muscle-bound professional athlete—but I meant it. "At the first sign of trouble, we'll go."

"Thank you."

"You're welcome."

We reached the valet then, and we both adjusted our attention. TJ straightened his shoulders, handed over the keys, and climbed out. As he did, a second uniformed employee opened my door, and by the time I'd started to get out myself, my hockey player "boyfriend" was already in front of me, chivalrously holding out his hand. I took it and let him help me. It was more for show than for need, but as my feet tapped to the ground, the glitz seemed to envelope me, and I tightened my grip on him instead of letting go.

"Holy shit," I said under my breath.

TJ leaned down and spoke into my ear. "Fast food is looking pretty good now, right?"

"Maybe it is," I whispered back.

"Too late. Game-face time, babe."

In a practiced move, he realigned us so my hand was tucked under his elbow, and he ushered us forward, making short work of the wide steps leading up to the building. Somehow, we managed to bypass the majority of the crowd. One click of a camera. One hello to a person who recognized TJ. No more than that. But it was still overwhelming, even once we were inside. Every man at the event seemed to have donned an equally bespoke tuxedo. The women wore silk and satin and lace and velvet. There were scandalously plunging necklines. Skin adorned with diamonds and pearls. Clinking glasses. Laughter. Overly complex finger food and a ridiculous ice sculpture. In short, it was everything someone might envision when they heard the word *gala.*

My eyes scanned the whole group—or they tried to—in search of anyone out-of-place. It was a Herculean task.

"Who *are* all these people?" I blurted after a few seconds.

TJ chuckled. "No clue."

But just after he said it, a suited man across the room—all but invisible in a sea of other suited men—lifted a yell over the din as if to prove him wrong. "Hey, TJ! Everyone's been waiting for you, man! Get your ass over here! We're trying to take some team pics!"

The request was promptly followed by one directed my way, called out in a vaguely familiar voice. "Ivy! Leave the boys alone and come have a drink with us!"

I squinted through the throng in search of the speaker. A woman in a pink dress waved at me, then motioned for me to join her and the group of women she stood with.

Heather, I reminded myself.

And now that I'd recognized her, I saw that Charlene and Lisa were among the small crowd around her, too. They all waved. Even the few I hadn't yet met.

TJ lifted an eyebrow at me and spoke in a low voice. "Should we obey their commands?"

"It's a bad idea to let you out of my sight," I murmured.

He bent his head, his lips brushing my cheek. "I won't be out of your sight. I'll be just over there, getting a few candid shots taken with the guys."

"I should come."

"You'll hurt the hockey wives' feelings."

"I'm not worried about them," I told him. "*You're* my responsibility."

"Nothing's going to happen here," he said. "You told me so."

I had said that. But as soon as the words were out of his mouth, my worry spiked. What if something *did* happen here?

"Are you trying to make it happen?" I grumbled at him.

He chuckled. "C'mon, babe. Let me take some pictures with my teammates."

I made a face at him, stopping just this side of sticking out my tongue. But honestly, I was going to keep protesting. Play the new and needy girlfriend card. Make him let me come with him. But I barely had time to think before Heather came running over, her movements remarkably fast despite her spiked heels *and* the way her dress hugged her body. She grabbed my arm, tugging me away while talking enthusiastically about girl time and champagne. And TJ—the traitor rather than the troublemaker in this instance—offered me a helpless shrug. Then he slipped away to join the guys.

"Dammit," I muttered.

"Sorry?" Heather replied.

I sighed. "No. Nothing. Not you."

Her brow crinkled the tiniest bit but cleared quickly, and she planted me in amongst the other hockey wives, raving about my dress. Before I could stop myself, I told her that TJ picked it. A mistake. The women *gushed.* Not that I could blame them. Not if it were real.

Even though I was still keeping an eye on TJ—who kept looking my way too, and shooting winks when he caught me watching him—it was easy to get swept along in the hockey women's conversation. Heather and couple of the others were planning a charity event. Charlene had recently started the journey to get her Masters, and Lisa was in the throes of a startup business. They were all interesting, all smart. And they all worked so hard to include me that I felt terrible lying to them about my relationship with TJ. It only got worse when my smile faltered, and one of the others in the group asked me if I was okay. It took serious effort to keep from excusing myself and spinning dramatically away to take a breather in the bathroom.

Fieldwork. Am I right, Pint-Size? Charles's voice asked in my head in response to my near slip.

Mentally, I rolled my eyes. But it was a good reminder that despite my twinges of guilt, I was there in a professional capacity. My obligation was to TJ.

And speaking of TJ...

I tipped my head back to the group of hockey players, who were still taking photos. My so-called boyfriend caught me looking. Again. And he smiled, waved, and winked. But as Heather nudged me and made a teasing remark about the honeymoon period, and I brought my attention back to her, I felt a weird shift in the air. Like I was being watched.

The hairs on the back of my neck—all over my body, really—stood up. The women's conversation faded into background noise, and I sipped my wine. Which up to now, I'd been only feigning to drink. Scanning the room for the source of my disquiet, I took the smallest step away from the group. And the very moment I extricated myself from them, a man standing at the bottom of a set of curved stairs caught my eye. Or maybe it would've been more accurate to say *I* had caught *his* eye. Because there was no doubt, he was staring at me. No doubt at all.

Chapter Thirty-Two

My breath stuck in my throat. My pulse surged. But whoever the man was, he wasn't trying to disguise his interest in me in the slightest. There was nothing sneaky about his look. So, I went ahead and studied him in return, assessing with no holding back, either.

His stare raked over me in a way that was undeniably scrutinous.

Why?

There was nothing sexual about it. No thinly veiled desire, and I didn't feel a sudden need to fold my arms to cover my chest. But as much as that was a relief, it didn't answer any questions. He certainly wasn't someone I knew. I'd remember the steel-gray hair, wide shoulders, and unsettling fixation. Who wouldn't?

His gaze ran over me again, and as it came up to my face, I didn't look away. His eyes met mine. I lifted my chin a smidge. *What the hell do you want?* My bold, silent challenge didn't phase him and being caught in the act of studying me didn't make him back down. In fact, he set down his tumbler of amber liquid and stepped toward me.

Admittedly, there was a small part of me that wanted to bolt. Maybe more than a small bit. But I ignored the urge, and stood my ground, waiting for the man to reach me.

"You're here with Travis," he stated, his voice

cool, matter of fact, and either oblivious or indifferent to the women near me.

"I am," I replied.

He held out his hand, speaking again as I clasped his fingers in a firm shake.

"I'm Raleigh Swinter," he said.

My neck prickled as our palms separated. *Raleigh Swinter.* The same last name as Skye Marie.

I swallowed and glanced over to the hockey players. TJ was distracted. Doubled over in a laugh, to be exact. I brought my attention back to the man in front of me and met his eyes, carefully polite and friendly.

"Ivy," I said.

He raised a thick eyebrow. "Ivy?"

He left the echo of my name hanging between us. A question. Pushing for a last name, or at least a bit more info. But I wasn't handing anything over.

I smiled extra sweetly. "Yes, that's right."

Now his eyebrows knit together in irritation for a second before he quickly regained his impassive expression. "It's nice to meet you."

"Likewise." I added a tinkling laugh to my saccharine smile, then let out a ramble. "But are you sure this the first time we've met? I feel like I've been introduced to *so* many people over the last few days. It's hard to keep them all straight. Your last name is kind of familiar, but maybe you're a celebrity of some kind, and I should just *know* who you are, anyway."

His lips pressed into a thin line. "From that, I'm going to infer that Travis has told you nothing."

It caught me completely off-guard. "Sorry?"

"You wouldn't be making jokes if you knew who I

was."

"I—"

"Regardless, he's got a shit-ton of nerve, bringing you here." He said it like a sneer. "Though I suppose that's par for the Travis course. More balls than brains."

He took a step closer. He wasn't much taller than me, but he held himself like he was used to his mere presence being intimidating.

Like hell am I going to be intimidated.

I didn't budge except to straighten my shoulders and ball up a fist. If he touched me—and he was pointing a finger between us like he was going to—I'd be sorely tempted to deliver one of my well-practiced punches. Or maybe I'd straight-up break the offending finger. Decorum and public appearance be damned. But he didn't bring the digit to my chest like I thought he would. He just leaned closer.

"You should demand the truth from him," he whisper-snarled.

I still didn't back away. "The truth about what, Mr. Swinter?"

"You're his new girlfriend?"

"Yes."

"Then ask him what the truth is."

"I don't know what you mean."

"The truth about my daughter. The truth about himself. The truth about *anything*."

His daughter. Well, that explained more precisely who he was, anyway.

And the rest of it?

Another heartbeat passed with his eyes boring into mine, and then TJ's voice carried in, his tone casual. "Hey, babe. I've been looking for you. Whatcha up to?"

I spun and found him striding toward me, a small frown marking his forehead.

"Hey," I said back to him. "I was just making new friends."

"Oh, yeah?"

"Yes. I think you—" I cut myself off as I turned once more and realized Raleigh Swinter had removed himself from my company while I was facing the other way.

"Ivy?" TJ asked.

"Um."

Why was I hesitating? There was no reason for me to take a single thing that had come from the older man's mouth as truth.

And no reason to lie to your client about who you were talking to either, right?

Except for the potential for reminding him of his heartbreak once again. The look on his face when he'd talked about Skye…it was so sad that it'd made me ache. Truthfully, it made me hurt now, too. But even so, I couldn't make myself straight-up lie.

I cleared my throat. "It was Raleigh Swinter. But he's gone now."

TJ's face went stiff, and when his spoke, his words were flat enough to make me blink. "I'm sure Mr. Swinter had more important people to talk to."

Normally, I might've taken that as an insult. But right now, concern was my dominant feeling. Especially when I saw the way TJ craned his neck and glared around the room, finally finding and zeroing in on Swinter, who really was talking to another group. TJ had a flinty look in his eyes. A determined one. And his hand was curled, just like mine had been a minute ago.

Shit.

I slid my palm to his, tightly closed my fingers, then gave him a small tug. A silent sigh of relief escaped my lips when he let me pull him wordlessly away. *Thank God.* I didn't pause until we were a decent distance from Swinter, and before I stopped, I glanced back to make sure the crowd blocked the other man from view. When I did halt, we were about as alone as we could be given the circumstances. The nearest people were another couple, locked in an intense conversation. I turned to TJ, expecting him to offer up some sort of explanation. He didn't do anything even close.

"We're leaving," he said instead, pulling his hand free.

"We just barely got here," I replied.

"I've taken the obligatory photos. Checked in with my manager. Left a large donation and bid on an entirely useless crystal duck centerpiece in the silent auction. I'm ready to leave."

"When did you have time to do all that?"

"Not my first rodeo," he stated. "And you were tied up. Apparently."

"Are you *mad* at me, TJ?" I asked. "Because that hardly seems fair."

"Yeah, well. That's life, isn't it?"

He sounded so cold it startled me. But not quite so much as it surprised me when he spun on his heel and strode away without looking back. And worse, it stung.

I started to call out then stopped just in time. Yelling for him to wait would draw attention. So would chasing after him.

"Goddammit," I said under my breath.

I glanced around, worried someone might've seen our rapid extraction from the main event and assumed we were in some kind of fight. TJ needed that about as much as he needed to be seen losing his mind over Raleigh Swinter. Thankfully, everyone in visual range was distracted by the fact that a team from the catering company had just swept in with an enormous cake on a rolling tray. Even the other couple strayed toward the fresh excitement.

I took a breath and hurried to catch up before someone *did* take notice. But TJ's legs were long, his stride fueled by determination. And unlike me, he wasn't hindered by a dress. All of which meant I didn't manage to reach his side until he was bursting out some side door and into the chilly night air. Even then, my success was more because he'd stopped than anything else. I almost rushed right past him. He didn't look at me. He just bent over, hands on his knees, breathing far more heavily than a man of his athletic ability ought to from such a short, fast walk.

I put my hand on his back. "TJ?"

He shook his head, and guilt tore through me. I clued in that he was overwhelmed. This was the second time I'd inadvertently brought Skye back into his life. First with that stupid police-report and now with my interaction with the other woman's father. Why hadn't I walked away from Raleigh the moment I heard his last name? A dead woman couldn't make threats on someone's life. And why would her father bother after all these years? Maybe if it had happened right after, but now?

Why the hell did I keep talking to Raleigh?

Then I remembered my initial reaction when

thinking about Skye Warren. That strange twinge of envy. Was this about that? Was I so curious about Raleigh Swinter because he was TJ's ex's father?

My throat burned, and the guilt intensified. And belatedly, I realized my hand was still on TJ's back.

Shit.

I started to let it fall. But I barely put an inch between us before his fingers shot out and grabbed mine. Not quite roughly, he pulled me to his chest and held me there. I should've been fighting to get away. Not just because it was inappropriate for me to be held in a tight embrace by my client. Not even because my conversation with his ex's dad was the source of his distress. But because of my past. And with anyone else, under any other circumstances, the need to get free would've been automatic. Knee-jerk, even. Hadn't I just been thinking about breaking Mr. Swinter's finger at the mere idea of being touched? But with TJ, it was different. It'd been different this whole time. His wide frame wasn't intimidating; it was comforting. Solid and safe, even when he was the one seeking support.

"I'm sorry," he mumbled into my hair.

My chest compressed. He wasn't the one who should be apologizing.

"It's fine," I said into his chest.

"It's not."

"I wouldn't say it was if it wasn't true."

His body relaxed, and he loosened his hold on me, then leaned back and looked down at me without quite letting me go. "You're way more forgiving of crazy outbursts than I am."

I tipped my head up and met his eyes. Maybe I should've said *I* was sorry for being jealous of dead woman. Or at least acknowledged that I knew it was painful for him to revisit that part of his life. But it suddenly felt like too much. Something that would leave me far too vulnerable. So I kept it in.

"Only girl in a houseful of boys, remember?" I said instead.

He chuckled, but his gaze was serious. Maybe even guarded.

"Can we go?" he asked. "Please?"

For a second, I wanted to joke that his so-called crazy outburst a couple of minutes ago hadn't made it seem optional, but the pinch around his eyes stopped me. And hadn't I told him that at the first sign of trouble, we could leave? Skye Marie Swinter's dad definitely seemed to fall under that category for TJ. So I just nodded. The relief on his face was as immediate as it was palpable. The crease on his forehead disappeared, and he smiled a real smile.

"And then some burgers and fries?" he suggested.

"Yeah, still a no on that one for me," I replied. "Can you imagine getting ketchup on this dress?"

I gestured down at the yellow fabric for emphasis then wished I hadn't. Because it occurred to me that the ketchup on the red dress would've blended right in.

Goddammit.

I didn't need the reminder.

"How about some takeout instead, then?" TJ asked hopefully as we started walking toward the front of the venue. "Fried chicken?"

I glanced toward the building where the gala was continuing on without us. "You've got to be the only person on the planet who'd rather eat fast food than caviar."

"Have you ever *had* caviar? It's gross."

I pursed my lips. The truth was, I hadn't ever had caviar, and it did look gross to me. But I wasn't going to give him the satisfaction of being right.

"Maybe it's my favorite food," I said.

"Maybe that's what's going to cause our 'official' breakup, then," he countered.

"Oh, is that all it takes? I thought I was going to have to do something drastic."

"Like what?"

"I don't know. Public argument. I could throw a pie in your face."

"A pie?" he echoed. "How does that make sense? Maybe a glass of cold water."

"How about the caviar itself?" I offered.

"I'll consider the idea and get back to you." He nudged my shoulder, and I realized that somehow, in the preceding few seconds, our fingers had become entwined.

It's for the public's sake, I reminded myself forcefully.

And we *had* just rounded the corner. The steps to the main entrance were directly in front of us. But to be honest, there wasn't exactly much of the public left to worry about at the moment. The event was in full swing inside, so only a few stragglers stood around—two smokers, a woman on her phone, and a guy tying his shoe, to be exact. I didn't even see any sign of the flashing cameras that'd been hounding the crowd when we arrived.

"One sec," TJ said.

He didn't wait for me to answer. He just gave my hand a squeeze before letting it go and jogging up to the valet station, where he engaged in a chat with the man behind the podium-style desk. My mind wasn't as still as my body.

Was it really just my feelings that made it seem like TJ's reaction to Raleigh Swinter was a bit much, or was it more than that? Was I being ungenerous? Childish? Overly fixated? I didn't know. But I did wonder if I was entirely sure it didn't relate back to his stalker.

Because he's still keeping things to himself, isn't he?

If I could've rewound and mentally bitten my tongue to hold back the thought, I would've done it. But it was already out there, rolling around in my head. And that meant Raleigh's words came back to me as well.

Ask him to tell you the truth.

Because TJ *was* holding back. I could feel it everywhere, all the way down to my bones.

Yeah, but he told you some things were off limits. So it's not really holding back at all, is it?

I frowned. He didn't owe me more just because I *wanted* to know more. But it was my job to fix this for him. I couldn't keep putting his feelings above that.

Great. Now I'm contradicting myself. Are my feelings making me too sensitive or making me go out of my way to not be sensitive enough?

My hand tapped my thigh for a second. If I kept going in this direction, I'd soon lose all impartiality.

Focus, Ivy. Focus.

What kind of private investigator was I if every case I undertook became personal? I *had* to ask TJ about Raleigh. There was so much animosity there that it just made sense to pursue it. And it wasn't as though any other leads had cropped up yet. Skye Marie's dad was the only person who'd shown any outward dislike for TJ.

I frowned harder. Did that make him *less* suspicious? Maybe so. Because why go to all the trouble of the notes and the stalking only to confront me in a public place? The only way to figure it was to ask TJ a few more pointed questions about the Swinters. Something I dreaded.

TJ was jogging back to me now, keys dangling from his forefinger.

"It's a two-minute walk to the truck," he said. "Figured it was a waste of time for the valet to do it when we could get there faster ourselves."

I nodded. I didn't relish the idea of standing around waiting. The culprit could be anywhere. He or she could be any*one*. Raleigh Swinter. Or even the guy who'd finally finished tying his shoe and was now intently studying his phone without glancing our way.

TJ held out his arm, and I took it, glad to be on our way. He was quieter than usual, but I was okay with that. I was honestly a bit worried I'd blurt out some of my concerns if we started talking. The silence mitigated that. But once we got back to his place, I'd dig in a little more to figure out if there was any reason to investigate Raleigh Swinter. Respectfully. Professionally. Maybe I'd check in on my brother, too, and run it by him to get his thoughts. I wouldn't tell him about *my* feelings, obviously.

Yeah, no shit.

But realistically, I'd have to be conscious of giving something away. I couldn't even *hint* at my self-doubt or where it was coming from, or he'd break out of the hospital, put on wig, and try to be TJ's fake girlfriend in my stead. Inwardly, I snorted at the image. But it was likely close to true. And I'd far rather have him believe I was bowing to his more extensive experience than for him to become aware that it felt entirely too normal to be walking through the street with the client's fingers threaded through my own.

And yet...you're not pulling away, are you, Pint-Size?

I couldn't muster up an eyeroll. Because I *wasn't* pulling away. Instead, I ignored my brotherly subconscious and opened my mouth to ask TJ if we were almost at the truck yet—it seemed like more than two minutes had passed. But at the same moment, we went around a corner and came face-to-face with the vehicle's grill. And there, on the hood of his truck, was a now familiar-looking note. White paper. Pasted-on letters. A fresh reminder that the threat hadn't eased.

Chapter Thirty-Three

"What the fuck?" TJ said, his voice low and his gaze whipping back and forth as though he'd find the culprit lingering nearby.

I, on the other hand, was momentarily still. Transfixed by the experience of seeing one of the notes appear live. When I'd been looking at the small collection of them amongst TJ's things, they'd seemed half-comical. Not because of the content but because of the medium. I'd thought then that it was like someone had watched one too many kidnapping movies and taken their lead from that. But now, seeing the effect here, I knew I'd been wrong. It was truly creepy. The effort of cutting out those letters. The painstaking application of them, one by one. And the way they stood out from the white paper...

My body unfroze, but only so it could shudder for a second before I regained my composure.

"TJ," I said softly, "I just want to point out that this would be a good moment to call the cops. And before you argue, I know it's not what you want to do, but there could be real evidence here. Fingerprints. DNA. What are the chances some epithelial skin cells didn't get attached along with that glue?"

His answer came quickly, and though the words themselves could've been taken as angry, his tone was as soft as mine had been. "You think I don't know that, Ivy? I've told myself a hundred times the police would be able to fix this. But then what? Where does that leave me?"

"Alive." The word barely made it through my lips.

This was part of the job. Keeping clients safe. Advising them of the options. But I couldn't seem to manage to keep myself at any kind of emotional distance. The idea that someone might kill TJ cut at me.

You're a disaster.

I didn't know if it was Chuck in my head or just my own conscience, but either way, it spurred me. I'd kept TJ out of harm's way so far, hadn't I? And it'd been only a few days. I *would* get this solved.

"Okay," I said firmly. "No cops. But I had to remind you."

"Thank you." He flashed a quick, somewhat cheeky smile. "For understanding *and* for reminding me. I love being nagged and understood."

I rolled my eyes, but my heart wasn't in it. I'd nag him to death if it kept him from, well...death.

"Let's have a look at what it says before we move it," I suggested.

I channeled some confidence to go along with my words, and I stepped forward. TJ moved too, but he was a heartbeat behind. And the slight lag created a small space between us. Barely a foot. But it was just enough to let me see a sudden flash of someone furtively ducking away from a nearby bus shelter. And my reaction was automatic. Note forgotten, I yanked my dress to my knees and hollered over my shoulder.

"Wait here!"

And I launched myself after the rapidly

disappearing figure.

Behind me, I heard TJ call out my name, followed by the sound of his feet hitting the pavement, a clear indication he wasn't going to listen. But I didn't bother to look back. I was *going* to catch this guy, and I was going to do it now.

My target went around a corner.

I pulled my dress higher and lengthened my stride and reached the same corner in seconds. I half-expected him to be gone. My heart had already sunk. My feet had slowed. But there he was. Standing still in the spotlight of a dim streetlamp. Hedged in by a parked cube van that completely blocked the next alley and a chain-link fence that surrounded a playground. He was stuck.

He swung back as though to make a break for it in my direction. At the same moment, I sped up and dashed forward.

C'mon, c'mon.

He turned again, his hands finding the fence. Up, up, he pulled himself. But he wasn't fast enough; I was there.

My hand shot up and grasped the hem of his hooded sweatshirt, and I yanked with all my might. For a second, he maintained his grip. Then he came tumbling off the fence, his fall aided and abetted by gravity. Just in time, I stepped sideways. Except as he sailed by, something clunky smacked into the side of my face hard enough to make me yelp and jump back even more.

A weapon. He's got a weapon.

"Ivy!" TJ called out from behind me.

"Get down!" I hollered.

I didn't check to see if he listened. My attention

focused on the man, my eyes roaming for whatever it was he'd used to hit me while I prayed it wasn't a gun.

"Please," he said from his spot on the pavement. "Don't hurt me."

It wasn't an unexpected plea. And it could easily be a ruse. But as my heartrate slowed and my vision focused a bit better, I saw that his posture matched his words. He was curled up, his arms over his face.

"It was just a picture," he added.

My brow creased. "What?"

He dropped his arms, but he remained submissive. "I knew the truck belonged to someone from the gala. I took a picture of the note, but that's all. And it was in public."

I chanced a look over my shoulder. TJ *had* obeyed my yelled order. He was crouched down beside the cube van.

I brought my attention back to the cowering man, and it was then I realized what had hit me in the face. A camera.

Still, I didn't let my guard down.

"Who are you?" I asked, my tone authoritative—like I had a right to an answer.

"Stevie Styles," the man replied. "From *The Daily Local*?"

"The online news rag?"

"I prefer to think of it as a celebrity tell-all site," he said.

I pressed my teeth together for a second, then blew out a breath and called to TJ. "It's not him."

In a heartbeat, he was at my side, his hand resting on my arm just above my elbow.

"This guy's a reporter," I explained.

"Why doesn't that seem any better?" TJ asked.

Stevie Styles shifted to a sitting position then reached around to grab the fence and pull himself to his feet. "Who were you guys expecting?"

I narrowed my eyes. "None of your business. *Less* than none of your business."

But he'd clearly regained some of his confidence, because he shook his head. "The news literally *is* my business. And whatever's going on with you two…it's news."

"Give me the camera," I snapped.

His hands tightened on it. "No."

I took a step forward, but TJ tugged me back, speaking to Stevie as he did. "What if we offer you something better?"

I flicked a look his way, and he gave my elbow a reassuring squeeze. Even so, I was suddenly so apprehensive that my mouth went dry, and my palms grew clammy. What was he going to give to this reporter?

"You delete the photo—for good—and we'll tell you something no one else knows," he said. "And we'll toss in a *different* photo. An authorized one."

Stevie's interest was visibly piqued; he leaned forward. "I'm all ears."

TJ squeezed me again, which only made me feel worse. Now a lightheaded sensation hit me. But I couldn't muster a protest.

"This is my girlfriend," TJ said, then dropped his voice to a conspiratorial level. "But she's not *really* my girlfriend."

I wanted to gasp out a protest. I *would* have if it weren't for the fact that staying on my feet required concentration.

The reporter's eyes tipped my way, his gaze burning. "Go on."

"She's my fiancé," TJ whispered.

His statement ought to have made me feel at least a little better. He wasn't confessing our arrangement. Which I ought to have realized he wouldn't do. But was this any better? Sure, it was in line with the story we'd fed to TJ's manager about the seriousness of our relationship. But that was because we needed to make sure Bram didn't think he was breaking the terms of his contract. But telling this to a *reporter*? That made it fodder for public consumption.

I swayed again and managed to find my voice, albeit in a smaller way than I would've liked. "TJ."

The only acknowledgement I got was one more squeeze. Other than that, his whole focus was on Stevie Styles.

"You delete that picture—permanently—and we'll pose for an engagement announcement," he said. "It'll be an exclusive."

The reporter looked toward me again. "You on board with this?"

I forced a nod. What else could I do? We couldn't chance letting a photo of the note getting out. And we'd already set up the scenario, hadn't we? At least this way we could control the narrative. Better that than someone else getting wind of our supposed engagement and running away with the story.

"Okay," Stevie agreed. "You've got yourself a deal."

TJ smiled. "And with no threat intended, you can imagine how upset we'd be if you didn't honor the arrangement."

"Are you kidding?" the other man replied. "An exclusive story about the Troublemaker's engagement is far better than whatever the hell I took a picture of before. Watch."

He positioned the camera in front of his body, clicked through, then turned our way. In bright lettering, the screen announced that it currently contained zero photographs. He clicked again, and now the screen confirmed there was also nothing archived.

For the first time in an excessive number of minutes, I relaxed. My shoulders dropped, and my breaths stopped burning. It wasn't ideal, but it was a relief that no one would see the note. And even more of a relief that the reporter seemed to have no clue what he'd stumbled upon.

"Thank you," I said. "We appreciate your discretion."

"Happy to oblige," Stevie stated. "Now. The light here obviously isn't the best, but if you guys pose in front of that big van, I think I can make it look good. Does that work for you?"

Eager now to get it over with, I grabbed TJ's hand and tugged him to the makeshift backdrop.

"How's this?" I asked.

"Great," the report said. "All I need now is the perfect kiss."

"What?"

Stevie laughed like I'd said something hilarious. "The money shot. Every good engagement shoot has one. And since I'm only *getting* one shot, I wanna make sure it's that one."

Shit.

I swallowed and turned to TJ. He had to have an argument against the idea, didn't he? Some very reasonable excuse as to why we couldn't kiss for the camera. Lord knew my own mind had just gone blank. But as our gazes met, his hand found my cheek, and his head tilted down. He wasn't protesting at all. And to be honest, neither was I.

My eyes fluttered closed.

On autopilot, I pushed to my toes.

And TJ's mouth found mine, locking there and blocking out the world.

Chapter Thirty-Four

A hundred pinpricks of heat exploded along my lips. They danced up my face and made my skin tingle. They slid into my mouth and down my throat and stole my breath away.

Without meaning to, I lifted my arms to TJ's shoulders and pressed my hands to the back of his neck. His palms landed on my hips, tugging me closer. And there was heat there, too. Searing from his fingers and through my clothes. Rising between us. It was like a wild, living thing seeking a home in all the places where our bodies met. And I wanted more. So much so that when TJ pulled back, finishing the kiss by pressing his forehead to mine, my eyes flew open, a demand ready to fall from my lips. But the world came back into focus. *Stevie Styles* came back into focus.

Shit. Oh, shit. This is worse than the goddamn note.

I wriggled free and opened my mouth, but TJ beat me to it.

"You won't be using that one, Mr. Styles," he said without looking away from me, his voice a little rough.

The reporter chuckled. "Yeah, no. That was more money-shot than I was counting on. I didn't even click. Wanna try again?"

I shook my head, but TJ was already leaning in again. Thankfully—and regretfully too, if I was being truthful—his lips brushed mine in a firm but nearly chaste peck. Then camera flashed, and he quickly stepped back.

"You good, Mr. Styles?" he asked.

"Have you set a date?" the other man replied.

"Not yet," TJ said. "But if you give me your card, I'll be sure you're the first person to get a heads-up."

"Not necessary," Stevie told him. "I already got way more than I could've been hoping for. You two lovebirds have a nice evening."

I let my eyes sink shut for a few seconds, trying to calm the race of my heart and the rapid speed of my breathing. I waited until the sound of the reporter's footfalls had faded before daring to open them again. When I did, I expected to find TJ watching me. My face was pre-emptively red with embarrassment, and I mentally fumbled for some excuse for my overly enthusiastic response to what was supposed to be a staged kiss. *Was* there any excuse for that? But he was looking in the other direction anyway, his hands jammed into his pockets. A heartbeat passed, and he spoke up, but only so he could ask me the exact same question he'd posed to the reporter just a couple of moment earlier.

"You good?"

I blinked. "What?"

He just repeated himself. "You good?"

I couldn't pretend it didn't nettle me. That was it? He wasn't even going to acknowledge the kiss? He was going to talk to me the same way he talked to Stevie Styles?

Maybe because it was just a show. It's not like any of the rest of it's real.

I set my jaw and nodded.

At what felt like snail's pace, we made our way back to TJ's truck. We were quiet again, but this time around, it was unpleasant. For me, anyway. I kept stealing little glances at him, trying to get a read on what was going on in his head. His face was as impassive as I'd ever seen it, and the more minutes that ticked by, the more it bothered me. How was it possible he'd made my whole body light up with one kiss, and he didn't seem at all fazed? By the time we reached the truck, I was bristling with irritation. My hand kept opening and closing, and the punching bag at the gym flashed into my head. What I wouldn't have given to be hitting it right this second.

I'd let myself get far too involved in my role as TJ's fake girlfriend, and my teeth wanted to gnash together. Worse, I'd known it the whole time, but I'd done nothing to stop it. And worse than worse, I knew better than most. Someone might assume I'd learned my lesson. But nope. Apparently not.

I walked faster.

Part of me knew I was being ridiculous. Overreacting. Oversensitive. Over everything. Not to mention the unprofessional piece.

Well, on the bright side...hurt feelings are better than what happened last time. The thought made me flinch, and I sucked in a breath. *But the real goal is no feelings.*

Maybe Charles and his obnoxious need to protect me were valid. It was a deflating idea. One that sucked at my lungs and made them burn all over again. But did he have a point? The last time I'd dived into fieldwork, I'd gotten in over my head. And now this?

I didn't *want* him to be right. I didn't even want

him to be in the same *room* as being right. I wished I couldn't see his point of view, and I almost wished I'd never agreed to take this job so I wouldn't have to seriously consider what happened.

Damn you, Chuck. And damn you, TJ, too.

I was so caught up in my thoughts it took me an extra minute to realize my hockey player companion had suddenly stopped walking. I only noticed *then* because a cool gust of wind kicked up on the side of me where he'd been. It drew out a shiver, and I spun around. We'd reached his truck—gone past it, in fact—and though he stood just in front of it, he wasn't paying any attention to it. He'd shoved his hands back into his pockets and had a strained look on his face.

"Ivy, I'm sorry," he said. "What happened back there…" He gestured in the general direction from which we'd come. "It shouldn't have."

All the embarrassment I'd been fighting came roaring back to life. He was *sorry*? Somehow, that was so much worse than everything that'd been going on in my head.

"It was just work," I replied with far more neutrality than I meant. "No apology necessary."

"That's not—" He ran his hand over his hair and muttered something incomprehensible then tried again. "I'm not—I don't—For fuck's sake."

"Seriously, TJ. We have more important things to worry about than putting on too good a show for Stevie Styles."

"It's really not—" Now he cut himself off with a growl that managed to come across as helpless.

This is getting worse by the second, Pint-Size, Charles said in my head.

I breathed in and out and in and out again, trying to find a smidge of inner calm. Whatever TJ was attempting to communicate, it wasn't helping in the slightest.

"Let's pretend it didn't happen," I said. "Do you want to grab the note from your truck?"

His mouth worked silently, and he shook his head like he was going to argue. But after a quick narrowing of his eyes and a second headshake, he strode over to his vehicle and did as I'd suggested, snapping the paper up then holding it out.

I didn't take it from him. I just stared down at the creepy lettering and read the message.

PROCEED WITH CAUTION.

I forgot about my feelings. I didn't *quite* forget about the kiss along with that, but it did manage to slide to the back of my mind.

"Shit, TJ," I said. "This is too damned generic."

The words could apply to almost anything. Crossing a road. Getting into a car. Walking up a flight of stairs.

But we have time, I reminded myself. *He's sticking to the pattern.*

"Two days," I murmured, bringing my eyes back to TJ. "We should be safe for that long."

"Great. A countdown until my career explodes."

Something about his sarcastic statement caught my ear and made a skin prickle.

"Say that again," I told him.

"What?"

"The thing about counting down until your career explodes."

"Not something I want to dwell on," he said.

"I know. But…" *But what?* "Let's get in the truck."

TJ frowned at my lack of explanation, but he didn't argue. He tucked away the threatening note, unlocked the doors, then held mine open for me. And by the time he was in the driver's seat and turning over the engine, I'd figured out what had tickled at my brain.

"What if that's their goal?" I asked. "Ruining your hockey career, I mean."

TJ guided the truck on the road. "Then I'm sure they could've found an easier, faster way to do it."

"But what if that's part of it?"

"What do you mean?"

"What if they're doing it slowly so that you feel it coming?"

"That's—" He stopped as though searching for the right word, then shrugged.

I filled it in for him. "It's vengeful. Way more personal than someone just trying to hurt you."

TJ's posture tightened. Did he see the new potential motive as changing things? Because I sure did.

"Can you think of someone—literally *any*one— who might want to see your career ruined?" I asked.

His thumbs tapped the steering wheel, and for a minute he was quiet. Visibly lost in concentration. I waited it out. But when he spoke up, it wasn't to give me a real answer to my question.

"How can something be more personal than wanting someone dead?" he replied instead.

I stared straight ahead as I responded. "Because dead is final. Suffering, not so much."

He was quiet again. For longer this time. I focused on the windshield, watching the streetlights and city blocks go by and ignoring the way my brain tried to replay that kiss. Or *tried* to ignore it. But it wasn't easy. Leave it to me to misread a situation so badly. To read into all the moments over the preceding couple of days. Even that conversation we'd had while he was asleep.

Then again, I'd spent the last four years totally avoiding men and romance—totally avoiding social activities except with my brothers—so was it that surprising I'd mix up the signals? I mean, sure. TJ might find me attractive in a general way. I wasn't so down on myself that I didn't think I could date if I wanted to. But he didn't lack the ability to separate our fake relationship from the real thing.

Ugh. Just think of this as wakeup call and move on.

At last, TJ sighed. I stifled a relieved one to go right along with his resigned one. Thank God the silence was over.

"I just don't know," he said. "I told you before that I can't come up with a single person who might hate me enough to murder me. I wasn't a stellar guy for a while, sure, but bad enough to kill? I don't think so." He shifted uncomfortably in his seat. "But what if I accidentally did something that made someone think I wrecked their life?"

My hand got halfway to his arm before I clued-in to what I was about to do and pulled it back. Somehow, touching him had become a habit in a matter of days.

Professional from here on out, I told myself sternly.

"When we get back to your place, we'll go through everything again," I said aloud. "We'll doublecheck that anti-fan mail. We'll look at every line of every letter. And if we don't find anything there, we'll cast a wider net. Look online. Go through social media comments."

"Do you think we missed something? 'Cause that online part would take a hell of a lot longer than two days," he pointed out.

I managed a joke. "Oh, you're *that* popular, are you?"

TJ offered a chuckle, and I smiled, too. But neither of us seemed truly amused. And my mind was already moving forward. *Had* we missed something? Or to put it more accurately had *I* missed something? Were we about to have to put ourselves in lockdown in order to figure this out? Even if we did, would it be enough? The warning note really didn't offer any hint of what was to come.

PROCEED WITH CAUTION.

And as I rolled the words over in my head, I swallowed. Because truthfully, they could apply to the investigation itself.

Chapter Thirty-Five

By the time we pulled into TJ's driveway, the clouds had rolled in. I made another joke, this one about his house being a lightning rod for bad weather, but it fell short when an actual bolt of lightning pierced the sky right after I'd spoken. We hurried inside and separated to get changed out of our gala clothes. Once I was clad in sweats and a T-shirt, I took a minute to fire off a text to my brother, who was up late and doing fine. After answering a few questions about the case, I signed off with a fib about heading to bed now, and made my way to living room, where TJ waited.

I stopped just outside the space, holding my breath and studying him for a second. He was facing slightly in the other direction, but I had a perfect view of his profile. Had he showered? His hair looked damp, and I swore I could smell a hint of freshy, soapy scent as well. He definitely hadn't shaved. His tanned jaw had a graze of stubble, a few shades darker than his hair. I hadn't noticed any roughness during our kiss, but then again, I hadn't noticed much of anything but his lips. Which, at the moment, were pursed in concentration.

His lips. Dammit. My breath caught in my throat, and I forced my attention away from his face. *C'mon, Ivy. Get your shit together.*

My eyes landed on the coffee table. TJ had laid out the same boxes we'd gone through before, but as I took a step toward them, I paused, distracted again. He hadn't put on the fire or made hot chocolate like he'd done during the other storm. Now that I was thinking about it, the lights were on their brightest setting, too. A sharp contrast to the gloom visible through the nearest windows. Almost excessively so. Was he doing his best to diffuse any semblance of romance? Not that I could blame him. And not that I disagreed with the setup, either. It was better, really. Like drawing a line.

"Hey," I said, sinking down onto the nearest couch like I'd just walked in rather than had been standing there staring for at least two minutes.

"Hey," TJ echoed. "Everything all right?"

I nodded.

"Good," he said.

But instead of joining me on the couch, he seated himself on the floor on the other side of the coffee table.

I opened my mouth then closed it.

This would be a lot easier if he didn't smell so nice, wouldn't it?

Viciously, I shoved aside the unbidden question and grabbed the nearest envelope. I got only as far as sticking my fingers into it to retrieve the letter inside before another flash of lightning made me jump. A resounding boom followed it, and the whole place plunged into blackness. For an extended moment, my pulse surged. It was so dark that I couldn't see anything, which made me want to brace for *every*thing.

"TJ?" I whispered at the same as he said, "For crying out loud. Again?"

My body slumped. There was a shuffle, and I knew he must be standing up. Then, as though to prove my assumption correct, lightning crashed all around the house and lit up the room brighter than a camera flash. TJ was on his feet, rummaging through the cabinet on the other side of the room. As the flash ended, thunder drowned out the sound of his movements, but moments later, I felt him drop down beside me.

"These are electric candles," he said, his voice low and close. "Which seems like a contradiction or something. But hang on."

I sat perfectly still as his clean scent filled my nose and his arm brushed against mine. A few additional seconds passed, and a small orange glow bathed a few inches of table in something that could barely be called light. TJ was fumbling with the next electric candle—more like tealights for inside jack-o-lanterns, from my perspective—but the switch didn't seem to be working. He tried it about ten times, muttering to himself, then gave up and grabbed the next one. He worked his way through nine more, and only a single other one actually turned on.

"Well, I guess that answers the question on whether I'm an ideal companion for an apocalypse adventure," he said. "Apparently, my prepper skills leave something to be desired."

"Lucky for you, I'm here for the danger," I replied. "If you were *good* at prepping, you wouldn't need me quite so much."

He laughed, and it was a relief to hear how real it sounded. But my nerves barely loosened before TJ ruined it with his next statement.

"Trust me, Ivy. I need you."

My tongue stuck to the roof of my mouth, and I swallowed and stared at the two artfully flickering tealights.

So much for a lack of romance.

Dammit, I really needed to find a way to stop my brain from continually pointing these kinds of thing out.

"That's probably my cue to start earning my keep," I made myself say lightly.

I adjusted my body, trying to put a gap between us as I reached for the envelope I'd unconsciously abandoned when the lights went out. It backfired. The couch cushion sagged, and now our legs were touching. And seriously. Why *did* he have to smell so good all the time?

"Ivy."

Even though I *knew* he was right there, his voice beside my ear startled me. I turned. And he was more than right there. I could feel his breath on my lips.

"You didn't let me finish apologizing before," he said.

I inched back, but there was no way to gracefully extricate myself from him or the sunken couch cushion, and I gained only the smallest smidge of room. "Because there was nothing to apologize for."

He shook his head. "I don't think you understood."

"What's to understand? Whatever we do in the name of solving this is just what *has* to be done. I'm not worried about it."

"See?"

"What?"

"You saying that *proves* you didn't understand why I was apologizing."

Somehow, *he* managed to adjust enough to give us a bit of space. But it didn't do much good anyway because he also reached out and touched by face. The tips of his fingers ran from the top of my cheek to my chin, leaving a trail of heat in their wake and shortening my breath before he dropped his hand.

"It was an excuse," he said softly.

My reply was a whisper. "I don't understand."

"Yeah, I know. Isn't that what I just told you?"

His lips curved up, and I could practically feel them all over again. My eyes fluttered without my permission. I wanted to groan. I had to keep him talking, or I'd probably climb into his lap.

Professional. But I could hardly hear my own thoughts over the thump of my heart.

"Make this make sense, TJ," I said, failing miserably at anything even *close* to detached.

"It was an excuse," he told me again.

"What was?"

"The ruse for the reporter."

I still wasn't following. His mouth turned up even more.

"You're so...*capable*," he stated.

"Why does that sound like an insult and compliment at the same time?"

I didn't need to keep him talking. I was fooling myself. I needed to jump up, run to the bathroom, and splash a whole bucket load of cold water over my face. Maybe over my whole body.

"Just a compliment," TJ said.

"Then it definitely has a *but* coming after it," I replied.

"You're so capable, but..." He cleared his throat.

"In case you were wondering, this is the worst apology I've ever received."

"I'm embarrassed."

It wasn't anything I would've expected to hear, and my eyes stopped their flutter. "What?"

He shrugged, but the gesture seemed anything but casual. "I try hard nowadays not to be too much of an asshole, but with you...tonight...I couldn't help it."

"Okay, I officially have *no* idea what you're talking about. Nothing you did tonight was asshole-esque in any way. And you're sorry for kissing me because of a ruse that was meant to follow the *existing* ruse?"

At least my confusion had let me regain control of my faculties. I shifted on the couch again, this time managing to pull back enough that one wrong move wouldn't send my mouth headlong into his.

"I wanted to kiss you, Ivy," TJ said, and I swear to God his cheeks were pink.

"You..." I was at a momentary loss. "That's it?"

"What do you mean *that's it*? I saw an opportunity, and I jumped on it."

It took a second because I was still hung-up on the fact that he'd admitted he *wanted* to kiss me, but finally, my brain kind of put together what he was getting at. Sort of. It was like he'd used the fiancé angle and the resulting kiss for the sake of the kiss itself. Now he felt bad about it.

"I could've just refused," I said slowly.

"Could you?" he replied.

"Of course, I could've. I'm a grown woman."

"But you were doing it to fool the stupid reporter. I wasn't. False pretenses."

Maybe he had a point. Or maybe he *would* have had a point if not for one small detail.

"I wanted to kiss you, too," I blurted.

"You did?" He sounded ridiculously hopeful.

I straightened my shoulders. "I'm not that good of an actor."

He let out a breath. "I'm sorry anyway."

"Sorry you kissed me?"

"Sorry I did it dishonestly."

I didn't know what to say. Pretty much anything felt like the wrong thing. Accepting his apology made it seem like he'd done something bad. Not accepting it felt unnatural. I'd already admitted that it was reciprocal, which went against my resolve to make sure things stayed within professional bounds.

Maybe it's good to have it out there, I reasoned. *Maybe it's the best way to put things back into the box where they ought to have stayed in the first place.*

But when I opened my mouth, something else came out instead. "If it would make you feel better about it, you could kiss me again."

Chapter Thirty-Six

I regretted the words as soon as they were out of my mouth. My face was as hot as it could get. I was desperately glad it was dark. Especially since for an extra long moment, while I was dying inside, second by second, TJ said and did nothing. He just stared at me. His gaze, darkened to deepest ocean blue, pinned me where I sat. But right around the time when I was beginning to think we might stay stuck in the frozen tableau forever, he cleared his throat.

"How would it make *you* feel?" he asked.

Now it was my turn to stare at him. I didn't know quite what to say. Something Chuck and all my other brothers would've probably found amusing, given how they often told me I always had an answer for everything. But how *would* it make me feel? Lost in the moment. Covered in goosebumps. Wanting more and more.

But also...

Bad about myself and my inability to do what I wanted and keep things above board. Maybe like I was wrong and not good enough for fieldwork after all. And most of all...vulnerable. The worst feeling of all.

Unexpected tears stung my eyes, and I didn't drop my gaze quickly enough to disguise them.

"Whoa," TJ said. "I'm not *that* bad of a kisser, am I?"

A watery laugh escaped. "No, not at all."

"Good. Because my ego was about to take a serious blow."

"It was a great kiss, TJ."

"Let's not exaggerate too much. My ego doesn't need stroking anymore than it needs to be beaten down."

I laughed again and wiped my eyes, oddly unembarrassed by the fact that my emotions were on display. "I ruined that moment, didn't I?"

"Honesty never ruins anything," he said.

I opened my mouth to agree, but Raleigh Swinter's face filled my head. *Tell him to tell you the truth.* And even if the moment hadn't been ruined before, it was ruined for me now. Was TJ being honest with me? And if he wasn't, if he was still holding something back, then how could he cling to the claim that being truthful was the best way to go?

Ironic much?

Another man's face floated to the front of my mind, overtaking Raleigh's, and my throat went dry. And TJ was staring at me expectantly, which made all *three* men's faces blur together. I shuddered, abruptly nauseous.

"I don't think we're going to get much done here in the dark," I said. "We can pick this up again in the morning."

TJ frowned. I knew what must be running through his head. I'd said we were safe for two more days, but now I wanted to give up some of those precious hours. And we hadn't even been discussing that in the first place. Our conversation had been personal. He'd asked me a question I hadn't really answered. So what switch had flipped? But he didn't say any of that.

"To be honest with *you*, Ivy..." he said instead. "A relationship of any kind isn't on my radar either."

I stiffened. "Who brought up anything about a relationship?"

"No one. I didn't mean—"

"Look. Don't get me wrong. You really seem like a nice guy. And like I said before, I wanted to kiss you, too. There's not much point in lying about it, and I don't want you to feel like you took advantage of the situation or of me."

"Ivy."

I stood up. I was fully aware I was being prickly. And maybe slightly petty. But I wasn't going to back down.

"I have some shit in my past, too," I said.

"I think it's safe to say that we all do," he replied.

"Exactly." I stood up. "I'll see you in the morning, okay?"

I didn't wait for him to answer. And I didn't look back. I hurried away, almost at a run by the time I reached my temporary bedroom.

Well, I guess that ends the brief run of not *being embarrassed by my feelings,* I thought as I closed the door behind me and pressed my back to it.

I tried to laugh and failed miserably. I also stayed where I was, half-expecting, maybe half-hoping TJ would follow me. I even braced myself for it. But there was nothing but silence. Several minutes passed before I finally conceded that he wasn't coming. As I gave up and eased away from the door, exhaustion hit me. The preceding days had been trying. I'd been bombed. My brother was in the hospital. The case had forced me into a role that might be classified as my worst nightmare. It ticked every box that would rehash my trauma. So why was I so hurt by TJ telling me he didn't want a relationship? It wasn't like *I* wanted one. And why did it bother me so much that I thought he might be keeping more from me, when I knew perfectly well that I was keeping at least as much from him?

I sank down onto the bed, sat there for a second, then climbed right in and pulled the covers up over my head. I closed my eyes and tried to make my mind go blank.

Fat chance of that, it said in reply, tossing out a reminder that even if I went to sleep now, it wouldn't change a single thing about what I had to do.

I flipped over. Once. Twice. Three times.

I lay on my back and stared at the ceiling.

I closed my eyes and counted to three hundred.

I even screamed into my pillow in hopes that it would release something enough to send me over into dreamland.

None of it helped.

I finally had to accept that no matter what I did, no matter how exhausted I was, it wasn't going to be that easy.

"Oh, so this is *easy*?" I grumbled.

What's bothering you most, Pint-Size? my brother's voice asked.

"Everything, Chuck. All of it."

I tossed back the blanket and swung my feet to the floor.

But what *was* bothering me most?

The conversation with TJ was an embarrassment. Clearly.

Not having any real clues was a frustration.

My inability to remain objective was a personal bone of contention.

"All of it," I repeated.

Except as I spoke out loud, Raleigh Swinter made another appearance. And yeah, honestly. What he'd said to me about TJ was definitely an issue. Even when I tried to remind myself that I shouldn't be listening to a complete stranger over a man I knew—or sort of knew and at least *liked*—I still couldn't shake it. Was it just about the idea that TJ was keeping a secret? What if whatever it was, it was the key to figuring out who was after him? Was there some other way I could find out, short of telling him what Raleigh said and demanding an explanation?

Because that *would do wonders for our trust, wouldn't it?*

But as I thought about it about more, I shook my head to myself. Trust wasn't the issue. I did trust TJ. Which went against both my experience and maybe my better judgement in general. Trust came with risk. Trust led to mistakes. Trust steered people wrong.

And yet...

My gut insisted TJ wasn't deceiving me with a willful intention to hurt me. It was almost like he was protecting him*self.*

"From what?"

Something to do with the Swinters? That seemed most likely.

Almost absently, my eyes wandered toward my phone. I'd plugged it in and left it on the nightstand after texting Charles. I'd already looked TJ up on the internet, but would it hurt to do it again?

Now my eyes went to the door. I envisioned TJ on the other side of it, and a little stab of guilt threaded its way under my skin. But this was business. Looking clients up online wasn't a violation; it was part of the job. There was no reason to feel bad about it. If anything, it was worse to think of it as being wrong.

With that in mind, I snagged my phone and opened the browser. But as my thumb hovered over the letters, I changed my mind and pulled up my contacts list instead. Quickly, I scrolled through to the person I wanted. *Gilly Rosefield.* I hesitated. Gilly was both a cop and a long-time a friend. She was also tall and blonde and curvy with a bubbly personality—a woman often underestimated in the same way people underestimated me. She'd used her considerable know-how to help me bust through a few blocked cases over the years, and she was always happy to cut through red tape in the name of justice. No one knew how to legally disperse information without bullshit like Gilly. But she was also someone who I hadn't contacted since everything had gone wrong for me during my last fieldwork stint.

I bit my lip, swallowed my worry, and typed up a message. *Hey, Gilly. Long time since we talked. Wondering if you might have time to do a quick check on a name for me?*

I wasn't expecting a reply right away if at all. It was late. She might be holding onto some resentment from the lack of contact followed by the spontaneous request. I wouldn't blame her. But I didn't even get to switch back to the browser before my phone dinged with an incoming message.

Ivy!!! Gilly had written. *Where've you been, girl?*

Figured you ran away and eloped or something. On night shifts this week, stuck at the station on desk duty. Blah. Bored. So, yeah. I'll look up whatever I can. Client or perp?

Smiling at her exuberance and immediate willingness to help without any caveats, I typed up a reply. *Client.*

Then I hesitated. My finger hovered over the phone and the send icon. Not just because I'd assured TJ—or to be more accurate, Ames Security had assured TJ—that we wouldn't involve the police but also because of the reporter and his engagement photo. Gilly was discreet. But she might be hurt I'd kept a supposed engagement from her. I didn't want to lie, and I didn't want to explain, either. Maybe by the time the photo was published, I'd have this figured out, and maybe she'd understand. But maybe not.

I hit the back button then typed, *Prefer not to say.*

Ooooooh, she replied. *Juicy. What's the name?*

Travis Jones.

Dude. The hockey guy?

That's the one, I told her.

Lucky, she wrote back. *He's cute, capital C. I mean CUTE. Or Cute? Gah. Whatever. Is he hot in person? No, wait. Don't answer that, I don't want to know if he's not. But I bet he is. Hang tight. I'll see what I can find.*

Impatiently, I waited. Tapping my foot. Scrolling through social media while *not* looking up TJ details. Several minutes ticked by, and I was about to text her once more when my phone binged again. The message was a long one.

Okay. It's a bit weird. Your buddy Mr. Jones was

involved in some kind of car accident. Not the driver. Not a passenger. Not even a witness.

That *was* weird. I frowned and kept reading.

Bear with me because some of this stuff was redacted. Something to do with an out-of-court agreement of some kind. A non-disclosure for a car accident? Sus. Anyway, I'm filling in a few blanks. So your guy showed up after the fact. Caused a scene. Looks like a rookie attended and made a statement. Then a lawyer got involved. No arrest, no charges. Any of that help you?

I stared down at the phone screen and asked myself the same question. The answer seemed to be a resounding *no*. Was this what he was keeping from me? If so, why? Did he think it was irrelevant?

My phone chimed yet again.

Oh, hang on! Gilly had written. *There's another name here. A woman named Skye Marie Swinter died in the accident. She was the driver, too. And it was her lawyer, not your client's, who got this gag order or whatever. Equally sus.*

My heart bottomed out. Of *course,* it was that accident. What else would it be? But I frowned a little harder. I already knew about Skye's death, so it couldn't very well be the thing TJ was so closely guarding. He hadn't mentioned he'd been to the scene. Was that "sus," as Gilly had said?

Slowly this time, thinking over how I wanted to phrase my curiosity, I typed another message to Gilly. *Is there anything else weird about any of is? Specifically from a police perspective, I mean?*

I dunno, she wrote back. *The whole thing seems a bit…off. I sound super police-y, right? But. Like, why did the deceased party have a lawyer? It's not as if she needed protection. Or like anyone else was hurt.*

I pursed my lips. I was pretty sure the answer to her lawyer question had something to do with Skye Marie's father. As far as the rest of it went...I wasn't sure. Gilly's text confirmed what TJ had told me. His ex was the driver and the sole victim.

Wait, though. What if someone else was *hurt?* The thought came so suddenly that I nearly dropped the phone. *What if that was the coverup?*

I started to type that out to Gilly then stopped. If I suggested it, would that prompt her to investigate more than I wanted her to? But my hesitation meant I didn't have to say anything because Gilly had already sent a fresh text.

I must be REALLY bored, she'd written. *'Cause I looked to see if any other weird stuff showed up around the same date, and I got nada.*

I exhaled. That answered that.

Thanks, Gilly, I typed.

Did I help?

Yes.

I feel like that's a lie, she wrote back. *But I'll accept it. For now. Dinner and drinks soon?*

For sure, I replied. *Call me in a week?*

I'll hold you to that.

:)

I sighed and squeezed the phone before setting it down on the nightstand again. Whatever giant reveal I'd been expecting, I hadn't gotten it. But I was surer than ever that TJ was keeping something close to his chest, and despite the lack of conclusive information from Gilly, I was also increasingly certain it all related back to the Swinters and Skye's accidental death.

I flopped backwards and pinched the bridge of my nose for a second before dropping my hand to my side and sighing once more. I tried to reassure myself that if TJ thought it was relevant, he'd share it. But I knew from experience that people tended to underplay things. Lord knew I'd done it myself.

I stretched out my arms and stared up at the ceiling, trying to imagine the scene of the accident. Trying to see TJ arriving after the fact. How had he learned about it in the first place? He and Skye Marie had split up a year or more earlier. Who would've called him? Not her dad.

I shifted a bit, and my gaze found the door. Again, I imagined TJ on the other side of it. Only now, my skin prickled. With curiosity. With unease. They battled each other for several seconds, but neither of them won out. And something else occurred to me. TJ had no police record, but he'd told me he'd gotten into a ton of trouble. And not the kind on the ice that earned him his nickname, either. Several times, he'd mentioned he wasn't a good guy, way back when. Had he specifically mentioned breaking any laws? I didn't think so. But why else would all those excessive stipulations be in his contract? It couldn't just be about his affair with his teammate's wife. It was more like a three strikes situation.

The uncomfortable tickle had made its way into all my pores. My skin was practically hot with it.

Could TJ have had his crimes—assuming he'd committed them—covered up?

My all-over heat seemed to burst. A chill took its place, and I shivered.

Was it possible? That kind of coverup would require connections. Money. A certain level of thoroughness. TJ didn't fit that bill.

You mean he doesn't seem *to fit it, right, Pint-Size? Because you know better than most how deceiving outward appearances can be.*

For once, I didn't tell my brother's intrusive voice where it could stick its opinion. Because it was right. There were few people who could attest so thoroughly to misreading a situation as I could.

Should I ask Gilly if she can find out more?

She typically shared whatever she could legally get her hands on. But I could press her to see if there were hints of buried transgressions. The thought of an affirmative answer nauseated me. The thought of not knowing was worse.

I was shivering harder now. Almost feverish. My teeth wanted to clack together in response. So I grabbed the blanket instead of my phone, wrapped it around my body, and pulled it up to my ears. I closed my eyes and waited for the cold to pass. My brain kept moving along.

If I was right, and TJ was keeping a darker past to himself, where did that leave the case? Where did it leave *me*? Honestly, I wasn't sure I wanted to answer that second question. But one thing was for sure. I was suddenly pretty damn glad things between us hadn't gone any further. I'd been down that road already, and I had no desire to do it again. Not ever.

Chapter Thirty-Seven

At some point, after lord knew how much tossing and turning, I fell asleep. I knew it because the sound of a slamming door abruptly jerked me awake. I sat up, disoriented and with my heart pounding so hard it almost hurt. It took a second for the room to come into focus. And when it did, the first thing that came back to me was the same question I'd been tormenting myself with prior to drifting off.

Is TJ really who he says he is?

I sat very still, listening for sounds that he was nearby. I heard nothing. But my body refused to relax. I stretched, trying to ease some of the ache caused by my bunched-up muscles. It didn't help much at all. I was wide awake, though, and a quick look toward the window told me it was light out. I'd slept for a good chunk of time. Probably not a bad thing physically *or* mentally.

I threw aside the blankets and put my feet on the floor, then listened again. Still nothing. Maybe TJ wasn't up yet. Maybe that door slam I'd heard had been part of a dream. But when I snagged my phone from the nightstand, I blinked at how wrong I was.

"Shit."

It was almost noon. I couldn't even remember the last time I'd stayed in bed past seven in the morning. From a job standpoint, I ought to be rushing out to see what my client was up to. But I didn't do it. Instead, I took my time. I stretched again. Then I reread the messages between Gilly and me. Despite the fact that my head was clearer now than it'd been when it was spinning last night, nothing about the information had changed. No nuance was missed in the name of exhaustion. TJ had still shown up at the scene of the accident somehow. He hadn't bothered to disclose that to me. And something was off.

I stood and stretched a third time before making my way to the bathroom, where I studied my appearance in the mirror for a solid minute.

Not too bad, all things considered, I finally decided.

Even so, I still didn't rush off. I turned on the shower, stripped down, and climbed in.

Was I stalling? Most definitely. But it wasn't just avoidance, and it wasn't just because I hadn't yet decided what I was going to do. It was also because I was afraid. A million doubts rolled through my head, and the hot water did little to help slough them off.

What lengths would TJ go to in order to keep his secret?

Was I in danger?

Could I even trust myself to know the difference?

I stayed in the shower until it started to get cold, and I took my time getting dry and dressed afterwards, too. I texted my brother and waited more than ten minutes for a reply that didn't come. But finally, I ran out of excuses for staying in my room. Firmly, I reminded myself that TJ had no idea I'd talked to Gilly. He didn't know I was unraveling *him* in an attempt to unravel the case. And he probably thought I was still irritated at him about the relationship conversation, which meant he was likely avoiding me as much as I was avoiding him.

I took a breath, marched over to the door, and flung it open. Nothing but silence greeted me.

I stepped into the hallway. The lights were out. TJ's bedroom door was wide open. And quite abruptly, my skin broke out in goosebumps. Why did the quiet suddenly have a sinister undertone?

I tossed a glance to the other end of the hall, half-expecting to find someone lurking in the shadows. No one was there.

I cleared my throat and lifted my voice to a level just below a cheerful yell. "TJ?"

When I didn't get an answer, I realized I wasn't truly expecting one. And I didn't bother to give it a second shot. I hurried to TJ's room, the light thump of my feet the only sound. His space was empty. I turned away quickly and headed for the main part of the house. He wasn't there, either.

My worry over him and his past slid to the back of my mind. Where was he? We still had twenty-four hours or so until his stalker was supposed to make another move. Could he have escalated? Taken advantage of the lack of my presence?

My professional experience took over.

I checked every room twice. I peered into closets. When that didn't pan out, I went back to TJ's bedroom a third time and stood in the middle of it, turning in a circle. A pair of shorts peeked out from a drawer, and it prompted me to remember he had a home gym off the mudroom. Hope bubbled as I rushed to look there. But I had no luck with that, either.

What about his truck? Is it here?

I sprinted from the home gym to the front room and pulled back the drapes. It was there. His truck sat just where he'd parked it the night before. I dropped the drape and exhaled. He hadn't left, then. Not in his own vehicle, anyway.

And you heard the door slam, I reminded myself. *He might be outside.*

"Right."

I strode to the front door, slipped on my shoes while pretending not to notice how at home they looked in TJ's foyer, and let myself out. The heat startled me. The sun was up in all its glory, the air unseasonably warm. A light sweat beaded along my forehead within seconds, and as I moved from the front steps to the yard, I was compelled to bend down and pull the bottoms of my sweatpants up to my knees. I started to right myself then froze. *A shoe.* TJ's white runner. It sat near his truck. Starkly out of place. And it sent a sharp spike of fear all the way up my spine.

Shit. Shit!

Staying in the awkward position and breathing shallowly, I scanned the area around the shoe then just past it. And there he was. Lying on the ground near a tree, his face pointed to the sky. Even from where I was, I could see the mark of crimson on the left side of his temple.

Oh, God. The worries I had about him hiding things from me completely fell aside. *Please, no. Not this.*

I righted myself, and my feet started to move again. Slowly at first. Weighed down by dread. Then they picked up. And in seconds, I was at a full sprint, charging across the lawn while my brain continued to reverberate with its plea.

No. No. Please, no. Please.

I reached TJ's side and collapsed to the ground beside him, saying it aloud now.

"Please, no. Please, no. *Please.*"

Tears blurred my vision.

"TJ. Come on."

Gently, I touched his cheek.

"TJ."

His lips parted, and he let out a small groan. My whole body shuddered with relief, and I sagged.

"Ivy?" he said, his voice shaky. "What just—shit." He sat up slowly, touching the blood-covered spot on his head and wincing. "Someone hit me."

I hated how vulnerable he looked. Which reminded me I hadn't even secured the area or looked to see if his attacker was nearby, waiting to strike again.

Goddammit.

"Sit tight." The command sounded strained and weak, even to my own ears, but I didn't try to fix it. "Don't move at all."

Wiping my eyes, I stood and swept my gaze over the area and inventoried everything in the immediate vicinity. I saw no evidence if whoever'd done this. No tire tracks. No flicker of someone watching to see what we did next. That didn't mean they weren't still here. My hand clenched. There were a dozen places to hide on the property. More than a dozen.

And this happened on my watch.

I didn't even know how long TJ had been out here. Or why. He could've been killed, and it would've been 100 percent on me. I was probably lucky the culprit hadn't had murder on the brain. Because there would've been nothing stopping him. At the thought, tears threatened again. I rolled my shoulders and ordered myself to calm down and approach this logically. If the person behind the attack had wanted TJ dead, then TJ would *be* dead. So maybe it was safe—or at least safe-ish—to infer our lives weren't presently under threat. But if that were the case, then what was the motive behind the assault? It was a damned good question.

I swung back to TJ. He hadn't budged. His hand was still cradling his injured head. My chest compressed so thickly that my lungs burned. And I knew what I had to do. But first, we needed to get inside.

I held out my hand and helped him up, and I didn't say much of anything as I led him back to the house. I didn't push forward until he was seated on the couch with a damp cloth pressed to his injury. And before I'd even spoken, TJ's expression had already drooped. He looked like he knew he was about to be dumped. And maybe that was accurate.

"I need to give your case to someone else," I told him, the words coming out in a rush.

"Why?" he asked.

The question was simple. The answer was complex. And I really had no intention of explaining it to him, so I surprised myself by being completely honest.

"Because I can't be objective about you, TJ," I admitted.

"That's a bad thing?" he replied.

"What just happened out there?"

"I assume someone hit me in the head with something, and I blacked out for a few seconds."

"I mean what just happened with *me*?" I amended, then sighed. "I woke up late, and you were gone. I searched the whole damn house and finally came out here to do the same. And the very moment I saw you on the ground, I lost it. If someone had been trying to do more than just hurt you, they would've succeeded."

TJ lowered the cloth and frowned, the crease his expression created making his wound all the more macabre. "That's my fault, not yours. I should've woken you up."

I sat down beside him. "Yeah, no shit. Part of it's on you. But it's not really you going outside with no warning that makes me sure I'm not the right person for this job. It's my reaction to you being injured. To thinking maybe it *was* worse. I didn't secure the area. I didn't focus on the possibility that whoever it was might still be hanging around. I just needed you to be okay. For *me*. And if I can't separate my feelings from—"

"Kiss me."

My heart skipped a beat, and I thought for a second I'd misheard. Or projected what I wanted to hear onto whatever he'd really said.

"Sorry?" I replied.

"Kiss me," he repeated. "Please."

"I can't do that. You're hurt."

"If that's the only reason you can't do it, then fine. But if it's because you're scared…"

I stared at him, narrowing my eyes. "Are you trying to play me?"

His lips twitched, but he somehow managed to

keep a straight face other than that. "I'm not that kind of guy. Plus, I hardly know you well enough to know *how* to play you."

My mouth opened and closed. He *shouldn't* know me that well. And I should've been offended by the idea that getting me to do something was as simple as challenging my need to prove that things didn't scare me. But there it was. And despite the blood on his head—despite everything—he looked *smug.*

"I'm not scared," I said, but it was bold-faced lie, based on the way my heart jackhammered against my ribcage enough to rattle my teeth.

"All right." TJ leaned back with a small shrug.

"I'm not."

"I said all right."

"But you didn't mean it."

"Of course, I meant it."

"Fine," I said.

"Fine what?" he replied.

"I'll kiss you." If it weren't for the words themselves, I would've sounded like a petulant five-year-old resentfully eating broccoli or something.

"Okay. Go ahead."

Simultaneously bristling with irritation and buzzing with anticipation and nerves, I leaned closer and tipped my head—and mouth—toward his. But just as I was about to close both my eyes and the final gap between us, TJ put his hand on my cheek and met my eyes.

"Is this what you want?" he asked with zero hint of his previous teasing look or tone at all.

"Goddammit, TJ. Yes!" The words burst out, and my face got hot.

He didn't laugh. He didn't even smile. He just dropped his hand and waited. And I finished leaning in.

Chapter Thirty-Eight

If someone had asked me five minutes earlier whether anything could beat a first kiss, I would've said no. Of course not. There's nothing like driving through that dam of pent-up want for the first time. But I would've been wrong. So, so wrong. This kiss...this *second* kiss...or third if I was getting technical...it was impossibly better.

TJ's mouth was a part of mine. An extension of the oh-so-sensitive skin there. Warm and firm. Yielding for a moment then melding together then matching my desire, point for point. When his tongue danced across my lips, there was no stopping the gasp that slipped out. And it earned a groan from him in return.

The third kiss became a fourth. A fifth. An endless succession, all of them bests.

His hands found my waist and pulled me closer. Our chests met. Mine melted into his taut muscles. A perfect fit. But it still wasn't close enough. I pushed forward. And forward again. And again. I was in his lap, but I didn't care. And even that wasn't as near as I wanted to be.

My shirt lifted, and his fingers trailed along the small of my back, and I realized there was only one way to be as close as I actually wanted to be.

"Ivy," he said against my mouth.

If he meant to slow the moment, he failed. Utterly.

"Say my name again," I breathed.

"Ivy." His voice wasn't just laced with heat; it was a molten thing, sliding from where our lips met to my every pore. "Ivy."

I put my hand on the back of his head and clutched his hair, the soft tendrils of it sending pinpricks of electricity through my fingers. He was leaning back now, his shoulders resting against the arm of the couch behind him. His mouth fell from mine but only so it could ghost kiss from jaw to my throat.

Fire licked over me. My breaths were short, torturous gasps.

I reached for his shirt. I *had* to take it off. Had to be skin-to-skin.

Now, now, now! a voice in my head demanded.

I couldn't remember ever wanting something so badly. But when I got the shirt up to his head, it grazed his injury, making him wince. I had to slow down. To be more careful.

Gingerly, I finished lifting his shirt. But the extra few seconds it took was just enough time for my brain to gain some control over my body.

What am I doing?

He was under me. My legs straddled his waist. His bare chest was enough to make me ache with longing. And yet there was his head wound, contrasting it all with the way its crimson stain marked his skin. It was a glaring remark on just how wrong it was to be here like this.

The heat—well, most of it—sapped away.

"Ivy?" TJ said my name softly now, questioningly.

"I'm just proving myself right." I had no idea if I meant the statement for him or for me—both, maybe. "I need someone else to do this."

For a moment, his lips quirked. I rolled my eyes.

"Not *this* this," I amended, easing off his lap and back into the seat beside him. "Your case."

"So long as we're clear on that." He lifted an eyebrow, then grabbed his shirt and pulled it back over his head.

"You can see why, though, right?"

"Only if I assume this isn't how you treat *all* of your clients."

It should've been at least a *little* funny. But given my history, it not only fell flat but also made my heart try to seize up. I wanted to dart a look around, too. I refrained. I schooled myself into meeting TJ's eyes, and I reiterated my point.

"Someone else needs to run this case," I said. "Charles is laid up, but I can ask one of my other brothers."

TJ shook his, which made him wince again, and I had to squeeze my hands together to keep from reaching out to soothe his obvious discomfort.

"How the hell will that work?" he asked without much vehemence.

"We'll just have to 'break up' sooner than anticipated," I replied.

"The whole point in this arrangement was to make sure no one knew I had a bodyguard so my reputation didn't get messed up."

"I know."

"I want to respect your wishes, Ivy." He paused. "Scratch that. I *do* respect them. But I can't fuck up my contract. I have too much on the line. We did that whole engagement thing with the reporter, too."

Now I winced. "We'll work something out."

"Like what?"

The first idea that popped into my head was that I'd continue to be his fake girlfriend until the case was solved. I could let someone else worry about the rest of it.

Think you'd be able to hand over the reigns on that, though, Pint-Size? Charles's voice countered.

He had a point. Plus, it was pretty obvious my self-control was lacking. I needed separation for myself, too. So, I didn't voice the suggestion aloud, and TJ took advantage of empty moment to make another argument.

"I don't trust anyone else," he said. "I *can't* trust anyone else."

My throat scratched. "I can't keep you safe, TJ. Your trust isn't well-placed."

His eyes met mine. "Why the hell not? Because you care if something happens to me?"

"Yes."

But it's not just that, I added silently. *There are things you don't know. Things that would make you regret hiring me in the first place.*

He shifted, reaching out his hands to clasp mine, and as he did, my eyes dropped. I frowned, distracted. There was something near his feet. A piece of paper, about five inches by seven inches in size. And even though there were a dozen other bits of paper around—the letters and envelopes and newspaper clippings—this one made the hairs on the back of my neck stand up.

"What is that?" I asked.

He looked down, following my gaze. "Not sure."

In reply, I reached out to pick it up, noting that it was speckled with mud. Maybe that was why it gave me the creeps. I ran my fingers over the dirt, the sensation intensifying because it was *fresh*. Damp. Like it'd been dropped outside very recently. I flipped it over, and a woman's face smiled up at me.

TJ inhaled an audibly sharp breath. "Fuck."

I jerked my eyes back to him. "What? Who is it?"

But before he even spoke, I knew the answer. It came as no surprise when he said her name in a bewildered tone.

"Skye Marie," he said. "What the *actual* fuck?"

"This isn't yours?"

"No. *Jesus*. No. I don't know where that came from."

But I had an idea. The way it was covered in fresh mud…

"I think whoever knocked you out left this behind," I said. "Maybe they tucked it into your pocket our something."

"Why?" He ran a hand over his head, his face pale. "Why would they do that?"

"They want you to know what this is about," I replied, sure I was right as soon as the words were out of my mouth, and surer still of what it meant. "He's getting ready for it to be over."

TJ went quiet. So did I.

I studied Skye's picture. She had the palest blond hair and startlingly dark eyes. A distinct mole marked a spot just above her left brow. That she was pretty wasn't in question. Even though she wasn't smiling, and her skin had an unnatural-looking translucence, I could see that she was the kind of woman who'd draw second glances. But for some reason, I couldn't picture her on TJ's arm. He was so…vibrant. Strong. And funny. Skye appeared, even in photographic form, like someone who needed to be saved.

Then again, maybe that's what made them work, I thought. *Maybe she needed protecting.*

I stole a glance at TJ. Is that what he needed, too? To play that role? To be the hero?

Unexpected resentment—ill-timed and self-centered—rose up in my chest. It wasn't what *I* wanted. I sure as hell didn't have a desire to be a damsel in distress. Just the opposite. And if that was the vibe I was giving off, then—

"She was nothing like you," TJ said abruptly, almost like he was reading my mind. "Sometimes, when I think about it, I can't understand how we got together in the first place. Which makes me feel like shit. Like a fraud. But she didn't deserve to die. Especially not the way she did."

Now I studied him instead of the picture. I'd been assuming his heartache was over losing Skye. Was I wrong about that?

"TJ," I said, "I think you need to tell me exactly what happened. Whatever's going on, it's about her. And I'm sorry. It hurts. I can see that. But I think she's the key to solving this."

He looked down at his hands, and for a second, I thought he might deny it. Or refuse to tell me. I heard Skye's father in my head for the umpteenth time. But then TJ sighed and started to talk.

He described meeting Skye Marie at a club. How she was carefree and gave zero fucks about what anyone thought. TJ had thought it was what he needed following his father's death. Someone who wouldn't judge him and wouldn't have expectations for his future. Somewhat ironically, they'd eloped. But it didn't take long before Skye's father had found out and demanded the marriage be annulled. She'd laughed in her dad's face, but Raleigh Swinter was a powerful man. A rich man. One with connections who could make things happen so quickly that the person on the receiving side of the action barely caught on before it was too late. And he'd been convincing.

I interrupted TJ then. "Hang on."

But he shook his head right away. "I know what it sounds like, and you're wondering how the hell I can tell you my former father-in-law hated me and wanted to destroy my marriage, then claim there's no chance he doesn't hold me responsible for his daughter's death."

"TJ—"

"It's not wishful thinking."

"You're going to have to give me a *really* good reason to believe that."

He lifted his head and met my eyes. "I'm sure because there's no way he'd threaten the father of his grandchild."

Chapter Thirty-Nine

The air seemed to have gone out of the room. I didn't know what to say. TJ kept staring at me. Waiting for a reaction. But my head reeled. It kept me from forming proper sentences. He was a father. His ex-wife wasn't just his ex-wife. She was his child's mother. And she was dead.

"I'm sorry," TJ said after a few heavy seconds. "I should've told you. But it's part of the arrangement."

"No," I replied. "Don't apologize. Please. It's just not what I was expecting to hear."

Truthfully, it was more than that. I'd inferred he was still grieving the loss of his loved one. I'd genuinely thought maybe he'd still been *in* love with her. Now I could see it wasn't that at all.

"We'd already split up when she found out," he told me. "It was…complicated. But there was other stuff that came before that. Like the fact that she overdosed."

His eyes lowered to his hands again, a clear indication of how painful the subject was for him. But he didn't stop talking, and his voice was mostly steady.

While he disliked Raleigh Swinter in a general way, the other man had been hard to argue with. Hard being a euphemism for a brick wall. TJ was his daughter's third husband. *Third.* And she was just rounding onto her twentieth birthday. She had a long history of drug abuse, and this was in no way her first close call. Raleigh had forked over a ton of money trying to get her clean, again and again. There was a new program available. An in-patient one. But it forbade relationships. TJ was young, too. And in love. Raleigh convinced him it was for the best for everyone involved, and he agreed to the annulment for Skye's sake. She entered the program, and she was in it for a full eighteen months.

"The first thing she did when she got out was to get fucked up all over again," TJ said. "And she got sent right back in again. Another year there. Then again. She was locked up in that facility for over three years, when all was said and done."

He learned all of that after. He hadn't seen her or spoken to her or even *heard* a word about her when it was happening. It wasn't until almost three *more* years had gone by that she came back onto his radar.

"She came to see me." Now his voice lost some of its evenness. "And I sent her away."

My stomach churned. I knew what was coming next, but I let him explain it.

"She was wasted. Drunk. High. And when I told her I didn't want to talk, she hopped in her car and *drove away.* I tried to stop her. I jumped in front of the vehicle. If she'd been able to see straight, she probably would've killed me, but she just clipped my leg. I called the cops. Gave her license plate number and whatever. It was too late." TJ drew a breath, blinked a few times, then continued with his story. "Fifteen minutes later, they called me back and told me she was dead. She hit a lamp post, head-on. No seatbelt. Going well above the speed limit. She didn't suffer, but she died on impact."

"I'm so sorry."

"Yeah. Me, too. I lost it for a while after. I blamed myself. Who wouldn't? I kept thinking that if I'd just let her stay, she'd still be alive. Christ. I know it wasn't my fault. But still."

I threaded my fingers through his and waited for him to catch his breath.

"Her dad tied shit up with a tidy bow," he said. "Paid off the cop who was first on scene. Made sure the papers billed the whole thing as a tragic accident. Threatened to make sure my name got dragged through the mud if I leaked anything. As if I would."

He stopped again, shaking his head. He brought my hand to his lips and gave it a quick kiss, then exhaled.

"But I guess it messed me up more than I thought. I was already on the downward slope, you know? Between my dad and whatever else. After that, I was more destructive than ever. Even though I'd spent the time Skye was in rehab trying to make things better, it was like I'd done none of the work. The whole time, I knew it was ironic. Getting wasted because my ex-wife had gotten wasted, too, and accidently killed herself. Wrecking my life because she'd wrecked hers. I got arrested. Drunk and disorderly. Destruction of property. I want to say it was a slow decline, but it was just a decline. That's when the affair happened, and my career tanked.

It was around then that Skye's dad showed up again. Raleigh Swinter had bailed TJ out. He'd been keeping tabs and finally had enough. And he told TJ the truth. Skye Marie had given birth while she was in rehab. A son. His name was Travis, too. And if TJ wanted anything to do with the kid, he had to agree to clean up his life and get his career back on track.

"Cue Bram," TJ said. "Raleigh introduced us. Used his influence to work out representation. He also got me a lawyer who helped expunge some things from my record. We made a deal when that side of things was done. I'd spend a year—exactly three-hundred and sixty-five days—on the up-and-up, and Raleigh would let me into my son's life. I'm about to hit that mark. Three hundred and fifty days and counting. But if I don't follow through, he'll make sure I'm cut out of Travis's life for good."

"You couldn't have pushed for custody?" I asked.

He shook his head. "I don't know. Maybe? Probably? With Raleigh and his money, I don't know. I didn't want to take the risk. I've got a kid who doesn't know I exist. If I pushed things then, Raleigh would've been more than happy to tell him what a terrible person I'd been. That's not who I want him to see. This seemed like a better way to do things."

It all sounded needlessly cruel. Or at least very heavy-handed. Illegal, too. But it also made sense why TJ agreed to his contract. It explained why he was keeping things a secret and the reason for his reluctance to agree to the phony girlfriend scheme. And it only made me like him even more. But what it didn't do was offer up a suspect for the threats.

"I should've told you from the beginning," TJ said again. "If I'd thought this was going to be anything more than fake…"

For a second, his words distracted me. *Was* this more than fake?

Duh, my subconscious fired back at me.

The attraction was real. But was there more to it

than that?

Not unless you're being as honest with him as he was with you.

"TJ, I need to tell you something, too," I said.

"I'm listening," he replied.

I took a breath and launched into the story I'd never shared with anyone except my brothers and the police.

Chapter Forty

"Almost four years ago, Ames Security took on a case. A sibling set—a brother and sister—from a wealthy family had just lost their father, and they'd inherited a significant amount of money. Enough that they and their children and grandchildren and maybe even great-grandchildren would never have to lift a finger to work if they didn't want to. But they'd barely said goodbye to their dad before they received a blackmail threat.

"There was a video. The sister had made some regrettable choices when she was about twenty, and someone had caught her in the act. The two of them had thought they'd wiped out any trace of it, but whoever was blackmailing them showed them proof they were wrong. By the time they contacted us, they'd actually already paid the money, but they were worried about a second threat coming and wanted us to investigate.

"Charles hadn't wanted to take the case. He had a bad feeling about it. But I was almost the same age as the sister. And we'd just lost *our* dad. So, we did it. Me for their sake, Charles for mine.

"For a whole month, we practically lived at their house. We ate there. Slept there. They paid for everything. And even though we couldn't source the original threat, and a repeated threat never came, they didn't want us to leave.

"Charles was getting antsy. He'd passed over three other quick cases to stay on this one. We argued about it, and ultimately, I told him to go ahead and go. I'd stay behind and wait it out. Another week went by. He *did* leave. The moment he was out of the picture, I got closer to the sister. And even closer to the brother."

"It was a romantic relationship," I admitted. ...More than romantic.

It was electrically charged. Clandestine and exciting. He would buy me things and hide them in my room at their place and kiss me in every corner when his sister wasn't looking.

"Another month went by. The blackmailer still hadn't reappeared, and I was finding it more and more challenging to make excuses to stay. And even more difficult not to tell anyone about what was going on between the two of us. I suggested that Ames Security release them as clients and come clean about our relationship. He refused. Adamantly. So I kind of went behind his back and asked his sister if she thought it was necessary that we stay on.

"That's where things started to unravel." I plucked at my sweatpants, and TJ's hand came up to still the nervous movement. "She—the sister, I mean—got cagey. She told me her brother had never wanted to hire us in the first place. She'd insisted on it. Then she walked away. Literally, I mean. Just turned and left the room."

In retrospect, I should've seen that as a red flag. Because it was weird. If he didn't want us there, why was he had insisted on keeping us there? Why wouldn't she explain? But my feelings got in the way. I assumed he wanted me there because he'd liked me from the start.

"I made a joke about it to him," I said. "It backfired."

"I can still see his face. The way it got dark and angry and changed him into a person I didn't know at all. I could hear his voice, too."

What the fuck were you thinking, Ivy?

The question had been a slap. He'd always been so kind. So soft-spoken and tender. But I let it go."

"I guess I thought we were in love," I told TJ, working not to sound bitter and sad and probably failing at it. "It clouded things."

"At that point, it'd been three months since the case had started. Keeping the secret had made me tired. It wore on my relationship with my brothers. And yet I still didn't manage to see a problem. It wasn't until I walked into the kitchen one day and found the sister crying at the table that I had my first bit of doubt that something was off."

My voice broke as I recounted it. "She'd looked up then saw me and turned off her emotion with some invisible switch. Except it'd been too late. Seeing her like that turned on my *own* switch. She wouldn't tell me what was wrong, and honestly, I didn't ask. But my brain stored what I saw. She was doing something on a laptop. Not the same one she so often opened when I was around. Not the old clunker her brother favored in some throwback bit of nostalgia, either. It was one with a matte black cover I'd never seen before. Why would she have a secret computer? What was on it?

"I remember wondering why she'd hidden it for all those months, then suddenly look at it somewhere as open as at the kitchen table," I said.

"She wanted you to see her," TJ quietly replied, and I nodded.

It was what I'd assumed as well. And I used that as an excuse to hunt for it. It had taken a few days, but I'd finally found an opportunity to search her room when she was at a spin class. She'd hidden it under her mattress. I opened it right away. The password was the same one she'd shared with us when we first took on the case in what she called *the interest of transparency.*

"I still don't know what I was expecting to find," I said. "Maybe just the secret video of her doing whatever it was she'd done to get herself into this mess in the first place. Because it was the one thing she hadn't shown us, and we hadn't insisted on it for discretion's sake."

It hadn't seemed important to know *what* was on the video. Only that there *was* a video.

"Except it wasn't the video," I told TJ.

And despite what I'd just said, there *had* been a video. Just not like anything I would have ever expected.

My eyes closed. I couldn't stop them. It didn't help the rush of blood that surged through my head, and it didn't stop my breath from cutting away like I'd just been shoved underwater.

As I described what had happened next, it was like I was seeing it all over again. Watching myself from a bird's eye view.

There I was, sitting in front of the desk in her enormous suite of a bedroom. Settling the laptop onto that same desk. Staring down at the single icon on the screen. A blue video reel. It was puzzling, not so much because of what it was, but because it was the only thing there. No taskbar. No folders. Just that one thing. Almost in slow motion, I'd reached out and double clicked to open it and then balked at what I saw.

"It was a man," I said. "He was sitting in a chair. Tied to it. He had a white hood over his face, but it was covered in blood. And then a second man came into the frame. He poked the first guy with a long pole."

It'd been a broom handle, I found out later. Not that it mattered. But by that point, my brain had been trying to distract itself from what I was seeing.

What is it? I'd wondered, my eyes hanging on the pole.

The second man had given another poke. And another.

"He was dead." I wanted my tone to be flat, or least neutral, but my voice warbled, and I had to repeat myself to get control. "He was dead, and the guy poking him was my boyfriend."

"Jesus," TJ said. "Ivy, I'm sorry."

I shook my head. "It gets worse than that."

How can it? his eyes asked.

"To be honest, a lot of what came next is foggy." Subconsciously, I touched the back of my head.

TJ's hand came up to cover mine. "Head injury?"

"Yes. The doctors think it affected my memory." I hesitated, but if I was going to tell him the truth then I should tell him everything. "They also think it could have something to with me wanting to block it out, too."

"Makes sense." He said it with no judgement, and my shoulders let go of some of their tension.

"The police believed I must've made arrangements to confront him even though I hadn't looped my brothers in."

I managed a smile. "Sounds like me, right? I would've been pissed off and stubborn and wanted to take care of it on my own."

"I can neither confirm nor deny said allegations against you," TJ said.

I smiled again, and it was less forced this time. "Smart choice. But I do think they were right. They found a reservation in his name at restaurant in the next town over. That was his jam. Taking me to eat somewhere else so we could be romantic without anyone seeing."

My moment of levity faded, and my lips drooped so heavily that I could feel it in my chin. But I made myself keep talking.

"The police had found that reservation. But first, they'd found me. Crumpled in a heap in an alley a block from where we were allegedly meant to be having dinner. I was alive, obviously. But barely." I breathed out. "This all happened within hours of me seeing that video. The police put together a timeline that fit."

"How did he find out you knew?" TJ asked.

"I'm not sure. I have a memory that comes through in a recurring dream. I'm standing outside. Probably near the restaurant. He shows up with flowers, and I see his face. And then I know that *he* knows. And it all falls apart. I wake up."

"But they caught him."

"No." It came out in a whisper.

TJ's face was still, but there was an open curiosity in his eyes. I had to look away when I said the rest.

"I killed him," I stated. "His body was beside

mine."

TJ was going to argue in my favor. Tell me it was self-defence. Then he'd point out that I'd saved the sister, taken out a murderer, and solved the case. Because if I *hadn't* stayed around and *hadn't* gotten involved then the whole thing would've gone undiscovered. I tried to tell myself the same thing. Charles had said as much, too. The police concurred. And maybe it was all more than a little true. But I hadn't done it on purpose, and that mattered to me. So did one other key detail. But there were other important things to explain first, so I cut TJ before he could do more than open his mouth.

"My so-called boyfriend wasn't our client's brother. But the man in video… *He* was. The one my boyfriend had tortured and killed."

"What the fuck," TJ muttered, and I couldn't blame him.

"He was the one behind the blackmail, while our client's real brother was the one who'd called us. The one who'd insisted on it, which is what she'd tried and failed to tell me. But the blackmailer caught him, and it was too late. He couldn't *un*-call us. He thought it would be suspicious."

This was all stuff the cops had explained to me. The man pretending to be the brother had set up the scenario, used the blackmail video, and collected the money.

"But it wasn't enough. He came after them for a second amount, and they tried to fight back. They met with him in person, planning to trick him, and the result was what happened in the video I'd seen." I took a deep breath. "And like I said before, they'd already reached out to us, so they kept our appointment."

Based on that meeting, the blackmailer was somehow convinced we knew more than we were letting on. It was almost laughable. We'd known less than nothing. He could've cut us loose at pretty much any moment, and I would never have thought twice about it. Instead, he spent three months digging to figure out what it was we supposedly knew.

"Seducing me to do it," I said softly, my face hot as I expelled the words.

"It's not your fault," TJ replied, sounding like he meant it despite the cliched reassurance.

I shrugged again. "It's not even *about* fault, though. It's about *me.*"

"How is that different?"

"Because I don't blame victims for being victimized. I can't blame myself for it, either. Logically, I know none of what happened is my fault."

TJ studied me for a moment. "Except it's impossible to *be* logical when it's you."

"Yes." I nodded. "But that's not the key thing, either."

I squeezed my eyes shut. I envisioned the man I was talking about. Tall, dark, handsome. So very different from his supposed sister, which made utter sense once I found out the truth. I made myself see him now, holding in a shudder as the recurring dream came thundering in. Those dead flowers. The look in his eyes. And I forced out the truth.

"I don't *remember* it, TJ," I said. "I killed a man, and I know it was in self-defence, and I know he was a terrible person. A murdering, lying, blackmailing, piece of garbage who thoroughly tricked me. But *I don't remember it."*

Silence hung in the air for so long that I had to open my eye to make sure TJ was still there. And he was, of course. Sitting patiently. Blue gaze steady as he reached out and took my hands.

"This *isn't* about you," he said.

I wanted to believe him. I'd just iterated the very same thing, hadn't I?

And yet...

"How can I trust my instincts?" I asked, a desperate edge glazing the question. "How can I ask my brothers to trust them? How can I ask *you* to trust them? I've spent the last almost four years trying to...I don't know. I don't want to say, 'deal with,' or 'cope with,' or even 'reconcile with,' but to *something* with my past. Find a way to integrate it into who I am, maybe."

"And who *are* you?"

The reply could've been cheesy or trite, but something about the way he asked it made me stop and think. I couldn't come up with an answer.

"You're probably wondering how the hell I wound up being your bodyguard at all now," I finally said.

"The opposite," TJ told me. "I'm glad you aren't some cocky asshole who thinks he's indestructible. But you know what does suck?"

"What?"

"That some actual asshole made you doubt yourself."

"I fell in love with a murderer. I killed him, and I don't remember it."

"You're human." He shrugged.

"None of those things are average human things," I countered.

"Are you average?" he asked.

"TJ—"

He cut me off with a sudden kiss. It took my breath away, but when he pulled back, I shook my head and tried again to protest.

"TJ, I—"

Again, he swooped in. Longer this time. More thorough, too. Which meant it was harder to recover.

"Listen, you—"

Another kiss, this one quick but followed by a dozen more, peppered between my lips and my cheeks and my chin and my forehead. And still, it managed to make me heady.

"Are you just going to keep doing this?" I asked.

"Yes," he said. "Until you tell me who you are, or until you tell me to stop."

He kissed me again, riding the line just between tender and passionate. There was exactly a zero percent chance I was going to tell him to stop.

And he damn well knows it, too, doesn't he? So I guess the only option is to tell him who you are.

But the repeated attention directed from his lips to mine was making it pretty damn hard to concentrate.

"I'm *me*," I mumbled against his mouth.

"And you are?" he murmured back.

"Ivy Ames."

"Ivy Ames?" he echoed, turning it into a question.

"Yes," I said, sounding annoyed now. "I'm Ivy fucking Ames."

His laugh rumbled a pleasant vibration from his body to mine. "I'll accept that. What else?"

I don't know where they came from—maybe my irritation—but a sudden burst of descriptors popped into my head. Like I was back in high school and being asked to fill in an *All About Me* project.

I was smart. Strong. Stubborn. Determined. Unwilling to back down, sometimes to my own detriment. I loved my family. I missed my parents, especially my dad because my memories of him were fresher and the loss more recent. I'd had my heart broken. I was too prickly. I made mistakes. But I worked hard, and whatever the world brought me, I did my best to rise to the challenge.

"Imperfect." That's the one that made its way from my brain out into the world, and as silly it sounded, it was like a *pop*.

TJ pressed his forehead to mine. "Aren't we all?"

"Yes," I said, another *pop*. "Of course, we are."

"You say you can't trust yourself, but I think the real problem is that you haven't forgiven yourself," he replied. "You don't need to be perfect to do this job, Ivy. I'd far rather have authentic, imperfect you, anyway."

A third *pop,* this one courtesy of TJ.

I stared at him. My heart lifted. I felt lighter than I had in years. Specifically, since the moment I woke up in the hospital with a murderer's blood still on my hands.

I was imperfect. And that was okay.

"TJ…" I said. "Please kiss me again."

He obliged. Slowly at first, then with ferocity.

Our clothes found the floor. *We* found TJ's bed. And at least for a short while, the only thing that mattered was the two of us.

Chapter Forty-One

I didn't know how much time had passed. An hour? Two? With my body spent and now tucked perfectly against TJ's, we were stripped down and covered with only his cotton sheet. It was easy to lose track of the passing minutes. And if not for the fact that we were both aware that those same minutes were leading to the stalker's next move, we might've stayed that way for a lot longer.

"We have to get up, don't we?" TJ said into my hair.

"I didn't want to say it," I replied.

"I take it back, then."

"Too late."

"Dammit."

He kissed my cheek and slid out of the bed, and I let myself have an indulgent moment of watching him as he searched for his discarded boxers. I was about to make a comment about it not being fair that *he* was practically close to perfect when I notice a long, jagged scar across his lower back. It looked bad. Probably a hockey-related gash that hadn't healed properly, leaving the skin puckered and turned into a nearly bruised shade of purple.

I smiled to myself, then gathered the sheets around my body and stood up to search for my own clothes.

Once we were both dressed, I expected some

awkwardness. But there wasn't any at all.

Hands clasped, we made our way back to the living room, which sat exactly as we'd left it. Letters and papers spread around from the night before. The photo of Skye Marie sitting on the arm of the couch, her pretty yet haunted face staring back at us.

TJ sighed. "Even with all this, I still have no idea who would want to wreck my life."

I hesitated for single moment before confessing to having contacted my cop friend, Gilly. Thankfully, TJ didn't seem bothered by it.

"If you trust her, I trust her," he said easily.

I fought another smile, this one far too goofy for the current situation. "Well, if that's the case, maybe she can delve into things a bit more. You told me that Raleigh Swinter's lawyers had a few things wiped from your record, right?"

He nodded. "Just small-time, misdemeanor stuff. But if you think it might help..."

I fired off a quick text to Gilly then another to my brother to keep him in the loop.

"Can I ask you something?" TJ wondered aloud while we waited for a response.

Despite our recent intimacy, I had to beat back a tickle of trepidation. "Sure."

"Did you think *I* might be a murderer, too?" The corners of his mouth were lifted in a smile, but I flushed.

"Maybe not a murderer," I said. "That can't happen to a woman twice, right?"

"But you were worried I had a shady past?"

"You *do* have a shady past."

"Fair." He studied me for another second then

cracked another smile. "I forgive you."

"Gee, thanks," I replied.

"I like you, Ivy. A lot. And despite my past, I'm not the kind of man who does things impulsively. The commitment I made to get access to my son has been everything to me. I just want you to know that."

"Me neither. That kind of woman, I mean. And without the son."

He slid his hand overtop of mine and squeezed. A cementing of his words. Maybe a cementing of something more than that. Heat—a different kind—wormed through me.

"My brother is going to be *so* displeased with me," I said.

TJ laughed, but if he was going to say something in reply, he didn't get a chance. My phone chimed with an incoming message, and both of us immediately sobered. Reluctantly—both because I didn't want to let him go and because I wasn't excited to have to refocus—I pulled my hand free to grab the device from the table. Gilly's name was in the center of the screen, and I held the phone out so TJ could read the text at the same time as me.

Okay, my friend had written. *I don't know what the poop is going on, but I was up all night thinking about you—no, girl, not like that...lol—so I'm glad you messaged. But if you want me to dig into this kind of stuff, I'm gonna need a better explanation. Let's meet for coffee.*

"What the *poop*?" TJ murmured when he finished reading. "Are you sure she's a police officer?"

"I'm sure. That's just typical Gilly," I replied, smiling briefly. "Also, that's not the important takeaway here."

"You think we should agree to meet her." It was a statement rather than a question, and I nodded.

"She won't mess around, and if she can help us, she will," I said.

He looked away from me, his eyes finding something on the other side of the room. After a second, he pushed to his feet and walked toward the cabinet there. He flicked a latch on one of the cupboards, hesitated, then swung it open. He hesitated again before reaching inside and pulling out a tiny photo frame. His fingers tightened on it, and he brought it back to me and held it out.

"This is him," he said. "This is Travis. It's the only glimpse of him I've ever had."

"You've never seen him in person?"

"Nope."

It was indescribably sad, and as I took the picture, my throat doing its scratchy routine again.

The little boy in the picture was about five years old. Maybe a kindergarten school photo. He had his mom's pale blue eyes, but the rest of him was all TJ. His olive skin. The color of his hair. The shape of his nose. He was 100 percent his father's son.

"I've never shown anyone that," TJ added. "I've never even told anyone he exists. I've been too afraid to in case I fuck it up, and Raleigh manages to keep him away from me."

I brought my gaze to his.

"He's the thing I'm putting on the line," he said softly. "The reason I didn't just go straight to the cops. And I know I'm repeating myself here, but if you think talking to your friend will help us, then I won't argue."

I looked down at the picture once more. TJ trusted me. He'd not only told me as much in black and white but was showing me in no uncertain terms. It was a big responsibility. Something that rode the line of being a big privilege, too.

Are you up to it, Pint-Size?

I lifted my eyes and nodded. "Talking to Gilly is the right thing to do. You won't be any good to your son if you're not alive."

"That settles it, then," he said. "I'll grab my keys. You text your friend."

And five minutes later, we were in TJ's truck on our way to meet Gilly, who'd somehow turned a coffee meeting into a late pancake dinner. One *we* were paying for, apparently.

As we paused at the end of winding driveway, and TJ flicked on his signal, I opened my mouth to tell him I thought we should devise a plan. Maybe make a list of things we should and shouldn't talk about. Possibly come up with a code word in case he wanted to shut things down. But just as I started to speak, a flash ahead on the road caught my eye. A vehicle was headed this way. For a second, I just frowned. Where had it come from? There were no nearby neighbors.

"TJ?" I said, my pulse increasing.

He'd already moved his foot from the brake to the gas pedal. The approaching vehicle had gained speed, too. And it was gaining even more. What was—

No. Oh, no.

It was a white van. The *same* white van from the arena parking lot. It had to be.

"TJ!"

I reached over to the wrench the steering wheel

away from him. It backfired. As my hands found the leather, the van found us.

My eyes closed.

A terrible, metallic crunch filled the air.

Pain slammed through me.

I heard the whisper of a voice in my head.

PROCEED WITH CAUTION.

And everything went black.

Chapter Forty-Two

For the second time, I had no idea how much time has passed. Only when it happened now, it was sudden. One moment, I was bearing down for the impact of the van-turned-weapon. The next, I was lying flat on my back. And this time, the lost minutes or hours weren't accompanied by a pleasant sensation I wished would last so much longer. Instead, they were full of physical hurt and a deep-seated fear.

My eyes were heavy. They refused to open more than a flutter.

Every bit of my body ached in some way—bruised ribs, a throbbing head, and a burn in my right arm were the most noticeable.

But worse than that was the feeling that wherever I was, however much time had gone by, I wasn't alone. There was a rustle around me. The sound of someone else's breathing. And I knew—I just *knew*—it wasn't TJ.

TJ.

His name sent my heart racing. Where was he? I very nearly asked the question aloud before I caught myself and clamped my teeth together. And the action brought awareness of a metallic taste in my mouth. Blood. Not surprising. But it made me want to gag, and I had to fight that, too. And in the end, neither my silence nor my refusal to react to the tang on my tongue did me any good. A man spoke up just then, confirming his unwelcome presence.

"I know you're awake, Ivy," he said. "Your breathing changed, so you can stop pretending."

I didn't move. I wasn't sure I could anyway. And I was also too busy trying to figure out why he sounded familiar.

My eyes attempted again to open. Again, they failed.

"I gave you something," the unseen man informed me. "A mild sedative. But don't worry. It wasn't much. I just needed to get you here, and it will wear off soon."

Like that's my biggest worry, I thought, mentally probing the rest of my physical state in search of some vain hope that I could extricate myself from this situation.

But I quickly realized it wasn't just my injuries or the sedative holding me captive. My hands were bound together in front of me, and my ankles were roped to each other as well.

"Why?" I managed to croak.

Maybe if I got him talking, I could buy myself some time.

"Because your boyfriend—pardon me, your *fiancé*—took something from me," the man replied.

He went on for a moment more, but my brain was slippery from whatever drug he'd used, and something about his first statement distracted me.

What is it? I couldn't quite grasp it. *How do I know this guy?*

"Where's TJ?" I said aloud, my voice a tiny bit stronger.

"Alive."

Well, that was a relief. A muscle or two unbunched. But how long would he *be* alive for?

My eyelids fluttered and lifted. They stayed open for just long enough that I got a glimpse of my surroundings. I was in a poorly lit room of some kind. The walls were strange. Not painted. They almost reminded me of being in an unfinished building. Except they were…metal? My eyes sank shut. Fresh bits of information filtered in. Like the strange smell in the air. It reminded me of winter. And the air was cold, too.

Where the hell am I?

And why did it seem like I should know? Just like it seemed like I should know the man who held me.

"What—" My question cut off in a squeak, and I had to cough and try again. "What do you want?"

"I want him to *know*," the man said. "It's as simple as that."

My fingers twitched. My toes tingled. How could I get free? I needed a better look at the room. And at my captor.

C'mon, Ivy. You're better than this.

"To know what?" I asked.

"What it feels like to lose the person you care about most," he replied.

A small detail in my brain clicked. This man was— or had been—romantically attached to TJ's ex. He blamed TJ for her death.

That gives me something to work with, doesn't it?

"You're talking about Skye Marie," I said weakly.

"No shit."

"Then you're making a mistake."

"How so?"

Was I going to tell him the truth about TJ and me?

I paused. Manifested another cough. And thought about it.

Confessing to the fakeness of our relationship might save TJ in the short run. It might get *me* killed immediately, though. Especially if he saw my bodyguard status as a bigger threat than my fiancée status. I needed more information.

"Untie me, and I'll explain," I offered.

The man laughed. "Fat chance of that."

"Do you *want* to be wrong about this?" I replied, my voice getting stronger. "It'd be an awful shame to have gone to all this trouble only to find out you weren't making TJ suffer the way you planned."

He went quiet. Thinking. Weighing the odds on whether I was trying to trick him. I used the extra moments to peel my eyes open again. I had more success now. The room came back into focus, the same as before, assaulting more senses than just my sight. The strange walls. The odd smell. That cool air.

Where the hell am I? I thought again. *Seriously.*

A light shuffle came from my left, and I let my head tip that way. And there he was. His back to me. His hands in his pockets as he studied something on that part of the wall. I strained to see what he was looking at. Was it a picture of a hockey player?

No, not a picture. A poster, my still slightly sluggish brain corrected.

If my eyes could've widened, they would have. The person on the poster had to be TJ clad in his uniform and gear. Identifying him made the details of my surroundings fall into place.

I'm somewhere in the arena.

It wasn't exactly a relief to know it, but at least it

was something.

The man sighed and spun back to look at me. And no wonder his voice sounded vaguely familiar. No wonder he'd assumed I was the key to TJ's suffering. My captor was Stevie Styles. The alleged reporter from The Daily Local who'd taken our phony engagement photo.

Shit.

"Either way, Ivy, it doesn't make a difference," he said. "I'm going to do what I'm going to do, and TJ will pay for what he cost me. Time to go meet up with your fiancé."

Stevie moved quickly then, his hands clasping the fabric that bound my wrists and yanking me to my unstable feet. He pulled again, but my body screamed a protest. I let out a cry, too. Then I swayed and stumbled, and I would've fully hit the ground if not for the fact that he held me up.

"I can't walk like this," I pointed out, the statement as strained as it was factual.

Lord, how it hurt. Sweat beaded along my forehead even though we hadn't gone anywhere yet.

"I really can't," I said.

Stevie narrowed his eyes, but he had to see I was right. I *couldn't* walk. And after a moment, he bent down and loosened the rope at my ankles.

"That's all the give you're getting," he stated.

He tugged me once more, and now I shuffled along. I wanted to come up with a solution. A persuasive argument. But my movements were agony. All the aches and pains I'd felt before were amplified. Almost blindingly so. I had to have broken ribs. Maybe a broken arm, too. I was for sure concussed. Every step made my surroundings wobble, and I couldn't see where we were headed. So when the world suddenly exploded from dimness into bright white light, I simply stopped short, eliciting a curse from the man in front of me.

We'd exited whatever room we'd been in, and now we were in the arena proper. The Surrey Slammer's home ice. We were up high. The nosebleed section. And though my rapid blinking told me that every seat in the house was empty, it also told me the whole place was lit up like game day. Even the screen and scoreboard shone. And—*oh, God.*

For just the briefest moment, my pain slipped to the wayside. There, in middle of the ice below, was TJ.

Chapter Forty-Three

The world tilted and spun. TJ was splayed out. He had rope around each wrist and each ankle, and the ends of his bonds had been secured to spikes driven into the ice. His pose was sacrificial.

But he's alive. Stevie said so. And there'd be no point in any of this if he weren't. I latched onto that. There was still hope.

My captor gave me another tug, and I forced my attention toward him. There had to be a way out of this. Something I could say or do. A way to make him see reason, and if not, a means of overpowering him.

C'mon. Think!

But the reprieve from my injuries had subsided. My body was hollering again, and Stevie had increased his pace in a way that forced me to concentrate on not tripping. He pulled me into the stands and then toward a set of the cement stairs. I assumed when we reached them, we'd head down toward TJ. Maybe it would give me time to form an idea. But I quickly realized I was wrong about our trajectory. When we got to the stairs in question, Stevie pulled me up instead of down.

What are we...shit!

My eyes lifted with my thoughts, and I saw what waited above. Maintenance scaffolding. Hundreds of feet from the ice below. The perfect place to send someone plunging to their death.

Stevie increased our pace, and I had to work even harder to stay upright as we continued the ascent.

"TJ isn't responsible for Skye's death," I said.

Stevie paused and spun back. "Is that what he told you?"

"She drove drunk."

"True. But why do you think she did that?"

I seized on the chance to prolong the conversation. "They had an argument. He told me about it."

"And let me guess…he also told you it was because she wanted him back," Stevie replied.

"Yes."

"That's bullshit."

He pulled yet again, and I had no choice but to go with him.

"What makes you think it's bullshit?" I asked, still trying to stall.

"Because she was with *me*," he replied.

"Maybe she changed her mind," I said.

Do you really think it's wise to antagonize him, Pint-Size? I shoved aside Charles's voice.

This was *my* case. These were *my* choices to make. And Stevie had paused once more, spinning to fix me with an angry look.

"It was money she was after," he snapped.

"Her father is rich," I argued. "Way richer than TJ."

Saying his name made me want to flick my eyes toward his still body, but I forced them to stay on my captor.

"Her father is an asshole," he replied.

"But she and TJ had already split up. Why would—oh."

The baby.

She'd been going to use their son as a meal ticket.

Stevie nodded. "That's right. Their goddamn kid."

A wave of emotion rolled through me. And questions, too. Why hadn't Skye gone ahead with her plan? Why had she left without telling TJ the truth about little Travis? Was it guilt? Anger? Something else? All those years that TJ had lost, not knowing his little boy. And maybe he'd never know why.

My captor hadn't stopped walking through the interaction, and we'd reached the top platform. In front of us was a door. Beside us was a railing. In a second, we'd be out there on that scaffolding with nothing but air and us below us. Unsurprisingly, dizziness threatened.

"Why now?" I gasped out.

Stevie stopped, thank God. "You know why."

"I don't."

Honestly, I didn't *know* whether I knew, and I wasn't going to try to come up with an explanation, either. Not when asking him meant further stalling.

"Because he's getting his shit together," Stevie said. "Because of his new contract. Because he was supposed to keep suffering, and because I've been watching all these years to make sure it stayed that way, and now…it hasn't. And I think that's about enough show-and-tell."

He gave the hardest yank yet on my wrists, pushing his way through the door at the same time. Abruptly, the air felt thinner. Colder, too. A shiver racked my body, and I involuntarily resisted being pulled forward. Which is when it hit me. Stevie held me captive. His fingers were tight on the fabric binding me. But one wrong move, and the balance of power could be shifted. And if I needed any confirmation at all, I just had to look down to his feet as I continued to resist. They needed to work to stay in place.

I gave another small tug back. Yes, he was struggling to maintain control. I tugged again. This time, it forced him to use his other hand to grab the nearest thing to hold onto—the railing.

"If I fall, you fall," he said calmly.

Exactly, I thought, giving one more tug.

He held fast. And my own feet, still bound, tried to slide out from underneath me. I kept going anyway. Inching back. Stevie's arm was stretched out all the way. Any second, he'd have to let either me or the railing go.

I pulled again. Except now, Stevie pulled back. Hard. Twice in a row. It took serious effort to keep from sliding forward. What was he doing? He really *would* send us both over the edge if he kept it up. He gave a third yank, and I wobbled, my shoulder smacking the railing while my stomach plummeted to my feet. Before I could stop myself, I looked down to the ice below. Vertigo slammed into me. I tried to focus on TJ, to use him as an anchor, as a lifeline through the fear. It worked for at least a moment. He needed me to come out alive, needed me to save him. And I needed it, too.

The dizziness waned. I breathed in and lifted my attention back to Stevie. He was watching me, almost impassively. Like he was just waiting it out. And a chilling realization washed over me. His indifference wasn't a sign of recklessness, but a calculated resolve. He didn't care if he died. Maybe he even wanted to. A ghost of a smile touched his lips, like he'd spotted my understanding.

"Any second now," he murmured.

I sucked in a breath, but whatever response I'd been forming slid away as TJ's voice echoed through the arena.

"Ivy?"

He sounded weak and confused, but the empty space made my name echo anyway. And Stevie's smile widened.

"Up here!" he called.

I don't know what I expected next. Some kind of explanation. An exchange of some sort. But apparently, Stevie had said all he needed to say. With no further warning, he gripped the fabric that bound me, and he launched himself over the edge of the scaffolding.

Chapter Forty-Four

It was mostly—maybe all—luck that saved me. As Stevie's dead weight dragged me down, my body went flat and my tied-up feet hooked over the metal behind me, stopping me from going with him. At the same time, my bound hands automatically clamped down, gripping my captor's wrist, leaving him suspended. And there, I stayed. Breathing hard. My torso wide across the scaffolding. The ice left waiting as I held the man who'd just tried to kill us both.

From below, TJ hollered. I barely heard him. I was too focused on keeping Stevie from plunging to his death.

Why don't you just let him go? a voice in my head asked.

And maybe I would've been justified in doing it. Or maybe there wasn't anything *maybe* about it. But suddenly, instead of being here in the arena, I was thrown back. Through blurred eyes, I saw a different scene. I relived a different confrontation, somehow squishing the whole thing into seconds, but absorbing it all at the same time.

There I was, just outside the fancy restaurant in the heart of Vancouver. There was my date with his flowers, walking past the restaurant, stepping into an alley. I'd followed, unaware that my trap for him had become his trap for *me,* and merely thinking overconfidently he'd taken a wrong turn. But then he'd faced me. And there was his expression.

He knows that I know, I'd thought in that moment, four years ago.

My pulse trilled. This wasn't part of my plan. We were supposed to go into the restaurant, where I was going to coax out some kind of confession. I'd been going to pretend to agree with his decisions, even the murder and the blackmail.

"Hello, Ivy," he said, his voice slow and dark and knowing.

Somehow, in a heartbeat, he adjusted his position, quite abruptly ensuring I had no way out. It was then I noted something else. Along with the bouquet, he held a knife.

He stepped closer. I stepped back. My mouth opened.

"You're going to want to keep quiet," he said.

My chin lifted in my typically defiant way. "Why the hell would I do that?"

"Because if you don't, my 'sister' will die, too."

Aha! a voice in my head—a voice in the present—said. *That's why I didn't call for help right away. Not weakness. It was for the chance, however slim, that my silence might keep someone else safe.*

My wannabe boyfriend dropped both the flowers and any hint of pretense. He lunged toward me, snarling. But I wasn't going to be easy prey. I dived out of his path, and he fell forward, his knife clattering to the ground. We were both on the cement, both heaving labored breaths. For a heartbeat, neither of us moved. Then his eyes left mine.

The knife.

Almost in unison, we reached for it. It was short-lived battle. He won, but only because his reach was longer. And because I'd thrown myself down, he had another advantage. Longer arms. While his fingers closed around the handle of his weapon, mine barely stretched past his elbow. I switched my goal. I grabbed hold of his arm and dug my nails in as hard as I could, pinching him through his suit jacket. He didn't drop the knife, but he did try to shake off my hand, and the slight distraction was all I could hope for anyway.

I twisted my body and freed my other hand, driving it into his gut. He grunted and swore. I ignored him, clambering to try to get to the damn knife. My fingernails found his wrist, tearing at the skin. For the second time, the weapon fell from his grasp and went clattering away.

Gasping, I went after it. But I wasn't quick enough. Or strong enough. Or *anything* enough.

He overtook me. He pinned me to the ground, towering over me, his wiry frame—the same body I knew so well—sinister in its sinewy strength.

Why wasn't someone coming? Why hadn't someone heard us?

Now's the time to scream, Ivy. Because if you don't...

My mouth dropped open, but before I could let out a sound, the heel of his palm smashed into my jaw. Pain ricocheted up my face. Stars dotted my vision.

How, Ivy? How? How did you think you loved this man?

I opened my mouth again. His hand now found my throat, squeezing and squeezing. Uselessly, my hand flailed. My feet tried to kick.

Losing. I'm losing.

There was a dimness encroaching on my vision. On my brain.

I bucked. My shoulders lifted the barest inch before he shoved me down again so hard that my head hit the concrete. For the second time, I saw stars. And that dimness expanded. My hands continued their efforts. Flopping. Sliding. Skimming. And—*the knife.* It was there. He'd abandoned it in pursuit of punishing me without the aid of his weapon.

Something in me reared up. A desperate drive to survive. A last-minute surge of fight.

My fingers wrapped around the hilt. I brought up the blade and plunged it into his side. Not a death blow. Nowhere near it. But violent and painful nonetheless, and he rolled off me.

Freedom overwhelmed me. I sucked in what felt like breath after breath before I could pull to my knees then stagger to my feet.

He was on the ground. Face up. Hand covering his wound.

Help, I thought stupidly. *He needs a doctor.*

I sought my purse. My phone. I'd call 9-1-1. I'd get him the help and—

"Ivy."

I whipped my eyes back to him. He was up again.

I moved backward.

"You're going to have to kill me, Ivy," he said.

How, how, *how* had he come between me and the escape route once more?

"I don't want to do this," I whispered.

"Me or you, Ivy. Me or you."

He launched himself at me. At the same moment, I

raised the knife. When our bodies met, the blade plunged into his chest. I'd tumbled back then, and the last thing I'd seen before my head hit the ground, knocking me unconscious, was the look on his face. The certainty he was going to die. And as the memory seared itself into my brain, filling the hole that had been there for almost four years, the present came back into focus. I shifted the barest inch on the scaffolding, and I saw that same expression in Stevie's eyes now.

It's not happening again. It won't be me or him.

Sirens cut through the air, spurring me to work harder.

"Hold on," I said. "I'll pull you up."

I strained. And strained. My shoulders burned. Tears slid out. And suddenly, there was a second set of hands beside mine.

"I've got him," TJ said. "You can let go."

Can I?

I thought about the man I'd killed. About the internal battle I'd been waging ever since. Could I let go? *Yes,* I thought, *maybe I can.* And I inhaled and loosened my grip, and let TJ take over. At least for now.

Epilogue

Two months later…

Ivy couldn't skate. She just couldn't. My mouth twisted with amusement as I watched her keep trying. She was so damned stubborn. So damned cute. Though she hated to hear about the latter of the two things, even from me.

"Stop looking at me like that!" she called from across the ice.

"Like what?" I replied innocently.

"Like it's *funny.*"

"It *is* funny."

"It's not."

Except it was. The way her legs didn't cooperate with her feet. The way her arms swung around. My face wanted to split into a grin, and I couldn't fight it.

"Come on," I said encouragingly. "You can do this."

"Not helping!" she yelled back.

"Dad?" my son said from his spot beside me.

My heart skipped a small beat the way it always did when Travis called me that. For over a month now, we'd been having these weekly visits. Tonight, we had our first planned sleepover. Somehow, in the way only kids could, and in a way that definitely irritated his maternal grandfather, he'd adapted to the new arrangement in his life. Almost like he'd been waiting for it to happen.

It'd been a bigger adjustment for me. Fatherhood. Being nice to Raleigh Swinter. Waiting for the police and lawyers to put Stevie Styles behind bars for his crime while convincing Bram I hadn't *really* broken the terms of my contract. And falling in love with Ivy for real under the scrutiny of her gaggle of older brothers. Yeah, the last eight weeks had been a wild ride.

Wouldn't change it, though, would I?

Hell, no.

"Dad?" Travis said again, tugging my arm this time.

"Sorry, bud," I replied. "Lost in my head. What's up?"

He lowered his voice. "What if she actually *can't* do it?"

A chuckle escaped my lips. "Then I guess we're going to be here a while."

"You could always meet her halfway," Travis offered, then paused and added, "But she might not like it."

His was right. On both counts.

"I'll give her another minute," I said.

"Then what?" his son asked.

My fingers slid into my pocket and squeezed the ring box there, and I smiled. "Then I'll give her another minute after that."

And a million more, too. Or that was the plan, anyway.

"Dammit, TJ," Ivy said. "Could you come and help me?"

"Anything for you, babe."

A word about the author…

Amazon bestselling author, Melinda Di Lorenzo, lives on the West Coast of British Columbia. Being sandwiched between the Canadian Rockies and the Pacific Ocean provides the perfect backdrop for crafting her books. Melinda writes across a variety of genres, including: suspense/thriller, romantic suspense, romantic comedy, women's fiction, and YA. When not at home with her handsome hero of a husband, her kids, and her pets, Melinda can be found running the trails or at the soccer pitch. melindaread@shaw.ca

Thank you for purchasing
this publication of The Wild Rose Press, Inc.

For questions or more information
contact us at
info@thewildrosepress.com.

The Wild Rose Press, Inc.
www.thewildrosepress.com